When Cupid gets i
You're heading for

Blind Dates and Other Disasters

Blind Dates and Other Disasters

Ally Blake
Fiona Harper
Barbara Hannay

Harlequin Mills & Boon Limited, Eton House,
18-24 Paradise Road, Richmond, Surrey TW9 1SR

BLIND DATES AND OTHER DISASTERS
© Harlequin Books S.A. 2011

The publisher acknowledges the copyright holders of the individual works
as follows:

The Wedding Wish © Ally Blake 2003
Blind-Date Marriage © Fiona Harper 2006
The Blind Date Surprise © Barbara Hannay 2005

ISBN: 978 0 263 88534 7

10-0211

Harlequin Mills & Boon policy is to use papers that are natural,
renewable and recyclable products and made from wood grown in
sustainable forests. The logging and manufacturing processes conform to
the legal environmental regulations of the country of origin.

Printed in the UK
by CPI Mackays, Chatham, ME5 8TD

The Wedding Wish

by Ally Blake

When **Ally Blake** was a little girl she made a wish that when she turned twenty-six she would marry an Italian two years older than her. After it actually came true she realised she was on to something with these wish things. So next she wished that she could make a living spending her days in her pyjamas, eating M&Ms and drinking scads of coffee while turning her formative experiences of wallowing in teenage crushes and romantic movies into creating love stories of her own. The fact that she is now able to spend her spare time searching the internet for pictures of handsome guys for research purposes is merely a bonus!

Come along and visit her website at www.allyblake.com

This book is dedicated to Mark, my angel,
who looked after me, brought me M&Ms
and made me feel like I had it in me all the time.

CHAPTER ONE

'I'M GETTING married,' Holly announced as she slammed her briefcase on the desk in her office at Cloud Nine Event Management, fifteen minutes later than her usual start time.

'You're doing what?' Beth's voice rang metallic and loud from Holly's speakerphone.

Holly sat down, crossed her legs, noticed a run in her stockings, and her mood went from bad to worse. She grabbed a new pair of stockings from the neat pile stocked in her bottom desk drawer, before moving into her private bathroom to change from frayed to fresh. She had to raise her voice for it to reach the speakerphone, but in her current temper that was not a problem.

'I said I'm getting married.'

'But I can't remember you dating any man more than once in the last six months, much less becoming familiar enough to want to *marry* one of them.'

Holly's assistant Lydia chose that moment to enter the office. She stopped in her tracks, the coffee she carried all but sloshing over the sides, and stared at the speakerphone as though it had produced an offensive noise. Holly came back into the room, new stockings in place, and waved a 'hurry up' hand at Lydia who placed the cup down without spilling a drop.

With no apology, Lydia joined the private conversation. 'Did I hear you guys right? In the time it took for me to make Holly a cuppa, she's hooked herself a fiancé? That's saying something for instant coffee.'

'Is that you, Lydia?' Beth asked.

Lydia leaned towards the speakerphone, articulating her words as though speaking to someone hard of hearing. 'How are you, Beth? When is the baby due?'

'I'm fantastic. Baby Jeffries should be here in a month or so—'

'Ah, guys,' Holly interrupted, 'major life decision being made here.'

Lydia mimed buttoning her lips shut tight.

'Sorry, sweetie,' Beth said. 'Blame Lydia. You know if anyone asks about the bubby, I gush. Do go on.'

'Thank you.' Holly took a deep breath and launched into her story. 'This morning, as I walked the last block along Lonsdale Street, this...*man* all but barrelled me over. Everything I was carrying went flying. My briefcase ended up in the gutter, pens rolled down the road and all my precious papers scattered across the footpath. And as I was on my hands and knees crawling around collecting my materials *he* had the nerve to tell *me* to watch where *I* was going.'

'Was he cute?' was Lydia's instant response.

Not cute, Holly remembered. She pictured early morning sunlight glinting off light flecks in hazel eyes. Tired dark smudges underneath those eyes. Sympathy she had felt at his exhausted expression. His scowl as he had realised she had dropped everything she was carrying. The same scowl that had extinguished her sympathy. The rich, deep voice with a hint of a foreign accent as he had said his piece. No, cute was not the word.

'Tall,' Holly eventually established, 'dark mussed hair. Matching dimples. Smelled nice. But that's irrelevant.'

'Irrelevant?' Beth said. 'He sounds perfect.'

'I reckon,' Lydia agreed.

'Just when you stop looking where you are going, he finds you. It's kismet.'

Holly rolled her eyes, picturing Beth reaching for one of her New Age books to justify the incident.

'He did not find me, Beth, he berated and bruised me. See.' Holly pointed out a light scrape on her knee to Lydia, who pouted in appreciation.

'And this is the guy you're going to marry?' Lydia asked.

'No! You've both missed the point.'

'Which is?'

'The point is, the whole horrible episode brought about an epiphany. My social life consists exclusively of attending parties we coordinate. But instead of meeting men, I meet male party personalities. They mislead me with an attractive, charming, confident disguise but there is never anything *more* going on behind the eye-catching masks they wear. The *gentleman* this morning was very attractive, uncompromising, and uncaring and was therefore the embodiment of all that is wrong with the men I meet. It's a foolproof theory.'

'I'm confused,' Lydia said. 'If not this guy, who on earth are you marrying?'

'That's the thing—I've decided Ben is going to find him for me.'

'My Ben?' Beth asked after a couple of seconds of bewildered silence.

'Of course. Can't you see it's the only way? Ben works in a big company, he's got plenty of staff under him, mostly young men he has hand-picked, and he knows me better than anyone apart from you guys. He's the perfect objective observer and if he can find me someone he likes then we can all be friends for ever. You know, live next door to one another, have neighbourhood BBQs, go on camping trips…'

'You hate camping—'

'I'm not joking, Beth. Come on, you have to see how flawless a plan it is.'

'And all of this came from banging into some very attractive, dimpled, nice smelling guy on the street?' Beth asked.

'It was like when we collided he smacked some sense into me.'

'Gave you concussion, more like it,' Lydia muttered.

Holly shot Lydia an unimpressed look.

'This guy must have been something to get you of all people talking marriage,' Beth said.

'Why me of all people?'

'Come on, Holly. You are the most controlled, independent woman I know. You keep a colour range of spare pairs of stockings in your office drawer, for goodness' sake.'

Catching sight of those very packets, Holly casually closed the drawer shut with her foot.

'And here you are,' Beth continued, 'wanting to put your future happiness in someone else's hands.'

'Ben is not just someone else and you know that. I trust him to make a good choice.'

'I can't believe you are making some sort of sense,' Beth admitted. 'All right, come over for dinner tonight so that we can ambush my poor, unknowing husband.'

'Thanks, Beth. You are the best friend in the whole wide world.'

'And don't you forget it.'

After Beth rang off Lydia peeled her lanky form from the chair and loped to Holly's office door where she turned back to ask, 'Did he help pick the stuff up?'

Holly dragged her attention away from the beckoning projects on her desk. 'Mmm, he dropped his bags and bent down to help almost instantly. But he was telling me off at the time so that's irrelevant too.'

'And you were walking with your head down, immersed in thoughts of what you had to do today, not looking where you were going, weren't you?'

'Sure…'

'But that's irrelevant, right?'

Holly narrowed her eyes, willing Lydia not to continue, but her mocking look was to no avail.

'A tall, dark, handsome stranger bowls you over and then gets down on his hands and knees to help. And you have decided this is a bad thing. I, on the other hand, would spend the rest of the day looking dreamily out the window if that happened to me. But no such luck. My morning consisted of being rubbed up against by a schoolboy on the train.'

Lydia sighed spectacularly and Holly could not help but grin at her amateur dramatics. 'You do realise that since I am your boss your job is to ooh and aah and say, "poor Holly", don't you?'

'I thought my job was to get you coffee and stand on chairs so that you can drape fabrics over me and hold all incoming calls from any men you may have had uninspiring dates with the night before.'

'Sure,' Holly agreed after a moment's thought, 'that too.'

Lydia left the room and headed back to her desk to prepare herself for a day of imagining walking up Lonsdale Street and banging into tall, dark, handsome strangers.

Jacob helped the driver haul the last of his luggage into the waiting taxi. As the car pulled away he ran a hand through his mussed hair, leant back onto the headrest, and was surprised to catch such a world-weary reflection peering back at him from the window.

Jacob's focus shifted and he watched the familiar hometown buildings flick past. He was not yet sure how he felt about being home. So far, so good. And a hot shower and a sleep in his own bed would only make it better. But how long would it be this time before he yearned to move on?

Either way Jacob knew Melbourne was a magnificent city. Take that enchanting woman he had just had an exchange with on the street. Now there was a real Melbourne woman. Pale smooth skin suited to the temperate clime, stylish to a fault, a compelling face, and subtle, easy confidence. You didn't find women quite like that anywhere else in the world. In any case he hadn't yet. During the drive home, his thoughts kept coming back to the brunette with the fiery blue eyes who had somehow roused his ordinarily controlled temper.

Jet lag. It had to have been jet lag.

'Babe?' Ben's voice called out from the front hallway.

Holly's hand leapt to her throat. She had not even heard the front door.

'In here, darling,' Beth called, sitting on an armchair they'd dragged into the kitchen to ease her aching back.

Holly understood Beth's raised eyebrows and tight mouth. *This is your last chance to change your mind,* her expression said. But Holly was not to be deterred. 'Just follow the delicious aroma of grilled chicken à la Holly wafting from the kitchen.'

Ben popped his head around the door. He leaned down and kissed his wife, not even asking why their lounge chair was in the kitchen. Holly offered her cheek for a kiss, which she duly received.

'To what do we owe the pleasure of your company,

gorgeous?' Ben leant over Holly to have a good look at dinner. She slapped his hand as he tried to grab a piece of potato.

Holly glanced once more at Beth, who gave her a discreet thumbs up. 'I want you to set me up with someone from your work.'

Holly clenched her face waiting for the inevitable 'no'.

'Sure,' Ben answered.

Holly was too stunned to stop him spooning a baby potato into his mouth. 'Really?'

'Of course. It's Derek from Payroll, isn't it? He's always had a thing for you, you know.'

'For starters it's not Derek. I mean, yuck.'

'Come on, Ben,' Beth said in support, 'you know she likes tall, dark and handsome. Derek's a weed.'

'Then who?'

Holly proceeded to explain her inspired theory and the mechanics of her plan with endlessly increasing enthusiasm until Ben could have no doubt of her sincerity.

'You two are serious, aren't you?'

'Deadly serious,' Beth agreed. 'I have mapped out her stars, and Holly is primed.'

Ben did a Groucho Marx with his eyebrows. Beth slapped his thigh playfully. 'Primed for a big change, you idiot. This is serious, Ben. She is getting on in years.'

'She's twenty-seven.'

'And I want to be her matron of honour while I'm still young enough and pretty enough to at least have a shot at outshining the bride.'

'You're nuts, the both of you. I shouldn't let the two of you alone in a room together. It bodes badly for the future of mankind.'

'But you will do it, won't you, darling?'

Faced with their excited united front, there was nothing Ben could do but agree.

CHAPTER TWO

So, THE next night Holly meandered through the outer bar of the Fun and Games sports nightclub on the arm of her best friend's husband. She was dressed to kill in a black silk dress: fitted, strapless and split to the thigh.

'Do you have anyone in particular lined up for me tonight?' Holly shouted in Ben's ear to be heard over the loud, pumping music.

'Actually, I stuck your photo on the wall in the men's washroom at work along with a note saying you would be here tonight. That way they can just come to you.'

'Not funny.' Holly punched Ben inelegantly in the arm. 'Why is the function here?'

'It's one of ours. It's Link's idea. We hold all of our functions in various clubs we own so we are constantly reinvesting in ourselves.'

Holly nodded, impressed. 'Ingenious. Pity all Lincoln Holdings events are managed internally. I could have a lot of fun with the budget you guys must have.' She huddled closer. 'Will the boss be here tonight?'

'Link? Sorry, Holly, you can cross him off your list. He's

been running the international operations from New Orleans for the last few years.'

'I bet he's tall, dark, and handsome to boot.' Holly pouted, bringing a smile to Ben's face. The smile probably meant his boss was a married workaholic with three whining kids, a pot-belly and high blood pressure.

He took her hand and led her single file through the swelling crowd, into the private function room hidden at the rear of the club. The room had been converted into a sort of theatre in the round. The high ceiling housed an elaborate lighting rig so bright it was almost blinding.

A cheerful murmur of voices and clinking drinking glasses echoing in the lofty space had replaced the raucous club music, soundproof walls thankfully shutting out the thumping beat from the previous room.

Holly excused herself several times as they edged past people sitting in their row. The numerous men in dinner suits sent a thrill of excitement running up and down her spine. She sat and turned to Ben, ready to ask what was behind the velvet floor-to-ceiling drapes in the centre of the room but her query froze on her lips. The curtains slowly rose into the rafters to reveal— A boxing ring!

Ben chatted to a couple of male colleagues in the row in front. Their eyes all gleamed like little boys in a pet store as they launched into a detailed discussion of the two men who were about to belt it out before them.

Holly tugged on Ben's sleeve. 'There's a boxing ring.'

He smiled. 'That's so that the boxers keep to themselves and don't spill out into the crowd.'

'But, I thought…I thought this was a business function. I thought we'd be sitting down, having dinner, and there would be refined and elegant men for you to introduce to me.'

'We're sitting. We're eating,' Ben said with a mouthful of

mixed nuts he had picked up from a nattily dressed wandering waiter. 'And this is Mark and Jeremy.'

The mundane middle-aged guys from the row in front smiled politely.

Ben's twinkling eyes fast lost their twinkle when Holly grabbed him gracelessly by the lapels of his tuxedo jacket and through clenched teeth said, 'But this was not what I had in mind.'

'Just relax. You'll enjoy it.'

Holly raised her eyebrows, pursed her lips and crossed her arms, demonstrating exactly how much she was enjoying the night so far. 'I am surprised that Lincoln Holdings would associate itself with such a primitive and politically incorrect enterprise.'

'All of Lincoln Holdings' staff from the managing directors to the custodial staff come together for these nights. It makes inter-office difficulties seem so small and petty when compared with what these guys go through to earn a living. You should know more than anyone that if a gimmick works, stick with it.'

'It's not just a gimmick, Ben, it's encouraging people to use their fists to sort out their differences. Whose idea was this in the first place?'

'Link's, of course,' Ben said, grinning. 'Forever inspirational.'

'Sounds like a thug to me,' Holly muttered.

'You thought he was ingenious ten minutes ago.'

'Ten minutes ago I was mistaken.'

Holly was suddenly glad that Ben's boss would not be at the function. If he were, she would have no problems letting him know what she thought of his little soirée, high blood pressure or no high blood pressure.

And she just knew that sitting quietly at home in her

'magic' briefcase—as Lydia called it—she would have a dozen more appropriate and inspirational function ideas and it frustrated her to distraction.

The white noise of the murmuring crowd rose to a crescendo when an announcer in black tie bounded into the ring and a microphone descended from the rafters. The crowd rose to its collective feet and Holly rose with it, shuffling her way back out of their row in search of a refuge.

Once inside the ladies' room, she slumped down on a very large round pink velvet ottoman, which sat alone in the middle of the vast space.

Her eyes were closed and she was plotting ways she could take revenge on Ben when the doors swung open. She opened her eyes, hoping to find solace with another woman in the same predicament as herself, but instead locked eyes with the least feminine person she had ever seen.

In walked a man well over six feet tall, his tuxedo precisely tailored to fit his athletic frame. He was so stunning it took her breath away. Maybe this night would not be a complete waste after all.

And then something about the furrowed brow and deep hazel eyes clicked in her memory. His neat, freshly cut hair framing his handsome, relaxed face had momentarily blinded her to the fact that she knew him.

He was the same brute who had knocked her down in the street the day before!

Her senses surged to full alert. He radiated charisma, confidence and composure. Any other girl would find it near impossible to stand firm against that killer combination of attributes.

But Holly was not just any other girl. Holly had protection. Holly had a foolproof theory and Holly had Ben to keep just this sort of guy beneath her radar.

So where was Ben now she really needed him? Hmm. No Ben. She and her theory would have to fend for themselves. And her foremost plan was to make the brute leave the room before he recognised her.

She shot to her feet, holding her clutch purse in front of her chest as a shield and said, 'Excuse me, this is the ladies' room.'

The man stopped short at her words.

'Actually it's not,' he said, the hint of an accent evident once more in his deep, rich voice. He pointed to doors on the other side of the room that Holly had not even noticed. 'That's the way to the bathrooms. This is a communal lounge.'

'Oh.' She sat back down.

All is fine. He will continue through to the men's room. Then I can make a run for it.

But he did not leave.

After several uncomfortable moments, she glanced up to find him leaning casually against the far wall, blocking the way to the outer door, watching her.

His amused gaze scanned her dark hair piled high in a mass of controlled curls, past her face, which burned under his intent look, down her exposed neck and shoulders, making her wish she had a wrap to cover them.

As his regard skimmed lower she followed its direction and noticed that the length of her crossed legs was fully exposed through the split in her skirt. Sheathed in shimmering stockings, they glittered from toe to thigh, and the light scrape she had received from their scuffle on the footpath showed red through the filmy fabric. She uncrossed her legs, quickly swishing the soft cloth over them, hiding the wound.

The gesture was not lost on him and a fleeting, and utterly knee-melting, smile washed across his mouth, for a brief moment revealing overlapping front teeth and those unforgettable dimples.

Strength, Holly. Strength.

Her only glimmer of hope was that there had not been one hint of recognition in those laughing hazel eyes.

It was her. It had to be. She was the woman with the briefcase and the temper.

She was dressed so differently and not yelling at him—Jacob ought not to have recognised her. But her gleaming dark hair, compelling blue eyes and natural elegance had meandered unbidden in and out of his mind so many times over the last day he had begun to think she had been no more than a jet-lag-induced delusion.

But she was real. And what a kick to walk through the door in search of a moment's peace and quiet only to find *her*, arranged before him like a delectable gift in such dazzling wrapping.

Jacob went to introduce himself. After all, they had met. Somewhat. And more to the point she could very well prove to be a delightful diversion during his hiatus here. Then he stopped himself.

She had recognised him too; it was splashed across her face, but she did not seem at all happy about it.

Sure, they had *clashed* rather than met, but that just made her all the more memorable. Yet instead of laughing it off or accusing him anew, she fussed and fidgeted and endeavoured to fade into the furniture. And despite her best efforts, that very bashfulness made her stand out like a luminous gem on her velvet cushion.

So maybe now was not the time to introduce himself. Maybe now was the time to enjoy watching her fuss and fidget some more.

* * *

'I know your face, but I can't seem to place you,' he said, staring at her as though sifting through his memory.

Help!

'Do you work for the company?' he asked.

Phew.

'No, thank heavens,' she said.

'You have something against Lincoln Holdings?'

She shrugged. 'I'm not a big fan of beer and boxing. So I guess that makes me not a big fan of Lincoln Holdings.'

He made no response, and seemed perfectly content in the long silence. On the contrary, Holly's right leg jiggled and her ears buzzed with every beat of her thudding heart.

'Are you planning on staying in here all night?' he finally asked.

'I hadn't really thought that far. I came with someone so I need the lift home.' She kept her eyes averted and her face turned as far away as was polite.

'I could organise a cab for you, if you wish.'

'No, thanks.' *Now off you go.*

'The least I can do is tell your companion you are in here,' the man said. 'I'm sure he would not want you out of his sight for too long.' And then he smiled again.

Holly felt like a whole family of butterflies had taken up residence in her stomach. It was unfair to have a debilitating smile like that in your arsenal. If he smiled at her like that one more time she would be reduced to a pile of quivering mush upon the fuzzy pink ottoman. It was maddening but she was drawn to him despite herself. So if he wasn't going to leave then she would have to.

'Maybe I should take a cab. Make Ben worry. He deserves it.'

'Ben?'

'I'm here with Ben Jeffries. One of the VPs.'

The man's attitude cooled so suddenly, it surprised Holly, then she remembered why she had embarked on her husband hunt in the first place. Her theory about the men she attracted. At parties.

He was no enigma, standing there seeming so cool and elegant. He had been wearing his party personality, he had been acting the part, just as they all did. He was good-looking enough to send a girl's stomach into a whole series of flips with one brief smile, and she had almost fallen for it.

The clang of a bell sounded from the other side of the door, followed by a loud cheer. Holly winced as she imagined the fighters coming together in a violent clash.

Her companion's attention focussed on her for one fleeting, intense moment, before he nodded, then headed back out into the throng.

The muffled sounds of the enthusiastic crowd outside infiltrated her conflicting thoughts. As she settled herself in for the duration it occurred to her that if it were not for that man's unpleasant behaviour at their first meeting, she would not have been sitting in a bathroom, dressed up, hungry and alone.

Smiling to herself, she felt much more comfortable thinking nothing but ill of him once more.

CHAPTER THREE

JACOB LINCOLN walked into his second-in-charge's office first thing Monday morning. He had been able to catch up for a brief hello and welcome home Saturday night but one subject had been bothering him since.

Without hesitation, Ben rounded his desk and hugged his old friend. He patted him on the back once more, as though making sure he was really there.

'I still can't believe you're back. And what an entrance. You sashayed into the match the other night, calm as you please, as if you'd never been away. Over the jet lag yet?'

'Pretty much. I had forgotten how cold and dry the air is in Melbourne. It hits you as soon as you get off the plane. I don't mind, though—I never could get used to the humidity in New Orleans.'

'Good. It means you're a Melbournian at heart.'

Jacob shrugged. 'Or maybe it means I should try San Francisco next.' Jacob sat down on the leather lounge chair on the near side of Ben's desk. His fingers unconsciously played with his bottom lip as he broached the subject that had been worrying him.

'At the fight, I met your date.'

Ben grinned broadly. 'So, you met the other woman in my life.'

Jacob's eyes narrowed at Ben's obvious affection towards a woman other than his pregnant wife. But Ben just burst out laughing.

'Don't look at me like that, Link. She's Beth's best friend. My poor wife can hardly walk up stairs any more, much less handle a nightclub function, so she asked me to take Holly. They've known each other for ever so when I fell madly in love with my wife, Holly came with the deal.'

Feeling undeniably better, Jacob leant back in the chair. 'What's she like?'

'You've met her. Short, blonde, heavily pregnant.' Ben reached for his wallet. 'I can show you a photo.'

'I meant Holly, and you know it.'

'Ah, Holly.' Ben put his wallet away.

'You get on well?' Jacob asked.

'You bet. So well, in fact, she has roped me into finding a man for her.'

'Really?' Surprising. She hardly seemed the type to need a blind date. But while he was in town…

'Not only a man,' Ben continued, shaking his head and smiling indulgently, 'but a husband at that.'

Whoa. A blind date was one thing…

He had been back in the country for just a few days and twice he had run into the same woman, and both times he had allowed her to get under his skin. He should have known better. So he swiftly latched onto the perfect balm for just that kind of irritant; she was on a husband hunt.

Suddenly San Francisco was looking better and better.

'She's cute, don't you think?' Ben asked with a glimmer in his eye.

'Sure.' If you called women with stormy blue eyes and legs that went on forever 'cute'.

'Did she happen to mention how she enjoyed the fight?'

'We met just before it began actually. But that didn't stop her pitching varied unflattering opinions about the match and my company in general.'

'That sounds like Holly. Did you… introduce yourself?' Ben asked, seeming to choose his words carefully. 'Did she know who you were?'

'She must have.' Jacob pictured her open book face and the recognition evident in every blink. 'What does that matter?'

'I guess it doesn't.'

Jacob stood and Ben walked him to the door.

'What are you doing for dinner tonight?' Ben asked. 'How does roast lamb grab you? Beth hasn't seen you for years and she would love to catch up before the baby's due.'

Though he had masses of work to do, the thought of such contented, uncomplicated company was too tempting to refuse.

'What time?'

'About seven?'

As Jacob left Ben's office he popped his head back in the door to say, 'By the way, I have never sashayed in my life.'

'It was horrible.' Holly was bent double with her bottom in the air and head pushed between her legs.

'Ben had a ball.' Beth did a far more gentle stretch with their yoga instructor watching her carefully.

'Of course he did. He's a man. And a Neanderthal at that, as I have only just discovered.'

'I promise if he'd told me beforehand it was that sort of function, I never would have suggested he take you. I'd told him a little about your dad, but not enough as it turned out.'

Beth laid a hand on Holly's arm. Holly shook it off, then instantly regretted the prickly move. She had long since let those memories lie and knew she was being overly sensitive.

'He thinks that Lincoln guy is "inspired",' Holly continued, her voice light. 'He has his head screwed on wrong. If he really wanted his employees to bond in one of his establishments, why not buy a health resort and send them there? I could do a better job planning their parties half asleep and with one hand tied behind my back!'

'Or with your head between your knees, evidently.'

Holly flicked her friend a smile from between said knees.

'So, did you meet any honeys?' Beth asked.

'Nah,' Holly said, steadfastly failing to acknowledge the picture of sparkling hazel eyes that had fast formed in her mind. Besides, he was no honey. He was the enemy.

'I'm not surprised. May I ask how you hoped to find a husband in the "communal lounge"?'

'By that stage all I hoped to find was sanctuary from the rabble outside.'

'You would hardly want that to be the story you tell your grandkids. "We met on the way to the toilet…"'

'What's the point?' Holly sighed as she slowly stretched her arms to touch her toes. 'I will find no husband. I will have no grandkids to tell stories to.'

'Well, if that's your attitude I had better cancel your dinner date for tonight, then.'

'Dinner?' Holly stood up so fast she had to steady herself so as not to black out.

Beth stood more slowly and waddled over to their bags. Holly followed at a trot.

'To make up for his dismal effort the other night Ben has organised for one of his work colleagues to come to dinner tonight. He had hoped the two of you could meet, fall madly in love and marry. But if you're not interested—'

'Of course, I'm interested. Do you know him? Is he nice? Intelligent? What does he do? No, don't tell me. I don't want to know. Is he cute?'

'Just be at our place by six-thirty, and all will be revealed.'

'Yeah, yeah, yeah. Okay.' She gave Beth a big hug. 'You guys are so good to me.'

'Even Ben? A minute ago he was a Neanderthal.'

'Ben a Neanderthal? Never. He's the most wonderful man in the history of the world.'

Beth nodded, agreeing wholeheartedly.

As the clock neared seven Beth screamed at Ben to take Holly into the front room and keep her there. 'If she asks me what he's like one more time, the pair of you will be sucking gravy from your shirts.'

Holly took a seat in the front room. She crossed and un-crossed her legs several times before settling on right over left. She nibbled at her manicured fingernails and her right leg jiggled up and down.

A sudden downpour made a soft, rhythmic drumming sound on the flat roof. Holly watched as rain created hypnotic rivulets down the window-panes. Each car driving past was heralded by a soft swoosh of tyres on the wet road surface. Headlights lit up raindrops on the glass to a blinding bril-liance, before fading as fast as they had arrived. But none heralded her blind date.

'Ben?'

'Yes, Holly.'

She knew that tone. Ben had already begun rubbing stiff fingers over the back of his neck.

'What does he know about me?'

'Are you sure you want to know? Are you sure you're not going to stop me as soon as I begin telling you?'

'I'm sure. Tell me. I can't stand it. I need to know something.' Holly's leg jiggled ever more violently.

'Okay,' he said. 'I told him that you were cute.'

'You said I'm cute?' Her leg jiggle slowed. 'You're so sweet.'

Ben mirrored her more relaxed behaviour. 'I told him that you and Beth had been friends for years—'

'He knows Beth well enough for you to mention I was friends with her?' she shrieked, and watched as a small muscle twitched in Ben's cheek. There was no stopping her. She was out of control.

'Maybe I should know who it is. No. I can't. Does Beth like him? What else did you tell him?'

Headlights flashed brightly through the window, though this time they shone directly through the lace curtains, and then switched off. Holly gulped as the engine sound stopped. He had arrived.

'I can't do this,' she whispered. 'Help.'

Ben stood and walked over to her, his jaw set. He grabbed her by the hand and pulled her to her feet. 'You want to know what else I told him about you?'

Ben propelled her to the front door. Holly knew that she had pushed him too far. She smiled in apology. 'I don't think I do.'

But it was too late. As the bell rang and just before Ben whipped open the front door he whispered in her ear.

'I told him you were on the prowl for a husband and he was candidate number one.'

CHAPTER FOUR

THE door swung open and Jacob found Holly frozen to the spot, her eyes wide and her mouth unnaturally ajar.

In that first moment, a broad smile swept across his face. He felt that same odd rush of warmth deep in the pit of his stomach that he felt each time he saw her.

Then he remembered Ben's revelation. The flowers he had brought for Beth drooped to his side. He glanced from Holly's curiously blanched face to Ben's apologetic one and he knew.

He had just turned up to a blind date with a husband hunter.

'Look, Holly. Flowers.' Ben grabbed the posy out of Jacob's hand and put them in Holly's, clasping her limp fist around the stems. 'Now, go put them in water.'

Ben spun her on the spot and gave her a little shove in the direction of the kitchen.

Jacob shrugged off his coat and shook his head to rid himself of a spray of raindrops that caught him on the way to the door, and then laid a friendly but controlling arm around his friend's shoulder. 'Is this what I think it is?'

'Mate, I'm sorry. I had a feeling neither of you would agree to come to dinner if I let on the other would be here.'

'You got that right.'

'If you are staying in town for any length of time you will be bound to run in the same circles so you may as well get to know each other.'

'Fair enough. But if that's all that this is, why is she acting like a living mummy?'

Ben flicked furtive glances towards the closed kitchen door. 'At times Holly can drive me around the bend, tonight being a prime example. And just before I opened the door I snapped and told her that—'

Ben stopped talking and swallowed. Jacob squeezed his friend's shoulder to hurry him up.

'I pretty much told her you knew she was "husband hunting" and that's why you were here.'

'You what?' Jacob dropped his arm from his friend's shoulder and took a step back, physically distancing himself from the shock.

'Look, Beth will be out any second, and she doesn't need too much excitement right now; so any shouting, and hitting, and telling Beth what I've done would create excitement. Please stay, eat a nice dinner. It'll all be over in a couple of hours.'

'I'll stay,' Jacob said through clenched teeth. 'For Beth.'

'Of course. And the shouting and hitting?'

'We'll save that for a rainy day.' Jacob grinned but it was all bared teeth and no pleasantry.

'And there's one more thing,' Ben said.

'What more could there possibly be?'

'It turns out Holly *doesn't* know you're Jacob Lincoln of Lincoln Holdings, which is a good thing as she really hated the whole boxing match and thus doesn't think much of him. You.'

Jacob blinked slowly. His mind was turning devilishly. Never one to shy away from a challenge—

'So, your Holly doesn't think much of me. Yet she thinks I have delivered myself here on a platter.'

'Yes. And?'

Jacob knew he had Ben worried. *Good.* 'Oh, I don't think you have the right to question me right now, my friend. No shouting, no hitting, now and for ever, as long as tonight you go along with whatever I throw at you. Deal?'

Ben looked over to the closed kitchen door. The water turned off and the kitchen door bumped as it started to open.

'Okay, deal,' Ben said.

Jacob slapped Ben on the back and grinned at his friend. But this time his smile was radiant with good humour.

Holly took her time fetching the food, and so gladly missed several minutes of chit-chat. That meant they were several minutes closer to the end of the night. Beth had just finished telling about the guitar lessons she was taking so she could play for her baby when Jacob informed the table at large that his younger sister was engaged.

'So that's why you're here,' Beth said. 'I knew it had to be more than just the temptation of my roast lamb. Have you met her fiancé?'

'I have. On Sunday. Nice guy,' Jacob said. 'This will be his second time around.'

'Divorced?' Beth asked.

'A widower.'

'Oh. Poor man. So he's older than Ana?'

'A good bit.'

'Doesn't surprise me, really, considering.' Beth brought her fingers to her temples and started to rub. 'Now, let me guess, knowing Ana, I bet he is in a caring profession. He's a...vet?'

'A triage nurse.'

Beth grinned. 'Oh, how perfect.'

'It would take someone with that sort of temperament to look after our Ana. She's quite a handful.'

'You would know.'

'No comment.'

Holly could tell there was some serious subtext to Beth's comments. She was intrigued despite herself, but her desire to stay invisible outweighed her curiosity so she let the conversation continue over her head.

'Anyway, good on him for taking her on,' Jacob said. 'I guess some people just like to be married.'

Holly stopped chewing and her cutlery stilled in her hand. *Did he seriously just say what I think he said?*

Ben coughed and she hoped he was choking on his potato. Beth's face, on the other hand, was all innocence. Perhaps Holly had misread the matter and Jacob was really talking about his sister, and not about her.

'Holly, could you please pass the broccoli?' Jacob asked.

Holly jumped in her seat at the call of her name. Her frazzled nerves were drawn as tight as Beth's new guitar strings. As she passed the bowl she locked eyes with the man across the table. He smiled bringing out his oh, so charming dimples.

He's the anti-husband, she reminded herself, *distant and indifferent. And his admittedly appealing dimples are, well, irrelevant.*

'Holly did the vegetables tonight, Jacob,' Beth said. 'She's a whiz with a steamer.'

Holly happily let go of the eye contact as she let go of the plate, and then shot Beth a quick yet entirely humourless smile.

'Anyway,' Jacob began again, 'Ana and Michael have known each other six months, been engaged for a week and are already talking kids.'

'Oh, that's wonderful,' Beth said.

'I'm all for short engagements,' Jacob said. 'She found someone like-minded, at the same point in his life, with the same goals and desires, and snapped him up. It was the smart thing to do.'

Was he serious? Holly had her reasons for embarking on her husband hunt, but what would Mr Standoffish be doing on a blind date with a woman he knew was after marriage? It made no sense. And, worse, it laughed in the face of her theory.

And who on earth was this guy? Ben had conveniently not let on what he did for the company. Maybe because Lincoln Holdings only kept him on in sympathy for some shocking flaw he hid under his cool good looks. Well, apart from the obvious personality defects Holly had already been subjected to.

To make matters worse, what if he eventually recognised her and let on that he was the guy on the street, the guy Beth knew had started her off on this crusade? If Beth knew, she would never let up about signs and primes and all sorts of gibberish. Holly was certain nothing bar that revelation could make this night more unbearable.

'I want kids, you know,' Jacob practically cooed. 'At least eight. No, eleven—a whole soccer team. So I should probably get started as soon as possible.'

Holly barely contained her groan. She lay down her cutlery, unable to stomach another bite.

Beth gave a painfully obvious nod towards Holly before asking, 'Do you have someone in mind to bear this football team for you?'

Holly glared ferociously at her friend, who refused to meet her eye.

'Not as such,' Jacob said, picking up a stem of broccoli on the end of his fork and twirling it before his eyes. 'But she would have to be a good cook. Though I would hope that she did not enjoy her own cooking so much that she not be able to keep her figure after the kids are born.'

What? Was this guy for real?

Jacob had trouble keeping the smile from his voice. Ben had his head buried in his hands, Beth's eyes were widening in shock with each absurd statement, and the lovely Holly was slumping lower and lower in her chair.

'Ben and I talked about this today. Didn't we, Ben?' Jacob casually cracked a knuckle or two as if to say, *Your choice: shouting and hitting or go with the flow.* Ben smiled ruefully and nodded.

'Constantly, mate. Hardly got any work done, we were so busy talking about kids.'

But Jacob wasn't finished yet—

'And I do like blondes. If I were to marry a brunette I would ask that she dye her hair. I mean, if she really cared for *my* feelings she would do that, wouldn't you think?'

Jacob revelled in the stunned silence that met his latest words. *Got 'em!*

'So, Holly, how about you?'

'Excuse me?' Holly squeaked.

'How many kids do you want?' Jacob asked.

Holly darted a hunted gaze to her friends but found no

help from their corner. Ben was finding his cutlery very interesting whilst Beth still stared at Jacob, her eyes bright with astonishment.

'Umm…kids?' she said. 'I haven't really thought about it.'

'No? I'm surprised at that.'

'Surprised?' Her voice was still an octave too high and barely above a whisper. She cleared her throat.

'Don't all women think of these things? How many and what you would name them all?'

'I guess,' Holly admitted whilst wishing she could dissolve into the floor.

'And haven't you had a distinct idea of the man you would one day marry?'

And then he smiled. From ear to ear. Adorably overlapping teeth, charming dimples and enough charisma to knock her socks off. If he had held up a big sign with an arrow pointing to himself it would not have been more obvious. He seemed so ripe he probably kept his grandmother's ring in the top pocket of his jacket every day…just in case.

She swallowed hard. Her brow was furrowed so tight it was giving her a headache. She knew her terrible poker face would be showing all the signs of the strain she felt. She could feel hot red blotches forming on her neck and cheeks. But she had no idea how to extricate herself from this nightmare.

Then suddenly Jacob's bright eyes narrowed, seemingly looking deeper and deeper into her own until she was sure she saw a softening. A melting. The impenetrable myriad hazel flecks in his gaze grew deep and kind and sad. For a flicker she sensed an apology, as real as if he had said it aloud.

And although she would have thought it impossible, it made her knees feel weaker than they had all night.

* * *

He had done enough. He had proven his point. After this performance, Ben and Beth would not dare to set him up on this kind of date again. And that was all he wanted from the night. So he changed tack.

'How about you, Beth? Did you think you'd end up with someone soft and fuzzy like young Benny boy?'

As Beth proceeded to regale the group with tales of numerous dream boys from her teens Jacob watched as Holly slowly relaxed.

Her natural colour had returned and he noticed again what an attractive woman she was—and just his taste. Not too tall, graceful, curvaceous, vivacious. And he had been lying earlier to rile her. He had never been one of those men who preferred blondes. Her lustrous, thick dark hair beguiled him. He found himself wanting to release it from its confining pins and feel its lush abundance sliding through his fingers.

With her head cocked, listening to Beth's funny stories, she surreptitiously picked up stray slivers of carrot and brought them to her mouth, daintily sucking them in with a swift sip. And each time she gave the tips of her fingers an unhurried lick, savouring the slight drops of honey. And Jacob was mesmerized. It was all he could do to stop himself from licking his own lips, she made it look so good.

'Don't you remember Gary Phelps, Holly?' Beth asked, snapping Jacob back to the conversation at hand. Holly even managed a small laugh. It was a pretty sound. Light and unselfconscious.

'He was so horrid, Beth.' Holly grimaced, but her voice had returned to a more normal timbre.

'He was not. He was lovely.'

'He was five feet tall and never washed his hair. I never knew what you saw in him.'

'Just because he wasn't tall, dark and handsome like every

boy you ever had a crush on didn't mean he couldn't be attractive to someone else. Namely me. And what a kisser.'

Holly flicked a sudden glance Jacob's way. If he had
blinked, he would have missed it, but he had caught its full
measure. It was a look brimming with suppressed attraction.
He should have jumped from his seat and run for his life. But
he didn't.

She had bruised his ego enough with her indifference towards his business practices. So he intended to soak up every
bit of positive attention she was willing to send his way. Just
to even the scales. That was all.

'Hey,' Ben called out, feigning a broken heart. 'You do
realise your husband and the father of your soon to be child
is sitting here having to listen to these stories of young love
which do not involve him.'

'Yes, darling but you have to remember that, out of this
long line of dreamboats, I chose you.'

'Very true.' Ben beamed lovingly at his wife.

Under the mask of laughing along with them, Jacob stole
a cheerful glance over Holly, and he found her leaning her
chin on her palm, watching Ben and Beth with a smile of
pure joy splashed across her lovely face. Her expression was
so tender it was luminous. And in that moment he thought he
understood her. It did not seem so very strange to want what
Ben and Beth had.

Jacob felt a sudden tightening in his chest. Not good. He
needed time out. He pushed his chair back and stood up.

'Excuse me, folks. I have to powder my nose.'

As soon as Jacob left Beth leaned forward and whispered
conspiratorially, 'What on earth is with him tonight, Ben?
All that talk of babies and blondes, that wasn't like the Jacob
Lincoln of old.'

'*Lincoln?*' Holly mimicked Beth's strained whisper, as it was the only way she could stop herself from shouting. '*He's* Jacob Lincoln? As in your boss, Link? As in Lincoln Holdings *Lincoln*?'

Ben flinched. 'Ah, yes. He's one and the same.'

'What on earth is he doing here? You told me he lived in… New Orleans or some such place.' And he was supposed to be balding, with a paunch and liver spots. Not…well, not so manifestly the opposite.

'He did,' Ben said. 'Then without telling a soul he moved back to Melbourne a couple of days ago.'

That first morning, standing on the corner, armfuls of luggage, faint accent. Holly dropped her face into her palms.

'That means I told him how little I thought of his boxing idea, not at the time realising that it was his idea, then accused him of going to the wrong bathroom, not at the time realising it was his bathroom. He's really Jacob *Lincoln*?' she repeated.

Ben shrugged and grinned contritely.

Holly's voice hissed as she turned on Ben, her pent-up mortification whirling into a terrible rage. 'And knowing all of this you set up this dinner, told him that I was "husband hunting", and that he was my number one contender?'

Beth also turned on her husband. 'Did you really do all of those things?'

Ben held his hands up in submission. 'Hey, you guys dragged me into this ridiculous plan of yours. So, I took you to a gathering teeming with numerous available red-blooded men and you hid in the bathroom all night. And then I ask the most eligible of all red-blooded men I know to dinner and you attack me.'

Holly was having none of it. 'But you told him—'

'The truth, Holly. But to tell *you* the truth I really did

wonder if my two best friends in the whole world might not hit it off.'

Beth's face softened easily. 'That's so sweet. Holly, forgive Ben.'

Holly sat back, all angered out. Her face was heated from her strained whispers and her head spun with the maze of words and deeds they had created for themselves.

Beth giggled. 'Now poor Jacob thinks Holly's hot for him. No wonder he has been acting so strangely.'

'Ah, well, actually,' Ben said, 'he knows the whole deal and has been pulling your legs all night.'

'Ha!' Beth said, clapping her hands together. 'Now that's more like the Jacob Lincoln of old.'

But Holly was not so amused. She was thinking. And planning. 'He knows the whole deal and he thinks I'm now sweating it.'

'Well, gorgeous, you have pretty much been sweating it all night,' Ben said.

'But I'm not now.' Now she knew the glimmer in Jacob's eyes had indicated he was enjoying an elaborate joke, not that he was sizing her up for a wedding dress.

Well, if it was fun and games he liked...

CHAPTER FIVE

WHEN Jacob re-entered the room Holly was standing by her empty chair, eyes closed, rocking her head side to side. He suppressed a grin as he settled back in his chair. He shouldn't have been worried; he still had the upper hand. He had the poor woman in knots.

As he watched she ran a hand up her side, and then back and forth across her shoulder, eyes still closed, head tossed back, leisurely massaging out those very knots. Her mouth dropped open and a blissful groan escaped her lips.

Whoa.

Jacob shifted in his seat, suddenly feeling mighty uncomfortable. He set his teeth and tore his eyes away before he would be forced to make another hasty exit to recollect his wits.

'What did I miss?' he asked, purposely not including Holly in his question.

But Holly had ceased her rub-down, and Jacob's gaze was magnetically drawn to the movement. He did not miss a single curve as her hand made its unhurried journey back down her side to rest provocatively on her hip.

'Nothing significant, Jacob,' Holly purred. 'I was just saying how much I was hankering for something sweet.'

Her lashes batted heavily against her cheeks, then her gaze fluttered and drifted to his lips.

The words 'then come and get it' sat precariously close to the tip of Jacob's tongue. *Get a hold of yourself,* he told himself. *You're imagining things. You're just tired. It's not been a week; can you still blame the jet lag?*

'Time for dessert, then, I think,' Beth said, her voice cheerful. Jacob flicked his glance to his other dinner companions. He had momentarily forgotten they were even there.

It took all of Jacob's concentration to focus on Beth, chatting to her about her nursery plans, resolutely ignoring Holly as she moved around the table clearing the dinner plates. His resolve weakened as he sensed her reach the back of his chair and it shattered when she bent to retrieve his plate and fanned a warm breath of air against his ear. It was all he could do to keep a straight face as a violent shiver racked his body.

Then, before disappearing into the kitchen, Holly turned and threw him a sultry wink.

Jacob stared at the closed kitchen door. She had assured him nothing significant had happened in his absence. She had fibbed.

In five mystery minutes, she had transformed from an overwhelmed young woman into a raging siren. And despite himself he was enthralled. Under that haughty façade lurked a hell-cat just waiting to claw her way out. It could be a lot of fun unlocking the door to that particular cage.

Jacob blinked his eyes back into focus to find Ben red-faced and shaking with laughter and Beth wiping tears of mirth from her cheeks.

And the truth dawned on him.

'She knows.' Jacob threw his napkin on the table in defeat.

'She knows,' Ben admitted. 'Shouting and hitting from you is nothing compared with the combined wrath of those two.'

'So,' Beth asked, her voice playful, 'are you going to propose to her now or after dessert?'

From the kitchen, Holly was glad to hear laughter.

She was about to return to the dining room to retrieve the cutlery when the kitchen door flapped open and Jacob joined her, cutlery in hand.

'Oh.' She took a step back, swamped by the man's considerable presence in the small kitchen. He leant past her to place the silverware in the sink, the sleeve of his dark grey suit jacket brushing against her arm. The sensation of the roughened wool against smooth bare skin was electric.

'I'm happy to clear. Go sit back down.' She waved him away with a flourish, and took two steps back leaving her flush against the kitchen cupboards. She desperately hoped he would leave her alone. But hoping did not make it so.

'Actually, I'm here to talk. The cutlery was just an excuse.'

'Oh,' she murmured again.

'That was some act you put on in there.'

Her blush was back. 'Your performance wasn't so bad either.'

He lowered his voice so that it washed over her as a soft rumble. 'Though I don't know that I can outdo your last turn—not with an audience, anyway.'

Gulp.

'So how about we call it even?' He held out his hand. 'Truce?'

Holly stared for several moments before reaching out and clasping it. His hand was soft and strong and she was thankful his palm was as warm as hers. When she let go she ran a nervous finger around the neckline of her dress.

'And I also wanted to apologise for that morning on the street.'

Holly's finger stopped, mid tug.

'That was atypical behaviour for me,' he said. 'And though I *was* jet-lagged, that was no excuse for bad manners.'

He stopped talking and Holly realised he was waiting for her to say something next.

'You didn't tell Ben that, did you?' she blurted out. Or Ben would have told Beth for sure and there would be no living it down. 'You didn't let on we had met before? That we met that way?'

'Ah, not as far as I remember.'

'Then don't. Please. For reasons inexplicable and uninteresting I would rather our first meeting stay our little secret.'

'Sure.'

Holly blinked. She had expected it to be harder than that. According to her theory he was supposed to be obstinate and unyielding.

'And one more thing, just to clear the air,' Jacob said.

'Go for your life.' So glad she was safe from Beth's karma and kismet conversation, Holly was ready to tell him anything.

'Do you mind telling me why you think you need Ben's help to find a husband?' He leant his large frame against the cupboards at her side and she had to look up to meet his eye.

'Oh,' she said for the third time in as many minutes, the blush now spreading all the way to her toes. 'Isn't that a little personal?'

Jacob laughed. 'Personal? You were ready to marry me before seven o'clock tonight.'

Holly's hands flew from where they gripped the cool kitchen sink to cover her fast-reddening cheeks. 'Don't remind me, please.'

She slowly lowered her hands from her face, thinking it must have been hot in the small room. His cheeks were as pink as hers felt. She wasn't just imagining it.

Then without warning Jacob raised his hand and ran a finger over a stray lock of hair that had escaped its confines. He slid it back into place behind her ear, his fingertip resting by her cheek for a few lingering moments. And during those long drawn-out seconds she could not have dragged her eyes away from his for all the world.

The scraping of a chair in the dining room brought Holly out of her reverie and she spun around to face the plates of dessert she had been preparing. Jacob cleared his throat and walked from the room without another word.

Holly went to pick up two plates and saw that her hands were shaking. She carefully placed the plates back onto the bench and took a couple of deep breaths.

'He's the enemy, remember,' she said aloud. 'The anti-husband. He was put on this earth to test you. If you can resist him, you can resist any of his kind.' She glared at her hands, demanding they not shake as she took the plates into the other room.

Hours later Holly helped Beth up to the master bedroom and left the men to say their goodnights downstairs. As Beth got into bed she said, 'He's a sweetie, Holly.'

'Of course he is or you wouldn't have married him.'

'I mean Jacob, you dope.'

Sweet's the last word I'd use, Holly thought. 'Yeah, well, the jury is still out on that one.'

'Promise me you'll give him a chance.'

Not likely. 'Sure, honey. For you, anything.'

'Good…goodnight…'

Holly kissed her sleepy friend on the cheek and headed quietly downstairs. The men's voices wafted up the stairwell. Holly stopped halfway down, her heart beating so loudly in her ears she was sure they would hear it too and know she was there.

'Give her a chance,' she heard Ben say. It made her smile, thinking how alike Ben and Beth were. But her smile soon faded at Jacob's response.

'Give me a break, Ben, I've been back in the country for a few days, and haven't even found the time to acquire a housekeeper. Besides which I have no idea how long I'm staying this time *and* you know my views on marriage. What were you thinking?'

She knew it! In that first instant when they had crashed together on the street she had seen it. She sensed this guy was the epitome of the inaccessible male. He was the antithesis of kind, committed Ben. Her theory had been right all along.

Holly strained to listen when there was a brief pause in the conversation.

'Unless of course she's handy with a feather duster…then both of our problems would be solved in one fell swoop.'

Charming! She waited for Ben's protest—which never came.

'Not likely, I'm afraid. A bit of a princess, our Holly.'

Ben! He always joked she would not know one end of a broom from the other, but did he have to describe her that way to a stranger? She pictured him describing her to other prospective men. 'She's a cutie, our Holly,' she could imagine Ben saying. 'She can cook up a storm but it will be you scrubbing the bathroom tiles.'

Great. No wonder his first attempts had been such failures.

Well, she would sort him out later so they could get this project back onto track.

Holly made great noise coming down the rest of the stairs, clumping loudly and whistling inanely.

'Isn't Beth asleep?' Ben asked, shushing her.

Holly clenched her fists at her side. 'Thanks for a *super* evening, Benny,' she said.

Jacob helped her into her coat at the front door. She wrapped a scarf around her neck but held onto her gloves, glaring at Ben and mouthing unpleasant promises as he waved goodbye and closed the front door with a soft click.

The rain had stopped but had left a slick sheen on the ground so Holly had no choice but to accept Jacob's elbow as they walked down the slippery front steps.

At the bottom of the driveway they reached Holly's car and she finally jerked her arm away. 'Thank you,' she said. Her breath showed white in the frosty midnight air.

'My pleasure.' He slipped his hands into his deep pockets.

'Look—' They both spoke at the same time. Jacob motioned for Holly to speak first.

'It's unlikely we will run into each other often, so, I think it best we just pretend we never met.'

'Sure,' Jacob said. 'No problem.'

Hmm. She had expected, 'If you say so,' or even, 'If you insist.' But, 'No problem'? Was she that easily forgettable?

Bothered beyond good sense, she mustered her haughtiest attitude. 'No matter what Ben told you, and not that it matters what you think, I am no princess.'

Jacob laughed, his head thrown back as he let out great effusive guffaws. Holly was shocked into momentary silence.

'You heard that?' Jacob finally asked, his eyes sparkling in merriment.

'Loud and clear. And I think that was extremely wrong of Ben and rude of you to even joke about such a thing.'

'Are you done?'

She looked up, surprised at his short tone.

'Well, yes, I thought that quite about covered it—'

Jacob leant over and placed a light kiss on her open mouth, succeeding in shutting her up. His hands remained in his pockets and her hands held her gloves in front of her at chest height. And since his toes were a couple of feet from hers, the only points of contact were their four, warm, amenable lips.

It took the merest moment for the unexpected tenderness of his kiss to wash its magic over her. On impulse Holly closed her eyes and tilted her head only ever so slightly. But it was enough.

Jacob took her hint and he leant that little bit closer to explore the warmth and thrill as unexpected yearning lit between them. And what started as little more than an overly friendly goodnight peck deepened into something very different. It was delicate. It was yielding. It was lovely.

After enjoying a few moments of unchecked ardour, they pulled apart.

Holly rocked back on her heels; luckily the car was there to catch her as she swayed. Her tongue ran over the back of her teeth and she could taste after dinner mints. She rocked forward as she opened her eyes and sighed, unconsciously biting her lower lip.

The adorable dimples reappeared on Jacob's smooth cheeks as he smiled. 'I think now it's time to go our separate ways. You and I have already created far too many inconsistent memories for one night.'

'Goodnight, Jacob,' Holly whispered, not trusting her husky voice.

'Goodnight, Holly,' he said, but his eyes were saying anything but. He let out a ragged breath, shook his head and turned away.

Holly dragged in a deep breath, revelling in the sweet smell of recent rain that wafted towards her on the light night breeze.

She opened her car door but turned quickly when she saw him coming back up the rise. She leant back on her car, holding her breath waiting to see what he would surprise her with next.

'I have to say this,' he declared, his face obscured by the darkness. 'You are an intriguing, vibrant and beautiful woman, Holly. Know your own worth.'

And then he turned and disappeared into the foggy night.

CHAPTER SIX

HOLLY waited until in between races to make her way from the big white marquee on the oval in the centre of the track where the Hidden Valley Greyhound Course fundraiser was being held. She stepped carefully, lifting her feet high as she made her way across the muddy dirt track.

Colonel Charles Lyneham, a long-retired Steward of the Course and her guest of honour, had gone for a walk around an hour before and had not returned, so Holly had set out to find him.

She ducked through a spot in the fence where the wire had broken away years before and headed up the old wooden steps to the grandstand. She checked in the clerk's offices, the betting areas and even in the car park. But the colonel was nowhere to be seen. She headed for the public bar, hoping she would not find him there.

As she rounded the corner the scene hit her like *déjà vu*. The smell of beer, mud and sweat. She, standing on the outside looking in, searching for someone she had lost. The only difference was years before her view had been from a couple of feet closer to the ground. At least now she was the right height to have a chance at finding a familiar silver-topped head standing tall above the pack.

She lifted on tiptoe but instead of finding said familiar silver-topped head, she recognised a pair of stunning, laughing hazel eyes looking her way.

Her heels dropped straight to the ground, her mind turning to the last time she had seen those eyes; midnight in a fog-shrouded street, after an exquisite kiss that had confused her exceedingly.

Suddenly a man reached out from the throng and grabbed her by the elbow, drawing her within the swelling crowd and giving her a big brotherly kiss on the cheek.

'Ben! What are you doing here?' Holly said, looking behind him half expecting Jacob to be hot on his trail.

'The company has a corporate box and Link sequestered it for the day. All the management guys are here for a welcome home bash. Come join us.'

'I can't, Ben. I'm here on a mission not a play date.' She tried to step back outside the bar but the crowd had long since swallowed them whole. 'Have you seen Charles Lyneham? He's with my party and seems to have gone walkabout.'

'The colonel? He's with us.'

Ben held her fast by the arm and dragged her through the crush. Bumped and jostled from all sides, she had no choice but to hug Ben's arm with both hands and hang on tight.

'Link found him wandering around outside after the first race,' Ben said. 'He coaxed him in for a tipple and he's been with us ever since. Now you'll have to come say hello.'

'Great,' Holly said. 'He's due to make a thank-you speech at our fundraiser in little under half an hour, and, the thing is, Charlie does not merely *tipple*. Now, thanks to your friend, if he's been in the bar *tippling* for an hour, it's very likely he will be there all day.'

Ben shrugged but had the good grace to look sheepish. 'Sorry, gorgeous.'

Jacob's hearty laughter rang out above their conversation and, despite her deliberate disapproval, she enjoyed every second of the delightful sound, an unwitting smile tugging at the corners of her own mouth. He certainly cut a compelling picture, standing taller than most of the others, one hand wrapped around a frosty glass of beer, the other tucked into the pocket of his suit trousers, and one foot casually resting on the bottom rung of a bar stool.

He was just ten feet away. The room was airless and muggy. Her face was hot and her palms sweating. And with each step nearer her heartbeat quickened.

She tottered after Ben, still holding tight so she wouldn't tumble and be crushed underfoot. She ventured a furtive glance around. No sign of Charlie, but she had no doubt he would not be far away.

Five feet. She felt eager and sick to the stomach all at once.

Come on, look up, see me. Let's just get it over with. Let's see if that kiss meant as little *to you as it did to me.*

'Link,' Ben called out over the noise.

Jacob looked their way. His ready smile brightened, and he winked as he caught sight of Ben. Then his glance shifted sideways to Holly and the smile changed.

His bright eyes darkened, clouded, his thick lashes descended mere millimetres until he was watching her from beneath them. The corners of his mouth fell. The warmth in his expression was more than a match for the heat pulsing through her body at that moment.

Then his gaze left her face to glance down to where she was hugging Ben's left arm tight to her chest.

She let go. Quickly. Hating the fact she must have seemed

so helpless, in her neat dress, her prim hair, clinging to Ben for protection against the unruly crowd.

Ben did not seem to notice, he just turned and smiled and placed a protective arm behind her back as he drew her into the group.

When Jacob looked back to Holly's face his smile was gone, and his once warm eyes were now cool and unreadable. He brought his glass up, and tilted it in her direction in an abrupt salute before drinking in a substantial mouthful and turning back to his men.

Holly's face burned. Sure, she had been the one to insist they pretend they had never met, but, still, she had not expected it to be so easy for him. In his company she could feel her pulse throbbing all the way to her toes. Yet this guy obviously felt nothing. He was too cool.

Ugh! Why had she expected it to be any different? She *knew* she had him pegged but for a moment had foolishly expected him to prove her wrong. Well, it looked as if her theory still stood the test. So be it.

She deliberately turned away from Jacob and assumed her most brilliant smile.

'I heard you gentlemen had waylaid a friend of mine.'

The men stopped talking as one.

'Sorry, Holly,' Ben said, 'it slipped my mind. Holly is in charge of the fundraiser under the big marquee and it seems we have stolen away her guest of honour.' He looked around, his hand never leaving Holly's back. 'Where has the young colonel gone?'

'It's his round, I'm afraid,' one young, good-looking member of the group said, his eyes on Holly, full of invitation. 'No way we could let him go until he'd paid his debt. So, you'll just have to wait with us until he gets back. And since this great lug won't introduce us, I'm Matt Riley. The new Accounts guy.'

'Nice to meet you Matt. I'm Holly Denison.' She shook his hand. It held hers for a fraction longer than necessary.

'I know,' he said.

Ben's joke came swimming back to her and Holly had visions of her photograph and phone number in the men's room at his work—

'I saw you at the fight.'

This guy was at the fight? He was one of the men she'd had the possibility of meeting that night? She took a closer look at the very real option before her. Tall, athletic, nice smile. Very cute.

Then from behind her Jacob openly scoffed. Holly spun on her heel and turned narrowed eyes his way, but to little avail. His distant expression was unaltered.

'You must have good eyesight, Riley. She was there for all of ten seconds.'

His gaze held hers without a hint of remorse. She glared back, her infuriated eyes daring him to go on and at the same time demanding he say not another word.

He turned to face Matt and shrugged. 'From what Benny boy told me, anyway.'

'Well, obviously ten seconds was enough to make an impression on me. But you did your runner before I had the chance to say hi.'

Holly spun back to face her new suitor and beamed, before flicking a smug grin over her shoulder at Jacob.

'You don't say.'

Go, Matt, she thought, *you're definitely younger, possibly cuter, and certainly more of a gentleman than the loud mouth behind me. Fair where Jacob is dark. Candid where Jacob is confusing. Yes, very cute indeed. But I think you know it too. Highly likely* another *party personality at work.*

Suddenly disinclined to play favourites, she broke away from Matt's concentrated attention and introduced herself to several other young men, most of them her age, a couple of them uncommonly good-looking. These guys were in the inner sanctum so they were obviously smart, successful and hand picked by Ben to work at Lincoln Holdings. This was exactly who Ben should have been setting her up with.

She was able to enjoy the possibilities for several moments until she once more locked eyes with Jacob. He wasn't smiling at her as the other men were; he was practically smirking. Sitting back, arms crossed, like an omniscient little devil watching over her. Evidently, he knew exactly what was going on in her mind.

Holly plastered the smile to her face and shrugged. Why deny it? What was it to him anyway?

'Holly, my sweet. How good of you to join us.' It was the colonel, back with a round of drinks. 'I would have invited you to come up here with me but it's been years since I have seen you step foot in this ancient inn.'

'Charlie,' Holly said, her antagonism subsiding in the company of the darling old man, 'you know I would go anywhere you asked me to. But we do have another arrangement today. Remember the fundraiser?'

Charlie nodded.

'The big marquee? Your thank-you speech?'

He stopped nodding. 'Oh.'

She studied him carefully for signs he had been drinking. He was sweating a little, but so was she in the hot, confined space. He was upright and his speech was not slurred. Shy of sniffing the drink in his hand she had no idea if he had been 'tippling' as Ben had suggested.

'I suggest we let Charlie finish his *lemonade*,' Jacob said,

'then we can all head down and listen to this great speech of
his. What do you say, Ms Denison?'

Lemonade? Holly looked up into Jacob's face in amazement. Gone was the smirk. In its stead was a raised eyebrow,
an easy smile. *How had he known?*

'Sounds fair to me,' Holly said, sending Jacob a terse nod
of thanks.

The colonel downed the remainder of his lemonade with
one swift, practised flick of his wrist. 'Off we go then.'

Holly turned towards the front of the bar and found she
was confronted once more by a seething mass of white shirts
and ties. She physically dreaded forcing her way through the
hot, sweaty throng. But then Jacob's voice bellowed from just
behind her.

'Clear the way, gentlemen! The colonel is coming
through.'

All of the men nearby acquiesced, and once the Chinese
whispers spread through the place a clear, snaking path, an
amazing sort of honour guard, formed from their table to the
door. The colonel smoothed down his suit and with head held
high traversed the way.

Holly felt a warm hand land softly in the small of her back.
She turned to find Jacob bowing gallantly towards her, his
face mere inches from her own.

'Shall we, Ms Denison?' He removed his warm hand and
offered his elbow. She looked into his quixotic hazel eyes
searching for a trap. Unfortunately they were as inscrutable
as he chose them to be.

Ahead of her the extraordinary meandering path was
threatening to collapse back in on itself. For once Jacob's
company seemed the lesser of two evils, so she took his arm
and walked at his side.

The back of Holly's hand rubbed against Jacob's shirt-cov-
ered bicep, the sensation heated, intoxicating, reprehensible.

Thankfully the awareness of that tantalising touch was short-lived, as soon the peripheral heat was all that registered.

The room was stifling, her view filled with sweaty, leering faces. Somebody trod on her foot and spinning around to apologise, they spilt drink down her side. She leapt back, clutching onto Jacob's arm with both hands. He immediately wrapped a protective hand over the top of hers, its warmth and tenderness calming her a little.

Feeling claustrophobic, she closed her eyes, and allowed herself to be led the rest of the way blind. Only once bright sunlight lit the inside of her eyelids blood red did she open them.

Finding they were now in the big open space at the top of the grandstand, she hungrily inhaled the fresh, cool winter air, her breath releasing on a shudder.

She turned to thank Jacob but he was in conversation with two of his men, pointing towards the track where Race Three had just begun. And Holly knew she would not get any sense from any of them until the event was over.

The first two races had been won by the favourites and Holly expected no different ending to this one. She remained silent, unmoved as the dogs rounded the final bend.

The sparse crowd in the grandstand rose to its collective feet and the men in her own party jumped up and down, yelling and screaming, and clutching their betting slips in tight, agitated fists. The favourite, Sir Pete, was a nose behind, and the possibility of an upset electrified the air.

'I don't know why they get so excited,' Holly muttered under her breath, 'Sir Pete will win.'

'Don't bet on it,' Jacob said equally quietly, his eyes bright.

'I never would.'

Then, in the last twenty metres, Sir Pete put on a

phenomenal burst of speed and finished two body lengths ahead of his nearest competitor.

'I hate to lose,' Jacob said through comically clenched teeth as he ceremoniously tore up his losing bet.

'So pick the favourite.'

A huge grin broke out over his face, its effortless brilliance surprising her, catching her unawares and sending a blissful rush from her neck to her toes.

'You are one surprising woman, Holly Denison.'

Definitely time to go back to her party.

CHAPTER SEVEN

ONLY when Holly made to follow her departing group did she find herself still attached to Jacob's arm. Flicking him an apologetic smile, she released her steel grip. But he pulled her back until she was flush against him.

'Not just yet, Ms Denison. Before I let you go, I have a question I simply must have answered.'

His voice was low and husky. His face was in shadow, and his dark hair in a halo of sunlight as he stood with his back to the sun.

'Ask away,' she said, her voice reedy.

'What on earth are you wearing on your feet?'

Holly blinked. Looked at her feet. And grinned. In all the confusion, she had plum forgotten.

'Haven't you even seen a pair of galoshes before, Mr Lincoln?'

'Of course. I have even seen ones that yellow before. But not, I must admit, on a grown woman, otherwise dressed to the hilt as you are. Is this some kind of fashion statement?'

'Hmm. You have been away too long, haven't you? Bright

yellow galoshes are Melbourne's must-have fashion item this winter.'

'Throw out the little black dress?' he asked.

Holly brought her spare hand to her heart and gasped in mock shock. 'Gosh, no. Never. But wear with the little black dress? Of course.'

Jacob nodded, his expression deadly serious, as though impressed by her wealth of fashion knowledge. He eased her into a slow ramble towards the grandstand steps.

'Now you've answered the what, do I get to hear the why?'

Holly paused a moment for effect. 'So my feet don't get wet.'

Jacob glanced at her sideways and raised one unconvinced eyebrow.

'Okay. After last night's downpour, I arrived this morning to find the ground below my marquee ankle-deep in mud. Rather than have guests whose only memory of the day would be their wet feet, and without having to move the whole she-bang up to a dreary old conference room with no view of the track, I brought in enough galoshes and warm socks to shoe my entire guest list.'

As her tale unfurled Jacob stopped watching the group ahead of him, and concentrated fully on her, his eyes growing bright with delight.

'And besides you, did *anybody* actually dare to wear them?'

'Sure. Everybody.'

Holly pulled Jacob up short as they had reached the fence line that separated the crowd from the track. Jacob looked about for the rest of their group and finding them heaving themselves awkwardly over the fence several metres away, he tried tugging her in their direction.

But Holly tugged him back.

She beamed at him proudly, then slipped effortlessly through the concealed hole in the fence that the others did not know was there. Jacob watched in amazement before following her through.

They trudged across the muddy dirt track, nearing the huge white marquee, which glowed brightly in the midday sun, the canvas roof flapping softly in the light breeze. The sounds of clinking glasses and happy chatter wafted across the way.

Holly smiled inwardly. Jacob looked so dubious. His expression was like a child's on Christmas Day, just before opening his present from Grandma. Would it be the monster truck he had been promised or would it be tartan hankies again?

Jacob's doubt was written so clearly across his face that Holly's inward smile twisted with sadness. She had the feeling that he probably always doubted good things could happen until he saw them with his own two eyes. This was a man who knew disappointment.

The men ahead of them lifted the flap and headed inside. Holly and Jacob came close on their heels. Enjoying the moment intensely, Holly made sure she got there first. She grabbed a hold of the big flap and feeling like a ringmaster, opened it with a flourish.

Jacob was astounded.

Inside the marquee were glass-topped tables, candlelight shimmered from every spare surface and even from makeshift chandeliers hanging low from the ceiling. Heaters were scattered discreetly throughout the tent. The walls crawled with ivy interweaved with daisies and daffodils. The effect was like a mirage, a dash of springtime in the middle of the gloomy, muddy oval outside.

He scanned the faces of the people in the room. Many

familiar, several famous. All laughing and drinking and obviously having a ball. And all were wearing bright yellow galoshes.

He turned to Holly, who was watching him with a satisfied grin splashed across her lovely face.

'I am impressed.'

'And your feet?' she asked.

Jacob lifted one foot and saw the kid leather was wet through and through. 'Ruined. Even my socks are soaked.'

Holly gave a quick nod to someone outside Jacob's field of view and within a couple of seconds a waiter arrived, the tray in his arms laden with a pair of brand new galoshes and a pair of thick cotton socks, both in size extra large.

'Do I have to?' he asked.

'What do you think?'

In answer Jacob grabbed the galoshes and pulled up a spare garden chair. He held up his wet leather lace-ups and the waiter swapped the ruined shoes for a cloakroom ticket and disappeared to look after other guests.

'There,' Holly said. 'Now you fit in. Now you're one of us.'

She turned away to give instructions to an earnest young man with a clipboard. She was efficient. She liked being in control.

And then he realised: she was happy because he had done what *she* wanted him to do. He bristled, hating the feeling of being constrained, of being dared to make a choice not his own.

He was a free man with nothing and no one holding him down. He had lived that other life, being beholden to someone else's needs and wishes. And he never wanted to go that way again. Then he stopped himself.

Relax. It's a pair of shoes. This is one afternoon. You can give over to someone else's wishes for one afternoon. It's not like you will be giving over the decision-making to the woman for a lifetime.

A lifetime. And he remembered. She was on the hunt for a husband and had convinced Ben to help her.

Why? She was gorgeous. Slim, with curves in all the right places and the sort of lush dark hair any man would love to run his fingers through. And he knew those legs of hers were long, lithe, and smooth, though right now half hidden beneath those ridiculous rubber boots.

She had been attracting plenty of interested looks since she had walked in, and earlier his men had practically tripped over each other for the sake of one of her smiles.

Jacob observed a couple of well-dressed sorts on the other side of the tent obviously talking about her. And he felt an unexpected urge to go to her. To shield her from their view. To defend her against their scrutiny.

She must have caught him watching her as she raised her eyebrows in question. She held up a finger to tell him she would only be a moment.

Her face was so open. She smiled, she frowned, and every thought was out there for all to see. And as he watched her face became more familiar and comfortable every second. It was not long before he felt as if he knew every expression her lovely face could generate.

Finally, she came over and slumped into a chair beside him and at once in such close proximity, away from the beer and the sweaty men, a sudden sweet scent drifted his way. It was heady and rich, like jasmine. It was her. And it rocked him.

Trouble. The word rang unbidden in his head. Without even trying, this one could prove to be a whole truckload of trouble. He should go. Back to his corporate box. Back to the office. Back to the other side of the world.

He should. But he couldn't. Not yet, anyway.

'You are a workhorse, Ms Denison,' he said, his tone chatty.

'All for the good of the racecourse,' she said.

'And all for the good of Cloud Nine's coffers.'

'Not this one, I'm afraid. This one is my own little baby and Cloud Nine have learnt to look the other way.'

'You are doing all this for nothing?'

'Don't get me wrong. I'm not footing the bill for all this grandeur. The costs for the day will come out of the takings, but I promise it will turn a very tidy profit.'

'Of which you will see not a cent?' Jacob could not believe he had heard right.

Holly laughed. 'You are such a doubting Thomas, Mr Lincoln. I promise I will not see even forty cents for a phone call.'

'Why?'

'These fundraisers make enough every year to keep the place running. If I took my usual percentage the day would be redundant.'

'But why here? Why this place? You said before you never bet. Do you just love the greyhounds that much?'

She pulled a face. 'Not at all. The whole half-starved puppies chasing a rabbit thing doesn't do it for me. It's just for the colonel, really.'

'How do you know him so well?'

She opened her mouth to answer but seemed to think better of it. She glanced around as though searching for a reason, or maybe a change of subject, and seemed to visibly relax when she saw the colonel coming her way.

'Holly, my sweet!' he said, his arms outstretched, ready to take her in.

She stood and gave the old man a big hug. Jacob felt an uncomfortable contraction in his chest at the sudden change in her. With him she was still the cool, confident, modern Melbourne woman, but in the company of the right person she blossomed into a completely different creature. Her smiles were softer, sweeter, with an abundant capacity for effortless delight.

'Charlie. Are you having a good time?'

'Always, my pet.'

'Are you ready for your speech? You are up in about ten minutes.'

'No problem. You are a sweet girl.' The colonel turned to Jacob. 'Our little mascot she was, always running around underfoot. Long hair flying behind her as she ran about the grandstands collecting old tickets, looking for the one that got away.'

A snippet of conversation from the grandstand snuck back into Jacob's consciousness. Not knowing how to fit the mismatched pieces into her story, he felt the fragment flutter away.

'And look at that little scar.' The colonel pointed at the bridge of Holly's nose and, though she swatted his hand away playfully, Jacob thought he saw a moment of panic in her action. 'Barely there now. All healed.'

Holly cut the colonel off, grabbing him around the middle and dragging him away, rolling her expressive blue eyes behind his back. 'Anyway, Charlie, it's all well and good taking us down amnesia lane, but it's time to get you to the stage. Excuse us, Jacob.'

And this time when she smiled it was just for him. And he knew, despite his very sensible inner protests, he was not going anywhere any time soon.

The colonel's speech went brilliantly. It was funny, sweet, and tender enough to have those listening make enough donations to run the old Hidden Valley Greyhound Course for another good year.

Jacob and Ben had waited for Holly. The other guys had gone back to the city to finish off their celebration, minus their guest of honour, and Holly offered to drop the two men home.

As the sun set over the all but empty racecourse they crossed the track in companionable silence. The ground had dried somewhat and they were all now in regular footwear. Though Holly, in her high heels, had a little trouble matching their long strides.

'Isn't this where you are supposed to lay down your coats for me?' she asked the men.

'I thought that was only for a queen,' Ben said from a few steps ahead of them.

'And we know you are only a princess,' Jacob whispered against her ear, sending thrilling hot shivers down the back of her neck. Holly poked out her tongue, though inside she was feeling far from flippant.

No matter how often she reminded herself of her perfectly good theory, she was beginning to sense there was more going on behind Jacob's taciturn gaze than she had at first thought. For instance, what sort of man would have the strength of personality to be able to persuade an alcoholic to drink lemonade in a public bar?

But maybe that was not the point. Maybe the theory just needed a little tweak. Maybe her archetypal Mr Standoffish *was* born with a conscience; just not with the commitment gene. He could be attractive as Adonis, and as intelligent as Plato, but would he be devoted as say, Ben?

That she very much doubted.

Jacob pressed a gentle hand to her back as they reached the gate to the car park. She leapt away from him as though his warm fingers were laced with fire. He did not seem to notice, he just kept herding her through the space and dropped his hand casually as they reached her car.

First Holly dropped Jacob back to the Lincoln Holdings offices where he was planning to put in a few more hours. He hopped out of the car, then peered through the driver window.

'Thanks for the lift.'

'No problem.' She had left the engine running at the ready for a quick getaway.

'And for the lovely afternoon. It was most…unexpected.'

She smiled, her lips tight, her hands clasping and unclasping the steering wheel. He was so close she could sense the remnants of his aftershave. Sweet and dry at the same time. Delicious.

He placed his hands on the bottom of the open window and leant in, his breath fanning her face as he spoke beyond her to Ben. 'See you tomorrow, Benny boy.'

Ben cocked his hand like a pistol. 'Shall do, boss.'

Jacob turned to Holly, his face still only inches from hers. It was all she could do not to close her eyes, drink in his delectable scent.

'I'll see you, Holly,' he said, and by his tone she believed it. He leant in and brushed a fleeting kiss upon her cheek. His lips were warm, soft, and gone all too soon. 'Promise me you will get Benny boy home to Beth in one piece.'

'I promise. Goodbye, Jacob.'

And as soon as his hands left the window she sped away. Allowing herself one brief glance in the rear-view mirror she saw Jacob standing in the road, his hands in his trouser pockets, watching her.

She kept her focus on the road ahead though her mind was

spinning in another direction. 'Have you found *anyone* else to set me up with?'

Ben paused, as he seemed to absorb this question. 'I'm sure I could rustle up a couple of possibilities.'

'Then do it. As soon as possible.'

'If that's what you still want.'

'It is.' He was watching her but she ignored him. She had said all she wanted to say on the matter.

'Consider it done.'

She nodded, then drove Ben home to his waiting wife.

CHAPTER EIGHT

THANK GOD it's Friday, Holly thought as the drinks waiter handed over her champagne glass of lemon, lime, bitters, and a dash of honey. She savoured a long, thankful taste before looking over the room. All of the guests at the Arty Pants Modern Art Gallery Charity Evening were smiling, chatting, and paying a good deal of attention to the art. All was well.

Until one man in the corner smiled her way. A man in an expensive suit, blond hair thinning and styled to within an inch of its life, strong tan, perfect teeth. Holly's smile faded.

Oh, boy, not another one. Do they pop out of an assembly line just to attend parties and openings and corroborate my theory?

The man raised his glass in salute. Holly gave him a short polite nod and then moved away.

Luckily Lydia had just arrived, back from a week assisting at a Star Trek conference in Sydney.

'Hello, gorgeous!' Lydia called out as though she were on the other side of the room, not leaning into Holly's arms for a fond embrace. 'Loving it all, Holl. Great food, fabulous music and a feast for the eyes. Speaking of which, that blond dish in the corner is eyeing you up.'

Holly shot a quick glance at the man. He was still watching her over his tumbler.

'Sorry, Lydia. Not interested.'

Lydia raised a thin blonde eyebrow in disbelief. 'Why? Do you have something better lined up for dinner already?'

'Hardly. The truth is, while you were away Ben set me up on a spate of blind dates and the thought of telling my life story one more time makes me feel sick to the stomach.'

'So the husband hunt is off to a flying start, hey?'

Holly shrugged.

'Of course, while you were off having wildly romantic nights with dozens of men, I was fending off pointy eared, eight-foot geeks in rubber masks. Though there was this one Klingon…' She smiled slowly, before shaking her head clear. 'Anyway, please renew my hope in mankind. Tell me they were all delicious.'

Holly laughed. 'Tiresome, more like.'

'Hmm. Tiresome, were they?' Lydia waved a hand, indicating her question related entirely to bedroom pursuits.

Holly grabbed the offending hand. 'Lydia!'

'Come on, then. Gory details, please. I expect to be swooning at the end of this.'

'No promises, but here goes. Wednesday's guy took me to a restaurant where we had to sit on the floor, which was fine, until he removed his shoes. Foot odour competing with curry is not a scent I will soon forget.'

'So buy him cotton socks. Ooh, and you could wash his feet every night. Terribly sexy. Next!'

'Okay. Last night my blind date picked me up from work. Nice car. Nice conversation. Nice guy. Until he took me via home to meet his mother. And that was before dinner.'

'You are too picky. Mummy's boys can be wonderful. I'll bet he even cooks and cleans.'

'You think I'm too picky? Well, then, beat this, one gentleman offered to sire me a football team.'

Lydia's effusive laugh rang across the room so that several people turned their way. 'Now that one is a definite keeper. If you don't want him, give him my number.'

Holly felt an unwelcome prickling in her stomach at the thought of giving Lydia's phone number to that particular blind date.

'I guess this means fending off next-morning phone calls from panting men is back on my job description.'

Holly did not have the opportunity to refute Lydia's claim as her acquaintance's eyes were fixedly focussed on something, or someone, beyond her shoulder.

'Now that tasty morsel was worth coming along for.' The younger woman nodded coyly at the vision behind Holly.

'Who?' Holly spun around to catch a glimpse of the object of Lydia's divided attention. She could not hide her gasp at the sight of Jacob Lincoln ridding himself of his coat by the front door.

Lydia whirled straight back to Holly. 'You know him, I take it.'

'Barely.' Holly turned away from the door, her cheeks heating madly, her eyes scanning the room for safe ground.

'Holl, you have a shockingly ineffective poker-face, you know. And if you are thinking you can avoid introducing us now, you are sorely mistaken.'

Lydia grabbed Holly by the elbow and spun her around to face the door. Together they watched the man straighten his tie, smile at the hat-check girl as he took his ticket, and then look up, overtly searching the room.

* * *

It took only a moment for Jacob to catch sight of the two women near the bar. The younger woman with the mop of blonde curls and hot pink feather boa wrapped around her thin shoulders was practically beckoning him with her eyes, whereas the woman with the sleek chestnut hair and vibrant form-hugging dress in a mix of eye-popping blues and greens seemed to be finding her shoes extremely fascinating.

Jacob took a deep breath, straightened his tense shoulders, pocketed his coat-check ticket, and made a beeline towards them.

Jacob's usually confident gaze was flicking from side to side, his hands were clenching and unclenching in his trouser pockets and Holly knew he was, for once, unsure of himself. Amongst the bohemian crowd in which Holly felt totally at ease, Jacob was visibly unnerved, just as she had been amongst the beer, boxing and betting.

She smiled. Now they were even.

Holly guessed he probably felt more than a little over-dressed, but he was disarming in his black dinner suit, crisp white shirt and lavender tie. He oozed masculinity amongst the eclectic group of buyers, dealers, artists, and hangers-on, standing out like a prize bull in a field of mangy goats.

He nodded his hello.

Holly nodded back, though her brisk glance barely connected with his. She could feel Lydia grinning enormously beside her and soon received a distinct jab in the ribs.

'Jacob, this is my assistant, Lydia Lane. Lydia, this is Jacob Lincoln of Lincoln Holdings.'

Lydia offered her thin hand to Jacob, hot pink fingernails glinting in the created light. 'Enchanted, Jacob.'

'The pleasure's all mine, Lydia,' Jacob said, his tentative smile showcasing his dimples.

'I never knew the man behind the name would be so young, and so damnably attractive. Either way, you are a breath of fresh air blowing into this old crowd.'

Holly tried hard not to laugh aloud at Lydia's lavish efforts at sophistication.

Jacob leaned in closer to Lydia, his voice secretive. 'I've never actually been to one of these evenings before.'

'Really?' Lydia whispered back. 'Why are you here to-night, then?'

'I was invited by the kind people of Cloud Nine Event Management.'

Holly looked up, her eyes narrowed, and finally connected fully with his. 'No, you weren't.'

Lydia coughed back a scandalized laugh.

'I mean, I don't remember seeing your name on the guest list,' Holly said more tactfully.

Jacob reached into his jacket pocket and pulled out his invitation. Holly grabbed it and saw that it was addressed to the chairman of the Find Families Homes Foundation, the main beneficiary of the night's takings. Her eyes flew back to his.

'That's you?'

'That's me.'

'But they're wonderful.'

'Meaning I'm not?'

Drowning in Jacob's amused eyes, Holly gulped down a lump that had begun to hinder her breathing. She looked to her drink for inspiration and, finding only bubbles that matched the sensations in her stomach, she reached deeper for an explanation.

'No, I mean they are so kind, one of my...Cloud Nine's favourites. Their board always sends the most *wonderful* appreciative notes of thanks for our efforts but they have never sent a representative to the actual events.'

'Well, I'm here now, aren't I?' The tinge of a Louisiana accent leant his naturally deep voice a captivating drawl and it washed like an intimate caress over her bare shoulders.

'Looks like someone did not do her research,' Lydia said. 'Not my fault, of course. I've been out of town.'

Jacob grinned.

'I have a question for you, Jacob. Lincoln Holdings runs all events in-house, don't they?' Lydia asked. 'Why is that?'

Trust Lydia to get straight to the point. Holly pricked up her ears, very interested in the answer.

'I like to stay in control, so I keep my interests close. I find no point in outsourcing work when I can usually do it better.'

Holly openly scoffed.

'Though Holly and I will agree to disagree on that point.'

'If you are not simply an A-list party-goer, and have no use for her professional expertise, how do you know my gorgeous young friend here?' Lydia asked.

'We've only met briefly once or twice...' Holly mumbled.

'Mutual friends set us up on a blind date...' Jacob answered.

The two spoke over the top of each other, with Jacob's deep, clear voice coming out on top. Holly groaned, wishing she had not felt the need to entertain Lydia with her blind-date disaster stories earlier.

'Oh, you have to be kidding!' Lydia jumped up and down on the spot, clapping her hands in glee, her ringlets bobbing up and down, all efforts at sophistication blown. And Holly knew Lydia would sooner not breathe than not comment.

'Were you the guy with the live-in mother or the one who

is planning on keeping Holly with child for the next decade? If he's the one with the foot odour, Holl, I'd wash this man's feet morning, noon and night.'

The one with the live-in mother? The one with foot odour? Had Holly been on further blind dates since meeting him? Ben had not mentioned a word of it. True, he had not asked Ben, just assuming the misguided idea would have lost its momentum by now.

But there had been others. And though that meant she was still forging ahead on her mad husband hunt, which he wanted no part of, he found he did not like the thought of her seeing other men one little bit.

'Come on,' Lydia repeated, 'which one were you?'

Holly watched Jacob under lowered eyelashes. Since Lydia's outburst, a small muscle in his cheek had been clenching and unclenching and his bright eyes were clouded by shadow. He turned an enigmatic smile her way, his stare so focussed it knocked the breath from her lungs.

'Well,' he said, his deadpan gaze never leaving her face, 'I hope I'm the one who spoilt her for all others.'

Holly's mouth flew open wide, ready to deny the ludicrous statement outright, knowing Lydia would otherwise lap it up.

And then it dawned on her. That was exactly what he had done. On her other dates she had been distracted. When they had picked her up, her mind had wandered to the night in the foggy street. When they had sat down to dinner she'd remembered Jacob in his impeccable suit, wearing those ridiculous yellow galoshes at the greyhound track. When they'd spoken they'd been drowned out by memories of Jacob's smooth, sonorous voice, rich with charm and that barely there accent.

She had not been looking for problems on her dates, but

looking for ways in which those men could measure up to this one. Having experienced his intelligence, wicked sense of humour, and looks so fine they made her knees weak every time she caught him even glancing her way, she was finding it hard to accept less in the other men she met.

But he so clearly did not match her criteria. Too detached, too independent, too…too much. Not like Ben in the least. And Ben was her yardstick when it came to husband material.

'How was the date, really?' Lydia said, breaking the silence.

'It was entirely dreadful…' Holly said.

'It was quite promising…' Jacob said.

And again, his answer came through loud and clear.

'Promisingly dreadful or dreadfully promising?' Lydia asked.

Before either could answer, Lydia's attention was drawn elsewhere. 'There's the superb St John. I have to congratulate him on his ace lithographs. I'll leave you two sweet young things to yourselves, then, shall I?'

Lydia left in a cloud of youthful perfume and floating pink feathers, and once more Holly was alone with Jacob. She knew she should bid him good evening and walk away. The less time spent in his complicated company, the better.

She searched for a way out, someone requiring her professional attention. But she only found the simpering blond gentleman eyeing her like a hawk. She glanced back at Jacob and in a heartbeat knew the blond would be the safer option.

But it was too late. She was drawn into Jacob's resolute hazel gaze and found herself rooted to the spot. She could not blame her bubbling drink for the hot flush creeping across her bare neck, as she had been drinking nothing bar lemon, lime and bitters with a dash of honey all night.

* * *

Jacob watched in fascination as the faint blush swept across Holly's delicate shoulders. He felt an unrelenting urge to stroke a cool hand along her neck to feel its warmth. Her face hid nothing of the tumult raging inside her and he was amazed. Amazed at her strong physical reaction to him, though not amazed at how much he enjoyed it.

'Why did you really come tonight?' Holly asked, her eyes hiding none of her uncertainty.

Jacob plunged his hands deep into his pockets, knowing from her tone they were safer there than coming anywhere near this volatile vixen.

'I had an opening in my calendar and the invitation offered free canapés.' Jacob knew his flippant responses would wear thin, but he had no intention of telling her he had spent so much time thinking about her he was getting little work done.

The truth was he had decided the only fix was to see her again. The fantasy girl he had progressively built in his head over the last couple of days could only be toppled once tempered by the real thing. The bundle of nerves before him.

The husband hunter—who it turned out was infinitely more tempting up close and personal than even her fantasy version.

'Where can a man get a drink around here?' He searched the room, saw the small bar, and taking Holly by the elbow, led her to the counter. 'Another for the lady and the same for me, please.'

'It's not champagne,' Holly said.

'That's okay by me. You don't drink?'

'Not when I'm working, no.'

He had forgotten for a moment she was working. Foolishly, he had been lulled into feeling as if they were just out for a drink. He and Holly, together.

Mistake.

Holly played with one of her dangly turquoise earrings as she turned to chat to the head beverage waiter, making sure the guests had so far been happy on the drinks front.

Jacob used the quiet moment to focus, to get back to the real reason he had come. The fact that she was on the lookout for a husband was not proving to be a big enough barrier to his temptation any more. So he took a good look at her, with every intention of finding as many faults as it would take to render her unappealing.

Her customary fringe was slicked from a dramatic side parting across her forehead, and hair was drawn into a low heavy bun at her nape, leaving her creamy shoulders bare. He wished she would wear her hair down for once. There, that was a fault. Wasn't it?

With a critical eye his gaze moved lower, meandering down the delectable curves enhanced by her stunning, sleek, psychedelic dress. The lustrous fabric fell to the top of her feet, thus hiding her lovely legs. She covered them too often. He knew he was stretching to find a fault with that, but a fault it had to be.

And then, as though she sensed the direction of his gaze, Holly's hand left her earring and ran down her leg to her foot, unconsciously rubbing the insole. Watching, enthralled, Jacob caught a glimpse of a simple gold toe ring on one sandalled foot and it surprised him. A touch of the gypsy amidst her cool glamour. He let out a deep breath, the simple frivolity of that one piece of jewellery promising so much more. So much hidden. So much waiting to be discovered.

Through her entire conversation Holly had been sure Jacob's eyes had not left her and as such she had barely been able to concentrate on the poor waiter, having to ask him to repeat himself on more than one occasion.

But when she looked up Jacob's wide eyes were on the

waiter, who was dipping a teaspoon in and out of their drinks.

'Is that honey?' he asked.

Holly merely raised her eyebrows as if to say, *You asked for it.* She took her drink and sipped at it happily.

Jacob took his, sniffed at it, stared at it, and shook the glass. And even put his ear close to listen to it.

'Why don't you just try drinking it?' Holly said, her voice full of laughter.

'And why don't you sit down for a second?'

'Fair enough.' Holly slid onto the bar stool next to his. She groaned in gratification as she eased the weight off her sore feet. 'So, why did you come back from overseas?'

'The time was right.'

She nodded, though she wanted more information. More background. Just more.

'And with your sister's impending marriage, I bet she's happy.'

'She is.' For a brief second he let down his guard and Holly saw the genuine affection he held for his sister. His face glowed with it. And it was lethally charming.

Now that was a definite chink in her theory. This guy was meant to have no attachments. He could be devoted to his business. Or even passionate about his car. But he was not meant to radiate such tenderness when talking of another person.

Hang on. The theory could still hold true; she would just have to make another slight modification. Blood relatives were an exception to the 'no attachments' rule. That seemed only fair.

'And the company?' she continued. 'Were your employees pleased to see you? Though it does mean they will have to start actually working, stop the three-hour lunches, and fire the in-house masseuse that Ben always raves about.'

'Are you kidding? That's the main reason I'm back.' He touched his hand to the back of his neck. 'I've had this dull ache in my third vertebra...'

'Sure you have.'

Feeling cosy and safe in the conversation, she could not stop herself from asking the question that had been foremost in her mind for the last few days.

'So are you here to stay?'

The sparkle left Jacob's eyes as he considered her for a long, agonising moment. Her heart seemed to stop beating as she awaited the answer.

'For now.'

She nodded, though her inappropriate angst had not been assuaged one little bit.

As though sensing the sudden weight of the subject at hand, Jacob turned the conversation to more ordinary issues. They talked about the gallery, and surprisingly Jacob knew a lot about the resident artist. He even had one of 'the superb St John's ace lithographs' in his apartment.

Her feet lightly aching, Holly once more ran a massaging palm over the arch of her foot.

'Long day?' Jacob asked.

'Long week.'

'Too many nights out, I think.'

She stopped rubbing and sat up, slowly, not looking his way. 'And I'd have to agree with you.'

'Maybe you should cut back?'

'Maybe I should.'

Holly's pulse was racing. The swirl of meaning behind their innocuous conversation reverberated in the air around them. Was he asking her not to see other men? Was she agreeing? Was she mad?

'What if...?' Jacob said, his voice trailing off.

What if, what? Holly thought, her nerves screaming in anticipation. She felt like a bell still resonating long after it had been struck.

'Dinner. Tomorrow night. Just you and me.' Jacob turned on his seat, his left hand coming down to rest upon hers. 'No strings. Just dinner.'

His little finger was stroking, playing, tantalising, sending hot, jolting shivers from her sensitive fingertips up her bare arms, melting the length of her suddenly rigid body. And then he smiled. *Strength, Holly. A smile is teeth and lips and muscles. Nothing more.*

'I won't demand any feet-washing at the end of the night. Unless of course you feel the urge…'

She pulled her hand away. She wanted strings. That was the whole point. Holly stood up behind the bar stool, putting herself a safe distance from his potent magnetism.

'It's never just dinner, Jacob. And neither should it be.'

'But—'

'But, you know my long-term plans. I want a husband. And you can't even tell me if you're still going to be in the country in a week, so I'm guessing marriage is not an option in your foreseeable future.'

All colour drained from Jacob's face and there was her answer. *So he loves his sister, so he supports charities, so he has a smile that liquefies all common sense. He is and always will be the indisputable anti-husband. There never was a safer bet.*

'I didn't think so. So there's really no point in having dinner, is there?'

For the sake of her own disobedient feelings she simply had to hit the point home as far as she could. So she lied. 'Besides which, you're simply not my type.'

Jacob blinked, his luscious eyelashes sweeping across his

beautiful chiselled cheeks. 'And those other poor saps during the week. Did they have the same advance warning I did?'

Holly shrank back from the bitterness in Jacob's tone and she knew she was doing the right thing, cutting off all further contact before it was too late. Before he made such a deep impression on her she could not simply theorise it away.

'Goodbye, Jacob.'

Holly walked away, feeling Jacob's slighted stare burning into her as she crossed the room. She latched onto the owner of the gallery and he kept her sequestered in his bawdy, noisy group until long after Jacob had grabbed his coat and left.

CHAPTER NINE

MONDAY morning Holly's intercom buzzed.

'Call on line three, Ms Denison.' The receptionist's fuzzy voice came through the speakerphone on her desk.

Holly looked apologetically at Lydia, who was standing on a chair in the middle of her office, her outstretched arms draped in several large swatches of fabric. 'Do you mind hanging in there for a minute? I'll be quick.'

Lydia strained dramatically under the weight. 'Get it, Holly, I'm just *fine* up here.'

Holly grabbed the phone and swung back in her springy leather chair. 'Holly Denison.'

'Holly. It's Jacob.'

Holly shot forward on her chair, her feet now both firmly planted on the ground. He needn't have introduced himself. That rich, masculine voice with its gentle American twang set her nerves on edge from its very first syllable.

Lydia raised her eyebrows and mouthed, 'Who is it?'

Holly shook her head, before pressing the phone firmly to her ear. After Friday night Holly had spent a restless weekend convincing herself turning him down was for the best.

But three little words were enough to have her doubting herself again. And if he was calling to ask her to dinner again, she did not know if she would have the strength to refuse.

'Yes, Jacob?'

'I have a party to organise and I want to employ your professional services for the event.'

She scribbled, *Lincoln Holdings—party* onto her note-pad.

Lydia could see the notebook clearly from her elevated position and her jaw dropped. Holly waved a frantic hand at her mouthing for her to dump the fabric swatches over the back of the chair and disappear.

Lydia mouthed, 'Good luck,' before she tiptoed out.

So he had not called to renew his dinner offer. Holly was glad he was not there in person to see her blush. He had obviously taken her at her word on that count. But that was what she wanted. Wasn't it?

Then it hit her what he *had* requested. Jacob Lincoln was offering Cloud Nine a gig. But she knew his idea of a party was very different from her own. She shuddered at the thought of having to search the local bars and pubs for a venue and putting up posters advertising a wet T-shirt contest with a free keg of beer being the first prize.

'I am flattered that you thought of Cloud Nine for the event, Jacob, but I'm not sure we provide the sort of parties that would suit your tastes.'

Jacob surprised Holly by laughing loudly on the other end of the line. 'Relax, Holly. I'm not after nude mud wrestlers. Besides, this is not for the company. It's a private affair. My sister Ana wants an engagement party. Something much more along the lines of what you created for the big marquee would be appropriate.'

This sounded much more up her professional alley but

Holly knew that the theme of the party was not what was really worrying her.

'Well, I am extremely busy at the moment but I could pass you on to another of our wonderful event managers who specializes in exactly these sort of—'

'Look, Holly—' his voice seemed to lose all patience '—this is just the beginning of what I am proposing here. If I like what you do with this gig, I will be offering you the entire Lincoln Holdings event management account.'

Holly blinked. Slowly. If she had had the strength, she would have pinched herself.

'The entire Lincoln Holdings account?' she repeated.

'Yes. We have been able to handle the workload internally until now but the company is leaping ahead internationally and the job is getting too big.'

Holly desperately tried to rein in her imagination, which was running riot with wild ideas.

'What's the catch?' she asked, hoping there was a great big one so she would have a sane reason to refuse.

'The catch is I don't want anyone else in charge of my account. I want you.'

Be careful what you wish for, Holly, for you just might get it. Those words echoed through her head as she sat in stunned silence.

He was offering her an account that her firm, amongst dozens of others, had been wooing without success for years. There was no way she could seriously convince herself or anyone else that she should turn this opportunity down. She had to do this party and it had to be perfect.

She sighed aloud. 'All right. I'll do it.'

'Don't sound so eager, please.' He laughed.

'I am, don't get me wrong. This is a huge opportunity. Though I can't help but wonder why.'

'Why not?' Jacob asked.

'Well, you've seen my work. And we both know I don't have the same tastes as you.' *And we all but had a fight the other night. And I had thought I might not ever hear that divine voice of yours again.*

Jacob laughed again and Holly grimaced, aware that she was fast finding the sound addictive.

'You really know how to sell yourself, don't you? I'm beginning to change my mind about the whole deal.'

Holly could not help but laugh as well. 'Look, I will happily take on your sister's engagement party and don't get me wrong, I will knock your socks off, it will be that fabulous. But I have a counter proposal.'

'Okay, let's hear it.'

She took a deep breath and went for it. 'I will deal with your sister alone for this party and when you give me the Lincoln Holdings account, which I am sure you will, I will deal with your promotions division, and not with you.'

'Well, now, that was more like it,' Jacob said, 'I was not sure that you had that self-protective spirit in you.'

His voice had reached her a little softer and definitely sexier, which was not what Holly had been hoping to bring out in him. She had merely been establishing professional boundaries. Not something she had previously thought sexy, but with Jacob involved…

'Thank you, I think,' she said, her own voice huskily mirroring his own. She cleared her throat. 'If you could pass on your sister's number we can get started right away.'

Jacob gave her Ana's contact details. 'And whatever Ana wants, Ana gets. The result of my being away so long. I am trying to buy back her affection.'

Holly knew from the warmth of his voice that this statement could not be farther from the truth. And again she wondered what sort of woman could secure such staunch and palpable affection from this man.

'So long as I don't have to help Ana choose between bronze and pewter candleholders. I've been there and done that and it wasn't pretty.'

'Pewter,' Holly answered without pause as she continued scribbling burgeoning ideas onto her notepad.

'See, that's just what she eventually chose. I think you two were made for each other.'

'*I think* if you promised to stay for ever she would prefer that to a party any day.'

Where on earth had *that* come from? Holly clamped a hand to her mouth to stop any further recriminating rubbish from slipping out.

'Would *she* now?' His voice whispered down the phone line silky smooth. The insinuation in his question clear.

Holly rubbed her suddenly throbbing temples. 'Ask her, Jacob,' she said, pretending she had no idea what he had implied, 'and see what she says.'

'I am sure you are right,' he said, his voice mercifully back to normal. 'I guess I'll wait to hear from Ana, then, to see how it's all going.'

'I would appreciate that. And Jacob?'

'Yes, Holly.'

'Thank you.'

'Don't thank me yet,' he warned her before hanging up the phone.

Holly put the phone down more slowly. Lydia was peering through the glass door with a big expectant grin on her face. Holly waved her into the room.

'So?' Lydia asked, her eyes bright with excitement.

'It may soon be safe to dummy up a press release saying we've landed the Lincoln Holdings account.'

'Yippee!' Lydia spun around in glee before slumping down on the chair she had been standing on earlier, the important swathes of fabric temporarily forgotten.

'You had no plans day or night for the next few weeks, did you?' Holly asked.

Lydia waved a 'no worries' hand. 'The Klingon can wait.'

Holly thought it better not to ask. 'The sooner we ready our other projects, the sooner we can reel in Jacob Lincoln.'

'You mean Lincoln Holdings, don't you?'

'Of course I do.' Holly swiftly changed the subject. 'Now, up you get, back on the chair so we can sort out these fabrics before lunch.'

Lydia grumbled as she stood back up on the chair and stretched out her aching arms, 'Sometimes I feel highly unappreciated.'

'I can't believe you just did that,' Ben said from Jacob's office doorway.

Jacob knew from Ben's smug expression he had been listening for long enough. 'Believe it, Benny boy. It's become too big for me and I've been contemplating outsourcing for some time.' *For three whole days, in fact.*

'This is the first I had heard of it.'

'This is the first you needed to hear of it. That's why the company is my namesake and not yours."

Ben sauntered into the room, and then lay back on a lounge chair against the far wall. He nonchalantly flipped through a magazine on Jacob's coffee-table. 'She didn't go on any dates this weekend, you know. I had a couple of men lined up, including the new Accounts guy, Matt Riley, the one who tried chatting her up at the greyhound track. But she baulked.'

There is no reason why that should concern me, Jacob thought, then realised he had stopped breathing.

'And young Matt's quite the looker, I am told by the girls in

Accounts,' Ben continued. '*Babeliscious* I think was the most common turn of phrase. Modelled his way through college, you know? But…still she said no.'

Ben's eyes left the magazine and zeroed in on Jacob, who hoped his face showed none of the curiosity he felt.

'You wouldn't happen to know why she has suddenly backed off, would you?' Ben asked.

Jacob merely shook his head, uncertain what state his voice would be in considering his suddenly dry throat. Maybe she had given up the hunt and had decided to become a normal single woman, capable of organising her own social life. Now that would be an interesting turn of events.

Then Ben said, 'Maybe she just needed to recharge her batteries. Ready herself for next week's multitude of contenders.'

'Maybe,' Jacob conceded, thumping briskly back to earth.

'Well, it's been easier than I thought it would be. She really made an impression on the bunch at your welcome home thing at the track. Once word got around *she* was open to being set up, I've hardly had to do a thing.'

'Lucky you.'

'Yep. I've met all sorts of great guys this last week. I had to cancel one guy's date but *we* got on so well I booked him in for a conciliatory lunchtime squash game.'

Jacob was determined not to give Ben the satisfaction of knowing that his comments were surprisingly hitting the mark. He was actually feeling pangs of something akin to jealousy.

'Was there something else I could help you with?'

Ben looked to the ceiling for inspiration. 'Nope.'

'I can find work for you if you're bored. I don't think my blinds have been cleaned in the years I've been gone.'

Ben looked at his watch. 'Sorry, Link. I'll be late for squash with my new friend.'

He stood and ambled back to the door before looking back with an easy grin. 'Just think, if Holly had not been run down by that oaf in the street the other week and been so turned off by him as to go on this husband hunt of hers, I would be eating lunch alone in my office right now. You've got to love the girl!'

'Who's an oaf?' Jacob called out but Ben had already gone.

So, Holly had been turned off by the 'oaf' in the street, had she? Jacob fumed. He grabbed a stick of gum and chewed it furiously as he swung sharply back and forth in his office chair.

No wonder she had begged him not to tell Beth they had met before. Turned off! She had been practically undressing him with her eyes that first morning, he was certain of it. The little fraud. She deserved to be found out for twisting that incident to suit her.

Unless she really had found him repellent from their first meeting. Every time he had seen her since she had been edgy and had made it clear she would rather be anywhere than in his presence. And she had flung the 'not her type' line in his face with convincing vigour.

All the better for him if that was the end of it. No use wasting time struggling to bat down his growing attraction to the woman if he held no appeal for her in the first place.

And then he stopped, mid swing, his feet planted firmly on the carpeted floor, and his hands grabbed his desk as he realised what Ben had unwittingly revealed. The one detail that made all of the above possibilities irrelevant.

He was the reason behind Holly's whole husband hunt.

'That's great Holly! What a coup,' Beth said over the phone later that night. 'And you'll love Ana.'

'Please tell me you can come.'

'Of course. Unless the baby makes other plans we'll be there with bells on.'

'Bells will not be necessary. Evening wear will be fine.'

Holly sat on her bed in her shortie pyjamas and thick socks, assuming the lotus position. She held the cordless phone to her ear, and rocked her neck back and forth easing out the niggling Monday-itis tensions.

'Ben tells me you cancelled on two of your hopefuls on the weekend.'

'Hmm. I needed a break.'

'Really? No other reason? No one take your fancy yet from the hundreds Ben has supplied?'

Holly heard the doubt in Beth's voice loud and clear. 'No one.'

'Not even Jacob?'

'Beth—'

'Come on, Holly. If it weren't for Ben I would grab the man with both hands and not let him go. He's the catch to end all catches.'

'You would not. He's so not your type.'

'Then whose is he?'

Holly let that one slide. 'And besides I feel like a movie star doing the talk show circuit. I need to come up with some new material before even I am bored with my funny stories.' After one final stretch Holly flopped backwards, her arms and legs spread diagonally across the bed.

'As long as this plan of yours has not fizzled out,' Beth said.

'I promise there has been no fizzling.'

'Good, because I had already decided that my matron of honour dress was going to be bright red, backless and very sparkly. Besides I did up a current star chart and you are primed for a liaison in July. In fact you are so primed you are about to burst. Maybe tarots would help—'

'No! I draw the line at tarot cards.'

Beth sighed. 'Fine. What are you doing tonight? Watching TV?'

Alone? Holly felt the inference come through loud and clear. She glanced at the silent TV at the end of her bed. 'If it weren't for your Ben we would still be a pair of old spinsters who loved to do nothing more at night than watch *Pride and Prejudice* and eat home-made caramel popcorn.'

'That was fun, though, wasn't it?'

'The most fun ever. But then Ben found you, and loved you and showed both of us how much better our nights could be.'

Holly sighed. She rolled over and scrunched herself into a warm little ball, with the phone cradled under her head. 'I've seen *Pride and Prejudice* enough times for one woman. You don't know how lucky you are, Beth. To have someone so decent and strong and dependable.'

Beth laughed. 'You make Ben sound like a St Bernard!'

Better a St Bernard than a Rottweiler, she thought as images of Jacob Lincoln with his dark hair, clear sharp eyes and his overwhelming personality bombarded her subconscious.

'Someone like Ben would drive you around the bend,' Beth said.

'Hardly—'

'For example, he keeps his socks, underpants and hankies in the same dresser drawer. You have a separate drawer for each and organise them by colour and fabric with seasonal adjustments.'

'How will I ever be able to look at Ben again without thinking about his underwear?'

'Seriously, though, one day you will meet the man for you. A man who puts honey in everything he cooks. A man who will be happy to let you name your first-born son Maximus as you have always wanted, God help the poor child.'

'I don't see what is so wrong with the name Maximus. It's a powerful and masculine name—'

'Will you stop kidding around and listen to me?'

Duly chastised, Holly shut up and paid attention.

'What I am saying is the perfect man for you is out there. But believe me he will be nothing like Ben. That's nothing against my husband. You drive him around the bend just the same.'

'Thanks.'

And Holly knew then that, though her friends would always be there with a shoulder to lean on, it would in all likelihood fall to her to find someone to love.

CHAPTER TEN

AT LUNCHTIME on Tuesday Holly escorted Lydia to the Lunar restaurant to meet Anabella for their first chat about her upcoming engagement party. Holly had spoken to Ana on the phone that morning and had found her bright and excited and was very much looking forward to meeting her.

Holly ordered her usual lemon, lime, and bitters with a touch of honey and Lydia ordered a pink lemonade spider with double whipped cream and chocolate topping.

Soon after Jacob Lincoln slid his impressive suit-clad frame onto the leather bench opposite her.

'Jacob! What on earth are you doing here?'

Why? Why are you here? Holly screamed inside her head. *Wasn't I perfectly clear? Did you not promise to leave the party to me? Without interference? Without walking in here unheralded, smiling at me like that, like a naughty little boy who knows his mother would never yell at him as long as he flashed those adorable dimples.*

Knowing she had been staring far too long, Holly glanced furtively at Lydia, and was glad to see she was being blithely ignored. In fact, as Lydia lowered her lipstick to her attaché

case and smoothed her newly glossed lips together her wide
eyes never left Jacob for a moment.

'I beg you not to throw that drink in my face, Holly,'
Jacob said. He sent her an enigmatic smile, as though he
knew something she didn't. 'New suit. And Anabella sends
her apologies but she suddenly had to go out of town…for a
week.'

Holly had to pull herself together. Lydia was now watching the two of them very carefully. 'I spoke to her only this
morning and she didn't say a thing.'

Jacob shrugged. 'As I said, it was sudden.'

'And her fiancé? He was unable to come in her place?'

'Well, he actually had to suddenly go out of town as well.
With Anabella. Skiing in New Zealand.'

'I see,' she said, desperately seeking a way to take control
of the situation. 'So why didn't she just cancel our meeting
until she comes back?'

'She wants the party booked for Saturday week but won't
be back in Melbourne until midday on the day before. She
gave me these notes and said to follow them as a guide, but
she would be happy with whatever you come up with.'

He reached over the table with a few loose sheets of pink
writing paper covered with loopy handwriting. Lydia's hand
slid across the table and snapped them up.

'I have a week and a half to organise a party for…how
many people?' Holly asked.

Lydia, who was poring over the pink pages, said, 'Three
hundred.'

'Three hundred people?'

'Of course it's people, though it doesn't specifically say
people in the notes—'

'Lydia!'

'We can do it easily, Holly,' Lydia said. 'Remember

the Newman do? We did that in just over a week and it was fab.'

Holly glared at Lydia, who just shrugged.

'What did I say? It's true.'

Holly sensed Jacob watching them, his head swaying back and forth as though watching a tennis match.

'Look, if you think you need help or if I should get someone else to do it—' he said.

Holly placed her hands steadily on the table in front of her. 'No, we will be fine.'

The waiter arrived and asked if they were ready to order lunch. Jacob raised his eyebrows at Holly and his look said it all. He had laid his cards on the table; he had changed the rules and made no promises he would not do so again. So much for professional boundaries.

But now it was her move. Order the meal or don't order the meal. Take the deal or don't take the deal. It was decision time and it was up to her.

So Holly ordered.

Soup of the day with a side salad. It would be served quickly and could be eaten quickly. Besides, the way her stomach was reacting she probably would not keep anything heavier down.

Jacob ordered appetisers and eye fillet steak. Well done. 'Cook it till it's unrecognisable,' he said, 'then flip it and cook it some more.'

'You should eat it rare. It's much better for you.' Holly nodded frantically at the waiter, willing him to change the order. Jacob shot her that peculiar enigmatic smile again and she shut up.

Lydia took a long, luxurious sip of her drink, the liquid gurgling loudly as it reached the bottom of the glass, then ordered a slice of apple pie with ice cream. 'The sugar stimulates me,' she explained.

Jacob laughed aloud and the young male waiter had to stifle a cough as he left.

'So how have you been, Lydia?' Jacob asked.

'Fabulous, Jacob. And you?'

'Fabulous.' His urbane voice gave the casual word a whole different feel. Long, drawn out, smooth. Holly took a large gulp of her drink.

'If you two are finished,' Holly said, 'let's talk about the party.' She stopped as Jacob held up his hands, his face contorted with mock apprehension.

'You promised me I wouldn't have to choose between pewter and bronze.'

'But—'

'No buts. Follow the notes if you must, but as I said on the phone you guys have carte blanche.'

It sounded perfect in theory, but Holly knew there was no way of pleasing a client without substantial input. One person's pewter was another person's bronze.

Obviously sensing the same looming disaster, Lydia whipped out the contract and gave it to Jacob. 'If you could just look this over, fill in your details and the party date, sign away and we have a deal.'

Jacob did as he was told, then Holly signed alongside his name. Lydia clapped her hands together excitedly as she took the signed contract and placed it carefully in her pink attaché case.

'Carte blanche,' Lydia cooed. 'My two favourite words in the whole English language.'

Jacob laughed aloud again. And Holly felt her skin resonating in response to the infectious sound.

'So, Jacob,' Lydia said, 'since we can't talk shop, tell

me why you had to stop Holly from throwing her drink over you?'

His eyes crinkled. 'Well, I just knew that she was expecting my sister and didn't want her to freak out.'

'Holly, freak out?' Lydia scoffed. 'She's the coolest cucumber you could ever hope to meet.'

'Do tell.'

'Sure. I mean, take yesterday lunchtime; these expatriate English people who were having a British-Australian dinner. We'd spent three full days with the client finalising the seating arrangements. We had even printed up these lovely table number cards. Weren't they lovely, Holly?'

'They were lovely, Lydia,' Holly agreed, flicking a quick apologetic smile to Jacob, who winked briefly before turning his rapt attention back to Lydia. Holly's skin tingled as though that wink had crossed the table and brushed along her cheek. She crept a stealthy hand from her lap to her face and rubbed at the wayward spot.

'Anyway,' Lydia continued, 'at the last minute the client realised that Joe was at table number three and Eunice was at table number four. They were both in the front row, both within spitting distance of the speaker, but Joe was sitting at a higher table number than Eunice. And this was cataclysmic. The client was ready to cancel the whole thing. In stepped Miss Cool Bananas here and said, Let's just rename the tables; not numbers, not letters, but names of small English towns. The client hyperventilated her agreement. There went our Holly into her "magic" briefcase and found enough fancy paper and a black magic marker to rename every table. And within minutes of everyone's arrival the whole room was in tears as they blabbed about the small English towns they all knew and loved and missed. Even Joe and Eunice were hugging each other and bawling their eyes out.'

Lydia took a deep breath and slumped back in her chair. 'Jacob, can you look around the corner and see if my apple pie is coming? I'm starved!'

It took a moment for Jacob to latch onto Lydia's sudden change of topic. He peeked. 'Not just yet.'

'Good. Holly, could you shove over for a sec? I have to take a pee before my pie comes.'

Holly obligingly moved out of her seat so Lydia could shuffle past. 'Thanks, gorgeous.' She flounced past Holly and skipped towards the ladies' room.

Holly slid back down into her seat, slowly and deliberately, already marking the seconds until Lydia's return.

'Isn't she exhausting?' Jacob said.

Talk about Lydia. Excellent. Safe ground.

'She's enthusiastic and imaginative and the clients love her. I'll probably end up working for her one day.'

After a moment's pause, during which time his mind seemed to be ticking over, Jacob asked, 'She called you "gorgeous". Ben and Beth both refer to you in that way as well. Do you just get that particular compliment a lot?'

'Hardly.'

Hardly a professional topic of conversation. Explain then change the subject.

'My dad called me that since I was little. And then one day when I first met Ben he called out "Hey, gorgeous" to Beth and I answered without even thinking. And he and Beth have called me that ever since. The guys at work heard Ben call me that at the Christmas party a couple of years ago and never let it go. I barely notice it any more.'

Jacob smiled. 'It suits you.'

'Please,' she scoffed, looking over her shoulder to check if Lydia was on her way back.

After another pregnant pause, Jacob thankfully changed

the subject. 'Did you really do all those things she said? Yesterday lunchtime?'

'In a manner of speaking. Though she makes it seem much more exhilarating than it really was. It was a fairly simple fix and we've had worse problems closer to the final hour.'

'There you go, selling yourself short again.'

'Fine.' She laughed. 'I was brilliant. I saved the day.'

'That's better.'

'But it's my job to fix those things, to smooth the way and make the events seem effortless whilst the client sits back and takes the honour.'

Watch and learn, buddy. This party of Ana's will blow your mind.

Jacob sat back and crossed his arms, mirroring her stance. 'Do you see yourself branching out with your own firm?'

'I love what I do and if I was the owner I wouldn't be able to do it. I'd have to concentrate on finances and payroll and other such icky things. I'm happy to play with other people's money.'

'And this way you could more easily take time off if you needed it.'

'I guess.' She wondered why he would focus on that aspect. 'But it would be decidedly more difficult to make the house payments if I was skipping off on cruises year round.'

'You own a house?' His eyes softened as he asked.

'It will be a few years yet before I can claim that distinction from the bank.'

'I see. But, if your circumstances changed, you *could* stop working altogether,' Jacob added, his hazel eyes now boring into hers.

'I guess I could.'

If I pick the right lottery numbers, or find a suitcase of money buried in my backyard.

And then it dawned on her. He was thinking that what she wanted most in a job was the flexibility to marry and have children as soon as possible.

How wrong he was! Or was he?

If she followed her plan through to its logical conclusion, wouldn't that mean a wedding, a honeymoon, and some day children? Holly felt a comforting blush creep over her as these ideas filtered through and meshed with her original plan just to find someone nice and compatible to spend her time with. She loved her job but the thought of a full life with a real family was intoxicating.

But hang on. This was not Beth having an innocent chat, and not a prospective husband seeing where her priorities lay. This was the man who, *if she played her cards right*, would be going a long way to funding her pay cheques.

But would he seriously reconsider handing over the Lincoln Holdings account to her if she was planning to start a family? If so, he was completely outside his rights.

But, closer to home, would she seriously consider starting a family if it meant losing the Lincoln Holdings account, which epitomised all she had ever wanted from her career, something she had been striving for long before the notion of a husband hunt had presented itself.

But before she could open her mouth to contradict him, or berate him, or promise to give up the hunt as long as he gave her the contract, the waiter arrived with their lunch, quickly followed by Lydia.

'Did you miss me?' Lydia asked as she climbed over Holly's lap and plopped into her own seat.

'More than life itself,' Jacob promised, shooting one final unreadable glance at Holly before tucking into his appetizer.

Her mind reeling, Holly could do little more than pick up her spoon and eat her soup.

Jacob stood outside Lunar and watched as Holly's chauffeured car drove away, the icy wind whipping through his lightweight suit barely registered.

'Holly. Holly. Holly,' he whispered aloud, 'what is spinning though that labyrinthine mind of yours?' Holly's uneasy expression as she'd slipped into the back of the car was branded on his mind.

He reached into his inner jacket pocket and grabbed a stick of gum. He threw it into his mouth and chewed furiously and began to walk the five blocks back to the office.

The day had not gone exactly as he had hoped.

When he'd known he would be taking the lunch in Ana's place, he had imagined Holly would be glad to see him, keen to thank him in person for the incredible opportunity he had given her. After an hour spent flirting over lunch, he would then help her into a cab, her hand resting for a few extra moments in his, tears in her eyes, thanking her lucky stars she had met him and for him having bestowed such an opportunity on her.

Admittedly, that had been a little optimistic. But from the panic in her expression he had even worried that she was planning on reneging on the whole deal. That was the last thing he wanted. He had become used to the idea of her running a part of his show.

So what was wrong with her? Why couldn't she be thrilled with what he was offering her? For the first time in ten years, he was contemplating handing over the public face of his company. Didn't she understand that? Understand the incredible chance he had taken?

For her?

As he'd watched her reactions with a studied eye at lunch she had fidgeted, blushed, and avoided direct eye contact. He knew he definitely did not repulse her as she had apparently claimed to Ben. Nevertheless, whatever she had felt that morning on the street had caused a strong reaction in her, and she'd created her husband hunt as a wall, an excuse not to face those feelings.

Since he'd unwittingly slung her into her current predicament, maybe he was the only one who could release her. He was simply unable to give her what she wanted most. But he could supply the next best thing—the job she had always dreamed of.

A car beeped its horn as Jacob stepped out onto the road. The street sign read 'Don't Walk'. But he needed to walk. He waited only a second for the car to pass, then jogged across to the other side and resumed his march, more determined than ever to find a way to make the obtuse woman appreciate that he was doing as much as he could for her.

'Come on, gorgeous. Spill the beans.' Lydia was sitting sideways in the back seat of the car, her seat belt stretched across her angled frame.

'About what?'

'About that whole weird and wonderful lunch, that's what. I was all ready to impress the socks off the sister in case you were still on audition or something and then in *he* comes in his three piece suit, and onyx cuff-links, all sophisticated and debonair and...I have stop for a moment and just say, yummy...'

Lydia paused to let this new assertion resonate for a moment until she seemed happy that her point had been made.

'To paraphrase, in comes the supreme Mr Lincoln. Then he sits across from you and he changes; he sort of melts as the look he gives you is all adorable and schmaltzy, like he'd prefer to be sitting on your side of the table just so he can look at you up close and personal.'

'Please!' Holly interjected, her cheeks fast burning up.

'I was there. I saw. And I also see you aren't wearing your lucky suit.'

'My what?'

'Whenever we meet with a new client you wear the charcoal trouser suit with the white sleeveless shirt with the plunging neckline and the sexy frill. But not today. Today you're suddenly going out of routine and wearing this dreamy new number.'

Lydia motioned to Holly's impeccable cream calf-length, fitted, square-necked dress.

'It is neither dreamy nor new,' Holly replied truthfully, but she knew that she had taken a great deal of care choosing what to wear to the lunch. 'And I did not know *he* was going to even be there today.'

'But you were going to meet his sister. And who would you more need to make a good first impression on than the sister? It all fits. The goo-goo eyes you two kept shooting at each other were so telling. So spill!'

'He attended my Hidden Valley day as well as the Arty Pants evening, liked them, then offered me the job.' Close enough anyway. 'He's a client, that's it.'

'Not if the divine Mr Lincoln has anything to say in the matter. You've got him hooked. Reel him in and be done with it.'

Lydia was such a dreamer, looking for romance in every chance encounter any time of the day or night. She simply had no idea what sort of person Jacob Lincoln was. She had not been there the other night to see the colour drain from his face at the thought of marriage. Goo-goo eyes or no goo-goo eyes, he was a hopeless case. No strings. No complications. No way.

CHAPTER ELEVEN

HOLLY spent Wednesday at the press junket for a new opera, which would be hitting town in the coming Spring. Thursday she managed the dressing of a debutante ball venue, which she then attended that same night. Alone. Stag. *Sans* date.

What with the party looming, she told Ben, she really did not have time to concentrate on her personal project. In a couple of weeks she would be back on track, but for now all dates were suspended. Suspended indefinitely if that meant landing the Lincoln Holdings account? Perhaps. She hadn't yet given herself the luxury of making that decision.

So in between more imminent projects Holly and Lydia had prepared a detailed preliminary plan for Anabella's party, and they knew it was going to be the best shindig they had ever thrown. But in order for this to be the best shindig they had ever thrown, the client had to be one hundred percent behind them and she knew she could not go any further without that surety. So last thing Friday afternoon Holly called Jacob.

'Holly! I'm surprised to hear from you—pleasantly surprised, of course.' His voice was loud and muffled as he was obviously talking on his car phone. 'What can I do for you?'

'The thing is I really do feel that I should show you our initial plans for the party. You know Anabella, and all I know is she likes pink paper. It'll only take a few minutes, I promise.'

'Sure. How about tonight?'

Holly looked at her watch. But she had no set plans and knew she should really strike before he changed his mind.

'Great.'

'Will Lydia be tagging along or will it be just you?'

'Just me, I'm afraid. Lydia's off to try out some new dance club in the city. The stamina of that girl constantly amazes me.'

'Then how about my place? I'm on my way there now.' She could hear the smile in his voice and it took all of her concentration not to picture him doing so.

'No, I don't think—'

'Why not? I'll cook. It's my turn.'

'There's no need for that. It will only take a minute.' Holly bit her thumbnail. 'Where do you live?'

'Port Melbourne.' He gave the address. On the water's edge and only a few minutes drive from work. She looked around her office. Fabric samples, menus and brochures swamped every spare surface. Quick decision, to stay late on a Friday night and clean up a week's worth of mess or—?

'Okay. How about I pop around in about half an hour? But please don't cook. I'll be out of your hair in time for the evening news, I promise.'

'I'll see you in half an hour, then,' was Jacob's only guarantee.

'Well, there you go,' Jacob said aloud as he hung up.

The excitement in Holly's voice when talking of the party

had been palpable. He had wanted to give her something to focus on other than her unreasonable husband hunt and it seemed this party had done the trick.

But why invite her over to your place? How does that help? Having her alone, at night, in your home, your private sanctuary?

No worries. It would be fine. This night would simply be the passing of the torch to their new professional relationship. And once that was established, they would be on stable ground. She would be happy professionally and he would be free and clear of any obligation he might have felt considering his part in her quest.

Okay, if it's a business meeting we should have an agenda. Much easier to stay in control of the situation if it's mapped out beforehand. First let her get comfortable with you as a business associate, second go over her presentation, and third send her home with the energy and high spirits to complete the project satisfactorily.

If dinner is involved, that's fine too. And maybe a bottle of wine. It will be business, not personal. All to ease the transition, of course.

He put his car in gear and barely kept under the speed limit all the way home.

Holly hurried into her office bathroom to grab a glass of water and caught sight of herself in the floor-length mirror. She was wearing her 'lucky suit', as Lydia called it, and was glad Lydia was not there to ask if it meant she was feeling lucky. And Beth would have a conniption fit at such a time, professing all sorts of fortuitous signs from her choosing that outfit on that day.

'It's nice and it's comfortable,' Holly said aloud to her reflection. 'Besides, tonight is just a presentation like you have done a hundred times before. Choosing to wear a particular outfit hardly portents anything out of the ordinary.'

She smoothed down the neat charcoal pinstripe trouser suit, and soft white sleeveless shirt with its plunging neckline. She ran her fingers through her hair, which for once she was wearing long and loose.

Blissfully ignoring her messy office, she popped the presentation in her 'magic' briefcase, hoping the information inside would work its magic that night, and headed out.

Walking along Lonsdale Street to where her car was parked, she passed the spot where she had first run into Jacob. A flash of intense eyes, mussed hair, hordes of luggage.

She had told Lydia that she had been head down, thinking of work that morning. But the truth was she had seen him exit his hotel. She had *watched* him, arms full of luggage, chill wind whipping his hair about his face, beckoning the hotel doorman to remain inside, insisting he stay out of the cold.

He had been so handsome, huffing and puffing in exertion as he had navigated his way, unassisted, to the kerb. And she had been smitten.

Holly slowed as she passed the hotel, the memory of him dragging his tired eyes from the bustling traffic to glance in her direction sending a delightful shiver along her spine.

He had not let go of his cumbersome cases, or stopped heading to the edge of the road, but from that moment he had only had eyes for her. And that look, both exhausted and vibrant, along with its accompanying hint of a smile, had almost frozen her to the spot. Only the biting cold and primal need to get inside to warmth had kept her legs moving. He'd watched her with such unconcealed interest, though her extremities had frozen, her insides had melted. Her pulse had quickened, and she'd barely been able to focus from the blood pumping so hard and fast through her head.

She'd had no choice; she'd had to pass him to get to her office, the front door of which had been barely a block behind him. She had walked on, unsteady but determined, her knees shaking as she'd walked closer and closer, her breathing ragged, unable to drag her eyes away from the stranger in her sights. Then—

Bam!

How they had come to collide, she had no idea. They had both been walking towards one another, eyes locked, and in those last few seconds should have tacitly agreed to walk to one side, allowing the other to pass. But somewhere during those last few seconds, neither had been able to do as politeness dictated.

Mightily embarrassed at having found herself sprawled at his feet, and at the fact that she had been devouring him with her eyes only moments before, she had lashed out, and the exquisite spell that had woven its way around her heart had been shattered.

Having passed the hotel and rounded the corner, Holly shook off the disturbing memory. It was not at all productive thinking about it, not for their business relationship, nor if she had any serious hope of eventually finding someone else, someone compatible to spend her life with. No point daydreaming about someone so unsuitable and unattainable.

It was time she heeded her own advice to Jacob, and *pretended it never happened*.

Twenty minutes later Holly stood outside a large five-storey apartment building in Port Melbourne. She pressed the intercom button for the penthouse, no less.

The street was bustling with young people rugged up in overcoats on their way to pubs and popular restaurants along the water's edge. A fair way down a long jetty, the cruise ship the *Spirit of Tasmania* waited silently to take her human cargo on her nightly trek across Bass Strait.

After about a minute, Jacob's voice answered, 'Holly?'

'Yep.' Her teeth chattered from standing in the biting cold.

'Come on up.'

The door buzzed and Holly scampered inside, thankful to be warmed by central heating once more.

She approached the security guard at the desk and he checked her name against a list before pointing the way to the lifts.

As she rode the lift to the top floor Holly prepared herself for a glimpse into Jacob's private world. If a man's home was his refuge, she craved to see what Jacob's home would divulge. Floor five lit up and the doors opened. The sweet fragrance of soy sauce and honey and tremulous strains of jazz music wafted into her cubicle.

Holly had thought her own home attractive and quite substantial, but this was something else. Jacob's home was neither stark and intimidating, nor overtly manly. Instead, with its open-plan, blonde polished wood floors, strategic ambient lighting and elegant neutral furniture it was tasteful and welcoming.

A stainless steel kitchen took up the right side of the huge room. A three-piece lounge suite filled the left side facing a fireplace, above which two oversized abstract prints of American jazz singers held pride of place. A shiny golden trumpet was the only item adorning the mantel.

On a raised platform at the far end sat the dining suite. The entire far wall was comprised of ceiling-to-floor tinted windows. The multicoloured twinkling lights of the city skyline and the glow of the fast-setting sun shone through the extra-thick smoky-grey glass producing a mercurial spectacular view.

She called out, 'Hello? Anyone home?'

Jacob poked his head out of a hidden doorway on the far side of the kitchen. 'Grab a drink from the bar in the kitchen. I'll be with you in a sec.'

His head disappeared again.

On the kitchen bench Holly found Jacob's tray of spirits lined up with a crystal decanter and crystal glasses. Ignoring the offer, she discarded her briefcase on the floor next to the bench and did a turn about the room.

She ran her hand across the back of the soft cream lounge, scanned the titles of the numerous books lining the long hip-high bookshelves that separated the dining room from the lounge. She walked up the three steps to the raised level and marvelled at the city lights reflecting off the glass-topped dining table. She could feel the cool of the coming night radiating through the thick glass of the window. She moved to stand so close her breath formed on the window.

'You like?'

Holly turned with her hand at her heart as Jacob's soft voice scared her out of her reverie. She had not even heard him come up behind her.

He handed her a glass of red wine and she took a quick sip. Peeking over the top of her wineglass, she noticed his hair was still damp as evidenced by the smooth comb lines running through it. And even through the intoxicating aroma of the heavy red wine she could smell mint. Toothpaste? Then she remembered seeing a few faint shiny patches on the floor on her way in. It suddenly registered that the patches were in fact wet footprints and that she must have caught him in the shower.

She turned back towards the window, hoping he had not

noticed her blush. 'How could anyone not like it? Your apartment is lovely, Jacob. And the view is breathtaking.' She swept a hand in front of her, encompassing the entire panorama.

'This was the first residential property I bought,' Jacob said.

'You own the building?' Holly asked, spinning back to face him, her intrigue overcoming her embarrassment. *Marble floors, a security guard, city views. Phew.*

'I did. I financed its refurbishment several years ago and then sold it off piece by piece, keeping the best apartment for myself. Admittedly I made no money on the deal, I came out even for the first, and hopefully last, time, but I think the sacrifice was worth it.'

'Indeed.'

'Every time I come back it makes me wonder why I ever chose to leave.'

Holly took another sip of the delicious wine, entranced by the city lights reflected in Jacob's eyes and unable to swallow down an unreasonable hope that he would never leave again. As though sensing the acute emotion she could not contain, Jacob took a small step forward, bringing them to within a foot of each other.

She felt a torrid tingling sensation well up in her feet as all of the blood seemed to have ventured further north.

The cool perfumes of mint and now shampoo fought for her attention. With them came jumbled scented memories of fresh rain.

She watched Jacob's hand leave his glass and slowly, slowly ease its way towards her. Her breath caught in her throat. Her hands felt slippery and warm as she clutched the glass to her chest.

Her eyes closed, too heavy with expectation to remain open any longer, and she waited, unable and unwilling to prevent whatever was about to happen.

CHAPTER TWELVE

AND then the music stopped. The jazz CD had finished. With a slight cough Jacob stepped that same small step back to his original position.

This movement snapped Holly out of her trance and after blinking rapidly several times she too moved, willing her numb legs to step smartly around him and down the steps towards the kitchen.

'I have the presentation in my bag,' she prattled as she moved further and further from the window, and from Jacob, her heels clacking on the polished wood floor, the noise comfortingly louder than the beating of her heart. 'Maybe we should sit on the couch and I'll go through it with you quickly so I can get out of your hair.'

She placed the half-empty glass on the kitchen bench and reached down to grab her briefcase.

Jacob had moved down to the bookshelves and was restarting the CD in the discreetly concealed stereo. As the soft strains of the mellow song wafted from numerous hidden speakers around the apartment Jacob turned to face her.

Holly stood, rooted to the spot. The moment was upon her.

This was what she had so keenly wished to see. The man in his environment.

The reality was a man a couple of inches over six feet, with thick springy dark hair, rich hazel eyes frayed by long, dark lashes. A man whose slightly crooked smile could turn her knees to butter and whose occasional dimples made her lose her focus and resolve every time they surfaced. A man wearing velvety soft chocolate-brown trousers, a lightweight sweater, which emphasized the width of his shoulders and the well-developed muscles beneath, a silver and gold two-tone sports watch, no rings or other jewellery. A man content to spend a Friday night at home on a comfortable couch, sipping on a good red wine and listening to lazy jazz music.

Jacob walked towards her and she saw that he was also a man wearing no shoes. *So that's how he crept up on me so quietly,* Holly thought as her eyes snapped back up to his. The cheeky look in his eyes dared her to accuse him of anything.

As he approached her she stood her ground, her briefcase held like armour in front of her. Once at her side he leaned towards her. Her breath caught in her throat and she could not move. Then at the last second his hand reached out, grabbing her red wine glass from the kitchen bench top. Then just as casually he turned and strolled towards the lounge. He had not come within a foot of her yet she was shaking from his proximity.

'Are you coming?' he called over his shoulder.

Holly released the deep breath she had been holding, gathered her wits then walked over to join him. He had lounged on one of the long four-seater couches in his usual idle manner and she joined him there, though far enough away that their knees had no chance of touching.

'What important details have you got to show me?' Jacob asked, amusement lacing every word.

Holly glared at him. 'You may not think this meeting will be valuable, but if it means that Anabella's party is the better for it then why object?'

Rather than be offended, he looked at her with respect, as he always seemed to when she stood up to him. 'Go ahead, then. Though I must say I never once said your coming here would prove invaluable.'

'Yes, well, good, then,' she stammered as she collected her thoughts. But once she clapped eyes back on her party notes, her confidence returned. This she could do in her sleep.

She went through every detail regarding venue, catering and décor, leaving not a single suggestion out. She finished her presentation with the fact she had chosen a luxurious banquet hall owned by Lincoln Holdings, as she already knew he preferred to use his own establishments for his events. When Jacob did not respond she looked up to find his eyes spectacularly crossed.

'What was that for?'

He uncrossed his eyes and grinned. 'First things first, Holly—you do realise that I am a man?'

She had not met a man more obviously masculine. 'For the sake of argument, yes.'

'Well, then, you must understand that I find words such as "georgette" and *"decoupage"* mind-boggling.'

Holly went to interrupt but Jacob held a finger to her lips, shutting her up quick smart.

'Believe me, I am not diminishing what you do, I hired you because I admit you can do it better. If you came here for my approval, then you have it. Book everything. Hire everybody. Just go right ahead. But first things first, stay right where you are.'

He quickly pulled his finger from her mouth, kissed it and placed it back on her lips before bounding out of the chair and jogging into the kitchen.

'Now, I have to give this a quick stir and add the veggies for half a second and then I will be able to blind you with my culinary talents.'

'Oh, no,' Holly said, shoving her bits and pieces quickly into her briefcase, fighting the urge to vigorously rub away the warm impression his finger had left on her lips. 'I thought I made it clear I wasn't staying for dinner.'

As she passed by the kitchen her nostrils were filled with that same delicious soy and honey aroma she had smelled earlier. Her stomach grumbled and she placed her hand over it to quell the noise, hoping Jacob had not heard.

'Do you have dinner plans already?' he asked. *Another hot date with a potential husband,* was left unsaid, but it echoed clearly enough in the air between them.

Holly opened her mouth to answer and in the moment during which she should have come up with a believable lie, she wavered, picturing her dark, empty apartment and the leftover tuna casserole she was planning to reheat.

Still she was about to decline when she caught the look on Jacob's face. Though he was acting cool, aloof, indifferent, he was obviously sweating on her answer. His lips had thinned, pressed together too tightly, he was stirring the dinner ingredients more vigorously than seemed necessary and he kept shooting her short, accusatory sideways glances. If she hadn't known him better she would have thought him jealous.

After several moments of telling silence, Jacob's shoulders relaxed, his thinned lips softened into his usual crooked, beguiling smile and she knew he had caught her hesitation loud and clear.

'Good,' he said. 'So stay.' He added the vegetables to the mix with a deft hand.

He seemed so relaxed. As if he had flipped a lever and they had gone from God knew what to business associates in the blink of an eye. Maybe he could turn his nature on and off like that but Holly was not so fortunate.

'Don't you find this in the least bit uncomfortable?'

'What's that?'

'That you know about my future plans and desires. I find it uncomfortable enough to face you as a friend of a friend, much less as a prospective client.'

That earned her another of his unreadable glances. 'I understand what you think you mean,' he said, 'but I just don't believe you.'

'Excuse me?'

He paused, stopped stirring and stared. 'The truth is I like you, Holly.'

Holly gripped her briefcase tight, clinging to it, feeling as though if she let go it would rise to the ceiling like a dozen helium balloons and take her with it.

He paused a moment to taste the stir-fry and, obviously finding it satisfactory, he finished his thoughts.

'My closest friends are your closest friends. My business and your business will be of great benefit to each other. So what if I know that your current goal is hooking a husband and I am still willing to have you over to my place on a dinner date? Maybe one thing does not have to exclude the other.'

Holly's knees all but buckled beneath her.

So much for his agenda. So much for it's business not personal. Who was he kidding?

She was one big spanner in the works of any agenda he could ever hope to follow. Standing there, her glorious hair spilling over her shoulders, her huge eyes pleading for him to put her out of her misery, one way or the other. It was all he could do not to just haul her off to his bedroom like some caveman and show her exactly how uncomfortable she made him feel. He didn't know what they were. But they were no more 'friends of friends' than they were business associates.

He should change his mind. Thank her for her thorough presentation and send her home. But the words that came out of his mouth were, 'It's not complicated. Let's stop avoiding each other when we could be having so much more fun enjoying each other. At least until the thing you most wish for becomes more imminent anyway.'

There. Now how's that for a spanner in the works?

Jacob wiped his hands on a clean teatowel, poured two new glasses of wine and grabbed two rolled-up napkins from the kitchen bench. He passed her on his way to the dining table, the determined look in his eyes daring her to disagree with his perfectly sensible proposal.

What thing? Holly wondered, the idea of she and Jacob 'enjoying each other' pretty much blotting out the rest of his speech.

Oh, a husband. A partner. Someone to love you. Someone like Jacob.

And like a bolt of lightning it hit her. Right in the stomach. Like a sucker punch. And she was lucky not to have collapsed under its weight.

Talk about complicating things. She was head over heels for Jacob.

Ever since she had seen him dragging his heavy luggage along the footpath, she had been lost. She had been filled with a longing, which she had mistakenly tried to shoulder onto someone else, anyone else, other than the one who had produced it in the first place. She knew without any doubt her husband hunt had been over from the moment it began.

He lay the glasses on the table, unrolled the linen napkins, which contained two sets of cutlery, and shifted a small vase of wildflowers so they would not hamper their view of one another across the table. Every move appeared to her in slow motion.

It cannot possibly be love, she thought. *I barely know him. But you can know someone for ever and not love them, so why can't the opposite be possible?* And the unremitting feeling of weightlessness since he'd admitted to merely liking her was like nothing she had ever felt before.

But he's not the marrying kind and has said as much from day one.

Remember?

And the whole perfect-husband theory meant you were not to fall for a guy like him. A guy who was self-important, shallow and self-serving.

Remember?

But she could not remember how she could ever have thought those things about Jacob. The man whistling melodiously along with the lovely music was confident, to be sure. But more than that he was protective and generous, kind and considerate. He was also barefoot and cooking up a storm. For her.

The stir-fry sizzled enthusiastically and Jacob jogged back to the kitchen and turned off the stove. He grabbed two dinner plates, onto which he heaped generous portions of the delicious-looking dinner.

'No more excuses, okay,' Jacob said.

Holly did her best to compose her features to appear the same as she had looked before her alarming revelation.

'I have cooked enough of this lip-smacking dinner for the both of us. You have no other dinner plans. You are here already. You are able-bodied enough to grab the bottle of wine and bring it to the table. Put down that heavy briefcase and come give me a hand.'

Okay, Holly thought, knowing something had switched inside of her and she was going to have a hell of a time switching back. *Whatever you say.*

CHAPTER THIRTEEN

HOLLY finished off the last morsel on her plate. She had long since discarded her suit jacket. But even in just her filmy frilly top, in the fire-lit room she was warm and cosy.

'That was heavenly,' Holly said, patting the napkin to the sides of her mouth and then placing it on the table.

'Hmm. Heavenly,' Jacob agreed.

Watching Jacob sitting back, his hands clasped across his stomach, a contented smile lighting his lovely face, it was too easy for Holly to let herself believe he was thinking the same thing she was. That it was heavenly enough just to be sitting there together.

'Where did you learn to cook like that?'

Jacob reached for his wine. His eyes seemed to narrow briefly as he took a determined gulp, but after swallowing the mouthful he answered her. 'I moved out of home when I was sixteen so if I wanted to eat more than tinned soup and toast I had to learn how to cook.'

'Sixteen, really? Were you young and rash and ready to take on the world?'

'It was more that I was determined to become somebody, to make money and keep it, and to never want for anything.'

'My biggest ambition at that age was to drive my dad crazy by running off to marry Toby Cox, the cutest boy in my class.'

'I guess some things never change.'

Holly blushed. As the corners of Jacob's mouth twitched in the hint of a smile she had a glimpse of the dimples, and it was worth every trace of embarrassment.

'Did your drive come from your parents, do you think?' she asked. 'They usually provoke fairly strong responses from kids of that age.'

'My strong response was that I did not want to end up like them. Well, not like my father, to be more precise.'

'Tell me more.' *Tell me everything.* Holly leaned forward with her chin on her palm, intrigued, and waited until he was ready to go on.

'By the time I was a teenager, more of his money was going on surreptitious boozing than paying the bills. Once I caught my poor mother searching Dad's jacket pockets for loose change in order to pay the milkman. And when she died, he barely left the house, and then only to head down to the local pub. So the day after my sixteenth birthday I left.'

'I had no idea, Jacob. I didn't mean to pry—'

'It's okay. I've never hidden my modest beginnings. In fact, it has been fairly well documented. "Poor boy makes good" is always a better headline than "Rich kid is still rich".'

Holly glanced at Jacob's half drunk glass of wine. 'Was he an alcoholic?'

Jacob smiled ruefully at his glass, gently swirling the contents.

'Possibly. Though I have always thought him more weak-willed than having an addictive personality. Being drunk was an excuse not to make a decision.'

'And you have based your life around not being like that?'

'Absolutely. It was the perfect example of failing to take life by the horns. I find no point in being tied down in one project. Take the risk, reap the rewards, and move on to the next venture.'

He sounded so earnest. But to Holly it felt as if he had said this same speech a thousand times in his head. And it broke her heart. She had known a man who had lived by that maxim and all it had done was hurt those who loved him most.

'And Anabella?' Holly asked, her voice soft. 'She's younger than you?'

Jacob dropped his intense gaze to the table, but not before Holly was certain she saw a wave of guilt pass over his absorbing hazel eyes.

'She was only twelve at the time. We wrote to each other a bit and she let on she wasn't happy, but at the time I figured it was more important for me to make money so that later she would be set.'

Jacob absently took a large gulp of wine.

'A few years later I came home, a man of means and experience, rid of my resentment towards my father. Or so I thought. I walked in to find half of the furniture gone, a pile of ironing covering the couch and Ana practically tied to the sink. She was only four years older but had aged so that I barely recognised her. Her clothes were ragged, and her hair had been chopped short, by her own hand, I later discovered. My bright, beautiful little sister was all but gone, replaced with this listless, miserable creature.'

'Jacob,' Holly whispered. She lifted a finger to cover her trembling lips, blinking fast to clear the tears blurring her vision. *What have I begun?*

Why did I begin? Jacob asked himself.

But he was unable to drag his eyes away from Holly's compassionate face. *When she looked at me with those big blue eyes and asked such a simple question, about cooking, what made me leap into this tale?*

It was like leaping off a bridge but all it had taken was for her to ask, and he had leapt. He felt as if he were dangling over the edge and that Holly had control of the only rope that could bring him back to safety. Yet he had complete faith that she would not let go.

And now he had started he knew there was no way he could stop until the whole thing played itself out.

'Angered beyond thought, and before I even had the chance to hug the poor girl, I forced her to tell me where *he* was. Down at the local pub, of course. I found him sitting at the bar, a frail shell of the man I had once known. I tossed him the papers to our family home. I had paid off his mortgage. He glanced at the papers, barely registering the fact of them, much less the enormous symbolic gesture of reconciliation I had offered him. I left in disgust, went home, collected Ana and left without a note, knowing that at least now he could wallow in his own self-misery with a roof over his head but without taking Ana down with him.'

'So you looked after her?'

Jacob nodded.

'But you were only twenty.'

'I know, but what choice did we have? So the next few years I was her rock, her whole life, until she managed to get back on her feet.' *I don't ever want to feel that exposed again. Having someone else depend so entirely on me. It was just so hard.*

Holly nodded. And Jacob felt sure it was not just an affectation. She had heard the unsaid words and she understood.

'What happened to your father?'

Jacob shrugged. 'He passed away about four years ago.'

'Before you left for New Orleans?'

Jacob inhaled sharply. *She doesn't miss a beat.*

'That week. After the funeral I made the move.' *Took off, more like it.*

'It all seems to have turned out for the best, don't you think? You've certainly done well for yourself and you and Anabella are on good terms.'

'But Ana has been spoilt,' he said. 'She's never been interested in holding down a job, and would rather burn her clothes than wash and iron them herself. And that's my failing.'

Holly had found out what she wanted to know. Her lovely Jacob had exhausted more emotions in the last years of his childhood than most people did in a lifetime. Then in adulthood decided if he had no feelings, they could never consume him.

How could she hope to bring someone back from that sort of pain? She had hardly experienced the kind of rich, fulfilled childhood and stable family that could make it all better for him.

But she would do her best to try.

'Jacob. Are you kidding me? You helped a child become an adult. Many people never get that chance.'

'I was clueless.'

'You were a kid. You can hardly have been expected to know all the answers.'

Jacob shifted in his chair, trying to throw off the strange feeling that had fast crept up on him. He found himself reaching for Holly's reassurance. And that was exactly what he had just finished telling himself he never wanted to endure again.

He felt that familiar old need to just run and run. But this time he would not look back.

And then Holly took his palm in hers.

'Listen to me.'

What choice did he have as she stroked the back of his hand? He listened.

'From what Beth has told me of Ana, she is compassionate and optimistic, serious and spirited. Without her specific blend of life experiences she may not have taken on that formidable combination of traits.'

His hand tingled from the inadvertent patterns she was weaving across his skin. 'You are probably right.'

'No probably about it, I am right. I truly believe a person needs highs and lows, comedy and tragedy in order to mature into a valuable, well-rounded personality. I mean, without the sad times how can you really enjoy the happy times? You know how it feels so good after a great big sneeze?'

Jacob was completely caught off guard. The corners of his mouth twitched in the beginnings of a smile. 'Sure.'

'Well, that's because of the intense discomfort and irritation preceding it. You know how it goes. That first slight tingle that makes your nose twitch, which then grows into that bothersome tickle that builds and builds into an exasperating itch. And then comes the sneeze and when it is released, ahhh, what a wonderful sensation. But that wonderful sensation is only the same non-sensation you had before the tingle even started. Basically the good feeling only exists because of the bad feeling prior to it.'

Jacob's laughter came more easily. 'I guess there is some peculiar sense in there somewhere.'

'Peculiar or not, it's true. Without understanding of deep sorrow there can be no appreciation of sheer joy.'

Holly patted him companionably on the hand, pushed her chair back and stood up. 'Now, my friend, could you please point the way to the little girls' room?'

Jacob pointed down the stairs to the doorway next to the

kitchen. Holly smiled her thanks and rubbed Jacob's shoulder as she passed him by, sending a wash of warmth from her lithe fingertips through his tense shoulder.

As she reached the door she turned back for a moment, as though she knew he was studying her, and smiled before disappearing into the room beyond.

A small smile played at Jacob's lips as he thought of his younger sister and her love of stray animals, her abhorrence of reality television and refusal to cut her long dark hair any shorter than her shoulder blades. Without those traits and without his support through those formative years, she would not be the same Ana.

With a deep, contented sigh, Jacob rose from his seat and cleared the table, whistling softly along with the upbeat jazz music as he did, a spring in his step and a serenity he did not remember *ever* feeling.

As Holly washed her hands in the bathroom sink she looked into the mirror. Her lipstick was all but gone; only a light burgundy stain remained on her full lips. Her tongue ran over her teeth, once again tasting the honey soy stir-fry Jacob had cooked.

In the corner of the mirror she caught sight of a bath, which was so huge it took up all of one corner of the spacious room. It was certainly large enough to fit Jacob's tall frame. Easily. As well as that of another person.

Her eyes swung back to the mirror so she faced herself head-on.

'Holly, get a grip,' she growled through clenched teeth. 'And get your briefcase and get out of here before you do something you can't take back.' *Something worse than just picturing him stripping off and lowering his long, muscular length into a hot bath filled with bubbles...*

'Holly!' she said aloud, bringing her hands to her face and slapping herself lightly. She had to shake off the growing ardour that mental picture had initiated.

Jacob was a guy who needed time and space. He needed patience and kind words. She felt as though he had made some progress out there tonight and the last thing he needed was some husband-hungry woman leaping into his arms and professing her undying love.

Once free of the bathroom, Holly found herself back in what she assumed was Jacob's bedroom.

The natural tones and unpretentious feel of the room matched the rest of the home. 'St John's ace lithograph' filled an otherwise blank wall above the bed head and bookshelves ran the length of one wall.

This could be her one and only time there and she could not resist soaking up as much of Jacob's habitat as possible. She ran her fingers along the smooth, clean horizontal planes of the bookshelves. Amongst the numerous books there sat a few photo frames; most housed pictures of Jacob with a thin brunette woman. Holly ran a finger over the girl's face, assuming it was Anabella. She had the same dark hair and deep hazel eyes and her smile towards her brother was bursting with love.

And between a pair of stout candleholders and a bunch of unused candles sat a pair of much-used boxing gloves in a glass case.

She stopped short at this last item, staring at the rough, rounded surfaces with their numerous cracks, bruises and stains. Looking closer, she even thought she could make out splatters of dried blood on the knuckle of the right hand. A chill ran down her spine as her mind clouded with a flash of images of how those marks and scrapes would have been achieved. She knew exactly what it took for a pair of well-worn boxing gloves to look like that.

Then she remembered that Jacob was the man who had organised those dangerous boxing bouts for his employees to 'enjoy'. She found it hard reconciling her memory of the antagonistic, commanding, condescending man of that night with the astute, intriguing, reflective man on the other side of the door.

But they were one and the same.

Jacob, whom Ben and Beth considered a close and worthy friend, who worried for his little sister, and who had unsuspectingly captured Holly's heart was the same ruthless and unfettered Jacob Lincoln of Lincoln Holdings.

The clink of china from the dining room jolted Holly from her puzzled reverie. Having no idea how long she had been snooping, she decided it was time to leave.

On her way to the door she passed a chest of drawers. Her mind reeling to a conversation she'd had with Beth a few days before, Holly turned back and opened the top drawer. She stared at the contents for a long moment before shutting the drawer quietly.

'Definitely time to go home,' she whispered aloud as she walked out of the room.

CHAPTER FOURTEEN

HOLLY walked into the main room determined to find her host so that she could make her excuses and leave. The table had been cleared and cleaned but there was no sign of Jacob. She moved to the hearth to wait for him to return. Her skin tingled from a mixture of the sizzling heat of the fire and a whole different warmth that had lit her from within since she'd come to realise that she was in love.

She caught sight of something hidden in a shadowy corner, and moved in that direction for a closer look, when the lights in that corner sprang on in a blinding flash.

Holly screamed as she spun around, her eyes searching wildly for Jacob. He was near the front doorway, his hands moving down from a bank of light switches on the wall by his shoulder.

'Sorry,' he said as he sauntered towards her. All signs of the reclusive man from dinner had vanished and he was re-placed with a Jacob she had not seen before. The approving warmth in his eyes was so unmistakable, for the first time she felt like she was the hunted.

'I didn't mean to startle you,' he said, his voice low and

husky. 'I knew you were heading to my bag so I thought I'd make it easier for you to have a nose around.'

'Your bag?' Holly asked, her voice barely above a whisper.

Jacob held out his arm motioning her towards the corner. She turned back to see a red punching bag hanging there sedately.

She swallowed hard. It was colossal. Taller than her by half. Thick metallic chains ran from both ends, connecting the bag to large matching steel plates bolted to the floor and ceiling.

Taking the last few steps towards the bag, she reached out tentatively and gave it a slight push. The heavy bag barely moved. She pulled her hand away as thought burnt by the touch, rubbing her fingers together committing to memory the rough, cool feel of the worn leather.

Jacob joined her, his hands on hips and his eyes bright. 'When I refurbished the place I had the roof and floor reinforced so as to take its weight. Do you want a go?'

He slapped the bag playfully a couple of times. Holly baulked, her pulse quickening in loathing at the thought. She backed away holding up her hands defensively.

'No, thank you.'

'Are you sure? It's great fun.'

'Sorry. I have no interest in beating up a big red bag that has never done anything to deserve my wrath.'

'It's good for releasing tension. And it's excellent exercise. It'll work muscles you never knew you had,' Jacob promised as he jogged up and down with loose fists raised at the big bag.

Holly kept walking backwards, putting herself as far from the bag and Jacob's flailing fists as possible. 'If I hadn't discovered those muscles to date I'm sure I can get through the next fifty years without them.' She kept her voice light, to stop herself sounding as she felt. Frantic. 'And aren't there better ways to release tension than hitting something or someone?'

'I can think of at least one.'

Holly stopped short. Her eyes flew to Jacob's and she was all but undone.

He had stopped bouncing around. His feet were shoulder-width apart, and he had steadied the heavy bag in two hands. His dark soft hair was tousled from the exercise and a lock flopped down his forehead. His eyes were bright and his breathing was heavy.

If her mind had not already been conjuring up inappropriate sensual images, she would have taken that as a serious invitation. And what an invitation that could have been. The man before her was so male, so virile it was enough to wrench any woman's heart. Add to that the 'nobody can touch my heart' aura he carried with him like a weight across his broad shoulders and he was an irresistible package.

But the fact that he had long since had Holly's for the taking meant she was in danger of seeing meaning in his looks and words that were not there. She could almost convince herself she saw her own desire reflected in his bright hazel eyes.

What a picture she makes, Jacob thought. Her blue eyes flashed and her own heavy breathing was more than a match for his. For someone he once thought cool and calm, she was the most emotive woman he had ever met. Every thought and fancy played across her face the second it crossed her mind. And if she wasn't careful, he would take the three steps over there and make good her very thoughts and fancies.

He had thrown the line out in jest. Sort of. But instead of a raised eyebrow and a haughty stare he had been hit with a look of undisguised passion. A silent submission. And it shocked him to his core.

What would happen if he made good on that throwaway invitation? What an encounter that could be. If only she were that sort of woman.

If only.

His mind had been spinning in that direction all night. Who was he kidding? It had been spinning that way for two weeks. And if that look was anything to go by, her mind had been spinning on a similar track.

But this was not a woman to be toyed with. Ben and Beth's best friend. He should never have cooked her dinner. She had been right about that from the outset. There was no point. It was too close to home. It would be too complicated.

But, oh, it would be so sweet.

Jacob ran a hand through his hair, took a step away from the bag. Time to wipe that mesmerising look from her lovely face. Time to change the subject.

'Do you really have such an objection to boxing or are you just claiming the accepted feminine view for my benefit?'

Holly blinked.

That's better. Dislike me. Fight me.

Then she lifted her chin in defiance.

Better still.

'And what would I be hoping to gain in coming across as acceptably feminine?'

He wanted her up and debating. Much safer than standing before him so quiet, so lovely, making him ache through wanting to touch her. He reached out and took hold of the bag once more, needing to distract himself from his runaway thoughts. Better his hands occupied there than reaching out for her.

'All I'm saying is that I'd rather hear your opinion than an expected opinion any day.'

There, that should get her worked up.

'Truthfully, Jacob, that is my opinion, expected or not,' she said, seeming to drag the statement from deep within her.

Jacob watched in chagrin as the fight drained out of her. She deflated before his eyes until she looked so sad, so tired, and so vulnerable, as though she had been pretending to be strong for such a long time and could do it no longer. She could not know how it affected him.

'This all frightens me a little.' She motioned to the punching bag. 'The first time we met you yelled at me, a complete stranger in the street, then there was that horrible boxing match at the Fun and Games where you advocated violence to your employees. Then I found those old gloves in what amounts to a shrine in your bedroom, and now this. There seems to be an unsettling pattern forming.'

The one word that had captured Jacob's attention had been the word 'frightens'. Only then did he detect Holly's panicky expression. Her hands were clasped defensively in front of her chest and her feet were planted firmly as though she was ready to fly at any sign of trouble. And she flinched with every random slap he gave the bag.

Jacob moved away from the bag, lightly taking Holly's arm to lead her to sit with him on the big couch by the fire.

'What are you frightened of, Holly?'

She didn't answer, just shrugged and swallowed hard, her big blue eyes wide, still focussed on the bag in the distance. Jacob kept hold of both of her hands in one of his. With his other hand he lightly stroked her hair to relax her and kept his voice deliberately soft.

'Big Red over there is just for fun and fitness. Though as a kid I had a good teacher who took me aside and joined me up for elementary boxing classes at a local gym. It taught me how to master my emotions and how to focus on the task in front of me. I put on matches for the staff to teach them those same ideals.'

'And the gloves?' she asked, her voice subdued and wavering.

'The gloves once belonged to Muhammad Ali and are encased in glass in the safety of my room as they are worth a small fortune.'

Holly seemed to have relaxed very little. Her eyes had softened and lost that startled look, but she still shook. Jacob's hands now stroked her hair from her face, behind her ears, around behind her neck. He still sought to relax her but he was also finding the touch exhilarating and was soon doing it for his own benefit as much as hers.

'It's no big deal, Holly. Really. I mean, Ana has a punching bag at her place. I dare say she uses hers more than I do these days. She loves it. Haven't you ever done kick boxing, or self defence classes?'

'I take yoga with Beth every week,' she answered quietly, and then a hesitant smile lit her lovely face. 'Just plain old yoga, not even power yoga.'

Jacob shifted in his seat. His heart rate rose after just one quick smile from her. Not sensible. He slowly drew his hands away from her, resting one on his thigh and the other along the back of the couch. He had more important things to get from this conversation than the delight of her touch.

'Holly, I haven't been in a fist fight since I was sixteen and have never used my skills outside of a ring. I promise. I have never hit a woman and never would.' He shot her a playful smile. 'No matter how exasperating I know some of them can be.'

But instead of laughing along with him as he had hoped, she flinched and shrank within herself. Did she have to be so sensitive?

Leaning forward, he raised her head with a finger under

her chin. 'Come on, Holly, this is ridiculous. I need to know that you believe me. I couldn't endure thinking that you were seriously fearful of me. Tell me you believe me.'

Holly swallowed hard as she looked into his pleading eyes. 'I believe you,' she said.

But Jacob saw the uncertainty. He also saw that this uncertainty was worrying her, as though she really wanted to believe in him. There had to be a significant reason behind this wish to believe and the idea invigorated him.

If she saw him as merely a client with whom she was having a business dinner, or even as a 'friend of a friend', it really shouldn't matter to her. But evidently it did matter. Before he could tell himself it was a bad idea, Jacob leant forward ever so slightly and she did not turn away.

Holly waited silently as Jacob's face came closer and closer to her own, until his lips touched hers, so lightly, just as they had that misty night on Beth and Ben's driveway. And just as readily the kiss turned into something deeper and more exhilarating.

Jacob leaned in a fraction closer, pressing his warm mouth firmly against her own, and Holly turned her head so that their lips met more fully. She was still holding her weight with her palms on either side of her thighs, her elbows locked.

After several moments of blissfully enjoying the sweet taste of Jacob's soft, supple mouth, Holly felt her arms go weak and her elbows unlocked, causing her to sink back ever so slightly. But it was enough. Jacob slid an arm behind her and leaned her back into the plush chair, guiding her, his strong arm taking her weight until she rested comfortably along the seat.

Desire raging through her, she felt his warm imprint along her receptive body, his heavy male scent making as much of an impression on her awakened senses as his strong insistent body.

Her breathing hastened until she felt as though she would pass out if she were not already lying down. Smooth and skilled, his teeth tugged lightly at her bottom lip, intermittently nipping and pulling away, creating a longing ache deep within her so that she found herself craning to meet his mouth. This was the Jacob she loved. Generous, sweet, intoxicating.

And all too soon, above the heady, insistent ringing of blood in her ears, came the shrill, insistent ring of the telephone.

'Shouldn't you get that?' Holly asked, whispering against Jacob's tender mouth.

As if in punishment for her even noticing the phone, Jacob shifted his attentions from her warm mouth to her ear, softly fanning hot, short breaths at the base of her lobe and raining delicate kisses along her exposed neck.

'The machine will get it.'

And so it did.

'This is Jacob, leave a message.'

'Hiya bro.' Anabella's cheerful voice came over the machine.

Holly placed her hands firmly on Jacob's chest; both of their faces turned towards the phone, though only an inch apart.

'The snow's fast and furious and so is the skiing. And no, I haven't broken a leg. Mikey says hi. How's the party coming along? Did you meet up with Holly as you promised? If she's as lovely as you say maybe you should ask her out. Sorry, I can't help it. When I'm in love I have to share it around. Anyway, let me know how it's going and I'll see you in a week. Love ya.'

The phone clicked as she hung up and the machine went through the beeps and whirrs necessary to reset itself.

Her senses slowly returning, Holly did not wait for Jacob to turn his face back to hers. She pushed at his chest to lift him and he conceded.

'I take it that was Ana.' She swung her legs back onto the floor.

'Mmm hmm,' Jacob answered, his eyes not leaving her. One of his hands rested lightly on her thigh and the other curled in and out of a lock of her hair.

'Look, I really should go.' If she didn't she could so easily fall under the spell of that strong hand and those mesmerising lips once more. All too easily. She should not have given into that sensational bliss in the first place. But how could she not? Though next time her common sense was unlikely to be saved by the phone.

'Why?' Jacob asked.

Why? Holly thought. *Because I am at once enamoured and afraid of you and at real risk of leaping into your arms and not letting go thus of making a complete fool of myself and sending you running for the hills.*

'I really had no intention of even staying for dinner and then afterwards…' She could not find the words to explain what had happened afterwards. 'This isn't what I expected.'

Jacob smiled. 'Let's just agree it has been a most unexpected evening on every count. In fact we seem to only ever have unexpected times together. I certainly couldn't call our encounters predictable.'

How easily he can joke. He really has no idea. Holly knew she should be glad. At least that way she could hopefully extricate herself from her own feelings without anyone ever knowing.

But she wasn't glad. She was frustrated. He was attracted to her, that much was obvious. But that much was as far as it went for him. And it wasn't enough. Not now. Not when she knew how she really felt about him.

Holly smiled shortly before easing herself away from Jacob's light touch, standing up and meticulously straightening her clothes. She looked around, not quite knowing where to turn next until Jacob stood and motioned to her briefcase by the kitchen.

'Right, of course. Thank you,' Holly said. She collected her jacket and bag, and headed straight for the lift. She pressed the button and turned to face Jacob who was standing only a couple of feet from her. She skittishly jumped back before remembering herself and holding out a hand for a businesslike handshake.

'Well, Jacob. Thanks for dinner and…well, dinner. It was really delicious.'

Jacob laughed softly before taking the proffered hand and shaking it with a serious expression on his face. 'And thank you for the presentation. It was enchanting.'

Holly looked at him blankly before he motioned to her briefcase and she remembered what had really brought her here in the first place.

'Of course. Well, I'm glad you like it. Come Monday morning I will get on top of it and I'll contact…I'll get Lydia to contact you later in the week with the final details.'

The lift binged and Holly let out a deep sigh of relief. The doors opened and she stepped inside. Jacob leaned in slightly, his strong arms holding the lift doors open.

'In case you were wondering, I did tell my sister you were lovely, you know,' he admitted, looking her directly in the eye, his dimples out in full force.

Holly stared back, suddenly feeling very close to tears. He *really* had no idea. Jacob leaned in and kissed her lightly on the cheek, but the kiss lingered longer than was merely polite.

Holly sighed at his velvety touch and when he pulled away she saw that his eyes were closed tight. It took great restraint for her to stay put and when the doors began to close it took even greater strength to stop herself from wrenching them open and dragging him into the lift with her.

As the lift made its way downward Holly leant back onto the cool steel wall. The mirrored door in front of her revealed a very different expression from the one in the bathroom mirror half an hour before. Her lips were plump and now devoid of lipstick. Her eyes were bright and shining, wide and shell-shocked.

She found she could not draw her eyes away from the image until it finally wavered and split in two as the lift stopped on the bottom floor and the doors opened.

Jacob turned off the lights in the kitchen, leaving only those mood lights by his punching bag on. He had changed into track pants and running shoes and was strapping his wrists. But for the first time since he had installed the bag he didn't have the energy or the desire to hit it. He used to exercise himself into a frenzy to dissipate his frustrations. But tonight, with Holly's few well-chosen words, the aching feeling of injustice that had resided permanently in the pit of his stomach for so many years had eased.

He bounced around a bit, stretching out his shoulders and neck before throwing a few warm-up punches at the bag. All of a sudden the image of Holly standing there looking almost frightened as he'd slapped the bag flooded his mind.

He wondered why she hated boxing so much. Sure, a lot of women screwed up their dainty noses at the sport as they thought they were supposed to do, but he knew Holly was not false in that way. She really had something against it.

He had opened up and told her more of himself than he ever had to a mere 'friend of a friend', yet she had said not a word of her family or past. Was she simply a good listener or had she deliberately chosen not to reveal herself? Jacob found himself disappointed that she had not said anything. Or maybe he was disappointed that he had been so caught up in his own regrets that he had not thought to listen to her in the same way.

This would take some looking into. Not because he was interested in her in any personal way, of course, simply because he owed her. She had helped him more than she could know. And he wanted to return the favour.

Who was he kidding? He was interested. More and more so every time he met her. She was captivating. And truth be told he could hardly keep his hands off her. That scent: it reminded him of apples in summer. That hair: so thick and soft and ridiculously shiny.

But what was the use? No matter how attracted they were to each other, she was searching for something that he was unable to supply. But now, having had a taste of the delights Holly had on offer, he found he could not let it go at that. She was addictive. And he was hooked.

So what if she's on the hunt for a husband? Why can't I beg a little of her time until he comes along? I know we can have fun together until her Prince Charming appears.

But Jacob knew that as each day passed he found himself hoping her Prince Charming would not come along any time soon.

Holly angled her car onto the clear seaside street. No matter how hard she concentrated on the road ahead she could not shake one particular image from her mind: Jacob, self-professed risk-taker who was loath to put down roots, had in his top dresser drawer socks only, all neatly arranged by colour and fabric.

CHAPTER FIFTEEN

NINE o'clock Saturday morning Jacob could wait no longer. He picked up the phone and dialled.

'Beth, it's Jacob.'

'Jacob!' Beth said, her voice bright with pleasure. 'You've just missed Ben. He's gone down to the Dairy Bell to get me some Chocolate Nut-O Heaven ice cream.'

'A pregnancy craving, I take it.'

'I wish! I've always been a chockie-ice-cream addict. Did you want me to take a message?'

'I actually wanted to talk to you.'

'Okay. Talk away.'

'Well, it's about Holly—'

'Ooh, about time. Hang on a second while I get comfy.'

He listened as shuffling, scraping noises came through the other end of the phone.

'Well, you came to the right person,' Beth finally said. 'First thing you should know is that she prefers tulips to roses. She can't wear silver, she's allergic, so gold jewellery is the go—'

'Hold on, Beth. That's not what I was after. I'm not looking to propose, no matter how much you may have been planning and hoping. I'm just a little concerned about her.'

'Okay. What are you concerned about?'

'Well, she came over to my place last night—'

'Really? That's wonderful. She never told me—'

'Beth!'

'Yes?'

'Let me finish.'

'Okay, sorry. Buttoning lips right now.'

He smiled briefly as he had a feeling Beth had mimed buttoning her lips for real.

'She came over to my place last night to show me the proposal for Ana's party and she stayed for dinner.' Jacob paused, wondering how to explain what had happened next; he could barely deconstruct the order of events himself. 'Anyway, after dinner she saw the punching bag. You know the one I've always had in the corner of the lounge room? And she freaked out.'

'Freaked out how?' Beth asked, and Jacob was sure he heard real concern in his voice.

'Well, she chastised me for the boxing match at Fun and Games and for my Ali gloves. But the punching bag had her quaking. She seemed almost frightened.' Jacob decided he would have to spell it out. 'Why is Holly so against boxing?'

'Why shouldn't she be?' Beth asked, her voice excessively light. 'Many women are. I find it repulsive, grown men beating each other up. All that he-man, master-of-the-universe stuff. Most unattractive.'

'But it was more than that. I know it was. Was she...has she been hit before? Is that it?'

'No, Jacob. She was not hit.' But Beth's pause spoke volumes. He was onto something.

'Well, then, what is it? She's all messed up about something and it's driving me mad.'

'I think you should ask her that, Jacob.'

'I did, sort of.'

'Well, it's up to her to tell you.'

'So there is something to tell?' Jacob persevered.

'Jacob, I can't.'

Jacob swore under his breath. 'I was expecting you to tell me…I don't know. Look I'm sorry. I shouldn't have come to you with this.'

'That's okay. Don't be sorry. Be careful.'

'I'll let you go. Say hi to Ben.'

'Sure.'

And then Jacob hung up.

Nine-thirty Saturday morning the phone rang. Holly ran out of the bathroom wrapped in a big fluffy towel. She ran on the tips of her toes so she would not leave wet footprints on the carpet, and grabbed the cordless phone from its cradle in the hallway.

'Hello?'

'Hello,' Jacob said, this time clearly not feeling the need to introduce himself. His voice low and ominous. And sexy and heart-wrenching.

'Hi.' Holly stood, dripping on the carpet, the phone clasped tightly to her ear as a heavy silence sizzled over the phone lines for a couple of uncomfortable moments.

'It's about Ana's party.'

'Of course.' She tried not to sound so disappointed. *What, were you expecting a proposal?*

'I'd like to change the location if possible.'

Holly frowned as her attention zoomed in on the party quick smart. She had spent a good deal of time picking out the perfect Lincoln Holdings-owned venue.

'All right. I had only pencilled us in at that banquet hall, so we can cancel no problem. Was there something in particular you did not like about my choice?'

'I would just like to hold it somewhere else.'

'Did you have this *somewhere else* in mind? Somewhere we can book with only a week's notice?'

'Actually I do. If I could pick you up at around noon I'll take you there for lunch.'

Lunch? Not likely. She had promised herself no more time alone with Jacob, if only for the sake of her own sanity. Beth often said, 'What goes up must come down', so shouldn't that be the same for love? If you could fall in love it should be just as easy to fall out of love, so that was what she was going to do.

She cradled the phone between her chin and her shoulder, grabbing her towel with one hand as she scrambled for a pen and paper with the other.

'There's no need for you to take me, really. Just let me know the name of the place and I'll look after it on Monday. During work hours.' *There, that should put him in his place.*

'Wouldn't it be better to have it settled straight away? Considering we do only have a week's notice, as you said?'

Holly gritted her teeth to stop herself from saying that was his fault, not hers. 'Okay. But how about I meet you there?' Besides, being in a restaurant they would not exactly be alone; maybe she *could* stretch the boundaries of her promise. 'Just give me the address—'

'Much easier if I pick you up. I'll see you at twelve.'

And then Jacob hung up. Holly looked at the phone for a moment before slamming it back down on the cradle. She picked it up and slammed it again for good measure.

'You are so infuriating!' she shouted to the empty hallway as she padded back into the bathroom.

* * *

At a couple of minutes before midday Holly's doorbell rang. She grabbed her bag, quickly checked her make-up in the hall mirror.

Feeling more nervous than before any of her blind dates, she ran a hand down either side of her baby-blue knee-length dress, fixed the collar on the matching cropped jacket, and checked her stockings had no runs. That morning every little choice had taken on new significance. Her dress, her lipstick, the way she wore her hair—she wanted to be as attractive for him as she could possibly be.

She pointed an accusing finger at her reflection. 'You have no will-power.'

Her breath caught in her throat at the sight that met her when she opened the door. Jacob stood before her in jeans, a bulky cream sweater and a soft brown leather bomber jacket. Even dressed down he was stunning. Her heart leapt in her chest and she knew, no matter how many times during the long sleepless night before she had told herself she was over-estimating her feelings for him, she was wrong.

She loved him.

Holly soon saw that he was giving her the same once-over but she knew that, sadly, his thoughts were less altruistic than her own.

'You didn't have to get all dressed up for me,' Jacob joked as he took the house key out of Holly's hand and locked the front door for her. He led her down the footpath.

'These are work clothes,' Holly said stiffly as her judgment came back to her. 'And this is a work meeting.'

'Yes, ma'am.' Jacob saluted. 'I didn't mean to intimate that I was in any way displeased. On the contrary, you look absolutely beautiful.'

He looked her over again, his eyes full of the praise he had willingly stated. Holly felt her self-restraint dissolving under his gaze.

Jacob opened the passenger door to his car and waited until she was settled before he jogged around to the driver's side. He gunned the engine and pulled out onto the road.

Holly waited for the other shoe to drop. She waited for the cross-examination or the apology or something, anything to be said about their surprising dinner the night before. But he sat back, whistling along with the jazz station on the car stereo.

'So,' Holly said, breaking the silence, 'where are you taking me?'

'Ah, now that would be telling.' Jacob tapped the side of his nose.

Holly laughed, dumbfounded by his playful mood. 'And what is wrong with telling?'

Jacob pointed at the car stereo. 'Don't you love this song? This version was recorded in nineteen sixty-eight in this little pub on Bourbon St—'

'Jacob!'

'You talk too much, woman. Life is too short for so many questions. I order you to sit back, relax, and enjoy the ride.'

Holly gave in. 'Fine.' She sat back against the lambswool seat covers, snug in the heated car listening to the soft jazz playing on the stereo. She turned her head to the side and watched Melbourne go by through the tinted windows.

Jacob glanced towards Holly several times, wishing he could decipher the thoughts behind her calm, cool gaze. He itched to launch straight into a direct Q and A about Holly's past that Beth had all but admitted was brutal.

But he also had the feeling she would more likely open the door and jump from a moving car than be forced to talk about it. He bit his tongue and drove. There would be time for questions later.

After fifteen minutes of companionable silence, Jacob pulled into a familiar driveway.

'This is Lunar.'

'It certainly is.' He chose one of the free staff car parks, pulled on the handbrake, shot out of the car and around to Holly's door before she had even unbuckled her belt.

'*This* is your suggestion for a new location for Anabella's party?'

'Why? You don't think it would be perfect?' Jacob took her by the hand and pulled her from her seat.

'Of course. I love this place and it's much more appropriate for what I originally had in mind. I have a good relationship with the owners so we may have some luck booking it on short notice.'

'I've already checked and it's fine.'

Holly was a little put out that he had gone over her head, especially after his constant avowals that he wanted to stay out of the loop. 'Okay. But when did you speak to the owners? Between last night and now? You could have told me earlier if you weren't happy—'

'I am the owner, Holly.'

'You? No, you're not. Herman and Gina have owned the place for ever.'

Jacob placed light hands on the tops of her arms as though he knew she would fall over without his support. 'Not anymore.'

He let her go, slipping his hands in his trouser pockets, and Holly felt bereft, cool where her arms had been lit by his warmth only moments before.

'The deal came through midnight last night. Sorry I couldn't say anything. Confidentiality clauses and all that. Besides, after meeting you here for lunch that day I had an odd feeling that you would pick Lunar for the party even without my advice.' He shrugged. 'No matter. It's all worked out okay in the end.'

Holly felt devastated, as if she had let him down. As if choosing Lunar would have been a sign and she had failed. She felt like running after him and tugging on his arm and begging him to believe it had been her first choice. Beth would have been tickled to see her reaching for signs in that way.

'Are you okay with it being here?' he asked.

'Of course. I adore this place. This has been my lucky place ever since I started out at Cloud Nine. I bring all of my new clientele here.'

And then something he had said another time came back to her.

'You're not going to refurbish, are you? You're not going to change Lunar and then sell it off, like you did with your apartment block?'

Jacob's eyes narrowed. 'You don't think that if you took clients somewhere else they would not sign with you, do you?'

'No,' Holly answered, though not sure if that was the whole truth.

'Because it is you they love, not the meeting venue.'

Her heart tumbled. There was one particular client she would do anything to have love her.

'Or the magic briefcase or the lucky suit.'

Holly noted mentally that she would have to kill Lydia. 'You didn't answer my question.'

'I've owned the place for about twelve hours—how can I answer that?'

'If you've been after it for ages then I am certain you know exactly what you plan to do with it.'

'Perhaps,' he answered under his breath.

A waiter led them over to Holly's usual table.

'Well, since we know Lunar is available and you know I approve we really don't need to stay, do we?'

'We are here now. It's lunchtime. We may as well eat.'

She sat back, fuming, crossed her arms and refused to look at the menu. After a few moments of uncomfortable silence, she found Jacob watching her intently.

'What? Do I have something on my face?'

'That scar.' He pointed to a small straight scar at the top of the ridge of her nose. 'How did you get that?'

Holly's hand flew to the spot; she knew exactly the scar he meant. She flicked her head in a practised move so that a lock of fringe hair fell to cover the exact spot. Still seething, she looked back up and with a false smile answered, 'It's nothing. Just a silly accident as a kid, that's all.'

'What sort of accident?' Jacob persisted.

'It really doesn't matter. It's not an interesting story, I promise.'

'Tell me anyway.'

'I'd rather not.' Holly knew her voice was rising but she could not help it.

'Come on. Holly, I know you are hiding something big. Something you would rather I don't know.'

Am I so transparent? she thought, close to laughing hysterically. He was being so gentle, so reassuring. But how would he be if she said, *Fine, Jacob. I have been hiding something. I seem to have fallen in love with you.*

'I told you about my family,' he said, 'about my childhood. I want you to know that you can share the same with me.'

Where had the teasing grin gone? That had been much easier to resist than the offer of solace and compassion from the man who had stolen her heart.

Holly swallowed hard as her ears began to ring and the

stories and memories welled up inside her. After years of learning to calm her nerves and the swelling tide that once overcame her, she suddenly felt a great desire to confide in this man.

She wanted him to know her inside and out. She felt that she would be cheating him if she did not share with him what he had shared with her. And she knew in her heart that he would not judge her. She uncrossed her arms, her hands slipping to take a hold of the napkin on her lap in a firm grip.

'You really want to know how I got this scar?' she asked quietly, needing a final push.

Jacob was shocked that she had demurred so soon. He sat forward, clasped his hands on the table, and looked deep into her troubled eyes.

'Yes, Holly. I really want to know.'

She began in a quiet voice. 'It was at the Hidden Valley Greyhound Course, of all places.'

Of course, Jacob thought, *the colonel mentioned it at the fundraiser.*

'I was there with my dad. He had gone missing, which wasn't unusual. For hours, which wasn't unusual. After a while, once I was hungry, I went looking for him. I was a kid but the guys there knew me well and I could go where I pleased. I headed to the bar, scampering between the tall tree-trunk legs of the regulars when one guy stopped me. Picked me up in his arms, his eyes bloodshot from drink, and he asked me what the hell I was doing there. He could barely hold himself up, much less me. And he dropped me. I landed badly, my face hit a bar stool and I was knocked out. I came to in the hospital.'

'Your father must have been beside himself.'

'Well, he certainly was not beside me. The colonel was there and he had taken charge. Carried me to the course ambulance and forced his way into that van with me to ride to the hospital. He stayed with me through the day and took me home to stay with him and his wife that night. And the next and the next.'

'Your dad?'

'He showed up about three days later. Turned up at the door with a big grin and a pocket full of cash and took me home.'

'Where had he been?'

She shrugged. 'Who knows. Back at the track, maybe? Or perhaps he had found a soul mate, another guy onto a good thing, a sure bet, a quick fix. Or maybe he had been in on a fixed boxing match and was just holed up in whichever motel we were currently living in, watching the fight on pay TV. Any of the above would have been a typical day in the life.'

'Was the man in the bar charged with assault?'

'Gosh, no. The racecourse could have gone under from something like that. Then where would my dad have been without a place to leave the kid on the weekends?'

He had never heard her bitter before. She was masking it with humour but the sadness shone through all the same.

'It was okay, really. Though the colonel has never forgiven himself for not reporting the incident.' Holly shook her head in genuine amazement. 'He saved me that day. Showed me what regular life could be, with rules and boundaries and a place to call home. I help him out every year now, help keep his dear racecourse afloat. I owe him that much if not everything.'

Jacob wanted to leap around the table, take her in his arms, and promise that nobody would hurt her ever again.

The waiter arrived with their drinks and Jacob took the quiet moment to absorb the story of Holly's upbringing and to try to reconcile it with the woman sitting before him.

She was so refined, so elegant, she knew where to eat, how

to dress, and organised A-list functions for the city's rich and famous. You would think she had grown up with money, with prestige, with a chauffeur and a grand home.

But she had created herself from nothing. The educated accent, the prestigious job, the VIP contacts, she had cultivated them from the ground up.

Yet underneath that perfect façade was a real fear of change, of being abandoned, being out of control. It explained her desire to contain the passionate and impulsive side to her personality. No matter how she waved away her father's lax responsibility, she was frightened that she had inherited his hot-blooded nature so she was constantly trying to be more calm, more patient and more composed.

As the waiter left Holly's mobile phone rang. She scrambled to answer it quick smart, as though it were a lifeline.

'Hello, Holly Denison speaking.'

Jacob sipped on his drink, watching Holly carefully as he listened openly to the one-sided conversation.

'Right, I see. No, I wasn't busy,' Holly said, deliberately not looking at him. 'I'll be right there.' She hung up her phone.

She pushed back her chair and stood. 'Jacob. I'm sorry. I won't be able to stay for lunch. One of my clients has a Women in Film luncheon on Monday and it seems the guest of honour is trying to pull out.'

'But it's your day off. Can't one of the others look after it?'

'Ordinarily yes. But this client is quite temperamental and will only deal with me. She won't even take Lydia's phone calls. I'm sorry.'

Jacob went to stand as well but Holly all but pushed him back into his seat.

'No, you stay. I'll catch a cab. I'll talk to you later in the week. Bye.'

Jacob could do nothing but watch her go.

CHAPTER SIXTEEN

LATE Saturday night Jacob rang the doorbell. He rubbed his hands together to relieve them of the freezing cold, and shuffled from foot to foot so his toes would not go numb. It took several moments for Ben and Beth to answer the door together.

'Jacob!' Ben said. 'It's almost midnight. What are you doing here?'

'You look terrible. Are you okay?' Beth added as she stepped around Ben to take a closer look.

'She told me.'

'Who told you what?' Ben asked. His hair was flattened on one side and Jacob worried he had caught them asleep.

But Jacob saw the understanding dawn on Beth's face. She took her husband by the arm, pulled him out of the way and motioned for him to go get tea, then guided Jacob inside and onto the couch.

'Holly. She told me about her dad at the racecourse. And the scar. And the colonel. And…that's all.'

Beth nodded and looked over his bedraggled appearance. 'Have you been drinking?'

'No. Though I wanted to. I have been sitting in a bar not far from here for the last several hours. Thinking and eating stale beer nuts.'

'And what were you thinking about?'

'I was thinking about finding the guy who gave her that scar and breaking his nose.' His fists clenched in his lap. 'Or finding her father and giving him a piece of my mind.'

'Not much chance of that. Holly's father died several years ago.'

'Good,' he whispered under his breath and was amazed at the vehemence in his own voice. It was rare for him to become so impassioned. Not over business ideas. Not even over Anabella. He'd thought he had long since learnt not to care so much. But in that moment he felt so worked up, he could hardly think straight.

Beth took him by the hand, drawing his lapsing attention to her face.

'I told you the truth when I said he never hit Holly, but his apathy damaged her in other ways.'

Jacob listened intently, latching onto Beth's every word as though they were the salvation that could drag him out of this unnerving mood.

'Her dad was a drifter,' she continued. 'He dabbled in amateur boxing but was never good enough to make a living, but unfortunately learnt enough to use his skills to settle disagreements when the need arose. He never held down a proper job for long. He usually lost them after turning up with a black eye from a pub brawl the night before or by just not turning up at all. I'm pretty sure Holly even saw her dad in a few of his later fights. All losses, from what I know. So Holly has understandably never been so hot for the combat sports.'

'Did you ever meet him?' Jacob asked.

'Holly's father? Yes, I did.'

Jacob stared at her, willing her to go on.

'I stayed with them during the holidays, first year uni. He was living in a caravan then. Had been for a year or so. The longest they had stayed in one place, I think. I liked him. He took us to the ballet and to this bizarre underground modern art gallery. He had more energy in his little finger than anyone I had ever met. I thought Holly was so lucky to have such a cool father.'

'But, he left her for dead in a bar.' Jacob felt his face growing red with anger. 'And from what I gathered him leaving her to her own devices for days at a time was not unusual. I would hardly call that lucky.'

'I know that now but at the time that wanderlust and lack of responsibility was tantalizing. For a college kid, still living at home, it seemed close to heaven. Little did I know Holly would have given away all her freedom to be able to live in a normal home like I did.'

Jacob bit his bottom lip raw. It hit him that Beth had just described his own life for the past ten years. Wanderlust, lack of responsibility, freedom. They seemed like such hollow pursuits when on the outside looking in.

Ben came in at that moment with a tray of coffee and biscuits. He poured some out for himself and Jacob, along with a herbal tea for his pregnant wife. She sent him a loving smile before continuing.

'It wasn't until after his funeral, when Holly and I stayed up all through the night and she told me the story of the scar amongst others. If he ever felt the need to travel or disappear the fact that he had a child in his care did not stop him. Sometimes when he did his disappearing acts he took Holly with him so that she would miss weeks of school at a time. Sometimes he would leave her in a motel with some cash and the manager's phone number in case of emergency.'

He pictured Holly, as a little girl, with long brunette hair flying behind her as she ran about the racecourse and he felt sick. 'She must have so much pent-up rage against the man for what he did to her.'

'I don't know about that. You would have had to see them together. It was amazing. They either adored each other or hated each other from one day to the next. He doted on her; she was his little angel, yet he left her. It has made her the resilient, ingenious, forgiving woman she is today.'

He knew she was right. Holly had said pretty much the same thing to him before, that it was the highs *and* the lows that created a well-rounded personality. But it still did not stop him feeling so much anger towards any man who could cause her that sort of pain. He leant his head in his hands, rubbing furiously at his red eyes. 'God. What a mess.'

Jacob finally came up for air and saw Beth smiling at him. How could she be smiling at such a moment?

'What?'

'You're the mess, Jacob. Holly's fine. She has her moments but deep down she is fine. She's taken from it what she can and grown up.'

'Then why did she say she is scared of me? Why does she run every time it looks like we may have a proper conversation?'

When neither of his hosts made to answer Jacob deflated, all but running out of fight. 'I just had to know what made her tick, didn't I? So, I sat there and dared her to tell me about the scar on her nose. I was such a bully. And that's the last thing she needs.'

Beth smiled. 'Don't worry about it, Jacob. Poor Ben knew none of this when he took her to that stupid boxing match of yours the other week. But he also knows she is big enough and old enough to look after herself. That night she made the adult decision to walk away, to simply not be a part of the crowd, and everything turned out just fine.'

But that was Jacob's main worry. What if because of a myriad unfortunate coincidences, she made the decision not to be a part of his life. The thought of her pulling away so far he would never see her again made something ache deep inside him. But before he had the chance to really think about what that ache could be Ben spoke up.

'What do you want from her, Jacob?'

'What do you mean?' Jacob asked, surprised by Ben's suddenly protective tone.

'I mean that you all but told me that you had no interest in Holly, yet all I can see is you actively pursuing her, creating this last-minute party for Ana. And now you sound like you are about to fall to pieces because she may be shying away from you. What do you want from her?'

'I don't know.' That much was true. He wanted his comfortable, impenetrable old life, and at the same time he wanted her. But he knew he couldn't have both.

Which was the bigger sacrifice? Giving up the seamless wall he had spent a good decade building around himself? Giving up the secure knowledge that nobody could touch him, hurt him, want more from him than he could ever provide?

Or giving up her? Giving up the chance to have her blossom in his arms? Giving up the conviction and hope and delight that he drew from her without diminishing any of her own conviction and hope and delight?

For the first time, in a really long time, he felt the choice was there for the taking.

'Well, maybe it's about time you should know,' Ben said, 'because if you don't want to pursue Holly seriously, you really ought to leave her be. And if you really do feel something for her, and want to know her and help her, you really should be talking to her about this and not to us. Now, it's almost midnight and Beth really doesn't need this sort of excitement right now, so I want you to go home and sleep this off and decide what you want. We'll support you either way, but only once you're sure.'

And then Ben stood up, bringing a shocked Beth to her feet with him.

Jacob rose too. 'I am sorry to have come at such a time. I should go home.'

He kissed Beth on the cheek and then patted Ben on the arm. 'I'll see you.'

'Monday at work,' Ben added, his expression uncompromising.

'Monday at work,' Jacob promised.

Monday, Beth and Holly met for an early morning yoga class.

'Have you spoken to Jacob recently?' Beth asked.

'No, not so recently.'

'Since the weekend?'

'Umm, no, not since the weekend.'

'When are you planning to speak to him again?'

'What is with all these questions, Beth? The party is in five days so I will most likely speak to Jacob before then. Does that satisfy you?'

'Sure. But does that satisfy you?'

'Excuse me?' Holly asked loud enough for the yoga instructor to look over at them with narrowed eyes. Holly smiled in apology before turning back to her friend. 'What do you mean by that?'

'Why don't you two just stop dancing around each other and go for it?' Beth asked in exasperation.

'Go for what?'

'Date him or kiss him or something. Forget about your grand theory. And forget about marrying him or anyone else for now.' Beth rolled her eyes in exasperation. 'You know how when you decide to buy a new pair of shoes, you can never find ones you really like. But as soon as you go looking for a new dress, you find the perfect shoes instead?'

Holly stopped stretching long enough to stare blankly at her friend.

'Just take each other for a test drive is all I'm saying. No expectations. No strings. Just become involved.'

No strings, Holly thought. *If only.* A week before she had scoffed at the suggestion but now she wished it were only possible. She wished she could confide in her friend that all of her wishes were coming true one on top of the other and she had no idea if they were really what she wanted in the first place.

She had found the perfect man, and had fallen in love. Wish number one come true.

She was on the verge of landing the job of a lifetime. Wish number two come true.

But they came with a catch. They were all wrapped up in the unknowable whims of one person. A person she knew was as attracted to her as she was to him. A person who had made her tempting offers but no promises. A person who had proven that when trouble arose, he flew the coop.

There was simply no way Holly could place her whole future happiness in the arms of Jacob Lincoln.

So what to do?

Pursue an affair and forget the job?

Take the job and hope her feelings would fade over time?

Or maybe it would be best to leave both prospects well enough alone and start afresh. She had been perfectly happy before bumping into him that day on the street. Maybe not perfectly happy but at least she did not feel as if she were being torn in a million different directions.

Couldn't she go back to the way it was before she had met him? Working day and night on myriad one-off projects?

Dating every now and then when she had the time and the inclination?

If only.

She told Beth all she was comfortable revealing right then.

'We have kissed, actually.'

:'What? When? What was it like? Why didn't you tell me?'

'Once outside your place and then at his apartment. It was lovely. And I didn't tell you because I don't know what to make of it all.'

'Did he kiss you or did you kiss him?'

'He kissed me. Both times.'

Beth threw her hands up in exasperation.

'Holly! What are you waiting for? He obviously likes you. I mean, he's spoken of nothing else since our little dinner party.'

'Really?' Holly asked, unable to contain the intense pleasure she took from that one tiny validation. She so longed to confide in her friend but once she said out loud how she felt, that would only make it harder for it all to go away.

'Really. He came around to our place all worked up about a conversation you'd had at Lunar.'

'Oh. That.'

'Yes, that. You told him about your dad, I take it.'

'Mmm.'

'I think he's pretty worried that you see him primarily as a man without roots and with your history that would make you understandably wary.'

Holly kept quiet. Wary of what? Her mind reeled with the possibilities but she forced herself to rein them in.

'Jacob is a free spirit, like your dad, he has a strong personality, like your dad, and happens to enjoy boxing, like your dad. This does not mean that he would ever leave you alone for weeks at a time without telling you where he is or where he's been.'

'I know he wouldn't.'

'I know you know.' Beth took her gently by the shoulders and made sure Holly looked her straight in the eye. 'Then why are you using it as an excuse not to go for broke with him?'

Holly struggled to free herself from Beth's strong grip, not wanting her friend to see the truth was hitting home. But she failed.

'Because Jacob is a good man and I think he really cares for you, and if you can't bring yourself to trust a man as good and kind and eligible as him then I don't see that there can be any hope that you will be able to find anyone you can trust.'

Holly looked up at Beth, tears welling in her eyes. 'I have never pretended to *like* Jacob. In fact, I have made it clear to you and he alike that he is not my type. Sure, we may have kissed and I may be…attracted to him, but that's all.'

That is so not all. But by God that will be all by the time I have worked him out of my system.

'I think my trusting him or not is irrelevant. Thanks for the advice, but it's really not necessary at this time.'

Holly gently pulled away from Beth, walked through the class to collect her towel, and left the room.

Friday night Holly relaxed by her roaring fire. She had just that day handed over the moment-to-moment management of Ana's party to Lydia. Lydia had all but knocked Holly off her feet as she'd lunged at her and enveloped her in a massive clinch of thanks. Holly had no doubt Lydia could handle any last-minute changes and she also knew there was no way she would be in the right frame of mind to look after them herself. She still had not decided if she would even turn up at all.

The phone rang at Holly's side.

'What time should I pick you up for the party?' Jacob asked not finding the need for even a 'hello' this time.

Holly sat bolt upright wondering if her thoughts had carried across the miles and reached him. She hadn't spoken to him in days, managing to avoid his phone calls and ignore his messages. But hearing his voice glide down the phone line, she was promptly sucked back into the same weak, deep, heartbreaking sensation she had tried all week to put behind her.

'You can't pick me up, Jacob.'

'Why not? I have a car. I have a driver's licence. There's nothing stopping me. And don't tell me you're not coming because it would simply kill Ana and I know you don't have it in you to do that.'

At least the question of her not going had been decided for her.

But despite his flippant tone, she could tell he felt as strained as she did. And she knew without a doubt it was because he was feeling sorry for her. It always happened that way. Once anybody found out about her childhood, they changed around her. They patted her on the arm and smiled softly, as though any sudden movement would set her off. And she could not stand the thought of looking at Jacob through her own eyes filled with love, only to have him looking back at her in pity.

'I too have a car and do not need a lift as I am perfectly capable of driving myself to the party in said car.'

'Fine. Then you can come and pick me up.'

'No! Besides, I have to get there early and—'

'No, you don't. I already know you've handed over control to Lydia for the day. She told me. You will be a guest just like any other.'

Once again, Holly silently cursed Lydia for her big mouth.

'I just think it would be best if we make our separate ways to Lunar tomorrow.'

'But *I* think we should go together. A real date this time, not just us bumping into each other or working together.'

'If Beth has been match-making just forget about it. Please don't think I asked her to—'

'Holly.' His voice sounded nervous and it stopped her short. *'I'm* asking you if you would like to come to the party with me as my date. Not through Beth. Not through Ben. *I* would like to spend the evening at your side.'

Unbidden tears welled in Holly's eyes and ran down her quivering cheeks.

'I don't think that's such a good idea,' she whispered.

'Why not? Do you already have a date?' Jacob asked, his tone joking.

'Yes, I do,' Holly lied before she knew what she was doing.

'You do?' he asked, obviously shocked. 'Hell. Holly, don't tell me you are back on the husband hunt again!'

It was time to put her personal affiliation with Jacob to rest. Once and for all. It was the only way she could have the peace and quiet and time to heal her heart and he would not feel the need to see her out of pity. And what better way than to use his own presumption?

'I was never off the hunt. Just took a hiatus until I got some…work out of the way. Now we're back into the swing. Me and Ben.'

'You can't be serious.'

'Well, I am.' She felt her voice becoming slightly hysterical. 'Anyway, Ben and Beth are picking me…and my date… up. It's simpler for me to go with Ben and Beth. It's just simpler.'

'So, you'd rather go with Ben.'

'And Beth,' she repeated.

'Why did you choose Ben to look for a husband for you?' His voice was low and flat, the earlier emotion now completely sapped away.

'Well, I love Ben, and I knew that he would only set me up with someone he thought would be nice to me.'

'Are you sure that it isn't simply because, as you said, you love Ben?'

Holly's eyes grew wide in shock; she clutched the phone hard and pressed it tight to her ear.

'Jacob! You can't think that of me. That is a terrible thing to say. I mean, Beth is my very best friend in the whole world.'

'We can't choose who we love Holly.' His voice sounded subdued and wounded. It took all of her self-control not to unreservedly agree with his sentiments and tell him who had really stolen her heart.

'Even so, I am not in love with Ben. Ben is lovely and he puts up with me, which is a big plus in his favour, but I've never, ever seen him as anything more than a big brother.'

After a long pause during which Holly felt her heart beat faster, Jacob whispered, 'Come with me, Holly.'

'I can't,' Holly choked out, her emotions rising in her throat.

'Fine, then. I'll see you there. And if there is no mystery date on your arm I will know why, no matter how you try to justify your actions.'

And with that, Jacob hung up.

Holly stared at the phone in her hand for a number of seconds before she placed it in its cradle. She thought hard and fast before picking up the phone and dialling.

'Hi, Beth,' Holly said.

'Holly? How you feeling?'

'Fine. I'm fine. Sorry for the yelling and—'

'Oh, shut up,' Beth said, laughing. 'What can I do for you?'

'I need you guys to find me a date.'

'Not that again. I made a promise to Ben that we would never spring anything like that on him ever again. Ever. Or at least this week anyway.'

'Look, I don't want a life partner this time. Just someone who isn't busy tomorrow night.'

'But you are busy tomorrow night, with Anabella's party.'

'That's the point. I need a date for the party.'

'Well, not trying to sound like a broken record but…if I'm not mistaken Jacob was going to ask a certain young lady we both know and love so your problem may be solved.'

'But that is the problem. I don't want to go with Jacob, so I told him that I already had a date, so now I have to take someone else with me so he will stop bugging me. How about Derek from Payroll?'

Beth paused meaningfully. 'Okay, let me get this straight. You are asking me to set you up with Derek the weed so that the gorgeous, charismatic and highly eligible Jacob Lincoln will stop bugging you?'

'That's right. Derek seems harmless enough and I need harmless right now.'

'Now you are really worrying me. It's one thing deciding to get married without even having a boyfriend, but wanting a date with Derek the weed over Jacob the hunk is a whole different kind of madness.'

'Beth, you don't think I have a crush on Ben, do you?' Holly said, unable to hold it in any longer.

'Whoa. I certainly didn't see that one coming.'

'Well, do you?'

'No, I don't.'

'Jacob thinks I'm in love with Ben.'

Beth laughed sweetly on the other end of the phone and Holly could have strangled her. She felt so rotten she was sick to the stomach and all Beth could do was giggle.

'Jacob does not think you have a crush on Ben, honey. Jacob is having a hard time figuring you out, that's all. And I think it's hard for him that you are not falling into his arms as readily as he is used to, or as readily as he is falling into yours.'

Holly's head swam.

'Now, as for Ben, I know he represents safety and contentment to you and that's what you think you want. But what you actually want is someone who loves you.'

'So, Jacob is wrong?'

'About this, yes. But about knowing that he should be the one at your side at the party, no. About that I believe he is very right.'

'Beth,' Holly pleaded. 'I can't. Please call Derek for me.'

'Okay,' Beth sighed. 'I'll call the weed. But only because I gain so much enjoyment from your lunacy.'

'Thank you.' Holly breathed a sigh of relief. 'I'll talk to you later.'

'Bye, sweetie.'

And they both hung up.

CHAPTER SEVENTEEN

SATURDAY night Derek was unable to pick Holly up as he did not own a car. He had offered to meet her at the bus stop since they were on the same route but Ben and Beth kindly intervened and offered to pick them up at their respective homes.

Lydia was already waiting outside Lunar when they arrived and in her simple, elegant suit, slicked-back hair and glasses perched on the end of her nose, she was a revelation.

'All's well, Holly,' Lydia whispered, her buoyant effervescence seeping through the conservative exterior. 'I've never seen any event go so smoothly. The chefs are smiling, the bar is well stocked, and the guests of honour are relaxed. It's a miracle.'

'Enjoy it, Lydia. You're doing great.'

Holly was instantly on the lookout for Jacob, telling herself she wanted him in her sights so that she could avoid him. But there was no avoiding the willowy young woman who swooped upon her as soon as she entered the main room.

'You just have to be Holly!' the woman exclaimed.

Holly then noticed the crooked front teeth and dimpled

cheeks. 'And you must be Anabella. You look so much like your brother.'

'I know, though hopefully I'm at least a little *prettier*. Now let me have a good look at you.'

Anabella held Holly at arm's length and looked her over like an old aunt who had not seen her niece since she was a little girl.

'I believe the word Jacob used was "gorgeous",' Anabella said. She turned to Beth and Ben, her eyes twinkling indulgently. 'And from what I hear, you two introduced my darling brother to this one.'

'Not quite,' Beth said, 'though we have helped them along as much as possible, I cannot claim ownership of orchestrating their first meeting. It was purely accidental. Kismet, I say, though some people beg to differ.'

'I heard. Bumped into each other in the street and he had to help her pick up her belongings. I couldn't stop laughing when he told me. My big burly brother helping a damsel in distress. Priceless!'

Holly could sense Beth glaring at her open-mouthed; shock, confusion, an inkling and then complete understanding playing across her face. Holly shook her head, *no*, but she knew that would not be the end of it.

'This sensational hunk of a man is my fiancé, Michael.' Ana pulled a stranger forward. He was slightly shorter than she was, several years older with a neat, greying beard and greying hair at his temples. He was as soft as Ana was striking and his eyes rarely left Ana's face. 'Mikey, this is Ben, Jake's right-hand man, and Ben's wife, Beth, and inside her big tummy is their first.'

Holly felt an ache deep down inside her as she stood there surrounded by such an abundance of love. Her eyes reluctantly roved over the crowd looking for a certain familiar face.

'And this gorgeous creature,' Ana said, looking to Holly, who snapped back to attention at the sound of her nickname, 'is the woman who has sent Jacob into such a mope the last few days. I really can't forgive you for that, Holly. Whatever you did it has made him a nuisance to live with.'

'Who is a nuisance?' Derek had returned from depositing the ladies' coats in the cloakroom.

'Derek,' Beth said, her eyes bright with laughter, 'this is Ana and Michael, our gracious hosts. Ana, Michael, this is Derek Gordon. He works in Payroll with Lincoln Holdings.'

'I'm here with Holly,' he clarified to the group in general.

Holly saw Ana shoot a questioning look to Beth whose furrowed brow and shaking head were enough to explain the situation. That was all Holly needed, for word to get back to Jacob that Derek was superfluous.

'Well, it is nice to meet you, Derek,' Ana said.

'Likewise, I'm sure,' he answered, looking anywhere but at his hosts. 'Holly, it's time we circulate.'

He took Holly by the elbow and dragged her away. They reached the bar in record time and Holly ordered a glass of champagne.

'No, Holly,' Derek insisted as he pulled the glass from her hand and handed it back to the astonished bartender. 'You don't need a simulated high tonight. You just leave that up to me.'

He ordered two matching cranberry juices. 'Good for the kidneys.'

Holly defiantly pushed the juice aside, grabbed her original flute of bubbly and took a great big swig. As she spun around, aiming to get as far away from her appalling date as soon as possible, she stepped smack bang into an unmovable object. It was Jacob.

'Oh, hello, Jacob,' she said breathily. Though his beautiful hazel eyes glowered down at her, her heart danced a rumba at his presence.

'Where is Ben?' he asked.

Holly came back down to earth with a thud.

'He is with Beth, I expect.' Holly made sure her tone was light in front of Derek, who she knew was hanging on every word.

'Really? I would have thought you would not have let him out of your sight.'

'Yes, well, you thought wrong. Beth and Ben were chatting away with *another* happy couple when I last saw them.' She maintained a warning glint in her eye. 'We met Anabella and Michael at the front door.'

Jacob's eyes narrowed slightly as Derek moved in close behind Holly and wrapped an arm about her waist.

'I know you, don't I?' Jacob asked, sounding terribly imperious as he stared down his nose at the offending arm.

'Sure do, Mr Lincoln. I work for you. Derek Gordon. Payroll.'

'He's with you?' Jacob asked Holly, his tone incredulous, ignoring Derek's outstretched hand.

'Surely am, dear fellow. All it took was six months of badgering before she finally acquiesced. Helpful hint. Persistence, dear boy, will never let you down.'

Holly took a quick sip of champagne, willing herself not to thrust away Derek's wandering hands.

'How are you enjoying the party?' Holly asked, trying to deflect Jacob's attention away from her crumbling charade. 'Is it everything you thought it would be?'

It was perfect and Holly knew it. There was not a thing he could possibly fault. But he merely shrugged and shot a meaningful glance at Derek.

'Don't draft the press release just yet.'

She all but coughed on her champagne bubbles. Was that another hint that she would have to choose between a man and the job? He was playing with fire if that was the case. That was one too many times he had changed the rules to suit himself and she'd had enough.

'Oh, don't worry about that, Jacob,' she said through clenched teeth. 'Knowing full well your aversion towards obligations, I wouldn't dream of banking on a guarantee from you.'

Jacob flinched and she knew every word had hit its mark. He paled and a pair of misshapen red blotches stained his smooth cheeks. He looked as though she had slapped him square across the face.

But she kept her eyes locked onto his, determined not to budge, not to back down, not to be moved by his wretched expression. If she had set out to make him hate her, she might have succeeded.

Jacob finally dragged his tortured eyes from her and seemed to notice Derek anew, his expression hardening until it closed to her completely.

'I guess when Holly began this husband hunt of hers she opened her eyes to previously unexplored avenues of experience.'

'What's this?' Derek asked.

Holly was instantly red-faced. *Touché*.

'I guess she has made her choice. Well, I will leave you two lovebirds to it. I've never seen Holly look more lovely or happier than she is tonight and I guess she owes it all to you. Looks like the best man won here, Derek.'

Jacob nodded gravely and walked away.

'If what he said was true,' Derek said, 'though you seem a right corker of a girl, I promise I won't be proposing to you before the night is out. I hope that doesn't put a damper on your evening.'

Holly was finally able to drag her eyes from Jacob's retreating back. 'Not at all, Derek, I promise you with all my heart.'

'Good, good. Never actually met him before, you know. Seen him in the halls and that. Seems a decent enough fellow.'

'Yes, he is decent enough,' Holly agreed as her eyes were once again drawn to him. The most decent man she had ever met; a man with a good heart, a remarkable mind, and no false airs. And she had just cruelly thrown his deepest regrets back in his face, all to cover up her own feeble fears.

She watched Jacob circulate through the crowd. Ana came bounding up to him and enveloped him in a bear-hug. Over her shoulder Jacob said something to Michael, which sent the reserved man into uproarious laughter. Ana pulled away and hit Jacob playfully on the shoulder and he winced in mock pain. Holly could see even from that distance the love and respect Jacob brought out in people just as he had so easily brought it out in her.

And now she had done her best to make him hate her. Oh, what had she done?

'Well, come on, then,' Derek said. 'We had better find our table. Don't want to get there and find someone has switched our place cards.'

The dinner felt painfully slow as Holly counted every passing second until it would be polite to leave. The highlight of the dinner was when she danced with Derek; he motioned to the staircase, which led to several well-appointed rooms above the restaurant. 'The stairway to heaven,' he called it. And he was deadly serious.

Despite herself, she cracked up laughing. And at that moment caught Jacob watching her. For a split second, she felt his fuming gaze from across the room. Then he blinked, the cold façade once more on show, and her heart sank even lower.

After the speeches, Holly excused herself and went to the bathroom. And Beth followed.

'The man, on the street,' Beth began without preamble, 'the one who started all of this in the first place—'

'It was Jacob,' Holly admitted, knowing it was too late now to continue the cover-up. 'Just back from New Orleans.'

'Tall, dimpled, nice smell?' Beth shook her head. 'I should have known. See, I told you that first day it was kismet, and you didn't believe me.'

'I do now.'

'You do?' Beth laid a slight hand on Holly's arm. 'You love him, don't you?'

'I do, Beth. Stupid me, I really do.' Holly leant into her friend's warm embrace finally feeling lost, but with that came enormous relief as now she could hopefully begin to find a way out. Now she had said it aloud she wouldn't have to shoulder the load on her own.

'You're not stupid. It's natural.'

'But he doesn't love me,' Holly said between gulping breaths as she swallowed back the tears that threatened to spill.

'I wouldn't know about that. I know for a fact he has spent the whole evening watching you and Derek with a great scowl on his face.'

'I was mean to him.'

Beth laughed. 'He's a big boy. He can handle mean.'

'Then he feels sorry for me.'

'Well, maybe he does. And maybe he just cares.'

'That's the very worst part. I don't think he does. I think

he has spent a lifetime cultivating the ability not to care. And, like everything he puts his mind to, he is very good at it.'

'So do all these latest philosophies complement your grand theory about men and marriage or are we putting that behind us now?'

'Way, way behind us. The whole thing showed cracks from day one. Yet I kept insisting Ben take me on the hunt as I tweaked and fine-tuned along the way to suit my own capricious wishes. Oh, Beth. I am so sorry. I feel like the last three weeks have slipped through my fingertips. It's all been a total waste.'

Beth pulled Holly back up straight and wiped two soft fingers under her welling eyes.

'It hasn't all been a waste. You put on a great party. So, enjoy that success. We can sort the rest of your life out tomorrow.'

Holly nodded, and Beth gave her a kiss on the cheek before leaving her to tidy up.

The party was still in full swing. No matter what, the evening had been a marvellous success. The plates had been licked clean. Not a soul had yet left. And the dance floor was packed. But as Holly moved towards the solitude of the balcony, no matter how hard she rationalised that this was all she should have hoped for, her heart wished for a great deal more.

Once outside, she had barely had time to take a deep breath of the crisp evening air when she heard the glass door slide open and close behind her. It was Derek.

'Go back inside, Derek. I won't be long.'

Without saying a word, he came up behind her and wrapped his arms around her waist.

'Derek, please! What are you doing?' she yelled as she struggled to free herself from his grasp.

He spun her around roughly. There was hidden strength in his thin arms. 'We're grown-ups, Holly. Don't pretend you don't know what I am doing. Why else would you ask me out after all this time?' His hands gripped her under her arms, his bony fingers digging into her flesh.

'No, Derek! I just thought you might like a night out with people you knew.'

'And you thought I might make Mr Lincoln jealous.'

Holly stopped struggling and looked up into Derek's leering eyes, stunned at his perception.

'I'm no fool, Holly. I saw the way he looked at you with unsatisfied desire. I know that feeling well enough to recognise it in a fellow man. And I figure the way to do my good deed, to make him properly jealous, is to do to you what he obviously has not yet managed.'

Derek pushed Holly back against the hard metal railing, bruising her spine, pinning her so close she could not reach her hands in between them to push him away. She beat furiously at his hunched back as he ravaged her neck with rough, biting kisses.

'No! Derek, stop. Please!'

Before Holly needed to say another word Derek was wrenched away from her. Through her tousled hair she watched Derek cower with his hands over his face. A fist swung from Derek's left and landed on his jaw with crunching impact. He spun around and crumpled to the ground landing spread-eagled, almost on top of her feet.

Holly gasped and sprang back. Her eyes swung up to meet Derek's aggressor.

Jacob stood, feet shoulder-width apart, his head held high, rubbing his right fist with his left palm. His eyes were bright and his nostrils flared with each ragged breath.

Holly herself was slack-jawed, panting, and dry-mouthed

and she could not draw her eyes away from the potent sight before her.

Jacob took one step forward to make sure she was okay. Holly flinched only slightly at his sudden movement but it was enough to stop him dead in his tracks. His eyes softened and his throat worked with several uneasy swallows.

'Jacob. I...thank you. I mean, he was...' She desperately fought back the tears that were threatening to spill now that her adrenalin rush was dissipating. 'He was determined. If you hadn't have come out when you did—'

'I know. You don't have to say it,' Jacob whispered, the confusion and worry etched on his beautiful face.

'I'm...I'm fine,' Holly insisted, her tears now flowing freely.

'Holly.' The word wrenched from Jacob's straining vocal cords. 'Please let me come to you. I need to know you are not hurt.'

She held up a hand so that he would keep his distance; she was shaking enough without having to deal with him standing so close, looking at her like that. Then she looked down at Derek's prone figure. And she stood outside her own raw emotions for a moment and realised he hadn't moved a muscle since he'd dropped.

'Jacob, you knocked him out cold. With one punch.'

'I know.'

'You're a trained fighter. He could sue you for assault and he would probably win.'

'Do you think he *should* win such a case?'

'I think you have had so much practice and experience and you have such innate passion, Jacob, and I'm not sure that you can control it.'

'Hell, Holly, do you have any idea what I could have done to Derek if I had the inclination to punish him and not just to get him away from you? But more importantly do you have any real idea of where my passion is directed? Where it has been directed for the last weeks? Where I wish more than anything else in the world it was directed right now?'

She had stopped breathing, suddenly acutely aware of the fresh evening breeze caressing every single hair on her bare arms. A sprinkling of sensitive goose-bumps sprang up and a sensuous shiver quaked through her from top to toe.

As though instinctively sensing her surrender, Jacob stepped over the prostrate payroll clerk in one swift move and gathered her, pliant and ready, into his arms. She melted against him instantaneously, all of her anxiety and fear dissolving in his protective embrace. Their lips met in a crushing and desperate kiss as though they were unlucky lovers who had been waiting a lifetime to consummate their obsession.

Her arms wrapped around his neck relishing the sensation his soft, springy hair created over her sensitised fingertips. His arms wrapped tight around her back, brushing over the spot where the railing had only moments before bruised her. But his strong hands felt like a balm, a warm, sure comfort against all her hurts. Holly stood on tiptoe and Jacob curved against her so that they could be as close as could be whilst still standing up.

The kiss found its own fervent rhythm as tongues and lips melded in one great fierce, hot union that both bruised and mollified the pair. They squeezed together tighter, needing and gaining from each other a sense of unity and belonging and devotion.

'Holly?' a voice queried from the doorway.

Holly and Jacob leapt apart as thought hit by a bolt of electricity. Holly instinctively tried to pull away and straighten herself out but Jacob looked down upon her kindly before planting one last kiss on the tip of her nose.

Lydia and Ana stood in the doorway, looking from them to the unconscious Derek, their mouths hanging open in matching 'O's.

'Lydia,' Jacob said calmly, 'could you please bring Dr Thomas out to check on Derek here? He is unconscious, but with some smelling salts he should be fine. Unfortunately there will be no lasting damage bar a rather nasty headache.'

'Ah, I would get Dr Thomas but he is otherwise engaged with Beth,' Lydia explained, her eyes wide and glued to the man on the ground.

'Beth?' Holly stepped forward and grabbed Lydia by the arms. 'What's wrong with Beth, Lydia?'

'Nothing's wrong,' Lydia promised. 'She's just having her baby. That's all.'

CHAPTER EIGHTEEN

JACOB ran down the hospital hallway alone, and rounded the corner to find Ben and Holly clinging to one another in a tight embrace. He stopped his run so abruptly his shoes screeched loudly on the linoleum floor. But neither of them even noticed.

'I'm petrified, Holly.' Jacob could hear Ben's strained voice.

He watched as they pulled apart and winced as he saw that Holly kept hold of Ben's hands. 'Don't be. She's stronger than the two of us put together.'

'Should I go in yet?' Ben asked. 'Do you think they are waiting for me?'

Jacob waited for Holly's endearment, for a profession of her feelings. Knowing it could not possibly be true, but petrified into inaction just the same. But then she let go of Ben and ran two rough hands over his hair, messing it up so badly the worry left his face and he relaxed with laughter.

'Ben,' Holly said, 'I'm sure this baby is not waiting for even you. Go get 'em, tiger.'

A nurse came through the swinging doors and took Ben through to the maternity rooms.

And Jacob realized that what Holly had said was true. There was nothing more between her and Ben than affection. He felt a great weight lift off his shoulders. When he had accused Holly of secretly loving Ben, he had been searching for a fault, for a reason not to feel the intense affection for her that had grown so rapidly since he had first spotted her.

But just now, watching her play down her own worries for Beth to give all of her consideration to a friend in need, he knew there was no reason to be worrying.

He swallowed down the tender lump that had formed in his throat. He so wanted to reach out and take her in his own arms and make sure that *she* was the one feeling fine.

As though finally sensing Jacob was there, Holly drifted over towards him like metal to a magnet. He held out an arm, she came to him, and he gathered her close to his chest. And it felt so right. Never before had he felt safe and protective all at once. And rather than sending him running to the far reaches of the earth, there was nowhere else he wanted to be.

But his pleasure was short-lived as Ana, Michael and Lydia arrived. Jacob watched helpless as Lydia wrenched Holly from his arms and hung onto her like a baby limpet. And even with Ana and Michael tugging on his arm and barraging him with questions and attention, he felt alone. And he knew just what he needed to make that feeling go away.

A couple of hours later, Ana, Michael and Lydia had fallen asleep. Lydia had curled up in a big armchair, her feet tucked beneath her. Ana's head rested in Michael's lap and his hand lay protectively in her hair where he had been stroking her until he too had nodded off.

Holly glanced at Jacob to find him watching her. His hair was dishevelled, his face tired, he looked so much as he had that first morning not so long ago. No wonder she had been instantly smitten. He was so artlessly captivating, especially in those rare moments when his guard was down. She licked her dry lips and ran a hand over her hair, suddenly wishing she had a comb and a compact and a tub of lip-gloss at hand.

'Come with me to grab a coffee,' Jacob whispered, his low, smooth voice echoing faintly across the spacious room. 'I want to talk to you about something.'

'Shouldn't we stay? I want to be here in case something happens.'

'It will only take a few minutes. We can bring some coffee back for these guys who will soon need something and I can't carry them all on my own.'

Holly nodded. She peeled herself from her chair, making sure not to disturb the others.

In silence she followed him into the lift. What was so important Jacob wanted to talk to her about it, now of all times? It couldn't be about the job offer. That would be so inappropriate. Maybe he was going to tell her he was leaving again. She shuddered at the thought, and obviously mistaking her action Jacob shrugged off his suit jacket and lay it softly around her bare shoulders.

She smiled her thanks, careful to contain the absolute love she felt for him at such a kind gesture.

They exited the lift and she followed him into the all-night cafeteria. They ordered a couple of take-away coffees and found a table in a quiet corner by the window.

Holly sipped on her coffee and waited for Jacob to talk, more nervous than she had ever been in her whole life.

'I wanted to apologise.'

'What for this time?' She tried to keep her voice light.

'For the suggestions I made about you and Ben.'

'Oh.' Wow. That wasn't what she had expected at all. 'Well, thank you.'

'I know now why you chose Ben. You were looking for a type that he represented, someone dependable. I understand that.'

Jacob was looking down at his hands. They were wringing the life out of the edge of the tablecloth.

'I didn't see all that before, because, you see, I…I was jealous.'

Her heart sang. *Jealous?*

'I didn't want you turning to him for answers when I felt like you should have been turning to me.'

Her heart sank. 'To find me dates?'

'Hell no!' He raked a forceful hand through his sexily unkempt hair. 'That was the last thing I wanted you to be doing. Running about with every Tom, Derek and Matt.'

'The last thing you *wanted*?' *Please, Jacob, please tell me what I want to hear.*

He locked gazes with her, his expression pained, as if he had gone through the wringer. It mirrored Holly's own feelings exactly. Holly did not look away. Could not.

'It's the last thing I *want*.'

Was he really saying what she hoped so desperately he was saying? This was the moment she had to make sure. One way or the other.

'Then what do you want?' Her voice sounded as though it were coming from a great distance away.

He looked deep into her eyes, so intensely her knees threatened to melt under the heat.

'You.'

He wanted her! He really wanted her. But was that enough? She loved him. And if he did not love her back with the same force and hopefulness, it would never be enough. Unable to voice a single sensible thought, she kept quiet and let him speak.

'The minute Ben told me that you were on a husband hunt,' Jacob continued, 'I pictured myself in the role. Whereas the thought had always brought me out in a nasty rash before, I felt this sense of ease wash over me, like I had been waiting to picture myself in that role all my life. Well, it has driven me around the bend. I can't sleep, I'm barely eating and no matter how hard I try I cannot keep my thoughts or my hands off you. What do you think we should do about it?'

You tell me, she thought, but her throat was too tight with emotion to say the words.

'Well, I've had plenty of sleepless nights to think about it and I have come up with a solution.'

He paused, only long enough to unwrap his hands from the tablecloth and smooth them on top of hers. He enclosed his warm palms around hers, the sensation creating waves of heavenly heat along her arms.

'Marry me.'

'What?' Holly squeaked, loud enough to turn a few nurses' heads.

'Marry me, Holly.'

'But…why?'

He rolled his eyes comically. 'Why not? Why shouldn't a man madly and hopelessly in love propose marriage?'

'Madly? And hopelessly…?'

'In love. Because that's what I am, Holly. You hardly gave me much choice, turning up everywhere I went, never letting me forget for a second what a talent and a whirlwind and a knockout you truly are.'

'You turned up everywhere I went—'

'Either way, every time I thought I had managed to rationalise my growing feelings away, there you were, so beautiful and charming and absolutely lovable. I had no chance.' He smiled at her, his dimples growing deeper as his eyes softened. 'Then at last I realised I did not want the chance not to love you. I wanted the chance to love you more than anything else in the world.'

'Oh, Jacob. I had no idea.'

'I realised as much. So all it took was a horrifically expensive party to prove it to you. Then I found this great last-minute ski holiday deal and encouraged Ana and Michael to go.'

It slowly dawned on her what he meant.

'You sent Ana away?'

'Well, they were planning on going away anyway—they just weren't planning on going quite so soon.'

'So I would have to organise the party with you?'

'Uh-huh. I told you I buy my way into the women in my life's affections. But then you had to go and spoil it all by not coming to the party with me. That was not part of the grand plan.'

She blushed for the first time, though her confidence was soaring sky-high. 'My turn to apologise?'

'I should think so. You could have at least picked someone like Matt Riley to flaunt in front of me. Feeling envious of a man like Derek Gordon does not do much for a man's ego.'

Holly buried her face in her palms. 'Please don't remind me. That was not one of my more sensible plans.'

'As opposed to husband-hunting all because some oaf in the street gave you a bit of lip?'

Holly dropped her hands to the table.

'How did you know? Ben! Did Ben tell you? Or was it Beth? I knew she would not keep out of it. Lydia? It was Lydia wasn't it? That girl cannot keep her mouth shut—'

'What does it matter now?' he asked. 'I have been smitten

with you since before I knew that juicy bit of info, though how could it not help?'

He grinned and Holly slapped him on the arm. He caught her hand and brought it to his mouth for a soft, tender kiss.

'The truth is, ever since I spotted those ridiculous yellow galoshes covering up your breathtaking legs I have been yours for the taking, Ms Holly Denison.'

'At the greyhound race?' she asked, her eyes riveted on her hand where he continued to rain short, sweet kisses.

'Mmm hmm. To see a woman like you, a woman with such finesse and such class, happily slap on a pair of rubber boots to help an old man out of a fix, in that moment, I was gone.'

He had loved her for so long. Since before she had told him about her pitiable childhood. All that time he had been protective and supportive because he loved her, not because he felt badly for her. It was too wonderful.

That was more than she needed to hear to dump her cup and leap from her chair onto his lap. She buried her face in his neck, running a spray of kisses across his chin and face and then onto his heavenly waiting mouth. All too soon he pulled away, though she clung, determined never to let him go again.

'What do you have to say for yourself, Ms Denison?'

Finally unwilling and unable to hide her intense feelings, she let the love shine through her eyes. 'I love you with all my heart and soul, Jacob Lincoln.'

He rolled his eyes to the heavens. 'Well, that much I knew already.'

She stared in shock.

'Haven't you been told you have the most useless poker-face?'

Holly could do nothing but continue to gape.

'I mean, Ms Denison. You haven't answered my pressing question.'

She couldn't answer him yet, though her heart screamed the answer out so loud she could hardly think straight.

'Jacob, I adore you to the bottom of my heart. But I could not live with myself if because of me you felt trapped. You once told me you refuse to get bogged down in just one project—'

'You are not a project, Holly. You are the woman I love. It's true that I spent my adult life convincing myself I wanted to be free, but it was a false freedom because I carried my own wall with me everywhere I went. Then you came along equipped with just the steps I needed to get over that wall.'

His voice was low, lilting, and indulgent and made her light-headed as well as light-hearted.

'It took you three weeks to climb a bunch of steps?'

'It was a tall wall.' He punctuated his words with a trail of soft, warm kisses across her shoulder and she had to force herself to stay on track.

'But my hunt for a husband, that must have planted the idea in your head from the outset—'

'Holly, will you just shut up? This is my final offer. Take it or leave it.'

She shut up.

'Work with me at Lincoln Holdings. Live with me at your place or mine, I don't care which. If I decide to go away, it will only be with you at my side. But above all things, marry me. That I'm afraid is the clincher in this deal.'

'But, I thought you would only hire me if I wasn't married.'

He stared at her in bewilderment. 'Now how on earth did that silly idea get stuck in that beautiful head of yours?'

'At Lunar, when you were hounding me about playing my cards right, I thought you were intimating you would not be keen on hiring someone with plans to become pregnant.'

Jacob reached up and ran his agile fingers through a loose

tendril of Holly's hair. 'So you have plans to become pregnant, do you? Well, if you have *plans*, then who am I to argue? I'm convinced! I think we should put aside several days, maybe even weeks to focus on nothing but this plan of yours.'

Holly all but swooned. It took all of her remaining wits to gather her strength for one last important question. 'And, by the way, what are you going to do to Lunar?'

'Marry me and you can have the damn place as a wedding present.' He grabbed her around the waist and leaned in so she could taste his warm breath on her lips. 'You talk too much, woman. Yet I have still not heard the one word I am looking for.'

But before she could put him out of his misery he proceeded to stop her talking in the tenderest manner possible.

'Mr Lincoln? Ms Denison?' a nurse called out from the far end of the room.

They both turned, though this time Holly kept a tight hold of her man.

'Mr Jeffries is looking for you.'

'Is everything all right?' Holly asked.

The nurse smiled. 'Everything's fine. They would love you to come and meet their new baby daughter.'

Holly looked to Jacob and saw his eyes were glistening with emotion.

'A daughter,' he whispered. 'A daughter who will be loved and cared for by two wonderful parents.'

'And two thoroughly devoted godparents.'

Holly leaned in and lightly kissed away his beautiful tears.

Holly leant over her friend, who woke up from a quick nap.

'Holly, you're here.'

'Of course I'm here, you numbskull.'

'And Jacob?'

'He's here too.'

Jacob moved away from his position at the doorway and joined Holly, laying a hand on her shoulder.

'We saw her,' he said, his voice thick with emotion, 'and she's beautiful.'

'But she looks nothing like Ben,' Holly joked.

'I thought the same thing,' Beth said with a weak smile. 'But don't tell him that; he thinks she's his spitting image. What he doesn't guess won't hurt him.'

Holly nodded and Jacob winked conspiratorially. Beth's heavy eyes glanced from Holly, who was still wearing Jacob's suit jacket, to Jacob, whose hand was now lightly playing with Holly's hair, and her smile turned to a grin.

'You two look like the cats who got the cream.'

'You're not the only one with good news tonight,' Holly said.

'Really? What's the news? Who has news?'

'We do.'

'Well, come on, don't leave an exhausted woman on tenterhooks, I'll as likely fall asleep before you tell me as not.'

Holly looked to Jacob and felt herself glowing under his adoring gaze. He nodded at her, a loving smile radiating down upon her as he gave her shoulder a supportive squeeze. Holly dragged her eyes from the man she loved to face her beloved friend, and said:

'I'm getting married.'

* * * *

Enjoyed Ally Blake's fresh, fun, flirty style? Then look for
The Wedding Date!
Coming soon from Mills & Boon® RIVA™!

Blind-Date Marriage

by Fiona Harper

As a child, **Fiona Harper** was constantly teased for either having her nose in a book or living in a dream world. Things haven't changed much since then, but at least in writing she's found a use for her runaway imagination. After studying dance at university, Fiona worked as a dancer, teacher and choreographer, before trading in that career for video-editing and production. When she became a mother, she cut back on her working hours to spend time with her children and, when her littlest one started pre-school, she found a few spare moments to rediscover an old but not forgotten love—writing.

Fiona lives in London, but her other favourite places to be are the Highlands of Scotland and the Kent countryside on a summer's afternoon. She loves cooking good food and anything cinnamon-flavoured. Of course she still can't keep away from a good book or a good movie—especially romances—but only if she's stocked up with tissues, because she knows she will need them by the end, be it happy or sad. Her favourite things in the world are her wonderful husband, who has learned to decipher her incoherent ramblings, and her two daughters.

For the unknown man I soaked
while driving through a puddle

CHAPTER ONE

JAKE knew only two things about the woman he was going to meet: her name was Serena and her father had money.

Serena.

Sounded kind of horsey. She probably wore jodhpurs. Mel had refused to comment on whether she was pretty or not, so she probably looked like a horse as well. He could see it so clearly: the gymkhana trophies, the chintzy bedroom. Serena wore her mousy hair in a bun and had too many teeth.

He stepped off the kerb of the busy London street and zig-zagged through the gaps in the traffic. Headlights lit up his knees as he squeezed between the bumpers. A horn blared.

That was why he liked to walk. It gave him a sense of freedom in the midst of the cloying traffic. He wasn't about to take orders from anyone, especially not a pole with coloured lights on top.

Once on the pavement again, he stopped to shake the drizzle off his hair. It was more mist than rain, only visible in the orange haloes of the street lamps, but somehow he was wetter than if he'd been hit by big, splashing drops. He was going to look less than perfect when he arrived at the restaurant.

His long strides slowed as he contemplated the evening ahead. Should he be marching this briskly towards the unknown? Probably not. But he wasn't going to be late. He speeded up to his former tempo. This evening he would be polite, he would be charming, and then he would be high-tailing it out of there as fast as possible.

As long as Serena didn't have a horsey laugh to match her appearance, he could endure the temptation of the pocket-sized window in the restaurant toilet. At least he hoped there was a window. Just for emergencies.

He should have checked.

In future he would do a reconnaissance of any potential venues when forced on blind dates by his meddling little sister.

Not that there was going to be a next time if he could help it.

He was still a bit hazy about how she'd talked him into going on this one. Mel had rung him at work and slipped it into the conversation while he was studying a balance sheet and saying 'mmm' and 'yup' at suitable intervals. Before he knew it, he was meeting a total stranger for drinks and dinner at Lorenzo's.

One day he would have to put his foot down with Mel. She'd been able to wind him round her little finger ever since she'd bestowed her very first smile on him. He was pretty sure she knew he hadn't been listening when she'd arranged this date. Most likely she'd planned the exact timing of her call to maximise his suggestibility.

He cut through a little park in the centre of the square rather than keeping to the busy street. It was a refreshing change from the unrelenting grey of the city. Not that there was much green within the park's wrought-iron railings at this time of year.

At least it smelled like November—acorns and rotting

leaves. He took a deep breath and savoured the warm, earthy aroma. That was when he became aware of the tramp, more noticeable by his body odour than his appearance. He might easily have taken him for a forgotten coat on the bench otherwise.

The old man was oblivious to the rain. Saliva trailed from his open mouth down his chin, and the wind rolled an empty beer can to and fro beneath the bench. Jake removed the copy of the *Financial Times* from under his arm and spread a few pages over the man's shoulders and torso, making sure he didn't accidentally touch his coat. Hopefully, by the time the pages were wet through, the old guy would be sober enough to move himself somewhere drier.

He hurried through the park gate and re-entered the rush hour. The restaurant was only a few minutes away now. He didn't go in for that kind of place much. Lorenzo's was an odd choice for horsey old Serena.

According to the brief review he'd read on the internet, the restaurant was a small, family-run affair—nothing special in his book. He preferred places that were obviously exclusive now he could afford them. Give him women with diamonds, men with fat wallets and waiters that bowed any day.

However, the food was supposed to be tasty, and the critic had raved about a cannelloni dish. Not that it would make any difference to Serena. She was probably going to push a couple of lettuce leaves drenched in balsamic vinegar round her plate and complain about how everything went to her rather expansive hips.

The escape window was sounding more tempting with every step. Perhaps he should pop round the back and check the exact dimensions before he went inside?

He was so lost in thought that he didn't see the blocked drain. He didn't see the deep puddle that had collected over the top of it. He also didn't see the sports car driving up behind him.

He did, however, see the great tidal wave as car met puddle. He watched, helpless, as in slow motion tendrils of spray reared up and soaked him from head to foot.

She saw the wall of water in her rear-view mirror and gasped.

She'd been so busy daydreaming about the evening ahead she'd forgotten to manoeuvre round the small pond that always appeared on this corner in bad weather. Without thinking whether it was a good idea or not, she pulled the car to a halt, got out, and ran straight up to the sodden figure on the pavement. He didn't look as if he'd moved at all. He was just staring down at his dripping suit with his arms aloft.

'Oh, my goodness! I'm so sorry—'

He lifted his head and glared at her.

'Are you okay?'

One eyebrow shot up. At least she thought it did. It was hard to tell under the dark hair plastered onto his forehead.

'You're soaked! Let me give you a lift to wherever you were going. It's the least I can do.'

She'd been talking to him for a good fifteen seconds, but suddenly she had the feeling he was only just taking a good look at her. He was staring. Hard. She looked down at her suede boots and ankle-length skirt. Sure, she was getting a little soggy as she stood here in the rain, but it wasn't as if she'd come out with her skirt tucked into the back of her knickers. At least she didn't think she had.

When she looked back up he was smiling. And not just the polite tilt of the mouth you gave waitresses when they brought you a drink. This was a real one.

A shiver skittered up her spine. That was a great smile. She looked a little closer at the face it was attached to.

Nice.

This was one cute guy she'd drenched.

'You were saying…?'

She shook herself.

'Yes. It's just—I…I mean it's the least I can do. Drop you off somewhere, that is.'

'That's probably a good idea. I'm not sure I'm in any fit state to go out to dinner like this.'

Her hands flew to her mouth. 'I feel just awful… Well, that settles it, then. I've ruined your evening. I'm dropping you off somewhere dry and warm. No arguments.'

He looked her up and down, a crinkle at the corners of his eyes. 'No arguments from me. Shall we?' He motioned towards the car. 'Nice wheels.'

The drizzle was making a more concerted effort at proper rain, and a drop splashed on her forehead. Without talking further, they both ran to the low-slung metallic blue sports car and climbed inside.

She watched him shake his head and run his fingers through thick dark hair as he sat in the passenger seat. He looked even better with it slicked back. She could see his face properly. How did eyes that cool blue manage to smoulder? And look at that firm jaw. He looked like a man in control of his destiny. She liked that.

'The car's not mine, actually.'

The smile was back. 'What did you do? Steal it?'

'No, of course not. Mine's being repaired. I borrowed this from my…a friend.'

She wasn't about to tell him she was riding round in her father's car. It had mid-life crisis stamped all over it. Not that her father's crazy behaviour had started in his fifties. He'd got a head start in his teenage years, and had never stopped long enough to mature.

She didn't like admitting to her parentage when she met a man who caught her eye. She'd learnt the hard way to keep dear old dad out of the picture until it was safe to drop the bombshell—and even then she was never one hundred per cent sure if *she* was the main attraction.

The smouldering eyes were looking at her intently. 'A friend?'

Drat! He'd spotted the little detour in her explanation.

He sat back in the seat and smiled, a wistful expression on his face. 'That's too bad. Tell him I think he's got great taste in cars…and women.'

She fumbled with the keys in the ignition.

Come on, girl! Think of something sparkling and witty to say! Tell him he's got the wrong end of the stick.

'So, where can I drop you off?'

Great. Really smooth. Well done.

'Great Portman Street. Do you know it?'

'I know someone who lives down that way.' She indicated and pulled away. 'It's not that far from here, is it?'

'No, but in this traffic it could take a good twenty minutes.'

'I know. Sometimes I think it would be quicker if I walked.'

'My opinion exactly.' He pinched at his trouser leg and inspected it. 'Although I can't vouch for it being the drier option.'

She sighed and started to speak, but he warded the words off with a raised hand.

'Please, don't apologise again. You did me a big favour, in fact. I wasn't looking forward to my evening, and you've given me the perfect excuse to bow out.'

'Really?'

'Yes, really. I was destined for a date from hell with a girl that looks like a horse—and I'm not sure whether it's the front end or the back end she most resembles!'

Her laugh was loud and unexpected.

'Well, consider me your knight in shining armour, then,' she added, giggles bubbling under the surface.

He laughed along with her. 'My eternal gratefulness, kind lady. In fact, I should thank you in some way. How about dinner?'

Since they were sitting at yet another red light, she shot a look across at him. 'Have you forgotten why you're in my car in the first place? You're dripping wet!'

'It wouldn't take me long to get dry and changed. We could nip out somewhere local. We'd be in a public place. You'd be perfectly safe.'

'How do I know that? We've only just met. I don't even know your name.'

'It's Jake.'

'Well, Jake, I still don't know you from Adam—except that your name's not Adam, that is.' Oh, God, she was rambling!

'Then why did you let me in your—I mean your *friend's* car, then? I could be anyone. I could be an axe-wielding maniac, for all you know.'

She went cold. He was right. She'd been so busy feeling bad for him she hadn't even considered basic personal safety. Her voice was braver than she felt when she answered.

'Don't be daft! I rescued *you*, remember? You're a Jake-in-distress. You can't possibly be an axe-wielding maniac!' *Could he?*

Now it was his turn to laugh. Her shoulders untensed, but she stayed quiet and concentrated on the traffic. Quicker than expected, they drew up in Great Portman Street.

'Which one?' She leaned forward and peered down the road. One side was almost entirely occupied by a red brick block of Victorian apartments.

'Right here. Top floor.'

'Very posh.'

She kept her eyes on the road as the car came to a halt. Even without the tell-tale reflection in the windscreen, she'd have sensed he'd turned to face her. Strange, she'd always thought that being able to feel someone's eyes boring into you was a load of poppycock.

'Come inside and have the grand tour.'

'You're very forward, aren't you?'

'I know what I want, and I don't stop until I get it.'

The implication of that sentence made her cheeks burn. She was very proud of the wobble-free voice that came out of her mouth.

'Sorry, Jake-in-distress, I have a prior commitment. Maybe another time.'

'Couldn't you stand him up?'

A reply like that would normally have had her spitting, but he said it with such lazy charm she found herself laughing.

'No.'

But she wanted to. Miraculously, the prospect of an evening with Charles Jacobs seemed even greyer.

'Too bad.' The tone of his voice said he respected her decision more than he cared to admit. 'At least give me your number.'

'Give my number? To an axe-wielding maniac? You must be mad!'

She smiled at him.

He smiled back.

Boy, those smiles got more brilliant with every outing. If she didn't get out of here quick, she was going to change her mind about dinner. Then Cassie would kill her for standing up the 'suitable' man she'd found for her, and that would never do. She was looking forward to the prospect of *another time* with Jake too much.

He reached into his pocket, fished out a business card and scribbled something on the back with a fountain pen.

'Have it your way. Here's *my* number, then.'

She took it from him. Even the little rectangle of card was soggy. She'd done a really good job with that puddle.

He looked her straight in the eye. 'Use it.'

Her gaze collided with his. He was so sure she was going to call. There wasn't a flicker of doubt in his expression. Women probably fell over themselves to follow his every whim on a daily basis. Part of her felt like throwing the card out of the window and into the gutter; the other part wanted to tuck it inside her bra to make sure she didn't lose it.

Her lips pursed. She meant to look peeved, but somehow a small smile escaped.

'Maybe. Goodbye, Jake.'

She put the car into reverse and started to move out of the parking space. Before she had a chance to pull away, he pounded on the window. 'Wait!'

She pressed the button and enjoyed his mounting irritation as the window edged down bit by bit.

'You haven't even told me your name.'

'So I didn't.'

'Well?'

'I get the feeling you're the kind of man who won't let a tiny detail like that stop you. You'll find out—if you want to badly enough.'

With that, she rolled up the window and drove away. She risked a glance in the rear-view mirror and a huge grin spread over her face. He was standing in the street with his mouth hanging open.

She didn't look back. Instead, she tooted the horn and did a little finger wave.

Now, *that* had been smooth!

Stupid, but smooth.

Stupid, because the only reason she hadn't told him her name was the funny reaction it provoked in almost everyone she met. She hadn't wanted to spoil the moment, hadn't wanted the delectable Jake to have the usual set of preconceptions about her.

What had her parents been thinking when they called her Serendipity? It was tantamount to child abuse! She'd been the target of bullies from her first day of school because of her name.

Why couldn't she have been called Sally or Susan? Nice, sensible, traditional names. No one would think Susan was a hippy wild child. And Sally was the kind of girl whose dad worked a nine-to-five job in an office, while her mum baked jam tarts and fussed over the amount of make-up her teenage daughter was wearing.

She sighed.

Daft to run away without telling Jake her name. Now she would have to look all eager and phone him if she was interested. Which she was. She should have given him her number and let him do the running—she'd always liked the old-fashioned idea of being courted.

She turned the corner and headed back towards the restaurant. Perhaps it had been worth not telling Jake her name just to see the look on his face as she drove away. At least she'd have something to smile to herself about if Charles Jacobs turned out to be as yawn-worthy as he sounded.

She looked at her watch as she pulled up outside the restaurant. Only half an hour late. If she smiled, and flipped her long dark hair around a bit, perhaps Charles wouldn't mind.

She hopped out of the sports car, ran inside, and straight up to the small bar that doubled as a reception desk. There were far too many bunches of plastic grapes and straw-covered bottles for the décor to be in good taste, but she didn't care. It was homey.

Someone was loading small bottles of orange juice onto the bottom shelf. She'd recognise that acre-wide Italian rump anywhere!

'Hey, Maria!'

Maria stood up so fast she sent a couple of bottles rolling across the floor. Her hands flew into the air and she yelled in the general direction of the kitchen, 'Gino! Our girl is here!'

A round, middle-aged man appeared from the door connecting the kitchen to the bar. 'We thought you'd been run over by a bus—didn't we, darling?'

She ducked behind the bar and gave each of them a kiss on the cheek. 'You fuss like an old woman, Gino. Now, tell me—and don't spare my feelings—what's he like?'

Gino made a dismissive wave towards her favourite table by the window. A monstrous potted palm blocked her view. She stood on tiptoe to get a better look.

The table was empty.

She turned round to Gino, eyebrows raised. 'He hasn't shown up yet?'

Gino shook his head, almost overwhelmed by the tragedy, and she swallowed the urge to chuckle.

'Oh, well. Bring me the usual. I'll hang around until nine. I got here late myself, so I can hardly moan.'

He'd better be worth the wait, though! She'd murder Cassie

if she'd set her up with a first-class loser again. Her friend knew she was looking to settle down, but couldn't quite get the distinction between *stable and reliable* and *utterly dull*. She'd only agreed to go on this date because it was less hassle than arguing with Cassie about it. If she said no, Cassie would only badger her for a fortnight until she gave in, so she might as well agree and save herself the earache.

Gino brought her a glass of her favourite red wine, and she sat at the table and scanned the rain-swept horizon.

She sat up and smiled as a man in a smart suit with a bunch of flowers passed the window, but he walked straight past the door and into the arms of a waiting blonde outside the tube station. Minutes ticked past. The only other person to enter the restaurant was a small bald man with bad teeth. She whipped up her menu as an impromptu shield and held her breath. Thankfully, he was greeted by a tall woman with equally bad teeth on the other side of the restaurant. She dropped the menu enough to peek over the top, then jumped as Gino appeared, apparently out of thin air.

'There's a message for you. *He* telephoned.'

By the look on Gino's face, it was not good news. She lowered the menu slightly and held her head high. 'Let me have it, Gino.'

'He said he's very sorry, but something came up.'

Something came up! What kind of lame excuse was that?

The puff of air she let out lifted her fringe.

'What did he say, exactly?'

'He said he was not able to come, that he's very sorry, and asked you to meet him tomorrow for lunch at Maison Blanc, one o'clock.' Gino wrinkled his nose at the suggestion of anyone eating somewhere other than his establishment, then he grinned. 'But he also said dinner tonight is on him.'

She slapped the menu closed and smiled like a cat.

'In that case, my good friend, it's the caviar to start for me, followed by the priciest entrée Marco can conjure up, and a glass of champagne for everybody in the room.'

Gino winked. 'That's my girl! You show him.'

The nerve of the man. Standing her up, then practically summoning her to lunch the following day, with no thought at all as to whether it was convenient for her. The fact she was free, and could go if she wanted to, had no bearing on the matter. He was an arrogant jerk to assume she was so desperate for a date that she'd trot along at his beck and call.

Not in this lifetime, buster! No way was she turning up tomorrow. He could be the one to sit and fiddle with his cutlery.

Dinner was good, but revenge on Mr Jacobs was even tastier. She enjoyed every bite, because with each mouthful she could hear the ding of a cash register. By the time she had finished her espresso, she was imagining the look on his face when he saw the total. She had a mind to turn up at Maison Blanc tomorrow, just to see him wince as she delivered the news in person.

Perhaps that wasn't such a bad idea after all. She could bat her lashes and give him the *Oops! Silly me! I never was much good at maths* routine. The added bonus would be that Cassie couldn't moan at her for not giving the latest offering in the husband hunt a fair go.

Thinking of Cassie, it was time to give her an earful. She took her mobile phone out of her bag and punched in the number.

Cassie was never one for pleasantries, and this time was no exception.

'How's it going? Isn't he hot?'

'Not noticeably.'

'Really? I was sure you two would hit it off. My new project worker has talked about her brother so much I feel like he's a long-lost friend.'

'Yeah? Well, he's also my long lost date.'

'What do you mean?'

'He didn't show, Cassie! Some sorry story and an instruction to have dinner on him. You can tell your friend that she'd better get as much visiting time in with her brother as she can, because he's going to have a heart attack when he sees his credit card statement.'

'Oh...'

'Yes, oh! You'd better be making that famous carrot cake of yours when I come for coffee on Wednesday, or I'll never forgive you.'

'Yes, ma'am.' She knew without a doubt that Cassie had just stood to attention in her living room.

'And no more setting me up on blind dates! Got it?'

'Got it.'

Yeah, right. She could practically hear the cogs whirring in Cassie's brain as she did a mental search for the next poor sucker.

'Try and resist the urge to find me a husband as lovely as yours is. We have very different taste in men, remember? I never could understand why you used to moon over the geeks with plasters holding their glasses together in school.'

'Darren Perkins was a god!'

'Of course he was. See you Wednesday—and don't forget the carrot cake. Bye.'

She sighed. If the truth be told, she was pleased her blind date hadn't turned up. But that didn't stop her fuming over her wasted evening. She could have taken Jake up on his offer of dinner. She looked at the phone sitting in her hand. She could still call him.

Was she really that brave? Wouldn't it sound a little desperate if she called him now?

He'd have had time to get in, have a shower and change into something dry. She could picture him padding around a smart flat with polished wood floors, low-slung jeans resting on his hips, his hair damp and smelling of shampoo.

She felt in her pocket for the business card and looked at the number. Her heart sank. The ink had bled into the damp card, making Jake's scrawl illegible. She could make out the first two digits—a three and a two. One of the numbers further along looked suspiciously like a seven. Or was it a one?

If she'd believed in fate, she'd have thought it was an omen. But she had outgrown the New Age hocus-pocus her parents had spoon-fed her since birth. She stuffed the card back in her pocket, doubly cheesed off at the invisible Charles.

When she'd finished her coffee she made her way to where Gino was serving at the bar.

'See you soon, Gino. Tell Marco his cooking was superb, as usual, and give my love to the rest of the family—especially Sophia and your adorable little granddaughter.'

Gino's eyes sparkled with pride. 'Sophia says Francesca is sleeping through the night now.'

'Well, you tell Sophia I will be offended if I'm not first on her list of babysitters when she wants to go out for the evening.'

One more hug for Gino and Maria and she was outside, breathing in the cold night air. The rain had stopped and the stars twinkled up above.

Time to go home and plan her next move.

She stood on the pavement and stared at her car, feeling oddly deflated. She'd been excited at the thought of another sparring match with Jake. Now she had no way of contacting him, even if she wanted to give in to temptation and phone him first.

She flumped into the driver's seat of her dad's car and flung her handbag over the passenger seat into the back, not caring where it landed. She pulled the card out of her pocket again and stared at it hard, willing the numbers to come into focus. If anything, they were even more blurry now. There was only one thing for it.

She jammed the keys into the ignition and stepped on the accelerator. She might not know his phone number, but she knew where he lived.

She took the quickest route she knew back to Great Portman Street—unlike earlier, when she'd taken a couple of scenic detours—and arrived there in less than ten minutes. Her parking left much to be desired. There had to be a good foot between the car and the kerb.

She turned the engine off and sat in the dark.

Funny—now she was here, her feet were decidedly icy. Not because of Jake—he was lovely—but because of what he might read into finding her on his doorstep. She was looking for love and commitment, not a fling, and turning up after ten o'clock, uninvited, would be giving a completely different set of signals.

It was exactly because of this kind of impulsive behaviour that she had ended up with some of the most worthless boyfriends in history. She reminded herself she'd turned over a new leaf. No more leaping before she looked, even if the man she wanted to leap onto looked as good as Jake.

She wound down the window and stuck her head out. Soft light glowed in a few of the penthouse windows.

Why did everything have to come down to such an all-or-nothing choice? If only there was another way to reach him.

She picked the card up from where she had flung it on the passenger seat.

Of course! Talk about missing the obvious!

She had been so focused on the telephone number on the back of the card she hadn't even thought about turning it over to find his business address. She could wait a couple of days and phone him at work. That wouldn't be too forward.

She flipped the card over and ran her eyes over the classic black font. An accountant. She liked accountants. They were stable, sensible, and nothing like the kind of men she'd learned to shy away from—musicians, actors, tortured artists.

Jake was looking better and better. He was smart and good-looking, and he must be clever. And he might, just might, be the kind of guy a girl could hope to settle down with.

Then she noticed the name along the bottom and almost dropped the card in shock. Charles Jacobs!

Charles?

He'd told her his name was Jake!

She was about to stub the offending card into the ashtray when she stopped. Jake could be a nickname. After all, she wasn't exactly using *her* given name at the moment. She'd started abbreviating it to Serena. It sounded a lot less flower-child and a lot more...well, normal, than Serendipity. She couldn't blame Jake if he wanted to liven up a stuffy name like Charles.

She looked at the card again and smiled.

Well, well. Charles Jacobs.

Lunch tomorrow was going to be fun.

CHAPTER TWO

JAKE walked into Maison Blanc ten minutes early. Being there first gave him the edge. When Serena arrived he'd be calmly seated at one of the little square tables with its crisp linen tablecloth. He'd make sure he had a good view of the entrance, and scrutinise every female who glided through glass door.

Maison Blanc was his kind of place. The décor was white and clean, full of straight lines. No fuss. No frills. The best feature by far was that he knew how big the bathroom window was. He'd fit through it, no problem.

He walked past the bar into the main part of the restaurant and scanned the entire room from left to right—then did a double take.

It was her!

The mystery woman. Here. Now.

He very nearly swore.

The woman he'd spent most of last night trying to forget, while he punched his pillow and ordered himself to sleep, was sitting at a table in the centre of the room, sipping a drink.

Suddenly he didn't know what to do with his hands.

She looked stunning. Her silky brown hair was swept up into a braided ponytail. Her large, almond-shaped eyes were accentuated with smoky make-up and she wore a soft moss-green cardigan open at the throat. He swallowed. Never had a cardigan looked so sexy.

She was warm and vibrant. A perfect contrast to the sterile surroundings. And something about her seemed indefinably exotic. He wondered if she had gypsy blood coursing through her veins.

She'd started to turn her head in his direction, so he dived behind a pillar and stayed there for a few breathless seconds. Then, when he was sure she wasn't looking, he slunk over to the bar and ordered something. He sat there, hunched over his glass, hoping to heaven she hadn't noticed him. But that didn't seem possible. He was sure every molecule in his body was screaming *Look at me* and waving its arms in her direction.

He risked another glance.

She was looking at the menu. He was safe, for now.

An enigmatic smile curled her lips, as if she were remembering a secret joke. In fact, it looked very much as if she were trying not to laugh.

His fingers traced the rim of his tumbler, but it stayed on the bar as he let his mind wander.

Last night, as they'd driven through the crowded London streets, he'd prayed that every traffic light would stay red, just to keep them locked in the private world of her car a few seconds longer. He'd been fascinated by her movements as she drove, hadn't been able to stop watching the little silver bracelet that danced on her wrist as she moved her hand from steering wheel to gearstick and back. Everything she did was fluid and graceful.

He'd even admired the cool way she'd pulled away and left him gaping in the street. It served him right for his lack of finesse. He'd been too sure she was going to call him. Minutes after her departure he'd been pacing round his flat, scorning himself for being so smug. He'd tried desperately to remember if he had any business contacts who could trace the owner of the blue Porsche.

But it looked as if he didn't need to worry about that. She was here. In fact, he didn't need to worry about anything—except, of course, that she would have a ring-side seat to his blind date with Serena.

Serena! He'd almost forgotten about her.

He looked at his watch. Four minutes to go. Time to pull himself together. He couldn't let her find him sitting at the bar all a-jitter. Perhaps the situation could be salvaged by a bit of quick thinking.

He summoned a waiter and asked to be shown to his table. With any luck he'd be seated in the corner, facing the other direction. Maison Blanc was large, and there were plenty of square white pillars to hide behind.

His step faltered as the waiter led him not to the far corner, but straight towards his mystery woman. Rats! He was going to have to walk right past her table. There was nothing for it but to ooze charm and hope the matter of a lunch-date with another woman could be swept aside once he'd claimed her promise of dinner *another time*.

However, his best, knock-her-socks-off smile never made it past the planning stage—mainly because the waiter had stopped at the table and pulled out the chair opposite her.

He just stood and stared.

The waiter fidgeted and she waved him away. Then she smiled at Jake. He wanted to crawl under the table and hide.

'Good afternoon, Mr Jacobs. I'm pleased you could make it—this time.'

'But you're… You can't be…'

'I'm Serena. Pleased to meet you, Charles—or is it Jake?'
He swallowed.

She couldn't be Serena—her teeth were far too lovely.

She cocked her head on one side, waiting. Reading his
mind, as it turned out.

'I wore my hair this way just for you,' she said, and turned
her head so the ponytail swished towards him. Then she leant
forward and lowered her voice to a conspiratorial whisper.
'Just so you could tell which end of the horse was which.'

Something inside him snapped to attention. She knew!
She'd been ready and waiting for him, and he'd walked
straight in to her little trap.

'Touché,' he said, his voice unusually croaky.

She was really enjoying this. Her eyes were bright and
smiling, but without a hint of malice. She wasn't angry, just
teasing him, asking him to share the joke.

He held his hands up in surrender. 'Okay, you got me.
When did you know?'

She took a sip of her drink.

'Oh, not until *after* you stood me up. I found your business
card in my pocket. An amazing coincidence, don't you think?
I suppose I could have phoned you this morning and warned
you, but the opportunity to have a little fun was too good to
pass up.' She stopped and gave him a very genuine smile. 'I
can't really be cross, can I? It was my fault entirely. You only
cancelled because I drowned you. I suggest we start again.
Deal?'

'Deal.' He dropped into the high-backed leather chair and
offered her his hand. 'Charles Jacobs. But nobody calls me
that any more—except my sister when she's angry with me.
My friends call me Jake.'

She clasped his hand and shook it. Hers was small and

delicate and unbelievably soft. The smile he'd abandoned earlier returned without his bidding.

'I don't think I need to tell you my name again, do I? I think, after today, you're never going to forget it.'

'You don't look like a Serena.'

'You don't look like a Charles, either. Why Jake?'

'Boys called Charles got punched where I grew up. Some of my friends shortened my last name and it stuck. It was easier, anyway. I'm named after my father, and it was a relief to have a way to tell us apart.'

'You didn't fancy Junior, then?'

Her smile was warm and easy. He didn't mind her teasing him one bit. Somehow it made him feel welcomed—part of an elite club where they were the only two members—rather than putting him on the defensive. People didn't normally get away with ribbing him like this.

'Don't say you think it suits me!'

She wrinkled her nose and shook her head. Her chocolate-brown eyes held him hypnotised. It took the waiter appearing for their drinks order to break the spell.

They both ordered something non-alcoholic. Thank goodness he'd remembered he was driving before he'd downed that Scotch in one! The waiter moved away unnoticed.

'Your turn to spill the beans,' he said.

'Which beans would those be?'

'You could tell me your name.'

She frowned. 'It's Serena. Don't you believe me? Do you think I'm really called Mildred or Ethel?'

'Of course I believe you. I just want to know the *rest* of your name. You can't be just Serena.'

'Why not? Madonna only uses her first name.'

'But she has a last name too—she just doesn't need to use it. The same thing wouldn't work for you. If I tried to look up Serena in the phone book, I'd never find you. You've got to give me a bit more. For all I know you could disappear again, like you did last night, and I'd be none the wiser.'

She looked thoughtfully at the tablecloth. 'Oh. I see.'

'So? Serena…what?'

She leaned back in her chair and crossed her arms. 'Sorry, Charlie, that's on a need-to-know basis only.'

He leant forward and stared straight into her eyes. 'What if I *really* need to know?'

'I'd have to be *really* convinced.' She laughed and waved her hand in the air. 'Telling you my last name is too much of a commitment; I don't like to be tied down. But don't worry. If I think you can handle it, I'll tell you.'

Jake smiled. A girl on his wavelength. No ties. No strings. Just seeing what the future brought, minute by minute. She was right: he would find out her name. He liked her style— she was keeping him on his toes. It was very refreshing.

Talking to her was easy. He hardly noticed the first course slip by. She was funny and articulate, and he found himself talking back in a way that would have surprised his business associates. Sure, he could turn on the charm when it suited him. It was hard-wired into his genetic make-up. He used it as a mirror, reflecting anything that tried to pierce his armour, so no one got below the surface. Yet as he talked to Serena he found himself giving away little snippets of information he didn't normally make public. Nothing big, just stuff he didn't normally share: what book he'd read most recently, what kind of music he liked. Silly things.

Halfway through their main course he stopped eating and watched her butcher her steak. When her mouth closed round the fork, her eyelids fluttered shut and she let out a little sigh of satisfaction. There was an air of primal sensuality about her. And for some reason he wasn't feeling totally civilised himself at the moment, either. It was as if all the layers of varnish he'd carefully applied over the years were peeling away, leaving him feeling like the gawky teenager he'd once been. He should be scared of that feeling.

She looked up at him as she finished chewing her mouthful, her eyes questioning.

'I didn't realise six ounces of sirloin could be so riveting.'

Caught red-handed—or red-faced, to be exact.

He said the first thing that popped into his head. 'I'm just surprised to see you demolishing it with such gusto. You look more of a beansprouts-and-tofu kind of girl to me.' He didn't know why. Perhaps it was the long hair, the intricate earrings that dangled from her ears, or the skirt that swooshed when she crossed her legs.

She dropped her knife and fork and scowled at him.

'I've had enough beansprouts to last me a lifetime, believe me! My parents were dedicated vegans until—' Her breath caught for a second. 'Never mind. Let's just say my love of animal flesh is probably teenage rebellion that's way past its sell-by date.' She grinned. 'Since I was fourteen I've been a true carnivore. In fact, I'd go as far as to say I've never met a bit of cow I didn't like.'

She speared the next piece of steak and blood oozed out of it.

Jake shuddered, unable to tear his gaze away.

'Aren't you going to finish your swordfish?'

He picked up his cutlery and shoved something from his plate into his mouth. He didn't taste what it was. He just had to remind himself to keep cutting and chewing until his plate was empty.

Serena eyed the dessert menu when her plate had been taken away. 'Aren't you having any?'

'Not for me. I don't really eat dessert. I think I'll just have a coffee.'

'Mmm. Perhaps I should too, but that chocolate concoction looks—'

Her mobile phone trilled.

'Excuse me. I forgot to turn it off. I won't be a second.'

'No problem.'

He leaned back in his seat and took the opportunity to study her while her attention was elsewhere.

'Hello? Oh, it's you. I'm sorry, but I'm in the middle of... No, don't do that! Just stay put, will you? Yes, but... Look! Just give the phone to Benny... Let me talk to Benny. I'm not getting any sense out of you...'

She mouthed 'sorry' at him and her cheeks flushed an appealing shade of pink. He shrugged. It was nice to see he wasn't the only one who could lose his cool.

'Just keep him there, will you, Benny? I'll be there as soon as I can... Yes...don't worry... Just don't let him punch anybody else...'

Jake's ears pricked up.

She snapped her phone closed and exhaled long and hard.

'I'm sorry, I need to go. It's an emergency.'

'Anything I can do to help?'

'No, I'll be fine. I just need to get to Peckham as soon as possible.'

Peckham? Why on earth was a rich girl like her going *there*?

'What for?'

'I've got to find a pub called The Swan.

She stood up, skirted the table, and gave him an absent-minded kiss on the cheek. 'Thanks for lunch. I really enjoyed it.'

And before Jake could argue she'd rushed out through the door and onto the pavement.

He dug in his pockets for his credit card and paid as quickly as he could. By the smile on the waiter's face, he guessed he'd left a ridiculously large tip. But he couldn't be bothered to do the maths, so he'd just rounded it up to the nearest hundred.

He shoved the door open and almost bumped into Serena, who was standing on the kerb, waving her hands around.

'What are you doing?'

'I'm trying to find a taxi! One minute the whole street is teeming with them; the next minute there's not one to be had for love nor money.'

He pulled her arm down and turned her to face him. Only then did he see the tremble in her lip, her pale face.

'Hey.' He slid his hand down her arm until he found her hand and gave it a squeeze. 'It'll be okay.'

She sniffed. 'I need to get to that pub as soon as I can, or there's going to be a huge amount of trouble!' She pulled away from him and ran to the kerb again as a black cab hurtled past. She looked as if she were about to sprint up the road after it when Jake reached for her again.

'I'll take you. My car's round the corner. I know a way round the back-doubles that'll cut out a lot of the traffic.'

Her eyes gleamed and threatened to overflow. 'Would you really? You don't know how grateful I am. But you've got to promise me something.'

'What's that?'

She grabbed both his shoulders in what, at that time, seemed like an overly dramatic gesture. 'You can't tell a soul about what happens when we get there. It's vitally important.'

Her words haunted him as he turned his car towards the river and headed over Vauxhall Bridge. He left the main roads after passing The Oval, and wove through the back streets. The climbing numbers on the milometer matched his growing unease. He hadn't been back this way for years, had promised himself he never would. He'd done everything humanly possible to claw his way off the high-rise council estate he'd grown up on.

What had she got herself mixed up in? Trouble in this neck of the woods normally meant something criminal. Although she looked unconventional, he hadn't taken her for the kind of woman who courted real trouble. She lacked a certain brand of hardness he was all too familiar with.

But appearances could be deceptive. He'd learned that from his father—living proof that even the tastiest-looking apple could be maggoty at the core.

His eyes flicked over to Serena in the passenger seat. He'd only just met this woman. She could be anyone, involved in anything. For Pete's sake, he didn't even know her last name.

However, his gut said he could trust her, and when he thought of her face when the black cab had sailed past, he knew it was right. Whatever she was involved in, it wasn't drugs or dirty money. She really cared about the man—he presumed it was a man—they were racing to rescue.

A few minutes later he pulled up outside The Swan, or as close as he could get to it. A clampers' lorry was just about to winch a car off the double yellow lines outside.

A metallic blue Porsche.

Blast! He'd forgotten all about the guy with the Porsche. What a prize doughnut he was! He'd raced halfway across London to bail her boyfriend out of trouble. The hairs on the back of his neck bristled as he imagined some T-shirted lout, who obviously didn't look after Serena the way she deserved to be looked after.

Serena jumped out of the car and raced into the pub before he could undo his seat belt. Was she always this impetuous? Or was it just that the Porsche guy was so great she couldn't wait another second to be with him?

His frown deepened and he pulled himself out of his car, straightened his tie, and followed her inside. The smell of stale smoke and beer hit his nostrils as he pushed the door open. This place was even more of a dive than it had been last time he'd been here—and that had to be a good ten years ago. The same torn, faded upholstery covered the stools and benches, only it was even more torn and faded than he remembered.

A couple of blokes with tattoos on their knuckles propped up the bar. He knew their sort. He couldn't judge them, though. If he'd had a little less luck, made a few different choices, it could have been him standing there, whiling away his dole money on watered-down beer.

He turned his attention to the overturned table and broken glass in the far corner. Serena was leaning over a man sprawled on one of the upholstered benches. She paused every few seconds to discuss the situation with a burly man in a leather jacket. Only when Jake was a few feet away could he hear any of her hushed, staccato phrases.

'What happened, Benny? How did you end up in this place?'

Benny, for all his height and width, hung his head like a naughty schoolboy enduring a scolding. 'Mike said he wanted to visit some of the places he used to play when the band was just starting out. It seemed like a good idea at the time.'

She rolled her eyes. 'It always does, Benny.'

'Sorry, babe.'

She rolled her neck, as if she was trying to erase the kinks.

'So what happened, exactly?'

'Mike got to reminiscing with a couple of the locals. We were having a great time, buying everybody drinks and walking down memory lane, then some of the younger crowd got a bit mouthy and Mike flipped. He tried to thump one of them and tripped over a stool. They laughed, so he took another swing and hit the barman by accident.'

Benny shrugged. 'His aim is terrible after a few pints. He only knocked a tray of empties out of his hands—didn't hurt him.'

'Well, thank goodness for that!' She laid a hand on his arm. 'Listen, Benny, you see if you can get him upright, and I'll go and chat to the landlord. We need to get out of here before the press gets wind of it.'

The press? Jake thought. A pub brawl wasn't even going to make page sixteen of the local paper, let alone the nationals. Surely she was overreacting?

She stepped back to go and talk to the man behind the bar, giving him his first good look at the Porsche-driving god she had come to rescue. He couldn't have been more surprised. Mike wasn't some hot-looking young stud with a washboard stomach—he was a bedraggled-looking fifty-something with a beer belly. What on earth did she see in him?

He looked back at Serena, who was talking earnestly to the landlord. Frowns were giving way to nods and half-smiles. She marched back over to them, a less serious look on her face.

'He says he's not going to press charges. I've offered to pay for any damage, and a little bit extra for compensation. He seems quite happy, but I still think we ought to leave before he thinks better of it. Hand over the cash, Benny, and I'll sort this out right now.'

Benny handed her a wad of notes from his pocket.

Jake had the uncanny feeling this was not the first time

she'd bailed the man out of trouble. It was almost as if she was on auto-pilot. Even so, she was marvellous. Nothing seemed to faze her.

Mike looked up at him. 'All right, mate?'

He held out his hand. Jake ignored it. The guy didn't seem to mind.

'She's great, isn't she?' he slurred, nodding his head towards Serena.

Jake resisted the urge to punch him.

'Yes, she is. You're very lucky she takes care of you like this.'

His head sagged. 'I know. She's the best daughter in the world.'

Daughter! Of course! He was so dense sometimes. He grinned to himself. Benny gave him an odd look, obviously wondering who the hell he was, and why he found the whole situation quite so funny.

Jake looked down at Serena's father again. Maybe his first impressions had been a little harsh, but jumping to conclusions about people was an everyday hazard when you had a runaway imagination like his. Mel was always quick to remind him of this fault. She said he needed to slow down and look at the facts, not just let his imagination fill in the blanks. He hated it when Mel was right.

Apart from being a little the worse for wear, Mike looked okay. In fact, he reminded Jake of someone. His forehead creased as he tried to find a match for the face in his memory bank. Nope, couldn't place it. It would come to him later. He was good with faces.

When they got outside, the clamping lorry was just disappearing round the corner with the Porsche strapped on board. All four of them stood and stared at the space where it had been parked.

'So much for a quick getaway,' mumbled Serena.

Jake was glad of the opportunity to be more than a spectator of the afternoon's increasingly bizarre turn of events. 'No problem. I can give you all a lift.'

Serena turned to look at him, as if she'd only just remembered he existed—a huge boost for the ego! Two hours ago he'd been having a rather nice lunch with the most fascinating woman he'd met in months, and now he'd been demoted to chauffeur and general onlooker. Oh, well, he might as well play the part.

'How about I drop Benny off at the car pound? I'll pay if you're short after forking out for damages in there—' he jerked his thumb in the direction of the pub '—and then we can get your dad home.'

She closed her eyes and breathed out through her nose. 'You know he's my dad?' she asked, without opening her eyelids.

'It came up.'

'Fabulous.'

Why was she so upset? It was hardly a matter of national security.

He put his arm round her shoulder and drew her to him. 'What do you say? Jump in the car and I'll take you somewhere warm. Let me return the favour and be your knight in shining armour for a change.'

To his amazement, she turned her face up to his and kissed his cheek. Her lips were warm and soft, and her hair smelled of lemons. When she moved away his cheek felt cold.

'You're a real gentleman, Charlie. Let's get going before anyone spots us.'

Benny wrestled Mike and his unruly limbs into the back seat, where he lolled against the door. Jake had the feeling he would have slithered onto the floor without the seat belt to hold him up. Serena took the passenger seat while Benny babysat Mike in the back.

No one talked as they sped back towards central London. They could hardly make polite chit-chat after the sort of afternoon they'd had. Even if they tried small talk, once they got past, *Isn't it getting dark in the evenings now?* or, *Very mild for November, isn't it?* they'd have lapsed back into the bottomless silence.

Jake turned the radio on low, to muffle the sound of Mike's snoring. He tuned it to an 'oldies-but-goldies' station. Nothing too offensive to anyone's tastes, he hoped. The opening chords of a song he hadn't heard for years drifted through the car. It reminded him of a summer on the housing estate when he and his mates had hung round the playground on their bikes. Before the see-saw had been vandalised. Before they'd started finding used syringes by the swings. He smiled and wondered what Martin and Keith were doing now.

Without warning, Mike burst from his coma and belted out the chorus of the song. He didn't have a bad voice. Jake glanced back just in time to catch a virtuoso air guitar performance.

That was it! He'd known he'd get it eventually.

Serena's dad looked like Michael Dove, the lead guitarist of Phoenix. This song had been one of their biggest sellers back in the late seventies. He breathed a sigh of relief. Not being able to place that face would have driven him mad all day.

He sneaked another look in the rear-view mirror. The resemblance was uncanny. This guy could make a good living as a look-alike, instead of getting wasted in dodgy south London pubs. Perhaps he should suggest it to Serena?

He looked again.

Yep, it was a great idea. Mike even had that same little scar on his lip...

'Jake!'

The flat of her hand hit him hard on the shoulder. Instinctively, he stamped on the brake pedal, suddenly noticing the brake lights of the car in front were a little too close for comfort. He forgot to put his foot back on the accelerator and looked into the back seat.

'You're Michael Dove.'

Serena groaned. He looked across at her. The car behind tooted its horn.

'You're Michael Dove's daughter.'

She looked back at him, her brows knit together.

'I know. Funnily enough, I have been all my life.'

Great! He was going to go all starry-eyed on her. Just when she'd thought she'd found a possible candidate for Mr Serendipity Dove.

Men responded in very different ways to the news that her father was a rock legend, but the outcome was always the same. It was the kiss of death. Whether they pretended not to care, or decided to use the relationship to further their own careers, it changed things for ever.

She looked across at Jake. He was very quiet.

'But I thought Michael Dove's daughter was called something freaky, like Stardust or Moonbeam.'

A voice yelled from the back seat, 'Moonbeam, my—'

'Dad!'

'But Mr Three-piece-suit here thinks your name is ridiculous.'

Jake shook his head. 'There's nothing ridiculous about being called Serena. I was just saying—'

Serena groaned again. Which was not good. It was a seriously unattractive noise, but she couldn't stop herself. Earlier this afternoon she'd been a woman of mystery: exotic, alluring... Now Jake could find all the intimate details of her life just by picking up a tabloid newspaper.

'Who's Serena?' her dad muttered.

Jake leant across the gap between their seats and whispered, 'He must be in worse shape than he looks.'

I wish!

At least then her dad would pass out and save her from any further embarrassment. When she got home she was going to empty every bottle of spirits in their Chelsea townhouse down the kitchen sink. Including the one he kept in his guitar case he thought she didn't know about. And the whisky that was hidden in a wellington boot beside the back door.

Her father continued to mumble from the rear of the car, more to himself than for the benefit of the other passengers.

'Elaine named her...she was so thrilled—we thought we couldn't have kids. Then fortune smiled on us...'

If there was an ejector seat in Jake's BMW, she was praying fervently it would shoot her through the roof this very second.

'There's nothing wrong with Serendipity. It's a beautiful name. Moonbeam. I ask you...'

Jake coughed. 'I beg your pardon?'

'You heard!' she snapped.

There was a crinkle in his voice when he spoke next. She could tell he was holding back a snort of laughter, but, give him credit, he managed to arrest it by swallowing hard.

'It seems you were a little economical with your name, Miss Dove.'

'Yes, well, so were you, *Charles*!'

'Let's just call it quits and agree we are creatures of a similar nature.'

She allowed herself a small smile.

'Maybe.'

She turned to look at her father. He was fast asleep, mouth hanging open, threatening to dribble on Benny's shoulder if the car swung him in the right direction. Once again he was oblivious to the upheaval he'd created in her life. But it was hard to be cross with him. There was something so child-like about him. He didn't mean to cause trouble; he just couldn't help himself. It was as natural as breathing for him.

She closed her eyes and settled back into the comfy leather seat, letting the endless stopping and starting of the car journey lull her into a more relaxed frame of mind.

Later, after they'd bundled Dad into the house and up to his room, and Jake had made his excuses and left, she sat at the kitchen table with a steaming cup of tea between her hands and wondered if she'd ever see him again.

She thought perhaps not.

CHAPTER THREE

SERENA stared out across the London skyline in an effort to distract herself from the fact that very soon her bottom was going to be frozen to the wooden slats of the park bench. The bench's position on the brow of a hill offered little protection from the wind, even though it circled a towering sycamore.

'It's lovely here. What a view.'

Jake smiled and offered her a plate full of goodies from the picnic basket balancing between them. 'A favourite haunt of mine when I was younger.'

'Did you live close by?'

'Not too far.'

She could imagine him living in Blackheath, the exclusive area south of where they now sat in Greenwich Park. Blackheath itself was a mile-wide expanse of flat grass, its only vertical feature the razor-sharp spire of All Saints' church. Along the fringes of the heath were creamy Georgian villas, and she could easily imagine a young Jake bounding out of one of them each morning—grey shorts, school cap, laces undone.

'You can see it from here, actually,' he said.

She stared hard, but couldn't work out where he was pointing. The houses were too blurry and indistinct at this distance.

'You're looking in the wrong place.' He put an arm round her shoulder and nudged her so she faced more to the west. 'You can't miss it. See the three tower blocks?'

'Beyond them?'

'No, *in* them. I used to live in the one on the far right. Fourteenth floor.'

She turned to look him in the eye. 'Really?'

'I could see this park from my bedroom window. A beautiful patch of green surrounded by pollution and concrete.'

She laughed. 'Very poetic.'

'Shh! You'll ruin my tough businessman image.'

'I'm not sure you're as tough as you look, Charlie.'

He gave her a sideways look. 'Why do you keep calling me that?'

'I don't know. It just seems to pop out of my mouth. It must suit you.'

His jaw hardened. 'I prefer Jake.'

'But it's not your real name.'

'Ah! So I get to use your given name as well, do I?'

'Good point. Jake it is.' She leaned back and looked up into the leafless branches above. 'Didn't you have a garden where you lived? Not even a shared one?'

She could hear him fiddling with the strap of the picnic basket. 'Do we have to do the childhood memories bit?'

'It's only fair. Even though I'm not famous myself, I'm related to someone who is, and that's good enough for the celebrity-hungry media. You could probably type my name into a search engine and find out what I had for breakfast last Wednesday.'

'I can think of better ways of finding out what you like for breakfast.' The edge in his voice was pure wickedness.

She rolled the back of her head against the tree trunk until she could see him. 'Nice try, but you're not going to throw me off track. I just want to know a little more about you. It's hardly a crime.'

'I normally get away with that kind of tactic.' He grinned, willing her to take the diversion he offered.

'I bet you do.'

His expression grew more serious. 'You're right. It's not a crime. I'm used to fluffing over the details my childhood. Some of my clients would faint if they thought a council estate yob was looking after their millions.'

Serena looked him up and down. How anyone could ever think of him as a yob was beyond her. Six-foot-something of pure elegance was standing right in front of her, from his cashmere coat to his hand-made shoes.

'There were hardly any trees on the estate, so I used to come here on the weekends—on days when the prospect of school was just too bleak.'

She picked up her plate—china, no less—and pinched a stuffed vine leaf between thumb and forefinger. Jake was staring at his old home, his eyes glazed with memories.

'I'd sit on this very bench and plot and plan my escape from the tower blocks. I'd watch the rest of the city going about its business and dream I could become a part of it one day.'

'Is that why you got into accounting?' She gave him a lazy smile. 'All that rabid excitement?'

'Ha, ha. Don't bother going down the all-accountants-are-boring route. I've heard all the jokes a million times. Anyway, at first I didn't want to be an accountant. I knew I needed money to get away from the estate, so I decided I'd better learn how to look after it properly. I got a job at a local accounting firm when I left school and it grew from there. Pretty soon I knew I'd found my niche, so I took the tests and worked hard until I qualified.'

'It sounds like you were very dedicated.'

'I wanted to get my mum away from there. She deserved something more than that.'

'I've heard those accounting exams are really difficult.' She sighed. 'I've never stuck at anything like that. We were always moving around too much. Dad was either on tour, or recording in some far-flung place.'

'What did you do about school?'

'Well, up until I was eleven or so my mum home-schooled me. My primary education was unconventional, to say the very least. By the time I was ten I knew all about trees and crystals and the constellations, but I was a little lacking in the maths and science department.' She struck a pose. 'But I was very good at improvisational dance and mime.'

Jake gave her another one of his heart-melting smiles.

'What happened after that?'

'Mum got ill and I was sent away to boarding school.'

His eyebrows lifted. 'I can't really see you in a starched school uniform, having midnight feasts with Lady Cynthia.'

'If only! Have you heard of Foster's Educational Centre in the West Country?'

He shook his head.

'One of the Sunday magazines did a feature on it a few months ago—I thought you might have seen it. Anyway, it's one of those so-called progressive schools, all fashionable psychology and no common sense. Complete nuthouse, if you ask me.' She winked at him. 'Needless to say, I didn't fit in.'

'No! Of course not. The thought never crossed my mind.'

'Actually, I'm not joking. The other kids laughed at me because they thought I was weird after my mum's special brand of education. And, since the teachers believed that expressing negative energy was important to our emotional development, it wasn't hard for the other kids to find ways to torment me if they wanted to. Which they did. I was fresh meat.'

'Ouch!'

'I left as soon as I could, and fled back to Dad. He'd just come out of rehab for his drug addiction. I'm assuming you know about that; it's pretty much common knowledge. He spent a few years living too fast and hard after my Mum died of cancer. He needed me home as much as I needed to get away.'

'What about a career?'

She snorted. 'Looking after Dad is a full-time job, believe me! I've been Dad's manager for the past five years. Consider me a personal assistant, troubleshooter and baby-sitter all rolled into one. The band don't do as much as they used to, but it can be pretty hectic at times.'

Jake handed her a glass of champagne. 'What would you do if you could do anything? Travel?'

She took a small sip and shook her head. 'No, not travel. My life has been nomadic enough. Something completely different.'

'Run away with the circus?'

She smiled at him and said nothing. It wouldn't do to reveal her real desires for the future. Announcing that your greatest wish was to become a wife and mother was like a starter's pistol for some men, and she wasn't ready to see this one disappearing in a cloud of dust.

Jake ticked all the right boxes: stable job, successful enough not to be after her dad's money, thoughtful, charming—the list was endless.

He put one hundred per cent commitment into all he did, and everything he did was first class. Just look at this hamper of picnic food from London's most exclusive department store. No ham sandwiches wrapped in an empty bread bag here.

But something inside her longed for ham sandwiches, lemonade, and children running down the hill with jam on their faces and grass stains on their knees.

She'd had enough champagne to fill a lifetime. It had lost its sparkle for her. Probably because she'd seen her father drink enough for two or three lifetimes. She'd been pushing him to get help for his drinking, and, although he denied it furiously, she thought he was almost ready to go back to rehab. The alternative didn't bear thinking about. Dad was the only family she'd got, and she was hanging onto him. Tight. Just entertaining any negative thoughts in that direction made her shudder.

'Cold?'

'A little.'

Jake put a protective arm round her and she leaned back on him. They said nothing more as they ate the last morsels of their picnic, but she took great care not to give Jake an opportunity to move away. The kind of heat he was generating had absolutely nothing to do with layers of jumpers and wool coats, and everything to do with the man inside them. If only she could hibernate like this, huddled up to him, until spring. It was wonderful to let someone else do the caring, just for a little bit.

When they had finished, Jake picked up the basket and offered a hand to help her up. Such a gentleman! He didn't release her hand when they started to walk down the path, and she didn't want him to. Even without the tickle of electricity that crept up her arm, the simple gesture of human contact felt good. It had been too long since she'd held hands with anyone.

They passed the Royal Observatory and took the little railed path that crossed the hill beneath it. Jake refused to release her hand as they negotiated the kissing gate there. It took quite a while before they untangled themselves enough to pass through. She had more than a sneaking suspicion that Jake had been deliberately clumsy with the hamper, just to keep them squashed up together while they swung the gate open in the confined space.

Once free of the gate, she was going to walk on, but Jake stopped moving and her arm tugged taut. She glanced back at him, puzzled.

He looked down at their feet and she followed suit. A brass strip was embedded in the tarmac, symbolising the point where the Greenwich meridian dissected not only the path, but the city. Jake hadn't crossed it, and they stood facing each other, as if at a threshold.

'Zero degrees longitude,' he said, looking deep into her eyes. 'A place of beginnings.'

If Jake thought today was only a beginning, it meant there was more to come. She couldn't stop her mouth from curling at the thought. 'Don't you think this is a bit surreal? We're standing so close, but we're in different hemispheres.'

'We're not *that* close.' He dropped the picnic basket by his side and took hold of her other hand. 'We could be closer.' In demonstration, he tugged her towards him so the fronts of their coats met and her eyes were level with his chin. She could feel his breath at her hairline. If she tipped her chin up just a notch his lips would be *so* close.

The heat of a blush stained her cheeks. No one had ever made her feel this way. The only point of contact was their fingers, yet her pulse galloped like a runaway horse.

'Still feeling strange?' he whispered into her hair.

'I think it's worse, if anything.' She swallowed hard, and raised her eyes to meet his. They were impossibly blue beneath his dark brows, and he wasn't smiling any longer. Deep in his eyes she saw a flicker of something previously hidden. Beneath the smooth-talking, city-slicker image, this was a good man, with a good heart.

His voice was warm on her cheek. 'A few more millimetres and we could really set the world spinning on its axis.'

'That was really cheesy,' she whispered back.

Still, it didn't stop her eyelids fluttering closed as his lips made the achingly slow journey to hers. In the moment just before they touched, she trembled uncontrollably.

It was everything a first kiss should be. Soft, sweet, full of promise. Never mind about separate hemispheres, they seemed to be the only two people on the planet. She clung to him and buried her fingers in his thick hair—the way she'd been longing to ever since their lives had collided in the rush hour traffic only a few days ago.

His palms cupped her face and his fingers stroked her jaw.

Never had she been kissed like this. It had never been anything more than a clashing of lips and teeth with the drifters she'd gone out with when she had been younger, and stupid enough to believe they could fill the empty spaces in her heart. Kissing Jake was so different. The sensation travelled from her lips right into her very soul.

Too soon he pulled away, tugged her crocheted hat a little more firmly onto her head, and led her down the path towards his car. All she could focus on for the rest of the afternoon was when—please, let it be *when*, not *if*—the next kiss was coming.

If Cassie had been any more desperate for information, she'd have been dribbling.

'I want to hear all the gory details.'

'I'm pretending I don't know what you're talking about, Cass. Absolutely nothing about my love-life could ever be described as "gory".'

'Not even the crash-and-burn flings of the past?'

'Yes…well… That was then—this is now.' She gave what she hoped was a superior look. 'I have evolved.'

Cassie grinned and shuffled a little closer. 'Come on, girl-friend. How's it going with the hot-shot accountant?'

'You know, Cass, a vicar's wife can definitely *not* pull off a word like "girlfriend".'

'Not even one with funky pink hair and a nose-stud?'

She smiled. Cassie was the most unconventional minister's wife you could hope to see. Her short baby pink hair stuck up every which way, and she had four holes in each ear and one in her nose. 'Not even close, darling.'

'Shame. I pick phrases like that up from the youth group. I hardly notice I'm doing it. Anyway, stop being the word police and tell me what I want to know. Resistance is futile. You should know that by now.'

'You never change, do you?'

'Not since that day I waltzed into the common room at Foster's and saved you from *another* year of sitting in the corner writing doleful little poems you wouldn't let anybody read.'

Serena gasped in horror. 'My poetry was never doleful! Rambling and self-indulgent, maybe, but never doleful.'

'Whatever. You needed a little livening up.'

'You certainly did that!'

'What did Prudence and her gang call us again?'

Serena clapped her hands and grinned. 'The freaky twins!'

'Joined at the hip for evermore!' yelled Cassie, punching the air.

'Until you met Steve, anyway. I should be cross, but he's such a sweetie I forgave you ten seconds after I met him.'

Cassie stared off into space and her streetwise demeanour melted. 'He is rather wonderful…'

'Do you remember what your parents said when you told them about him?'

'Do I? They totally freaked! I can still hear my father—' She dropped her voice an octave to a low rumble. 'Cassandra. You're only nineteen. You're far too young to understand what marrying into the *establishment* means.'

They both collapsed in a heap of giggles.

Serena sighed and wiped a finger under her eye. 'At least they came round in the end. They practically fall over themselves now to tell their friends that their son-in-law runs an inner city project for underprivileged kids.'

'Ah, yes, but the dog collar still makes them squirm.'

'And you love it.'

Cassie giggled into her coffee mug.

'You're a minx, Cassie Morton.'

'It's why you love me.'

'No, I love you because you're the best friend anyone could ever have.' All traces of laughter left her voice and she fixed Cassie with a solemn stare. 'You're right. You *did* save me that last year at Foster's. It would have been hell without you. I owe you big-time.'

Cassie's eyes sparkled. 'And I know a way you can repay me.'

Serena slumped on the kitchen table in defeat. 'Go on. Pass me the carrot cake, and I'll tell you everything.'

Cassie just smiled, cut a thick wedge of cake, and plopped it on a chipped willow pattern plate. Serena dragged it across the table towards her, dipped her finger in the cream cheese icing and tried to think of where to start.

She almost didn't want to share this with Cass, which was a first. Not that she thought she would jinx it if she talked about Jake, but because it all seemed too precious. She wanted to keep all the memories locked up inside her. She'd have to tell Cass something, though, or she'd get the thumbscrews out.

'He's definitely in the running for Mr Right. We've had dinners and picnics and been to the ballet. I always thought there was more to a date than standing in the back of a smoky pub watching my other half play pool. It's like being Cinderella…'

'You've got it bad!'

She stared at the carrot cake, but didn't take a bite, her appetite arrested by the thoughts swirling round her head. 'Do you think so? Is this what *really* falling in love feels like?'

'Well, that depends. How do you feel?'

She sighed. 'He's all I can think about. When I'm not with him I've got butterflies thinking about the next time we'll meet, and when we're together I get butterflies just because I'm with him! He makes me feel special. For the first time I think I've met a man who likes *me*. Not Michael Dove's daughter, but me.'

Cassie put her coffee down and cocked her head on one side.

'So, have you…?'

'Have I what?'

'You know.'

She took a large bite of cake and shook her head. Chewing

and swallowing was a great way to stall, but regrettably her mouth was soon free again. 'You know I vowed it would take a ring on my finger as a guarantee of intentions before…that. I've been foolish too many times in the past where men are concerned. My creep-radar is completely defunct.'

Cassie nodded. 'I know. Every loser carrying a guitar pick was *the one*.'

'You'd think I'd know better, wouldn't you? I mean, I've been around musicians all my life. I know exactly how reliable they are. But there's something about arty types I can't resist. I've tried to fight it, but every time I end up getting hit with a sucker-punch and I'm totally gone.'

'Knocked out and down for the count. It's never pretty,' said Cassie, screwing up her face.

Serena rested her chin on her hand and stared out of the window. 'I've tried to analyse it. It just doesn't make sense. The best I've come up with is that it's something to do with those wild imaginations that make every day a surprise, that passion for life—'

'The attention span of a gnat,' added Cassie, finishing with a huge bite of cake.

'You're so right. And that's why I've sworn off men like that.'

Cassie mumbled through a mouthful of crumbs. 'And why I'm doing the vetting from now on.'

Serena sat back in her chair and wondered if the reason she fell so hard and fast was simpler than she allowed herself to believe. Maybe her childhood had left her so desperate for someone to love that she grabbed anything that vaguely resembled the real thing with both hands. Of course it was invariably a mirage—looked good at the time, but ultimately left her feeling dry and unsatisfied.

That was why she was pacing herself this time, taking it

slow. Jake was different from anybody else she'd been out with, but it was still early days. She wanted him to be *the one*, but it was too early to tell.

She took another bite of cake. The ever-present butterflies did a little waltz as she imagined the fireworks that could happen once 'Prince Charming' had been well and truly stamped on Jake's forehead.

Jake couldn't walk past the painting without having a third go at getting it straight. He nudged the left corner a little. There. He took three steps back and tipped his head slightly.

Blast! It had looked better before he'd started messing around with it.

It was just that he wanted everything right. Tonight he was cooking Serena dinner, playing on home turf—a departure from his normal routine. Now he had the money to enjoy such luxuries, he liked to wine and dine his girlfriends at good restaurants. They seemed to appreciate it too.

The perfectionist side of his nature urged him to pull out all the stops when he took a woman out, and his competitive spirit made him want to do that little bit better than the next guy. Even if his relationships didn't last, he wanted his old flames to remember him as the perfect gentleman. It was a little vain, perhaps, but he liked to think at least one or two of his ex-girlfriends thought of him occasionally and let out a little *if only* sigh.

He lifted his hand to tap the frame again, but pulled it back before it made contact. What was wrong with him? He wasn't usually this jumpy before a date. Perhaps it was because Serena was so totally different from the type of woman he was normally attracted to.

Ever since he'd had hormones in enough quantities to notice girls, he'd pined after cool, sophisticated types. Like the girls from St Bernadette's, the exclusive private school only a mile or so from Ellwood Green.

It had never seemed odd to him that such a bastion of old money was so close to his home. The school had probably been built for the daughters of wealthy merchants when Deptford had been a bustling port. Now the docks were miles downstream, and Deptford was no longer the prosperous suburb it had once been, but the evidence was still visible if you walked the streets. You could be walking past boarded-up shops one minute and down leafy roads with ornate Victorian masonry the next. Little pockets of poverty and privilege, side by side, but worlds apart. London was like that.

He smiled. The girls from St B's had looked so good in their crisp white blouses and pleated skirts. He'd bet they'd smelled good too. Not that they'd let a grubby little oik like him close enough to find out. Perversely, the way they'd lifted their noses when they passed him in the street had only made him want them more. Probably because they represented everything he'd ever craved—class, style, money—although he hadn't analysed that feeling at the time.

Then, one day, when he hadn't reeked of the council estate any longer, the snooty noses had lowered and they'd given him sidelong glances from beneath their lashes.

How stupid of him not to have seen it before. He'd been dating St Bernadette's girls in one shape or form ever since he'd owned his first Rolex. Except Chantelle. She was the one exception—and his biggest mistake.

He glanced down at his watch. Scratches marred the surface in a few places, but he would never replace it. He'd saved every penny he could from his first pay packets at Jones and Carrbrothers until he could strut into the jewellers and slap down a wad of cash for it. It had been an important symbol. One that shouted, *I've made it*!

Once it had been paid for, he'd rented a shoebox bedsit and started the process of erasing his past—from the chain-store clothes to the flat vowels of his cockney accent. Nobody who met him now would ever suspect. He took great pains to ensure his rich clients would never guess their family money was being looked after by the son of a petty criminal.

He'd surprised himself by telling Serena his history. Okay, he'd left out some pretty major details, but he'd also let slip more than he usually did. Somehow it didn't matter if she knew. She wasn't impressed by his money in the slightest, which, after the initial dent to his ego, had been a huge relief. He was tired of women who earmarked him as a *good prospect*.

But it was more than that. Despite all their differences, they had a common bond. She knew what it was like to be an outsider too.

He walked out into the hall and headed back to the kitchen. The sight of the crease-free bedcovers through the bedroom door made his insides clench. An image flashed in his mind: he was standing holding a tray while morning sun filtered through the curtains onto a tangle of arms and legs in the duvet. Dark, silky hair sprawled on the pillow.

Abruptly, he reached for the doorknob and pulled the door shut. He had to get a hold of himself. Rushing ahead was definitely not the way to go with Serena.

He was courting her. It was an old-fashioned idea, but it fitted, nevertheless—and it was delicious. A tantalising game. They circled round each other, prolonging the inevitable, but the circles were getting smaller and smaller. Sooner or later there would be an explosive impact.

He would just have to keep himself on a tight leash until then. But that should be no problem. He was used to keeping control when it came to relationships. Women in his past had tried to push and prod him into doing what they wanted, but he'd always remained firmly anchored. He called the shots. He took the lead in pursuing his quarry at the start of the relationship, and he always decided when it was time to end it—normally the instant he saw the glitter of diamond rings in her eyes.

Mel said he was heartless, but he told himself it was for his ex-girlfriends' protection. There was no point giving them hope of a happy-ever-after. It wasn't in his genes.

Just as well he didn't have to worry about all that with Serena. Her heritage was flower-power and free love. As she'd said on their first date, they didn't need to tie themselves down. They could take the relationship one day at a time and see where it took them, which was great. He felt freer to be himself if he didn't have to worry about her getting the wrong idea.

He reached the kitchen and hunted for the corkscrew so he could open a bottle of Pinot Noir. He'd just pulled it out of the drawer when the telephone whined.

Please don't let this be Serena, ringing to cancel!

'Hello?'

'Hi, big brother.' Mel was trying to be chirpy.

'What's up?'

There was a pause and a heartfelt sigh.

'Mel?'

'It's Dad.'

Jake's back straightened. 'What about him?'

'There've been a few sightings lately.'

'On the Costa Blanca?'

'No, not in Spain—here.'

Jake marched across the kitchen and yanked the fridge door open, although when the blast of cold air hit his face he had no idea what he'd come to fetch, if anything. 'I've told you before. I don't care what that man does, as long as he doesn't come within fifty feet of me.'

'It's been ten years. Aren't you even curious?'

'No. He won't have changed. Don't fall for his flannel, Mel.'

Her tone was defensive. 'What makes you think I'm going to see him?'

'I didn't say you were. Are you?'

Silence.

'You were much younger than me when he left. You don't remember half of what went on—and there was lots of stuff I made sure you didn't find out. I know you've got these fairy-tale ideas that he'll come back and it'll be happy families, but it's not going to happen, Mel. He'll pick your pocket the same time as giving you a hug.'

Her voice was quiet. He knew she was on the verge of tears, but he wasn't prepared to have her hurt. He had to be tough with her now to stop worse pain in the future. All the same, he didn't want to unleash the anger reserved for his father on Mel.

He softened his voice. 'I'm sorry, sis, that's just the way it is.'

'I know. I just wish it wasn't, you know?' She sniffed. 'I thought I should tell you, that's all.'

'Thanks. I'm glad you did.'

Another sniff. 'Well, I'd better be getting on...'

'Take care of yourself. I'll see you on Sunday, okay? Don't cry for him, Mel. He's not worth it.'

'I'll try. Bye, Jake.' There was a gentle but despondent click as she put the receiver down.

Jake resisted flinging his phone against the dark slate tiles of the kitchen floor and carefully placed it back in its cradle. Hadn't that man done enough damage in the past? Why couldn't he have just stayed *disappeared*? He wrenched the door of the glass cabinet open. He'd bet last year's salary that the reason for Charlie Jacobs's return was not a good one.

CHAPTER FOUR

JAKE walked back towards the bottle of wine. Grinding the corkscrew into the cork felt good. Just the scent of chocolate and cherries as he poured it into a goblet eased the creases from his forehead. The doorbell chimed.

He walked into the hallway, glass in hand, and checked the screen of the video entry system. The camera looked down upon a head of dark, glossy hair. She was fiddling with her nails. Suddenly she turned and stared straight at the camera.

He actually jumped back slightly, almost as if he'd been caught spying. She gave the camera a saucy wink. It took him a good few seconds before he remembered to press the button, and the buzzer sounded long after she'd disappeared inside.

He swung his front door open and waited for her, heart thumping.

Calm. Calm.

Never lose your cool in front of a woman, remember? Who was he kidding? His cool had run screaming from the room the first time he'd laid eyes on Serena, and he hadn't found its hiding place yet. Still, better not to let *her* know that.

He held the glass out to her as she rounded the corner. 'Perfect timing.'

She took it and glided past him into the flat. 'That's what I like,' she said, and stopped to take a sip. 'A man who knows what I need even before I do.'

Jake took a little bow.

A naughty grin spread across her face. 'I'm getting a little 1950s flashback here. Shouldn't I be saying, *Hi, honey. I'm home?*'

'Not if you don't actually live here.'

She ignored him and waved the glass in his direction. 'By rights, *this* should really be a martini and you—' A finger lifted from the stem of her glass and jabbed the air. '*You* ought to be wearing a frilly apron.'

That was what he liked about her. She was always seeing things from a different angle. He pulled her close and kissed her ever so gently on the lips. When they pulled apart she whispered in his ear. 'Actually, I think you'll do quite nicely just as you are.'

He took her by the hand and led her into the kitchen.

'Dinner smells nice. Where did you order from?'

'*Chez Jake.* Do you know it?'

'I'm not falling for that one! Don't you know that's trick number five in the bachelor handbook on how to impress women? Order a good takeaway and pass it off as your own. And if I'm not mistaken…' She edged over to the bin and popped the lid up with a flourish of her hands. 'Ta-dah!'

The smug smile evaporated from her face as she looked down into the carton-free bin. Her eyebrows rose. 'You mean you actually cooked it all by yourself? I *am* impressed!'

'You haven't tasted it yet.'

'But you really cooked? For me?'

'Yes, I really did.'

A softness glittered in her eyes and she took a quick sip of her wine. When she looked up again it was gone.

He stirred the bubbling sauce. 'Would you take the wine and the glasses through to the dining room for me? It's just opposite.'

Serena hesitated, then walked over and gave him a feather-light peck on the cheek.

'Thank you, Jake.'

He stopped stirring and frowned. Thank you for what? It was only dinner.

Serena placed the glasses on coasters and surveyed the bone china plates, silver cutlery and elegant wine flutes that were laid ready on the table. Long-stemmed candlesticks flanked an arrangement of fresh flowers in the centre. Never in her wildest dreams had she imagined a man would pamper her so. Jake must be *really* serious about her. The ramifications of that thought made her heart skip a little faster.

The most she'd ever got from a boyfriend before was a packet of peanuts thrown across the pub table after he'd been to the bar. In her experience, musicians who knew she had a rich father didn't bother frittering their hard-earned cash on her—quite the opposite. But it wasn't the quality of Jake's chinaware that impressed her. It had taken time and careful thought to create all this—just for her. It was utterly seductive.

Jake called from the kitchen. 'Sit yourself down. I'll be there in just a sec.'

She pulled out a chair and did as she was told, still marvelling at his domesticity. A vase full of creamy white roses sat in front of her. They were lovely, buds loosening with the promise of the fullness. Just like the perfect blooms of a bridal bouquet.

Clinking dishes announced Jake's arrival. She was about to compliment him on the table setting, but all she could do when she looked up was hoot with laughter. Over the top of his jeans and shirt he was wearing the most hideous floral apron she had ever seen. Jake just grinned back at her, not fazed at all by the combination of psychedelic blue flowers and designer shirt.

He set the starters down on the table while she wiped her eyes, trying hard to leave her mascara intact. It took quite a while before the end of her sentences weren't hi-jacked by a burst of giggles.

'Where the heck did you dig that up?'

Jake did a twirl. 'You don't think it suits me?'

'Oh, beautifully! In fact, I think you should wear it next time we go out.'

'How about next Thursday? At your special birthday dinner?'

She gasped. 'How did you know it was my birthday next week?'

'A handy little tool called a search engine.'

He'd been looking her up on the internet? If anyone else had said that she'd have found it creepy—definite boyfriend marching orders! But she already knew Jake wasn't like that. Anyway, it would be highly hypocritical of her to be cross. Hadn't she visited his firm's website nearly every day, just to look at the pixellated little photo of him and convince herself he wasn't some longed-for figment of her imagination? She was secretly flattered he'd done something similar.

She tried not to look too gooey as she smiled back at him. 'So, where are you taking me?'

Jake put a finger to his lips. 'It's a surprise. But I promise you this: it's going to be a night you'll never forget.'

She hastily studied the goats' cheese salad in front of her. 'You're too good to me.'

He sounded shocked. 'I thought you'd be used to getting the princess treatment. I can't believe no one has ever looked into those big brown eyes and said you deserve the best.'

She swallowed a little lump that clogged her throat. 'Mum did. But that was a long time ago—a different life, almost. She died when I was twelve.'

He took her hand and she looked up into his bottomless blue eyes, so full of compassion. Suddenly it didn't matter if he saw that hers were tear-filled. He saw parts of her that other men hadn't even noticed, let alone understood. It was as if she was transparent to him. Yet she didn't feel naked or scared, she just felt *known*.

He pulled her hand towards his lips and placed the tiniest kiss on her knuckle. Nothing to prepare her for the shockwave that shot up her arm and bullseyed in her heart.

Her breath caught in her throat as he said, 'I'm going to have to do a lot of making up for lost time, then.'

Dinner was fantastic. The conversation was warm and intimate. If a world existed outside the candlelit cocoon they shared, she didn't want to know about it. She swallowed the last bite of her seafood pasta and relaxed back into her chair.

'That was amazing!' The corners of her mouth curled up. 'You could take the apron off now, if you wanted to.'

His eyes jerked downwards, then he laughed. 'I completely forgot I was wearing it!' He tugged at the ties behind his back and slipped it over his head.

'So where did you get it? I'm going to be very scared if I find out you have a row of them hanging in your wardrobe!'

'No, you're safe. This belongs to my cleaning lady. She

keeps it in the hall cupboard with her cleaning supplies. You don't think a single guy living alone is this good at dusting, do you?' He bunched the apron up and slung it under his arm. 'I'd better put this back. Do you want coffee?'

'Please.'

Serena busied herself with collecting the plates and followed Jake down the hall. So he didn't dust—who cared? Neither did she. But in every other way Jake was shaping up to be Mr Perfect.

By the time she'd wandered into the kitchen, Jake was pouring steaming espresso into delicate little cups. He took the dishes from her hands, passed her a coffee, then laced his fingers in her spare hand and tugged her towards the living room. 'We'll leave the washing up for now.'

'Fine by me.' Her eye was immediately drawn to the tall windows that almost filled one side of the room. 'Oh, wow! You've got a balcony! I've always wanted a balcony.'

'There's not much to see. In a densely populated area like this, it's just gardens and back windows.'

'Can I take a look?'

'Knock yourself out.'

She put down her coffee cup, unfastened the brass catch, and stepped through the French windows onto a narrow wrought-iron balcony. She could have spent an hour out there, listening to the shuffle of the wind in the trees and nosing into the uncurtained windows.

Jake's presence was noticeable more from the heat of his body behind hers than the sound of his footsteps. He draped his arms around her shoulders like a knotted pullover and she sank back into him.

'If I lived in this flat, I'd spend all my time out here.'

'Would you? I like the trees, but it's a bit too crowded. Still, it'll do until I've saved up for my house in the country.'

'Don't you think it looks magical? Especially now people are starting to put their Christmas lights up.'

Jake grunted. 'It's only the second week of December! Far too early for all that stuff.'

'So that's why your place is twinkle-free, is it?'

'I don't *do* Christmas lights.'

Serena thought of the dog-eared tinsel and her mother's hand-made decorations that graced the nine-foot tree in her living room. 'Shut up, you old humbug, and give me a kiss!'

She swivelled to face him and their lips met. All she was conscious of for the next few seconds was the heady mixture of Jake's lips on hers and the heat trapped between their torsos. Even after three weeks, his kisses had the power to reduce her nerve-endings to frazzles. If anything, there was a cumulative effect. It seemed impossible that each kiss could be sweeter than the last, but Jake was doing his best to give her solid empirical proof.

The mood shifted. What had started out as romantic and sensual was rapidly intensifying into something else entirely. Her guard was too far down. It was all she could do to lock her knees and keep herself from puddling to the floor. Jake's hand was under her jumper, caressing her midriff and snaking a tantalising journey up her body.

A tiny voice screeched at her from the back of her head, telling her it was too soon, too intense. She'd promised herself, no matter what, that she'd use her brain rather than her hormones to set the pace. If Jake really liked her, he'd wait…

Trembling, she let the cold air rush between their lips and slid round in the circle of his arms to face outwards again. Her heart stamped an angry beat in her chest and she took a few deep, cleansing breaths.

She closed her hands over the top of his, if only to stop the mesmerising rhythm of his fingers as he stroked her bare flesh. The slice of December wind against her face was a welcome jolt. Nearly as good as a cold shower.

However, Jake didn't seem to notice it. He nuzzled into the side of her neck and placed tiny kisses along her jaw. She had to do something to break the spell, so she straightened a little and ordered herself to pay attention to the view.

'Isn't it fascinating—looking into all the windows, watching other people go about their lives?'

Jake clasped her even closer, his breath raising the sensitive hairs inside her ears.

'Riveting.'

She struggled to ignore the exquisite tickle of his lips on her earlobe. She was pretty sure if anyone took an X-ray of her insides right now, they'd be staring at a quivering mass of strawberry jelly.

She picked a window and focused intently on a mother pacing a repetitive circuit with a tiny baby propped on her shoulder. Although the pane muffled any sound, she could tell by the infant's red scrumpled face that it was not in a happy place. Every few seconds they disappeared as the woman changed direction, but she always reappeared in the same place.

The hypnotic quality of her movements was certainly working on Serena, who suddenly noticed Jake's hands had worked free of hers. The combination of lips and fingertips was fatal. Her eyes slid closed and her lips parted. A tiny intake of breath that sounded very much like an *ah* brought her to her senses slightly.

Focus, girl. *Focus.*

She wrenched her eyelids open and searched for another window. Two floors down, she found one. A couple—

married, probably—pottered around their kitchen. He stirred a pot; she opened a bottle of wine. They were so unhurried, hardly making eye contact, but they moved around each other in a well-choreographed sequence they must have practised a thousand times, opening drawers and cupboards, dishing up their meal. She couldn't tear her eyes away. Even the movement of Jake's lips against her skin was almost forgotten as she watched them circling round each other in their seemingly mundane dance.

In the pit of her stomach, she ached for just a little of what they had.

'It's freezing out here, Jake. Let's go back inside.'

He made no fuss, only smiled at her and opened the door for her to step through. Once inside, he fastened the catch and closed the curtains, so not a chink of the outside world remained visible.

But in her imagination she could still see the couple, sitting at a little square table, swapping stories from their day at work. She gave him an easy smile, sweet with promise. He touched her hand as she reached for her glass...

Serena tried to erase the image by taking an active interest in her surroundings. Jake's furniture was expensive. Classic designs with a modern twist. She could have opened the pages of any one of the aspirational interior design magazines at the supermarket and seen something identical. Almost.

As she looked more closely, she noticed elements that jarred. There were too many books for a truly minimalist look—and not just work-related tomes. Novels, poetry and biographies jostled for position on the cluttered shelves. Colourful modern art canvases hung on the walls. She would have expected abstract designs in beige and brown, not Kandinsky and Chagall. In the corner, a glossy acoustic guitar with a ratty strap was propped up against a small table.

'Do you play?' she asked, nodding towards it.

'I used to.'

'Not any more?'

'Well…I pick it up now and again. I'm very rusty. I just don't have the time.'

'Play me something.'

Jake shifted in his seat. Ridges appeared on his forehead. 'You don't want to hear me twanging away after listening to your old man. I wouldn't compare favourably.'

'Pass it here, then.'

'Yes, Miss.'

She sat the guitar on her lap and, one at a time, pressed the fingers of her left hand onto the strings. It took all her concentration to strum the few bars of the only song she knew. It was about as comfortable and familiar as bungee jumping. She stopped mid-verse and looked at Jake. His eyebrows were hitched halfway up to his hairline.

'That has to be the worst rendition of "Scarborough Fair" I've ever heard.'

She bowed slightly in acknowledgement. 'The musical gene obviously took one look at me and decided to leap-frog a generation.'

'Not a carbon-copy of your father, then?'

'I don't think you'd find me half as attractive if I was.'

He laughed. 'You're right there!'

She clapped a decisive hand against the front of the guitar. 'Anyway, my point is this: anything you produce can only be a step up from my paltry efforts.'

He thrust out a hand. 'I don't think I can resist you in anything.'

She passed him the guitar and settled back into the sofa as he reprised the song she'd just butchered.

'You're good,' she said, when he had finished a verse and a chorus.

'I'll take that as a compliment, from a woman who knows what good guitar sounds like even if she can't reproduce it.'

'Did you ever think of taking it further?'

'A career, you mean?'

'I suppose.'

'Not really. I needed to be sure I could earn a living so I could get Mum and Mel off the estate. Accountancy won out over music in that respect, no question.'

'Do you ever wish you'd had another choice?'

He shook his head. 'My life is exactly what I planned it would be. I wouldn't change a thing.'

His answer made her heart sink a little. She knew she *wanted* safe and predictable in her future husband, but a wayward part of her still hankered after the creativity and verve of an artistic temperament.

Yes, and look where that has got you in the past! Stomped on, taken for granted and broken-hearted. Don't even go there!

While she had been arguing with herself, Jake had started strumming the guitar again. He was staring into space, not even watching his hands, yet they seemed to remember the chords of the haunting tune he played all on their own. She closed her eyes and let the gentle thrumming wash over her, until it petered out a few minutes later.

'That was beautiful. What was it?'

'Just something I wrote when I was younger. I've messed around with it for years, but I can never seem to find the right way to finish it.' He shrugged and slipped the guitar over the edge of his chair to rest against the bookcase. 'Guess I never will.'

'Don't stop. It's very relaxing.'

He swung the guitar back onto his lap and started picking away at the strings. She sipped her coffee and watched him lose himself in the rise and fall of the melody his fingers were weaving. He looked different while he was absorbed like that. Less polished, more vulnerable. A tingling feeling flared inside her as she realised she was seeing a side to Jake he normally kept well camouflaged. An imaginative, creative side that was totally at odds with the conservative suits and accounts ledgers.

Then it hit her like a kick in the stomach. This accountant had the soul of a musician!

It was at that exact moment Serendipity felt the familiar slap of a right hook out of nowhere.

'Jake, I'm scared! I don't know where we are!'

'All will be revealed shortly.'

She liked surprises as much as the next girl, but being dragged round half of London with a woolly scarf covering her eyes was too much. Jake had insisted on securing it round her head while they were in the taxi he'd hailed outside the restaurant. As if dinner at a Moroccan restaurant, sitting on cushions and feeling pampered and exotic, hadn't been enough, Jake now had something else up his sleeve. Something she was starting to wish would stay tucked up there.

She prised her fingers from the metal railing and let him guide her down a never-ending flight of stone stairs. It took all her resolve not to grab the rail and hang on for dear life. Every other step she felt she was falling, but Jake's warm strong hand was there, steadying her, making her feel safe.

Finally her feet reached a large, blessedly flat area. 'Can I take this off now?'

Jake's hand swatted her fingers away from the knot behind her head. 'Not yet.'

The scent of his aftershave clung to the fibres of the scarf, overloading her nostrils. It was as if he was wrapped around her. Apart from the odd twinkle of what she presumed to be streetlights through the weave, she could see nothing. The gentle slap of waves against stone told her they were some-where near the river—probably the Thames embankment.

Jake's arm circled her waist and he propelled her forwards into the unnerving clatter of footsteps that swirled around them. Wherever they were, it was busy. After a minute or so, he came to a halt.

'Wait there. I'll only be a couple of steps away.'

'No! Don't let go!'

'You'll be perfectly safe. I just need to have a word with this young man over here.'

She clutched onto him with her gloved hand, but he pulled away gently.

'Trust me. I'll be with you in less than a minute.'

She heard him take a few steps, and his murmured voice mixed with another. She shuffled slightly in his direction and bumped into someone.

'Sorry!' she exclaimed, not even knowing whether she was talking to the person she'd barged into. She didn't dare move again, so she just stood there, letting the crowds eddy past her.

His arm enclosed her again. 'This way.'

The hard stone beneath her heels gave way to a clanging metal ramp. Where on earth were they? Soon they came to a stop. Jake steered her to face a certain direction.

'Now, Serena, it is very important that when I say *go*, you take a big step forwards. Okay?'

She nodded, suddenly feeling as if she was about to walk the plank. The lapping of water was louder, almost beneath her feet.

'Ready…?' She clenched her elbows to her sides, palms raised in front of her to ward off the danger she couldn't see.

'Go!'

She clamped her already blindfolded eyes shut and took the biggest step she could—feeling it was more a leap of faith—then clung on to Jake for all she was worth.

'We're moving!' she squeaked, then gripped him even tighter as she realised they weren't just moving sideways, they were climbing upwards too!

Jake just laughed softly, and kissed her forehead.

'Happy Birthday, Serena.' He prised his arms from her grasp, gently freed the knot in the scarf and pushed it back over her head.

'You can open them now. It's perfectly safe.'

She parted her eyelashes slowly, dazzled by the twinkling lights all around her. They were inside something. Her eyes just could not make sense of what she was seeing. Images jumbled into her brain. Lights…metal…glass. Then it all fell into place…

'We're on the London Eye!'

'You said you'd always wanted to go on it that day we had lunch at Maison Blanc.'

'How sweet of you to remember!'

She fell silent and took a good look around her. They were alone inside one of the egg-shaped glass and metal pods on the giant wheel almost directly across the Thames from the Houses of Parliament. She'd never seen London look so beautiful. It hardly felt as if they were moving, but slowly they were climbing into the night sky. A whole city of Christmas lights below twinkled just for them. She pressed her nose against the glass and stared.

The unmistakable pop and hiss of a champagne cork made her turn round. He was smiling that wonderful, heart-melting smile of his, and pouring champagne into a pair of glasses that seemed to have appeared from nowhere, along with an ice-bucket.

'How did you do all this?'

'It took a little bit of planning, but it wasn't impossible. I told you we had a little catching up to do to make you feel special.'

'I think you've done it all in one night!'

'What makes you think this is all there is?'

'There's more?'

'You haven't had your present yet.'

She looked past him to the ice-bucket. No brightly wrapped parcel stood beside it. She bent down and looked under the oval-shaped wooden bench in the centre of the pod. Nothing.

'So where is it? No, don't tell me—you're having it helicoptered in when we get a little higher?'

He laughed and patted the breast pocket of his jacket. 'It's right here, but I was going to wait until we got to the top to give it to you.'

Serena swallowed. It was getting hard to think.

Her present was obviously very special. After all, he was making the act of giving it to her a monumental occasion.

And it was small enough to fit into his pocket.

It couldn't be…could it?

No. That was a stupid idea! It was far too soon.

Jake handed her a glass of champagne and stood beside

her to survey the patchwork of the London skyline. They sipped in silence as the pod climbed higher, but she couldn't concentrate on the illuminations on Battersea Bridge, or St Paul's Cathedral. All she could think about was what might be sparkling inside his suit pocket.

It seemed as if the wheel had gone into slow motion. It took a torturously long time for their pod to reach the apex. Just as they watched the one above theirs start to descend, Jake turned towards her and looked deep into her eyes. The entire herd of butterflies resident in her stomach stampeded and came to settle, fluttering madly, in her chest.

'I want you to know you are the most fascinating woman I've ever met...'

Her mouth went dry.

'I don't think anyone has had the effect on me that you do. And, because of that, I want to give you something that is uniquely for you—something I've never given to anybody else.'

Her eyes followed his right hand as it slipped inside his jacket and reached into the pocket that covered his heart. When it reappeared, it was holding a small, velvet-covered jewellery box. Square. Ring-sized.

One hand flew to her mouth and she clutched the glass of champagne as if it were a lifeline. She was no longer aware of the motion of the giant wheel. It seemed to have stopped on her in-breath. The world paused as they floated high above a sea of sparkling diamonds.

He faced the box towards her and gently eased the lid open, to reveal the most wonderful...

CHAPTER FIVE

EARRINGS?

She looked up at him. His eyes held a question.

She checked the box again, just to make sure she was seeing straight.

No, she was right. It was definitely a pair of silver earrings sitting on the velvet cushion. Actually, they were the most exquisite design of interwoven ivy, completely unlike anything she'd ever seen before. They were really...*her*. They just weren't...

She ignored the fact that her stomach had plummeted from where they were suspended mid-air to the slime-coated riverbed below, and choked out the only words that came to mind.

'They're...earrings.'

Jake frowned. He almost let that mask of his slip. Just for a split-second he looked really vulnerable. 'You don't like them?' He shook his head slightly. 'I was sure the designer's work was just your taste, but—'

'No, Jake. They're amazing. Really.'

He searched her face.

'Then why do you look as if you're just about to cry?'

She set her glass down on the bench, took his head in her hands and kissed away his frown. When she thought she'd stopped shaking enough to sound convincing, she pulled away.

'Jake. The earrings are stunning. Nobody has ever given me a present that suited me so well. In fact, they don't just suit me, they sum me up.' And she didn't have to lie. They were perfect. He'd obviously had them made just for her. 'I'm just crying because I'm so…happy.'

The first of a hundred tears was poised and ready at the corner of her eye. She hugged him hard as it escaped down her cheek and screwed her face up against his shoulder, willing the other ninety-nine to stay put.

'Let me put them in for you.'

She moved back enough to remove the hoops she already wore, and dropped them in her coat pocket. Jake took one of the delicate earrings from the box between his fingers and aimed for the hole in her earlobe.

'Ow!' The spike of the earring stabbed tender flesh.

'I'm hurting you.'

'No. Well, a little. Maybe I'm better off on my own.' She forced the corners of her mouth upwards. 'Why don't you get me a refill?'

By the time he'd returned, with a full glass of champagne, both earrings were securely fastened in place.

'You're sure you like them?'

She pressed a delicate kiss onto his cheek. 'I love them.' *I love you.*

'Well…okay. Good.'

They spent the last ten minutes of the ride in silence. He seemed a little distant. She hoped desperately that he hadn't caught her awkward stutter when she'd opened the box. It didn't matter that the little velvet cube hadn't contained what her over-active imagination had conjured up. They'd been seeing each other less than a month. It had been crazy to think…

She would probably laugh about it in the morning when she spoke to Cass on the phone.

The pod reached the landing and the doors whooshed open. Back into the real world. Dirt, noise, pollution. Nothing like the fairytale scene from the top of the wheel at all, really.

Jake stood in front of the black-painted door and waited for the chime of the doorbell to fade. Part of him wished she wasn't there, that the door would stay shut.

'Hey! Up here.'

He squinted and looked up. Serena was leaning out of a first-floor window, looking extraordinarily beautiful, with her dark hair falling forwards and a huge smile on her face. She was so pleased to see him. He felt like an utter heel.

She pointed to a narrow passageway at the side of the enormous Chelsea townhouse. 'Come round to the back door. I'll meet you down there.'

By the time he'd ducked under the ivy that threatened to block the path and pushed the heavy back door open, she was already in the spacious basement kitchen, filling the kettle. She heard the squeak of his soles on the tiles and left the tap running as she rushed over to give him a hug.

Her soft lips brushed his cheek. Touching her had seemed so natural only a few days ago, yet now he couldn't find the proper place to put his hands. He eased out of her arms and sat down on a stool near a breakfast bar.

She turned the tap off and clicked the kettle on. 'I'm very flattered you raced over here in your lunch break to see me.'

Jake shifted his weight on the stool. 'I have some important news.'

News you're not going to like.

'Good news or bad news?'

He didn't answer. She stopped getting cups out of the cupboard and took a good look at him. 'It's bad news, isn't it?'

'Good news, really,' he said, trying to smile. 'It just feels like bad news.'

That was the truth. He didn't want to do this, but he had no other option. He really liked her, and had hoped they'd continue to see each other for quite a while, but he'd seen the way she'd looked at the jewellery box the other night. It had taken him completely by surprise.

He'd thought he'd been safe from all of that with her. It had been short-sighted of him to go over the top with her birthday celebrations, but he'd enjoyed watching her face light up at each revelation.

So stupid of him to think he could do all that and not give her the wrong impression! She was a woman, after all. And, just like any other woman, she wanted more than he could possibly give. He was almost cross at her for making him believe otherwise.

'Jake, you're starting to worry me! Is somebody ill?'

'No. Nothing like that. It's just...I've been thinking about this for a while, and I know the time is right...'

She waved him on. 'And?'

'I'm opening a branch of my firm in New York.'

'But that's wonderful!' Pride in him radiated from her in bucketloads. He felt like something that should be scraped off on the door mat.

'There's a catch.'

'Oh?'

'I'm going to have to spend a lot of time over there in the

next few months. In fact, I'm due to fly out tomorrow and I won't be back until mid-January.'

Her cheeks paled. 'Not even for Christmas?'

'No. Mum and Mel might fly out for a visit, but I won't be back.'

'Then…when will I see you?'

'This is what I wanted to talk to you about.' He looked down at his bunched fists on the counter and deliberately splayed his fingers. Looking her in the eye was harder than it should have been. He'd given similar speeches before, but he'd never felt this awkward. He took a deep breath and squared his shoulders. He wasn't going to wimp out now. 'I'm not going to have much time for anything but the new office for a while, so I think we should cool things off for a bit.'

Her mouth dropped open, then she inhaled and looked away. She hadn't seen that one coming. 'Just exactly how cold are we talking about?'

Cruel to be kind, remember! Tell her.

'I don't think we should see each other any more. Long-distance relationships never work.'

'They can if you want them to. And you're not going to be gone for ever. There's the phone, and e-mail…' She trailed off. 'Oh. Stupid me. This is a brush-off.'

'I—'

'Don't bother, Jake. I can smell that kind of crap a mile off. I've heard it enough times to know when I'm sniffing the genuine article.'

He didn't know what else to say. All he could do was look at her angry, flushed face while his stomach churned.

'What's the real reason?'

'I'm going to be busy—'

She marched over to him and leaned across the counter to look him in the eye. 'I want the truth.'

He stared into her beautiful chocolate eyes. She was right. She didn't deserve side-stepping and half-truths. He could have waited a few more months to open the New York branch, and even then he needn't have stayed away for so long.

'You really want the truth?'

'I really do.'

'You're not going to like it.'

'I don't care. It's got to be better than playing second fiddle to four walls and a fax machine! I thought we had something, Jake. Something special.'

'We do—we did. But it's just not going to work out. It's better to end it now, before anyone gets hurt.'

Her eyes narrowed. She bit her lip and shook her head.

Okay, that had been stupid. She was hurt already. He knew that. That was why he was cutting her loose, to make sure he didn't do any more damage. And yet this goodbye was almost as hard on him as it was on her. This time he wouldn't be walking away without a backward glance. He was really going to miss Serena—her sense of fun, her warmth and openness, the sense that there was always another mystery waiting to be unravelled.

Then he knew why ending it with her was so hard. He'd never felt like this before, not even with Chantelle. Never considered the possibility that there was a woman out there who matched him completely. But here she was, standing in front of him, and if anything it made walking away worse. It was easy to waltz through life, believing he had immunised himself against fairytales, but it wasn't so easy to walk away knowing that if things were different—if *he* were different—he could have had it all.

The phrase 'if only' kept echoing in his head. If only he

could believe in fairytales. If only he could make her truly happy. If only…

She wanted honesty? She was going to get it. Even if it left him feeling naked. He owed her that.

'You thought I had something else in that little black velvet box, didn't you?'

Her lips started to form a denial, but the words never left her mouth. She let out a puff of air. Colour crept into her cheeks and she stared at the floor.

'Is that so terrible?'

'No. It's just…' God, he wanted to haul her into his arms and tell her everything would be okay. But he couldn't. It never would be where they were concerned. 'I'm not the marrying kind, Serena. I don't have it in me.'

She looked up, shocked, as if she'd never considered the possibility that, deep down, everybody didn't hunger for a soul mate.

'How do you know unless you try?' Her voice was soft and shaky. He knew it was taking all the guts she had to ask him that.

'I just know. It wouldn't be fair to carry on.'

She covered her mouth with her hand. A tear rolled down her face.

'If I really thought I could do the lifelong commitment thing, there's no one I've come closer to wanting it with—'

'Stop!' Her voice broke, and she took a large gulp before she continued. 'I don't want to hear any more.'

She walked over to the door and held it open for him. He hesitated, then decided to do as she asked. There was nothing he could do to make it better. She kept her head turned away from him. He kissed her lightly on the cheek, hoping it would say all the sorrys he wanted to. She squeezed her eyes shut as the tears started to run in thick trails.

He stepped though the door into the bleak winter sunshine. It slammed behind him, and as he walked up the alleyway he could hear her sobbing.

Serena grabbed the alarm clock from the bedside table, threw it somewhere else, and burrowed back under the duvet.

The ringing continued.

She poked her nose out and opened one eye to look at the clock. It wasn't there. Somewhere in her sleep-fog she knew there was a good reason it wasn't sitting next to the lamp, but she had no idea what that reason might be. The clanging of the alarm against her eardrums was making any efforts at conscious thought impossible.

Hair fell in front of her face as she propped herself up and tried to get her bearings. That was the thing about sitting up half the night crying into your cocoa—when you finally got to sleep, it was next to impossible to wake up again.

She spotted the alarm clock against the skirting under the window. The battery and casing lay a few feet away. Then what on earth…?

Phone.

She grabbed the receiver of the clunky old-fashioned phone next to her bed and jammed it against her ear. 'Yes?'

'Ren? Is that you?'

'Cass? What are you doing, calling at this godawful hour?'

'It's ten-thirty.'

'It can't be.'

'Well, it is. Look at the clock.'

Easier said than done.

'Okay, okay, it's ten-thirty. Where's the fire?'

'You were supposed to be here at ten, remember?'

Oops!

'Sorry. It slipped my mind.'

'Well, it can slide right back in again, then, can't it? I thought your New Year's resolution was to find something to do while your dad is in rehab.'

Serena flumped back on the pillows and flopped the duvet over her face, phone still clamped to her ear. 'That was almost a month ago. Everyone knows that New Year's resolutions expire on January the third—the fifth at the latest.'

'Well, you said you would help with the youth music project, and I'm counting on you, resolution or not.'

'You don't really need me. After all, what can I do? I don't know anything about kids. All I know is the music industry. I'd probably just be a liability.'

'I've had enough. It's exactly *because* you work in the music industry that you're going to be useful. It's a *music* project, remember? And they're teenagers, not toddlers. You'll be fine. To be honest, I think it's about time you stopped wallowing.'

Serena stared at the rose-printed fabric in front of her nose. 'I'm not wallowing.'

'Then sit up, take the duvet off your head, and get out of bed.'

Serena stuck her tongue out at the phone. That was the trouble with best friends. They knew too much.

'I'm allowed to be a little depressed. I loved him.'

She heard Cassie sigh. 'I know you think you did, but you didn't really know him.'

'I knew enough.'

'Not enough to know he didn't want to settle down and produce your football team for you. I would have thought that was a pretty important piece of info to have.'

Serena was going to say she *had* known, because Jake had seemed so…

She punched a fist against the duvet above her head while she tried to think of the word she was looking for. It was on the tip of her tongue…

Then it hit her. She'd said it herself. It was all about how Jake had *seemed* to her, the assumptions she'd made. Nothing he'd said, or done, had ever given her the impression he'd been looking for marriage. He'd just looked the part, ticked all the right boxes.

Pity she hadn't noticed that, somewhere in the small print, the *ready for commitment* box was glaringly empty. She closed her eyes and groaned. Had she really been more in love with the idea of Jake than the real man?

'Ren?'

'Sorry, Cass. Miles away.'

'Just be here by twelve, will you?' Cassie's voice had softened, but Serena knew she wouldn't leave her alone until she'd bucked herself up. There was no arguing with Cass when she got all matron-like.

'Okay, okay. See you later.'

She pushed the duvet away and let the receiver drop back into its cradle with a satisfying thunk. She swung her legs out of bed and sat staring at the wall. The floor was cold against her bare feet.

She couldn't stay in bed all day, moping about Jake. She had to do something before the pity party spiralled out of control. As it was, she'd probably pushed the share price of Cadbury's up single-handedly.

The house was totally silent. She could hear nothing but the ebb and flow of her own breath. For months she'd been badgering her dad to go into rehab. Now he was there, the house felt the size of the Albert Hall. She hadn't realised how much time and energy it took minding her dad until now, when it was somebody else's job for a bit. And, if things worked out, he wouldn't need her as much when he came back home in six weeks' time. What was she going to do?

She thought back to the conversation she'd had with Jake in the park that day. Running away with the circus was still an option. She smiled. A maverick tear escaped from one eye and dripped onto her pyjamas, and the brick of lead that had been substituted for her heart contracted.

I miss you, Jake.

But he was right. She had a life to lead. She needed to find some other purpose than running around after her father. And while she was working out what that was, she might as well go and help Cassie with *her* mission in life.

'Grab the bag from the boot and follow me.'

Serena did as instructed, then jumped back as the car's central locking system beeped. Only when Cassie turned a corner round a dingy block of 1960s houses did she start to jog after her.

'Cass, wait!'

Cassie stopped to let her catch up, then set off again at a blistering pace.

'Where are we? I thought this youth thingy was going to happen in the church hall.'

'Steve's decided if we really want to reach the kids on these estates, we can't expect them to walk into a stuffy old church.'

Stuffy? Hah! They could hear the electric guitar and drums three streets away when Steve was leading a service.

'St Peter's has the least stuffy services I've ever been to.'

Cass grinned with pride. 'I know that, and you know that, but the kids that live here don't. We've decided to revamp the old community centre here on this estate for the youth music project. If the mountain won't come to Mohammed...'

'I think you're mixing your faiths up.'

Cassie waved her objection away. 'It's the same principle.'

They stopped outside a low, graffiti-covered building in the shadow of a great tower block. The community centre had a row of narrow safety-glass windows that circled the building. Despite the grilles protecting them, every single one was broken.

'You can't mean to use *this* place.'

'We can. All it needs is a sweep-out, and a bit of a clean today. The glazier and carpenter are coming tomorrow, and then we're going to get busy with some paintbrushes. We have exactly a week to get this place ship-shape.'

'You keep saying "we".'

'Too right. Don't chicken out on me now, darlin'.'

Serena sighed and looked up at the neighbouring block of flats as Cassie unlocked the doors. Her heart skipped a beat.

This was Jake's estate.

He'd pointed out these very towers the afternoon they'd picnicked in the park. She glanced between the three blocks of flats that dominated the housing estate, but she had no idea which one had been his.

Cass's voice echoed from inside the community centre. 'Are you coming, or are you going to stand there all day and admire the scenery?' Serena followed her inside just in time to catch the pair of thick yellow rubber gloves that Cassie had flung in her direction. 'I'll move this old furniture out and you can sweep up.'

She pulled the gloves on and picked up a broom that was resting against the wall. She needed time to assimilate this new information, and she might as well do something mind-less while she did so.

A couple of hours passed quickly as they immersed them-selves in their tasks. Serena couldn't dispel the uncomfortable feeling she got from being on the Ellwood Green estate. It was as if she were trespassing. She couldn't help thinking Jake wouldn't like it if he knew she was here.

When they stopped for a break, Serena stared out of a jagged hole in one of the windows.

'That person's popular,' she said over her shoulder to Cassie.

'Who?'

'The person in that flat up there, on the second balcony. Quite a few people have gone in and out in the last hour.'

Cassie peered through a hole in the neighbouring window. 'I think I know who it belongs to.'

'You do?'

'He's definitely *not* the most likeable guy on the estate.'

'Then how come he's got so many visitors?'

Cassie slung an arm over her shoulder and shook her head. 'You really do live in the proverbial ivory tower, don't you?'

'What do you mean?'

'He's a dealer. Drugs.'

Serena gasped. 'But some of them are kids! Barely old enough to be out of primary school!'

Cassie shrugged. 'They use the local kids as look-outs and runners. In a couple of years' time, those same kids will be part of the network, earning them even more cash when they sell to their school-friends.'

She stared at Cassie in disbelief. 'I don't understand why they get mixed up with people like that in the first place.'

Cassie dragged her out through the front door and turned

her to face the car park nearby. 'See that big black BMW parked over there?'

She nodded.

'It's his—the dealer's. He's well-known round here. The kids in this place grow up with next to nothing. They see this guy, with his designer clothes, thick gold jewellery and flash cars, and they want it too. You can't blame them, really. They don't want to be stuck here for the rest of their lives, on the dole or in dead-end jobs like their parents. Who wants to wipe greasy tables or pick up rubbish for a living? Mr Big up there is the only role-model for success they see at close range.'

'That's so sad.'

'Exactly,' said Cassie, slapping a cloth into her hand. 'That's why this project is so important. It might not be much, but it's a start. We can show them there's something better to do with their time, that they have other options.'

Serena's face settled into a mask of determination. 'Let's go, then! What do you want me to do next?'

Cassie grinned and handed her a huge bottle of cream cleaner. 'See that little kitchen over there...?'

Serena had an epiphany while she scrubbed.

Her childhood might not have been perfect, but it could have been a hell of a lot worse! So she'd lost her mother. At least she'd had twelve good years before her mum died. Some of the kids on this estate had probably never even met their fathers.

She scraped frantically at a bit of burnt-on grime on the electric hob. She'd spent a lot of her life feeling rather sorry for herself, when really she had so much to be thankful for. The lyrics from some of Steve's 'happy-clappy' songs suddenly made a lot more sense.

* * *

The little kitchenette gleamed. Serena stood back with her hands on her hips and surveyed her work, glad she'd forced herself out of bed that morning. Okay, glad Cassie had forced her out of bed that morning. Helping Cass had given her an unexpected dose of perspective.

She wiped her forehead with the glove-free part of her arm. 'I need some fresh air,' she called.

Cassie appeared, with a full dustpan and brush in her hand. The dust in her hair had turned it a rather dirty shade of pink. 'I need something cold and fizzy. Do you want to nip out to the newsagents and get us something to drink?'

Serena peeled her gloves off and left them on the counter. 'Where is it?'

'Follow the path to the left, past the nearest block of flats. When you come to the end, go left again and you should see a row of shops.'

Serena nodded, checked her jeans pocket for change, then walked out into the bright January afternoon.

She had been walking for less than a minute when she became aware of someone behind her. Not too close, but close enough, keeping pace almost. She slowed down a little to give whoever it was a chance to overtake. The footsteps matched her own.

Her heart began to thump even before she picked up speed again.

This was ridiculous! It was probably some old lady on her way to the bingo. But if that were the case why was she scared to turn round and take a look?

She wanted to break into a jog. Instead, she tightened her stomach muscles and glanced quickly over her shoulder, hoping to be rewarded by a nod from an old dear in a tweed coat.

It was a man.

More than that was hard to say. His woollen hat was pulled down over his ears and a scarf was knotted round his neck, covering his chin and mouth. He'd burrowed even further into the turned-up collar of his scruffy grey overcoat when she'd sneaked a look at him.

He wasn't doing anything threatening, wasn't getting any closer, but it just didn't feel right. Her palms itched and cold air sliced her throat as she drew it into her lungs.

They were almost in the shadow of the tower. The path ran right next to the block of flats, under the overhanging balconies of the upper floors. It looked as if it was designed to be a shelter for the entrance, but it felt as if she would be hemmed in after the open space of the walkway. The only alternative was to turn and face him, and she certainly didn't want to do that!

Suddenly she was running towards twenty storeys of concrete and dirty glass. She shoved one of the heavy double doors open and jabbed a finger on the lift button, taking care to breathe through her mouth. The foyer reeked like a public toilet.

She glanced outside, through the glass-panelled doors. He was getting closer, but it was impossible to tell if he was just going to walk past or follow her inside.

The lift machinery was ominously silent. No distant *dings* of the lift on upper floors. No lights on the display. She pressed the button one last time, then darted up the staircase without waiting for a result. The sound of her footsteps bounced off the walls in the confined space. She counted off thirty steps then stopped, a foot poised on the next step so she was ready to set off again.

Nothing. No sound behind her. It would have been hard to climb those stairs without making a noise. She slouched against the wall and caught her breath.

What to do now? She didn't want to go back downstairs just yet and risk running into the grey overcoat. She glanced up the stairs.

Fourteenth floor, Jake had said.

Her feet set up a rhythm on the stairs again, slower this time.

Each landing looked like the last. The floor numbers on the walls were often obscured by neon spray paint. Nothing artistic, though. Just name tags and obscene phrases. Finally, she stood beside the plaque reading '14' and gulped oxygen into her lungs, her calf muscles screaming.

Her destination was a bit of an anticlimax. Somehow she'd thought she would have a sense of arrival, that something in the narrow corridor would shout, *Jake was here!* But all she saw was a row of identical blue doors. At the end of the corridor was a large window. She walked up to it and looked out on Jake's world.

The greyness seemed to spread in every direction from the base of the block of flats for miles and miles. The oasis of Greenwich Park was nowhere to be seen. She must be looking in the wrong direction.

In her imagination, she tried to picture Jake as he would have been fifteen years ago—baggy jeans with rips and a baseball cap. Would his dark hair have been longer and shaggier, or would it have been a crew cut? The image wouldn't come. She could only see him in crisp shirts and designer suits, his hair neat, never a tuft sticking up. She didn't know the Jake of Ellwood Green at all.

But she understood *her* Jake better—the need to succeed at his career, his love of fine things and first-class service. It was a world away from the scene she looked down upon now. He'd talked about how he'd wanted to escape, and he'd done it. She admired him for that. It was a testament to his drive and determination that *his* BMW was parked in the underground garage of his office, and not in the car park downstairs as he waited for the next knock on the front door.

She walked back to the stairwell and started her descent. Once at ground level, she stayed well back from the doors and searched for any sign of a grey coat. When she was sure it was safe, she eased the door open and peeked out, grateful for the relief from the acrid stench of the foyer.

No sign. She let out a large breath and waited, half-in, half-out the door, for another minute before setting off again.

It wasn't long before she spotted the small parade of shops. The newsagents sat between a boarded-up unit and a launderette.

She picked a couple of bottles out of the cold cabinet inside and took them to the counter. A pair of chatting teenage girls hushed and watched her hand over the coins to the shop-keeper. She stuffed her change into her back pocket and scurried out of the shop.

Jake's roots were here. It was his world. And she clearly didn't belong.

Jake rested his elbows on the bar of the trolley and scanned the luggage carousel for his cases. A willowy blonde woman on the other side of the conveyor belt made eye contact. Normally he would have stood up and smiled, but instead he picked a case to watch and pretended he hadn't seen her.

London was a big city, but a homing beacon was calling out to him. His mind was tuned to wherever *she* was. It had been the same in New York. A little *blip-blip-blip* constantly on his radar. And now he was home, it was stronger than ever.

CHAPTER SIX

Icy rain battered the windows of the community hall. Serena looked over to Cassie and sighed. It was eight o'clock already and no one had turned up, just like last week.

She glanced across at Mel, Cassie's project worker, who had propped her elbows on the coffee bar and rested her chin in her hands. Her heartstrings twanged unexpectedly. Mel looked so much like her brother—the same dark hair, blue eyes and intense expression—but, unlike Jake, Mel wore her heart on her sleeve. She didn't lock a little part of herself away from the world and smooth over the cracks with a smile.

It didn't matter. Where Jake wore his heart and what he did with it was none of her business. He was four thousand miles away. She closed her eyes and willed herself to think of something else.

Steve suddenly stood up from the stool he'd been perched on. 'We're going to have to call in reinforcements, gang! It's half term in two weeks, and we want the daily workshops full.'

'How are we going to do that?' Serena looked at the circle of empty chairs. 'It's going to take a miracle.'

A slow smile spread across Steve's face. 'Miracles are my speciality—or, in this case, yours.'

'Mine?'

'I don't know why I didn't think of it before! Your dad must have tons of contacts in the music business. Can you think of someone—*anyone*—who would help us out? We need a name. Someone to attract the kids.'

Serena looked at the ceiling and scrunched up her face. A couple of seconds passed and she smiled back at Steve.

'Actually, I *can* think of someone. And he owes me—big time. You'll get your name, Steve, and in time for the launch too. I guarantee it.'

Cassie bounded over and rested her chin on Serena's shoulder. 'Who is it, then?'

Serena just tapped her nose with her finger and said nothing.

Just when he'd thought he was wise to her tricks, she'd gone and done it again!

Jake stared at the phone on his desk and shook his head. One minute he'd been sorting his e-mails and listening to Mel yatter on about a great pair of boots she'd just bought, and the next he'd agreed to take a week of mornings off work for some project of hers.

He was going to have to insist on doing all communication with his sister face-to-face. She was getting far too clever.

'I can't believe it! I'm such a big fan of yours.'

Cassie was gushing. Honest-to-goodness, eighteen-carat gushing. It wouldn't be long before she shook the mystery guest's hand off. The guy didn't know what had hit him. Serena almost felt sorry for him.

She smiled to herself. And why not? She was feeling very

pleased she'd bagged an up-and-coming R&B star for the Saturday night launch of Music Week. He would generate a lot of publicity. Not only that, but he was leading a few workshops too. The estate grapevine had gone into overdrive and the community centre was packed. She studied the assorted crowd. Council dignitaries stood shoulder-to-shoulder with baggy-trousered teenagers.

Cassie finally let go of the poor man's hand. 'How ever did you manage this?' she asked Serena, eyes firmly fixed on the man flexing and stretching his fingers.

If only she knew! Who would have guessed those torturous hours babysitting little Kevin would have paid off in the end?

Big Kevin's voice was gruff in her ear. 'Yes, how *did* you wangle this one?'

'Shut up, Kevin,' she said through a clenched smile. 'Or I'll tell everyone how you used to do ballroom dancing in sparkly red jumpsuits.'

He glowered at her. 'That's blackmail.'

'Blackmail is such an ugly word. I prefer to think of it as reparation for the many pranks you played on me over the years.' Those dark times when her dad and Kevin's parents had partied until dawn and left her in charge of a twelve-year-old with a death wish. She punched his arm in mock cheerfulness. 'Remember when you *borrowed* my car and left it with an empty tank in Soho? Ah, those were the days.'

He grunted.

She hummed a bar or two of a Viennese waltz.

'Smile, *Kevin*, everybody's watching.'

'It's Daddy K to you.'

'Whatever.'

She tucked her arm into his and they turned to face the gathering crowd, their smiles little more than bared teeth.

A shiver crawled up Serena's spine. Someone was watching her—which was an absurd thing to think. At least two hundred people had their eyes trained on her and the boy wonder, but it still felt as if, somewhere in the crowd, a pair of eyes was pinning her down.

Her ivy earrings swung as she whipped her head around and met his stare.

Jake.

Her heart performed a perfect swan dive and burrowed into the toes of her boots. Never in a million years had she expected to see him here. The ghost of yesteryear, maybe, echoes of Jake that lurked in the stairwells and playground, but never the new, updated and improved version. She'd thought she'd be safe here.

Why? Why was he here? It made no sense. He'd run away so fast from this place there were still skid marks on the pavement.

Then she caught sight of Mel, looking from her to Jake and back again, and she knew why. What chance did they have against the combined forces of Cassie and Mel? Were they trying to set them up again, as if nothing had happened? Unbelievable! She was going to wipe that soppy look off Mel's face the first opportunity she got.

She looked back towards the door. It was still open. A couple of steps and she'd be out of there, running as fast as her high-heeled boots could take her.

Kevin—she refused to call him by his ridiculous stage name—tugged her forward as he approached a man in a wrinkled suit. But her boots stayed glued to the floor. She recognised the man as a local councillor who'd suddenly decided to champion the project now he had the chance of seeing his face in the paper.

Kevin took another step forward and her arm slid free of his, leaving her standing alone in the middle of the hall. The words *sitting* and *duck* came to mind.

Don't look at him. Don't look at him!

Oh, you spineless creature!

Jake hadn't moved a muscle. He was leaning against the wall, his brows crinkled together, giving Daddy K the evil eye.

He's jealous?

That was rich, considering who had dumped who! She straightened and stared at him until he made eye contact. Once that small victory was accomplished, she nudged forward and slid her arm into Kevin's again.

One of the helpers brushed past her.

'Michelle, could you shut that door for me, please? It's letting all the cold air in.'

The girl nodded and scurried away.

No more Miss Puffy-Eyed Wimp! She dug her heels into the ancient lino and did her best to ignore the heat of Jake's eyes boring into the back of her head.

An hour later the music was still pumping. Kevin was performing a couple of songs, and Serena felt like a three-year-old without her security blanket. She jostled her way through the crowd to the non-alcoholic bar and grabbed a bottle of mineral water. Then, just as she was elbowing her way out of the crush, she came face to face with the man she'd been doing her best to avoid.

Why did he have to look so gorgeous? Couldn't he have grown an extra head or broken out in boils in the last couple of months?

'Hello, Serena.' That much was easy to lip-read.

Hello, worm.

'Hello, Jake,' she shouted back.

He said something else, but she couldn't make half of it out through the throbbing music.

'Pardon?'

He leant in close to speak into her ear. After eight weeks and five days of no contact, he was pushing her into sensory overload. Not only was his breath warming her cheek, but he smelled so good! Like crisp clean shirts with a hint of after-shave.

'How have you been?'

It was just as well his questions were as inane as the answers that whirred through her head. He was far too close to make sparkling repartee a possibility. She would just be happy if her mouth moved and sound came out.

'Fine. You?'

'Fine.'

Both their pants should be on fire, figuratively speaking. She'd never seen him look so tense. Where was the effortless charm? Had he checked it in at Customs when he returned?

'We can't talk here.' His voice was just that little bit too loud in her ear and she pulled away.

'Who says we've got anything left to say to each other?'

She gave him what she hoped was a scorching look then wove her way over to the other side of the room. She undid the lid on her bottle of water and took a gulp.

'I don't want to leave things like this between us.' They were now far enough from the speakers for her to decipher his yelling.

She should have guessed he wouldn't give up that easily. On some level she'd wanted him to follow her, wanted a chance to vent her anger. The imaginary conversations she'd been having with him since Christmas could now become a reality. Perhaps then the words would stop circuiting her head as if it were a racetrack.

She screwed the lid back on her water bottle so tight the ridges burned her fingers. 'Don't pretend you care, Jake. You're the one who ended it, remember? Just be glad I'm moving on instead of stalking you.'

'Moving on?' He flashed a quick look at Kevin and the heaving mass of girls trying to storm the makeshift stage. 'You know it's not that I didn't like you—'

Serena lifted her chin and stretched her lips into a smile. 'Save it for someone who cares, Charlie.'

His jaw clenched so tight she thought his teeth would shatter. She'd hit a nerve. Good!

'You're a fake. Do you know that, Jake?'

She would swear she could actually hear his blood bubbling in response to that. Or perhaps it was the steady bass beat of Kevin's song.

'*Me?* A fake?'

'Yes, you. You look like a decent, caring man, but—' her voice was getting shrill '—but underneath you're a commitment-phobic coward like the rest of your species!' She finished her tirade and froze.

Everyone was staring at them. At her. And the music had stopped. While her lips twitched and she wondered how to dissolve into nothing, Jake grabbed her arm and yanked her out through the door.

He didn't need to shout outside. The barely contained whisper he used next was far more lethal. Her confidence evaporated.

'I didn't ever pretend to be anything I'm not. What are us guys supposed to do? Wear little flashing neon signs saying "Husband Material"? You jumped to your happy-ever-after conclusions all on your own. You saw what you wanted to see.'

Words tripped over her tongue and fell flat before they passed her teeth. What could she say? Jake smiled, but not one of his heart-melting ones. This one was cold and brittle, but his voice still came out even and normal. She hated the fact he could do that when all she could manage were squeaks and screeches.

'Anyway, you seem to have *moved on* to new pastures—or should I say happy hunting grounds? I hope the poor sucker knows what he's letting himself in for.'

'You arrogant—' She stopped herself before she said something really unladylike. 'What's so wrong with wanting a husband and a family? It's hardly abnormal! Isn't that what everyone's searching for—a little love and happiness?'

Jake stopped smiling and looked sheepish.

All the rage was suddenly sucked out of her. Why couldn't it have been him? Life was so unfair! She took a deep breath and tried to disguise her quivering lip by bowing her head.

He gently tipped her face up again by lifting her chin with his finger. 'Let's not fight. It's pointless. I've told you before that you're a unique woman, Serena. You're right, you deserve the love and happiness you're looking for.'

Oh, this was worse! His anger she could handle, but his pity…?

'Just not with you.'

'No.'

'Why not?' If she was going to embarrass herself past the point of no return, she might as well get the whole lot off her chest.

'I wouldn't make you happy. I'd break your heart.'

Too late. It's a done deal.

'How do you know unless you try?'

'I did try once. It was a complete disaster. I'm not about to mess up anyone else's life like that.'

Her stomach clenched at the thought of Jake with someone else, of him loving someone else. It wasn't that he *couldn't* commit, just that he wouldn't with her.

'There's not much I can say to that, is there?'

Jake ran his fingers through his hair. 'Look, I'm taking time off work this week, to help with some of the workshops, and if we're going to be around each other we're going to have to find a way to co-exist harmoniously.'

She sighed and nodded. He was right again, and it made her want to box his ears for being all reasonable and logical when her heart was fracturing into cold, solid lumps.

'Okay. Truce.' She offered him a hand and he took it, but instead of shaking it he just stood there looking at it, his fingers blistering her skin. Then his thumb brushed against the back of her hand, giving her a jolt of raw awareness.

They both continued to look at their joined hands.

He felt it too. He must do. For all his sane words, he was no more immune to the chemistry between them than she was. She looked up at him and saw the truth of it in his eyes as he leaned in to kiss her.

She knew she should push him away, but instead of resisting him with the hand that had flown to his chest, she slid it up behind his neck and pulled him closer.

Once they started kissing, they couldn't seem to stop. She'd kissed him many times in the few weeks they'd gone out, but this one had an edge to it. There was a hunger and a quiet desperation from him that had never been evident before. He kissed her like a drowning man gasping for air, as if he needed it to survive. Her foolish heart leapt at the knowledge.

It was Jake who dragged himself away first. She rested her

head against his shoulder, eyes still closed, and tasted him on her lips with her tongue. The courage to open her lids and look him in the face was nowhere to be found.

'I'm sorry, Serena. I shouldn't have done that. It was wrong to let…'

His voice was heavy with regret. If only the concrete slabs beneath her feet would open up and swallow her.

'What I was trying to say…before…was that we should try to remain civil—be friends, even.'

Oh, he really had no clue, did he?

Still, she nodded, opened her eyes and stared resolutely at his chest. Her hand was pressed against it again. She snatched it away.

'Of course. Friends.'

Then he turned and walked back inside, leaving her to prop herself up against the rough-plastered wall and wonder why she hadn't noticed sooner how cold it was outside.

Serena looked at her watch for the fifteenth time. Eighteen minutes past eight, Monday morning, and she was at the community centre, setting up for the day ahead. Mel had nipped out to the local shop to buy some more coffee, so she unstacked the chairs in blissful silence.

Come to think of it, Mel had been gone an awfully long time.

She stuck her head out through the front door and did a quick scan of the surrounding area. Mel's pink coat was visible some distance away. Her head was bobbing up and down furiously as she talked to a man in grey.

A cold wave crashed in Serena's tummy.

A grey coat. Just like the man who had followed her the other day. What if Mel was in trouble? She was just about to shove the door wider and race over there when Mel gave the man a hug and headed back in her direction.

Serena peered at the stranger. He had his back to her, and it was impossible to tell if it was the same person. This man wasn't wearing a hat and scarf. The only similarities were the colour of his coat and his height.

She shrugged and shook her head. Mel obviously wasn't bothered by him. She was probably just imagining things. Her nerves were wire-tight. It was hardly surprising if she was dreaming up trouble where there was none.

She let the door flap closed and returned to setting up the chairs and instruments for the 'Guitar for Dummies' workshop. Mel had shanghaied Jake into leading that one. She checked her watch again. Another thirty-eight minutes and he'd be here. She stood, chair held mid-air, and wished the sick feeling in her stomach away.

The thup-thup of the swing door announced Mel's return.

'I can't believe Mr Singh still runs the corner shop! I was always a little scared of him as a child, but he practically vaulted over the counter to shake my hand just now.'

'You were a long time.'

Mel paused. 'Yes…well, like I said, I was catching up with Mr Singh.'

'Who was the other man you were talking to?'

'What man?' Mel fiddled with her top button.

'The one in the grey coat.'

'Oh, him. That was no one. He was just asking for directions.'

Serena raised an eyebrow as Mel shrugged off her coat and busied herself putting the jar of coffee away.

Jake looked at the circle of faces in front of him and inwardly winced. A dozen or so teenage boys and girls were staring at him, waiting for him to impress them. He was having fantasies of making a break for it and leaving a Jake-shaped hole in the nearest wall. He'd been less terrified when Lord and Lady Balfour had summoned him to their castle to discuss streamlining their estate's finances.

Five hours of workshops this week—and there were four hours and fifty-six minutes left to go. The second hand of the badly hung clock couldn't clunk through the seconds fast enough. Then he could get out of this hellhole and back to his real life.

Knowing *she* was watching him didn't help. She was trying to pretend she wasn't watching, but she was. She was just as attuned to him as he was to her. He risked a look across at Serena. Her head was buried in a stack of registration forms. Then her pen stopped moving and she went still. A couple of seconds later she peered at him through her fringe.

See? Attuned!

The motley group in front of him began to get restless, and he turned his attention back to them. How did teenage girls manage that withering *you're-such-a-loser* look? It must be something to do with their overly tight ponytails.

When in doubt, he always fell back on his tried and trusted arsenal. He smiled, and the charm started to flow. It was like flicking a switch.

A loud *tut* from the desk near the door almost made him falter, but he launched seamlessly into his memorised lesson plan, starting with the basics: which end of the guitar was up.

Serena, meanwhile, sorted the registration forms into alphabetical order. Then into age order. Then by workshop choices. Anything to keep her eyes away from the far end of the hall.

The strangling of guitar strings didn't even register. All

she could hear was Jake's cool voice, carefully explaining basic chords. After their initial display of expected apathy, the workshop participants had settled down, and now hung on his every word. All but one.

A boy of about fifteen slouched in his plastic chair and hardly bothered to pretend he was placing his fingers in the correct position for E minor. Max something. She flipped through the registration forms again and found his.

Max Black. Age: fourteen. Address: Ellwood Green Council Estate.

Why was he here if he wasn't interested? Oh, right. Max had been recommended by his social worker in an attempt to keep him out of trouble.

She glanced across at the boy. It was stupid to think this way, but it felt good to know that there was at least one human being immune to the charms of Charles Jacobs, Jr. She was tempted to go and high five Max for that very fine accomplishment, because she was doing a miserable job of being immune to him herself.

With ten minutes of the workshop left, there was an outburst. Max had got fed up with acting bored, and tried to join in with the simple tune the rest of the group were strumming. Since he hadn't paid attention, his fingers tripped over the chord changes and he couldn't keep up.

Serena watched Max grind his teeth, then his face flushed deep pink—the only warning an explosion was imminent. He hurled his guitar on the floor, kicked his chair out of the way and stormed out.

The rest of the group froze, eyes wide. The gentle reverberation of the chord they'd just played hung in the air. They all looked at Jake and waited for him to go ballistic.

Of course he did nothing of the sort. He calmly righted

the upturned chair, sat the dented guitar up against it, and carried on as if nothing had happened.

From her vantage point near the door, she could still see Max. He was hovering in the shadow of one of the tower blocks. He was too far away to make out his expression, but even at that distance his anger radiated in waves towards them.

She forgot to shuffle her papers and looked back at Jake. Damn him for being so totally in control of himself! She would love to see him lose it—really lose it—just once. And damn herself for wanting him more each passing day, despite his iron-clad bachelor status.

Before she'd finished lecturing herself on the pointlessness of it all, Jake had wound up the workshop and the kids had trailed back outside. He'll probably want a coffee, she thought to herself, and was just about to ask him, heart pulsating in the back of her throat, when he sprinted out through the front door, leaving her gaping.

No more than five minutes later the door crashed open and he reappeared, frog-marching Max in front of him.

'Well, Max, the damage done to the guitar is fixable, but you are going to have to work off the cost of the repairs by helping out here for the rest of the week.'

Max grunted, and glared at Jake.

Jake glared back, unmoved.

'Forget it! I'm not sticking around this dump any longer than I have to. You can take your guitar and shove it—'

'Fine. But I'm guessing that your social worker doesn't want to hear about this. I heard that you were on your last warning. But if you want me to call the police and report the incident of criminal damage that just happened here, I will be most obliged to do so.'

Max said a word no fourteen-year-old should even know,

and his feet shuffled to a halt. He looked as if he'd been sentenced to fifteen years hard labour, not a few days of floor-sweeping and coffee-making. He turned to face Jake and shoved his hands in his pockets. Jake pointed at the far corner of the room.

'We need twenty chairs, in four rows of five, for the next class, and I think it's about time you made the team a cup of tea. Put the kettle on, and you can do the chairs while it boils.'

Max stomped off in the direction of the kitchen.

'You know he's going to spit in your coffee, don't you?' Serena said in a hushed voice.

Jake laughed. 'I'll give him the one he offers me.'

'You're too smooth for your own good. Do you know that?'

They smiled at each other. Serena forced herself to re-member he was the enemy—the man who'd stolen her heart, decided he didn't want it, yet still refused to give it back. She was giving him permission to shred it into tiny pieces by weakening.

And still she couldn't stop smiling at him.

The number forty-seven bus trundled over London Bridge and Jake's shoulders unknotted. For years the Thames had been a physical and psychological barrier to his past. The bus was getting more and more crowded, but he didn't mind a bit. He could take anything now he was back on *his* side of the river.

He jumped out of his seat to offer it to a silver-haired lady with a string shopping bag. Taking the bus had been a stroke of genius. Who knew how long his BMW would have remained unmolested in the car park on the estate?

Oddly enough, he'd almost forgotten he'd left it at the office when he'd seen an almost identical model parked a short distance from the community centre. At first he'd thought that Max was wreaking revenge by breaking into his car. The boy's spiky black head had been bowed close to the driver's window. Only when he'd stepped away slightly had Jake seen that Max was talking to the driver through the open window, and he remembered he'd left his own car tucked up safe and snug in the underground car park.

But he'd still felt uneasy—this time on Max's behalf. He knew how much that car cost, almost down to the penny, and it wasn't anything law-abiding residents of Ellwood Green could dream of owning. Max was skating on thin ice by associating himself with that kind of man.

Then the BMW had pulled away. He'd listened to the tyres screeching round the corner as he and Max had eyed each other on opposite sides of the road. Max's first instinct had been to cower slightly, but then he'd straightened and swaggered towards him. The kid had guts. As Max had closed the distance between them he'd puffed himself up even more, looking as if he was expecting a fight.

But Jake had known that letting rip at him right then would only have done more damage. Max was much more scared than he'd let on. It was frightening how well he could read the boy. Not so long ago he'd been wired the same way. Max was angry at the world and didn't know how to curb his frustration, but, properly channelled, that drive and energy could be his path to a better future.

Jake's thoughts drifted to the look of admiration on Serena's face when he'd returned to the centre with Max. Her approval shouldn't mean anything to him. He didn't want it. He didn't need it. And anyway, he'd promised himself he wasn't going to think about her.

He squeezed the red button with his thumb and heard the

ding as the 'Bus Stopping' sign lit up. He nudged his way to the exit and angled himself through the double doors as they hissed open.

His building was in sight. All he needed now was to change out of these casual clothes into his suit, and his armour would be back in place.

A vagrant was huddled in the corner of the entrance, the collar on his coat turned up and his hat pulled down against the biting wind. Security would probably move the man on shortly. Jake rummaged in his pocket for a few coins and dropped them at the man's feet.

The heavy plate-glass door was already half-open when the blood in his veins ran like ice.

'Three quid? You can do better than that for your old man. Can't you, son?'

CHAPTER SEVEN

THE door slammed closed and Jake turned to stare open-mouthed as the man pulled himself to his feet.

It had been more than ten years since he'd last seen his father, and the revulsion hit him like a shockwave, hurtling him back in time.

'I have nothing to say to you.' He'd rather pull out his own fingernails than call that man Dad. He started to shove the door open again.

'I've got a couple of words to say to you, though: *Serendipity Dove*.'

Jake stilled, raw anger pounding in his head. He turned. 'What about her?'

The slimy smile his father gave made him remember why he'd always wanted to punch him. Last time the old toad had turned up he actually had. He wasn't proud of himself, but it had been a drop in the ocean compared to his teenage years when he'd been on the receiving end. He stuffed his fists in his jacket pockets.

'A little bird told me you were an item.'

'Your little bird is out of date. It's ancient history.'

'Shame. There could have been a bit of mileage in that.'

Jake invaded his 'old man's' personal space so quickly his father took a step backwards. Soon he was backed up against the polished granite wall of the entrance, and the slimy smile started to waver.

'Now, hang on, Charlie—'

'Don't call me that! It's Jake or Charles, but *never* Charlie!' Jake got his face close enough to smell the stale tobacco on his father's breath. 'Let's get this straight. If you go anywhere near her, so help me, I'll see to it you're in no fit state to ever bother anyone again!' His fists were getting restless in the confines of his pocket, so he dug them in deeper.

'Okay, okay, it was only a thought!' His father wriggled free and put some space between them. He raised his hands in an attitude of surrender.

Jake shook his head. He knew all the guy's tricks, even after a decade. Right now he was trying to defuse the situation by oozing charm, so he could attack it from another angle. In Jake's opinion, the man oozed something entirely different.

'Come on, Charlie. We're two of a kind, you and me. I always had an eye for a pretty girl myself, you know.'

'And if I remember rightly, being married to Mum didn't slow you down at all, either.'

'Your mother and I had an arrangement.'

Jake barked out a hollow laugh. 'What? You mean the one where she stayed home and cried while you went out and gambled all our money away?'

'A man's got a right to a beer and a flutter on the gee-gees every now and then.'

Did he actually believe the rubbish he was spouting?

'It was Mum's money! Money she earned scrubbing other people's floors because you were too useless to hold down a job. Mel and I almost got taken into care after you split with all our savings. Mum only just managed to make ends meet and keep us together!'

His father looked up at the gold lettering painted on the doors to the plush foyer. '"Jacobs Associates",' he read. 'Seems like you turned out all right to me.'

'No thanks to you. Now, clear off!'

'I'd be happy to. Only funds are a little short…'

'What's the matter? Have you managed to fleece every middle-aged divorcée on the Costa Blanca?'

His father shrugged.

'I'm not giving you a penny!'

'Go on, son. Ten grand and I'll be out of your hair for good, I promise. You'll never have to see me again.'

'Your promises are worth nothing! Don't you think I know that? I meant what I said. I'm not giving you anything. Now, get lost!'

The saccharine mask dropped from his father's face, and suddenly Jake could see the real man he'd always known lurked beneath: mean, selfish and spineless.

'Go away and prey on someone else.'

'All right, I will. But don't blame me when it all comes back to bite you on the backside.'

Jake folded his arms, his back against the door as if guarding it, and watched in satisfaction as his father walked away.

'I'm nothing like you!' he shouted after him. His father didn't turn round, and Jake waited until the tatty grey overcoat had disappeared into the crowds, just to make sure he was really gone.

'Nothing like you,' he muttered as he finally pushed the door open, more angry at himself than he was at his father at that moment. Angry because he knew he was lying.

* * *

The snooker ball skittered around the rickety table, then dropped into a pocket.

'Yesss!' yelled Max, punching a fist in the air. Serena smiled as she sat perched on her usual stool at the coffee bar. What a difference from the surly boy who had sloped into the community centre at the beginning of the week!

His next shot was not so lucky. The ball bounced off two cushions, then came to a halt two inches from the intended hole.

Jake tutted, then lined up his shot. 'You shouldn't count your chickens, boy. Now, stand back and let me show you how it's done.'

Talk about excess testosterone! Why did the males of the species have to turn every little challenge into a fight to the death?

Max grunted, but stared at his opponent with an obvious case of hero-worship. Jake had spent a lot of time with him this week. Serena had the feeling that nobody ever took time to be with Max. The positive attention was having a transforming effect on him. He was still a bit mouthy at times, but he'd arrived early the last two mornings to help set up for the day. And now he was hanging around after Jake's workshop had finished just so he could grab a few more minutes in the presence of his idol.

The really tragic thing was that Serena only knew Max had turned up early because she had done exactly the same thing. For exactly the same reason. Pathetic.

'The heart wants what the heart wants,' her mother had always said, and her heart wanted Jake, however much her head declared it folly.

Jake manoeuvred round the snooker table to take his next shot and gave her an unparallelled view of his denim-clad rear-end. She dropped her head to the counter and covered it with her arms. Why was she torturing herself like this?

Her *perfect husband* tick-list had been abandoned. Jake had both fulfilled and exceeded it. She'd been looking for safe and reliable when she'd met him, but she'd found so much more. He was passionate and imaginative and intuitive. All the things she'd thought were reserved for the 'creative types' she'd discounted from her search.

She'd always assumed that 'settling down' by definition included a certain amount of…well, *settling*. It was a trade-off. Passion and excitement versus companionship and security. Then, just when she'd been ready to make the sacrifice, she'd hit the jackpot.

Oh, but life was never that easy. It gave with one hand and took away with the other. Mr Right was, in fact, Mr Wrong. As much as she wanted him, he didn't want her back.

She banged her head on the coffee bar a few times to scatter her thoughts.

'Serena? You all right?' It was Jake's voice.

Her own came out muffled from underneath her folded arms. 'Yes, fine. Just…resting.' *Lame, lame, lame.*

The clacking of snooker balls continued. A triumphant shout confirmed that Jake had snatched victory from under Max's nose for the umpteenth time. She lifted an elbow and peeked out. Max was collecting snooker balls and throwing them into a cardboard box with more force than necessary.

'Loser makes the coffees—that's the deal. Off you go, upstart!'

Max turned to put the box away and she saw a smile he'd meant to hide from everyone else. 'Get 'em yourself, Grandpa!'

Hair fell across her face as she lifted her head, and she brushed it away with her hand. Max was stomping towards her with a couple of dirty mugs hooked on his fingers. She took them from him.

'I'll do the drinks, Max. You've worked really hard all week. Take a break.'

Instead of looking pleased, Max's face clouded over. 'It's the last day today.'

'Not looking forward to school on Monday?'

Max mimed slitting his own throat.

'Eeewww!'

He grinned, pleased with the reaction, then turned to look at Jake. 'Do you think he'll come on Friday nights?'

'I don't know. Jake says he doesn't *do* long term.'

They both lapsed into silence as they waited for the kettle to boil. Thankfully, her mobile phone rang.

'Hello?'

'I feel like hell.' It was Cassie. 'Steve got me to take a theology course last year, so I know what I'm talking about. I won't be coming in this morning. You've got enough adults to comply with all the regs, haven't you?

'Yes, of course,' she lied. Steve and Mel had dashed off to some emergency, but she wasn't going to tell Cassie that. 'You take care of yourself, and I'll drop by later.'

Serena ended the call and stared at her phone. They needed to have two adults present at all times. It was fine to tell Cassie it was all sorted, but in reality there was only one candidate for the post, and he was supposed to be heading back to work in ten minutes.

'Jake? I wouldn't ask if it wasn't an emergency, but could you hang on until Steve and Mel get back?'

'How long?'

She bit the corner of her lip. 'One-ish. Can you spare the time?'

He walked closer, too close, and looked her in the eyes.

'Sure. I'll make a call or two to smooth things over. But I have one condition.'

'I'm not playing snooker with you again. It's embarrassing.'

'Not snooker. Dinner.'

Her heels echoed on the floor as she took a step back. 'I don't think that's a good idea.'

'Why? Has nutrition suddenly gone out of fashion?' He smiled a great, cheeky smile. She could feel herself weakening. Still, she set her face into a frown and answered him. 'You know why.'

'Lunch, then? It'll be time to eat when Steve and Mel get here.'

She shook her head, not trusting her mouth to comply.

'Go on, we'll get plastic-boxed sandwiches and eat them on a bench. They'll taste nasty. You won't enjoy yourself at all.'

Her lips found a different way to betray her and curled themselves into an answering smile. 'Rubbery cheese and hard white bread?'

'Deal.'

They were just going to eat sandwiches together. Friends did that sort of thing. The singing workshop was starting up. Rick, the choir leader from Steve's church, was teaching a group of twenty or so to sing like a gospel choir. They were making good progress. The main group had the harmonies licked, but the soloist was having trouble.

'Darren, you have to fit your part over the top of the choir, but still in rhythm with them,' Rick instructed. 'Let's go back to the basic harmonies and we'll add the main melody in later.' He raised his arms to conduct, and the group stilled.

Serena rested her bottom on the edge of the registration

desk and enjoyed the sound as the group started the intro to 'Oh, Happy Day'.

She was just starting to hum the missing melody when, from behind her, another voice broke in. It was rich and sweet, easily able to reach both high and low notes. Serena swung her head round and stared. One by one the choir members stopped singing until that one voice filled the low-ceilinged room and reverberated off the walls.

Her voice was hoarse with amazement when she finally managed to speak. 'Max! Where on earth did you learn to sing like that?'

Max went suddenly silent and his face reddened. He shrugged and returned to sweeping the biscuit crumbs off the floor. She walked over to the coffee bar where Jake stood, just staring at his number-one fan.

Make that his number-two fan.

'Are you sure I can't get you anything, Dad? A cup of tea? Coffee?'

'No, I'm fine. I just want to sit out here and enjoy the fresh air for a bit.'

Serena hovered behind the garden seat and stared at her father. He'd been back for two days and she was really worried. She was used to extremes from him. This wasn't normal. He was too quiet, too steady.

'Go on, petal. You've got things to do,' he said, without turning to look at her.

She shuffled her way back through the dew-soaked grass and into the house. After making her way up to the study, she turned on the computer and checked her e-mail, all the while resisting the desire to switch to her internet browser and click the link to the Jacobs Associates website. It ought to have been deleted from her 'favourites' folder ages ago.

Only two weeks ago she'd shared a lunch of shrink-wrapped sandwiches with him in the playground at Ellwood Green. She hadn't had cheese after all, but a ham sandwich and a can of lemonade. They'd sat and chatted while children shrieked and ran past them. Despite Jake's dire prediction, she had enjoyed herself quite a lot.

But he wasn't returning to the community centre for the Friday night sessions now school had restarted, and she didn't know when she would see him again. Which was her own fault; she'd told him not to call her. There was no point in all the flirting if it wasn't heading anywhere—or at least not anywhere near an altar. But still, a perverse part of her was disappointed he'd respected her wishes.

A ring on the doorbell saved her itchy mouse-finger from any further temptation. She made her way down the stairs barefooted, only to find that Maggie, the housekeeper, had got there first. She stood at the front door like a guard dog, her ample figure blocking Serena's view of the visitor.

As she reached the bottom step, Maggie turned. 'There's someone here to see you. He says his name is Charles Jacobs.'

Serena's heart flipped over like a pancake.

She ran to the door and squeezed past Maggie, only to find her smile evaporating as she laid eyes on the man standing at the top of the steps. It wasn't him—almost. It was as if Jake had been fast-forwarded twenty years. Creases appeared between her brows.

Jake's father? It had to be. The likeness was striking.

'Hello,' she said, tentatively.

He smiled. Jake's heart-melting smile.

'Good afternoon, Miss Dove. Could you spare me a few moments of your time?'

'Erm…of course.' Behind her, she was aware of Maggie

standing down from bodyguard duty and marching back to her vacuuming.

'Please, come in.' She opened the door wide and gave him plenty of space to come into the hall, then waited until he was well clear before she shut it again. He followed so close behind her on the way to the sitting room she was tempted to pick up speed.

She chose an armchair, feeling the need for her own space, and indicated that he should take a seat on the generous sofa. He eased himself onto the wide cushions, stretched his arms along the back and hooked his right foot across his other knee.

The smile came again. She sat up slightly in her chair and studied him. It was *similar* to Jake's smile, but it wasn't the same—something was missing.

'I'm afraid I don't really understand why you are here, Mr Jacobs. Can I help you somehow?'

He slouched even further into the sofa, and took his time looking around the room.

'Oh, yes. I think you can help me. Most definitely.'

Serena's heart began to pick up speed. 'Is there something the matter with Jake?' She started to rise, but sat back down abruptly when he shook his head, hand raised. His eyes gleamed. Her level of distress seemed to please him.

'No. Jake is fine. And he'll continue to be—with your help.'

'I don't understand.'

Charles Jacobs leaned forward, his smile knowing and self-satisfied.

'I know you've been seeing my son, Serena. And I think some of the gossip mags would pay well for that little titbit. However, I could forget about that kind of windfall with the proper…incentive.'

Serena laughed. 'I'm sorry, but you're wasting your time. Jake and I went out for a while, but we broke up months ago. Hardly front-page news. Your threat doesn't carry any weight, Mr Jacobs.' She rose from her seat and held the sitting room door wide. 'I think it's time you left.'

He didn't even make a pretence of getting up. 'Not so fast. If it doesn't matter to you, it might matter to Jake.'

'I can't see how—'

'Especially if I get a bit chatty and start to recount stories from his childhood. I don't think his titled clients would appreciate learning of his arrest for robbery and drug possession, do you?'

She let the door swing closed.

Drugs? Robbery!

'I don't believe it. Jake would never steal. He's just not like that.'

'Ah, well, I'm sure Jake has told you all about that little *misunderstanding*.'

Of course he hadn't! There was so much of himself he kept under wraps, so much he refused to share with her.

'But there are the records, you see. Someone could get the wrong idea. You know what they say about mud sticking, don't you? Who knows what damage a rumour like that could do?'

The man was pond scum! Ready to sell his own son for a quick buck.

However, she couldn't ignore him. That kind of information *could* hurt Jake's career, and the last thing she wanted was to see him suffer. Blood pounded in her temples.

Could she? Could she give in to him and make this all go away for Jake? His firm was everything to him. He'd built a career and a reputation, despite his father's actions. She couldn't let this slimy little man destroy all of that with one idle rumour, it just wasn't fair.

'How much *reimbursement* would you need?'

'Twenty grand.'

She blinked. He was slick, but he hadn't done his homework. He could have asked for a lot more. It would be easy. She was a joint signatory on several of the bank accounts, and her father would begrudge her nothing.

She walked to the window and stared outside. Dad was sitting on the bench where she'd left him. Could she really take his money and give it to Charles Jacobs? A pang of guilt speared her.

Jacob's beady eyes had been on her the whole time; she knew that without looking. Now she turned to meet his gaze. Eyes that same boundless blue, but lacking in any warmth or humanity.

He smiled, and her stomach churned.

'It's not much to ask for the man you love.'

She started. *The man she loved.* Heat rose in her cheeks.

'I told you. We're not seeing each other any more.'

It was too late. He knew. Betrayed by the fear in her eyes.

Her suspicion was confirmed when he settled himself on the couch again, a satisfied smirk on his face. He had her exactly where he wanted her.

'I presume you'll want cash? It'll take me a day or so to make the necessary arrangements.'

'Clever girl! I knew we'd get on famously.'

'How will I contact you?'

'I'll give you my mobile number.' He pulled a crumpled scrap of paper out of his coat pocket. 'Pen?'

Serena opened a drawer and threw a ballpoint in his direction. She wasn't going to get any closer than absolutely necessary. He scribbled something on the back of what looked like a bus ticket and crossed the room to hand it to her.

She took the ticket and stuffed it in her pocket, still keeping her eyes on him. He was too close, but her back was against the window and there was nowhere else to go.

He reached for a strand of her hair and let it slide between his thumb and forefinger. 'My son is a fool. He should never have let you go.' His breath warmed her cheek. Stale beer and dog-ends. She crunched her neck back in an effort to keep as much distance between them as possible.

'Never mind. We're like peas in a pod, me and Charlie. How about trading him in for an older, vintage model?'

She turned her head and his lips made contact with her cheek, leaving a slimy trail. While surprise had him at a disadvantage, she shoved him away with every ounce of strength at her disposal and rounded the sofa. It was a hell of a lot safer with a barrier between them.

She was so furious her voice cracked when she shrieked at him. 'Get out! You are *nothing* like Jake! Nothing! He's everything that you're not—good and kind and honest.'

'That's his reputation *now*! Wait until I've finished with him. It'll be the messiest trial by media you've ever seen.' He paused and allowed himself a sneer. 'If you love him, you'll pay. It doesn't matter what you think of me. Take it or leave it. It's that simple.'

'I'll leave it.'

'What?'

Under any other circumstances the look of pure bewilderment on his face would have made her howl with laughter.

'I said, I'll leave it, thank you very much.' Then she did laugh, but it was short and hollow. 'You know what? I bet if you tried this on Jake he'd send you packing.'

The steely glint in his eye told her she'd hit the bullseye.

'Well, I'm not playing your little game either, *Mister* Jacobs. So you can take your pathetic little blackmail scam and try it on someone—'

He lunged towards her, and everything seemed to slow to half-speed. She had a split second to consider the fact she'd pushed him too far before he made another grab at her. The sofa didn't stop him after all, as it turned out. She almost got away, but he caught the end of the crushed velvet scarf that was looped around her neck and pulled it tight, arresting both her escape and her air supply.

She stumbled, and the side of her face crashed against a bookcase, sending shooting pains across her cheekbone. The fingers of his free hand tangled in her hair and he yanked her back towards him. Her roots screamed for mercy.

As he swung her round to face him all that crossed her mind was how odd it was that a face blessed with good looks and bone structure could contort itself into such a picture of hatred. She was still staring at him, coughing and struggling for breath, when the door crashed open.

Jacobs almost dropped her in surprise.

'Get your hands off my daughter or I'll rip your head off!'

Never had she been so glad that her dad was a solid-set man with a glint of danger in his eyes. It was just that hard edge that had kept the band popular for so long.

The hands that had been merciless a few seconds ago now pushed her away. He might be tough with a woman half his size, but it was a different matter when he was faced with her father, the pit-bull.

She hardly noticed him scuttle from the room. All she could take in was her father. Suddenly he seemed bigger and stronger, just like when she was little and he had ruled the world.

They clung to each other for a few minutes. He held her tight and stroked her hair away from her face, the way he'd used to, and looked down at her with fierce protectiveness.

Her lips crumpled into a smile.

'Thanks, Dad.'

'Any time, petal.'

He had to know.

If his own father was going to sell him to the highest bidder then he had a right to be forewarned. She stared at the doorbell and, not for the first time that night, wondered if she'd made the right decision.

Fine time to discover a belated need to stand up for herself! Her moment of victory might send Jake's career into a nosedive. The tug of anxiety in her stomach was double-edged. There was the churning anticipation of the pain her confession might cause Jake, but also the more urgent, dragging need just to see him again, the sheer indulgence of being close to him.

She jammed her thumb on the button before she could think herself into chickening out.

CHAPTER EIGHT

JAKE looked up from the mound of papers on his desk. He'd been adding a column of figures in his head, and was only vaguely aware of a foreign noise. Although the flat was silent again, the subliminal memory of the door buzzer still hummed in his ears. The old leather chair creaked as he stood up.

He didn't need to ask his visitor's identity when he reached the intercom. A huge pair of searching eyes looked up at him, their beauty undiluted by the grainy black and white picture from the CCTV monitor.

The figures he'd been holding in his memory fluttered away.

She didn't speak. She didn't need to. Her eyes said it all. *Let me in.*

But he knew that opening the door meant more than giving her entry to his home. Two whole weeks he'd managed. Two whole weeks of ignoring the phone number he kept doodling in the margins of his spreadsheets. Not only was he putting himself in danger by letting her into his life again—letting her go had hurt too much to repeat the experience—but he was putting her happiness at risk too. She'd made that quite clear. And he wouldn't do anything to make her unhappy.

He waited a moment or two before he pressed the buzzer with an unsteady finger. When she turned the corner at the top of the stairs he was waiting for her at the threshold.

There were no hellos. They both knew they were way beyond small talk, were communicating with each other on a much deeper, more instinctive level. She spoke to a part of him that hid behind the logic and iron defences. For the first time in years he wished he were different, capable of saying *I do*.

He didn't want to break the silence. The air was charged with whatever was pulsing between them, and words would only break the bubble.

Serena looked away, and he knew she was ready with a pin.

'We need to talk, Jake.'

He smiled and reached for her hand, reluctant to make his mouth form an answer. Then she looked back at him and he knew there was no putting it off.

'Must we?'

She let out a breath and her shoulders drooped. 'You're not going to be smiling like that when you've heard what I've got to say.'

Her fingers slid out from between his and she folded her arms across her front.

'I'm listening,' he said, and motioned for her to go inside. She went through to the lounge and perched on the edge of an armchair without taking her coat off.

The eyes looked at him, pleading him to understand. Begging for forgiveness?

What on earth could she have to confess to? Only one horrible thought jeered inside his head. She'd found someone.

The husband-hunt was over. His stomach knotted at the thought, which was very hypocritical of it, considering he had declined the role. He could hardly gripe if she'd found a more suitable candidate.

But the fact that she was here at all acknowledged something…unfinished between them.

She leaned forward slightly, her hair falling in dark sheets either side of her face.

'I had a visit from your father today.'

'*My* father?'

'Yes. Charles Jacobs the elder. Not a very uplifting experience.' Her hand shook as she tucked her hair behind her ear. 'I think I may have made the most awful mistake.'

A smudge of deep pink lay at the point where her temple met her cheekbone. Immediately he was across the room, crouching in front of her. His fingers gently explored the bruise and raised area beneath. She flinched.

Blood began to pound so hard in his head he could barely see straight.

'Did he…did my father do this?'

She nodded, and her eyes glistened. 'I'm sorry.'

In one swift movement he launched himself to his feet. 'God, that man is a piece of work!' Long strides propelled him around the room. Where he was going was anyone's guess. He just needed to move.

'See—this is what he does. It's his MO. He acts like an animal, then makes you feel it's *your* fault. He twists it all around so you're not sure of your own motives any more. You start to doubt yourself… He's poison.'

He managed to slow himself down enough to sit on the edge of the coffee table opposite her. His knees brushed hers.

'Nothing about this is your fault! *Nothing*. Look at me.'

He waited while she edged her eyes to meet his gaze. His voice crept into a whisper. 'It's not your fault—got it?' She nodded, but his words didn't seem to have soothed her at all. 'I knew he could be violent, but I never dreamed… How could I have known he would take it out on you? He didn't give any indication…'

Before he knew it, he was striding again.

'Actually, I think I earned this little trophy all on my own,' she said quietly. 'It was nothing to do with you. Not really.'

He stopped to look at her, but she was staring at the grain on the wood floor.

She didn't get it. He could hardly expect her to. It had taken him years to unravel his father's lies and see them for what they really were. The man was a master manipulator. It was how he earned his living, after all. He sucked dry anyone unlucky enough to cross his path, then moved on to the next victim.

When he spoke, although his voice was low and emotion-less, the words scared him. 'I could kill him.'

Never before had he felt such pure hate. He'd thought he'd scraped that barrel well and truly dry. But, true to form, his father could always sink lower, and he realised there were depths to hatred he had never imagined.

'I'm going to find him and I'm going to… I don't know what I'll do, but he's not getting away with this.'

Where was his coat?

He ran into the kitchen and grabbed it off one of the high-backed stools, only vaguely aware of the sound of Serena's heels coming closer. When he turned she was right behind him.

'You stay here,' he ordered. 'He won't dare come here. I don't know when I'll be back.' He swung his coat on.

Too many words. He was wasting time. He just had to get

out through that door and do something. His father was a creature of habit. The events of the last few weeks confirmed the old leopard's spots were still firmly in the same place. He had favourite pubs and betting shops. It wouldn't take long.

Serena was still keeping up with him as he neared the front door.

'Jake, you can't… Will you just…?' She gripped his sleeve and gave it a violent tug.

'Don't worry,' he said, and gave her a kiss on the forehead. 'I won't let him touch you again.'

'Jake! Stop! Listen to me!'

He stopped halfway through the door. Something in her voice demanded he obey.

Her breath was coming in gasps. She inhaled deeply, then continued. 'I haven't told you what I came here to tell you! If you go off half-cocked now it will only make things worse!' Her eyes pleaded with him. He was a total sucker for that look. 'Come back inside and sit down, and let me explain everything. Please?'

She was right. He hadn't let her talk. It was just such a stab in the gut to think of anyone hurting her. The fact that it was his flesh and blood that had done the damage just twisted the knife further. He let her pull him back into the flat.

Now he'd capitulated, all the fight went out of her. She closed her eyes and massaged the lids by dragging the flat of her hand across each eye.

'Get us a drink, and let's discuss this like rational human beings.'

When he appeared from the kitchen, a glass of red wine in each hand, she had taken off her coat and was right in one corner of the three-seater sofa, back straight, ankles crossed. She took the wine when he offered it, and placed on the coffee table in front of her without tasting it.

He opened his mouth, but she silenced him with a look.

'Just let me talk. It won't take long.'

He nodded, then sat down on the opposite end of the sofa and turned to face her. She didn't look at him, but straight ahead.

'I came to warn you that your father is ready to ruin your career. He came to ask for money, to buy his silence.'

'About us? I told him we were—'

'Jake!' Now she turned to look at him.

'Sorry. Listening.'

'Not about us. About you, and something that happened when you were younger.' She picked at a nail. 'Something to do with the police.'

It was so hard to keep quiet. He was practically bursting to explain. Surely she didn't believe…?

'He said it would hurt your business if word got out. I almost paid him. But then I…well, I just couldn't. So now he's going to go to the press and see what he can get off them. I'm so sorry. I should have stopped him.' She looked up at him. 'You can talk now. If you want.'

Too many sentences battled to be the first one out of his mouth. He took a large gulp of wine to sluice the words away. She looked firmly planted in her seat, but he could tell she was walking a tightrope.

'It's okay. I know what he's like. He came to me first and I told him to get lost.' He paused and watched as she crossed, then recrossed her legs. 'I would be more upset if you had given in to him.'

'But your clients! Won't they disapprove?'

'It's possible, but it's not as bad as Dad made it sound. He's clever—a good enough con-artist to know you should always build a lie on a grain of truth. Yes, I was arrested at age fifteen for burglary. But I was very quickly released when, despite my protestations of guilt, they decided I was covering for someone else.' He leaned back in the sofa and stretched one arm along the back. 'What I don't understand is why my father went to you at all.'

Finally, she took interest in her wine glass. When she could delay it no longer she spoke. 'I think he was trying his luck at first. Then he realised there was some leverage to be had in the situation.'

'But we aren't even an item any more. Not officially,' he said, rather too quickly. 'I think we're something. I'm just not sure what.'

At least she looked relieved at that. There was hope yet.

'I think your father realised I still…' Half of him wanted her to say it; the other was half terrified she would. '…care for you.'

They sat and sipped their wine, neither knowing what to say.

'Serena?'

Her face flushed, and he knew without a shadow of a doubt that her heart had to be thudding like his. He shifted along the sofa again. Now he was close enough to smell her perfume.

'What if I told you I've missed you?'

He was coming closer. Her lips tingled in anticipation. Kissing him would be a really bad idea. It would only be harder to walk away again. But she couldn't move—didn't want to. Her hands reached up and cupped his face, making sure he closed the distance, leaving nothing to chance.

His lips were warm and soft and intoxicating. She responded with a hunger that had jump-started itself out of nowhere.

Just for a moment it didn't matter that this was the worst idea in the world, that it would only make things messy and complicated. She needed him. Needed this. Needed his lips exploring hers, craved his touch. Inside she smiled, triumphant in the knowledge that he was just as trapped. The fact they were both cursed with this peculiar insanity only bonded them closer together.

This was her last chance. She might never have him in her arms again, yet her love for him was spiralling like a cyclone out of control. She couldn't tell him how she felt, but she could show him. She would pour every ounce of her heart into this one kiss as her parting gift. Maybe somewhere, in the sections of his heart he had cordoned off, he would keep it, and one day know the treasure she had offered him.

So, as their lips continued to brush and tease, she explored the planes of his face with her fingers, ran her hands over his neck and chest, and tried to imprint every last contour in the nerve-endings so she would never forget.

He groaned, a sound from deep within his chest, and dragged her even closer to him. Their arms and legs tangled, and she continued her memory map of him by adding the toned muscles of his shoulders and back to her collection.

Whatever she was doing, it was spurring him on to even greater levels of need. Every cell in her body burst into flame. To make love to him would be the sweetest madness. She was almost tempted to throw herself off the cliff. But the wreckage of the morning after would be unbearable, knowing she would not have him for ever. She would never survive to find anyone else. There would be no hope of mending her broken heart in a few years and moving on.

As his mouth left hers to paint tiny kisses all over her face, she thought her heart would burst with the bittersweet sensation.

Don't punish me for this! I can go just a little bit crazy before self-preservation kicks in and I have to leave.

Then he stopped, so still she could feel his heart beating against her own ribcage.

She opened her eyes and focused on him. His pupils were so large they almost obliterated the brilliant blue of the irises. The expression he wore was—what? Surprise? No, guilt. He looked as if he'd just kicked a puppy. His tongue darted over his lip, tasting something. He suddenly looked ten years younger, confused and defensive.

'You're crying,' he said.

She pressed the pads of her fingers to her cheek and discovered he was right.

Without realising it she had broken the spell. Part of her screamed that it was too soon, she wanted more, one more taste of him. But there would always be that hunger for *one more*. Perhaps it was better this way.

She unhooked her leg from over his and slid away from him, tucked herself back into the corner of the sofa. He let her go, sat up himself, and ran a hand to smooth his tousled hair. Her fingers ached to rake through it and mess it up again.

'All this doesn't change anything, does it?' he said, his voice blank. 'We still want different things out of life. You want your Mr Perfect to have your two point four kids with. I'm not him. I'm not even close.'

She could agree. She could straighten her hair, put on her coat, smile nicely and tell him it had all been a terrible mistake. Then months from now, if they met, they would kiss each other on the cheek and pretend it didn't matter, pretend they hadn't thrown away their chance of happiness.

She couldn't do it. Tomorrow she might hide her head under the pillow and groan with mortification about what she was going to say, but tonight she didn't care. She had to understand.

'I think you're perfect for me.'

He pressed a finger against her lips. 'Don't.'

Her hand closed over his and she drew it into her lap.

'I'm not perfect, Serena. I told you before. You see what you want to see.'

She shook her head. 'No. At the beginning that was true. You fitted the picture of my identikit husband closely enough for me not to delve deeper—you were right about that then, but not now. Over the last few weeks I've seen the real you I'd only had a hint of before. The Jake who takes time to stick with an awkward kid that everyone else has written off. The Jake who takes care of his little sister and is always there for her. A Jake who is full of imagination, passion and patience.' Her voice caught in her throat and came out husky. 'The man who would have stopped at nothing a few minutes ago to defend my honour. The man who has captured my heart completely.'

Looking him in the eye right now was the bravest thing she had ever done.

'I love you, Jake.'

He didn't breathe out for a full ten seconds.

There. She'd done it. This was as low as she could go. The ground could go ahead and do its swallowing.

His voice was low and croaky. 'And I...haven't felt this way for a long time.'

Something inside her swelled. Maybe it wasn't as hopeless as she'd thought. Then he continued, and her hopes came crashing down.

'But I'm no good at long-term relationships. I'm a disaster waiting to happen.'

'That's the second time you've said something like that. Tell me about her, Jake?'

'More wine first.' He went to fetch the bottle from the kitchen, and when he reappeared she knew from his face it had just been an excuse so he could batten down the hatches, get his emotions firmly back under control. The way his jaw clenched told her he was having less success than he'd hoped.

Good.

He topped up both their glasses and sat down, keeping at least three feet between them.

'Her name was Chantelle. Her family moved onto the estate when I was seventeen. She was the prettiest girl I had ever seen. It took me two years to pluck up the courage to ask her out. I was sure she'd say no—but she didn't. A year later I asked her to marry me. I was sure she'd say no to that too, but she surprised me again. I couldn't have been happier.'

Knives were carving great chunks out of Serena as she heard this, but she had to know.

'So what happened?'

He refused to look back at her, and she watched his profile as he continued, brows heavy, holding his glass so tight between both hands she thought it might shatter.

'As the wedding date drew closer I started to feel differently. My friends told me it was just the wedding jitters, but I knew it was more than that. Suddenly she seemed demanding and needy, but that wasn't the case, really. She could feel me pulling away and she was scared. The closer we got to for ever, the worse it got.'

'Please tell me you didn't jilt her at the altar.'

'No. We broke up two months before the wedding. I was twenty-one; she was nineteen. Everyone said we were just too young.'

He looked over at her, pain etched in his eyes.

'I knew it was me. I couldn't give her the support and love she deserved. In the end, she couldn't take what she called my "emotional unavailability" any more, so she ended it.'

He drained his glass and sloshed more wine in to fill the space.

'And the terrible thing was, as much as I loved her, I was royally relieved.' He gave her a wry smile. 'It seems, much as I like to kid myself it's not true, I've got some of the old man's genes after all.'

'And there hasn't been anyone since?'

'Well, I've dated, but all my energy has gone into the business. I'm happy with the way things are. I don't want to change.'

Liar. The way he'd agonised over Chantelle told her he *did* care. He just pretended he didn't because it was easier.

'So that's where I am now. Which leaves us wanting different things. I can't promise you all my tomorrows.'

'Couldn't you promise me even one?'

'Of course!' He rammed his glass down on the table. 'But it's all or nothing with you, isn't it? I can't stop thinking about you, Serena. I think we could be good together. It could last for quite a while, if we give it a chance.'

Oh, goody!

Jake got up and walked to the window. Serena slouched against the arm of the sofa and stared at the wood grain on the highly polished coffee table.

His voice was so low she could barely hear it. 'Move in with me.'

'Pardon?'

Jake turned to face her. The scariest thing was that the expression on his face was totally serious.

'Come and live with me, Serena. I want more than dinners and trips to the opera. I want to do the everyday things with you: watch TV together, cook a meal, tell each other how our days have been over dinner.' He paused. 'I want to share my life with you.'

'For now.'

'Yes, for now. It's the best I can offer.'

It made her ache to see how hard he was trying. She knew this was a huge step for him, but the thought terrified her.

'I can't live with that level of uncertainty—knowing one day you might decide you're tired of me and I'll come home to find my stuff in boxes on the landing and the locks changed.'

Jake looked ready to hurl his glass across the room. 'I would *never* do that to you.'

Serena scrunched up her face with her hands.

'I know, I know. I'm sorry, that came out all wrong. What I'm trying to say is that I don't want to waste time on a relationship that's not going to last. I would just feel like I was marking time until it all fell apart.'

'Right now, I can't ever imagine that happening.'

'But you can't promise it won't.'

'Even if I did, it might not change anything. Look at the divorce rate. There are no guarantees, even with a marriage licence.'

'But at least those people start out knowing they want the same thing, Jake. I want a family—a real family—children and dogs and a house that's always a little bit messy.' She looked round the room at the spotless furnishings. Not a coffee ring or a speck of dust in sight. 'I don't want to live in a slick city apartment while my biological clock ticks away my chance of all that. You don't want children, do you?'

He shook his head.

'That's a deal-breaker for me, Jake. I desperately want a family, and if we're just living together and "seeing how it goes" it's not enough. Children deserve a mum and a dad who are going to be there for them. You of all people should know about that.'

Jake was very quiet, just looking at her. The pained expression on his face told her this was hurting him just as much as it was hurting her. She thought he was going to say something, but the words never came. Probably because there was nothing to say. No way past this. No future for them.

She bowed her head and let the tears that had welled up fall into her lap. Jake was across the room in a second, hauling her into his arms, kissing her neck and face. It took all the effort she had to wrench herself away from him.

She dug her hands into the corners of her eyes and scrubbed away the tears. 'No, Jake. It's no use. We'd always be pulling in opposite directions.'

'In other words, I'm a waste of your time.'

Good. Anger was good. If he kept kissing her like that she'd forget why she had to be strong. And if she wanted babies she needed to be strong. She was going to give them all the stability and comfort she never had.

Now she understood. She knew Jake was not the man to give that to her. He was afraid, too scared of being like his no-good father to give love a real chance. Hedging his bets, as he wanted to, wasn't real love. It was like riding a bike with stabilisers for ever because you were too petrified you wouldn't whiz down the path like the other kids.

She got up, put on her coat and started buttoning it up.

'I think you're right. We *are* wasting each other's time. Tragic, but true.'

Her disobedient fingers finally managed the last button.

'What are you going to do about your father?'

He walked back over to the French doors and stared out the glass. 'I don't know. I expect I'll talk to the police. He can't go around demanding money from people like that. It's time I stopped pretending he didn't exist and dealt with him.'

She walked over to him and kissed his shoulder. He wasn't

going to turn around from looking out of the window. She knew that.

'Goodbye, Jake. I'll never forget you.'

Serena's key twisted in the lock and she pushed the door open.

Silence.

No lights were on. She fumbled for the switch in the hall and dropped her handbag on the floor.

'Dad?'

Maggie had gone to St Albans to visit her son, but someone should be here. Dad should be here. She shrugged off her coat and left it in a heap on the floor, then ran down to the kitchen. A tap dripped in the dark. The kettle was cold.

She took the stairs two at a time and raced to his bedroom, her heart hammering.

Empty.

That was when she really started to panic. She slumped onto the bed and picked up one of his discarded shirts and hugged it.

What *was* it with the men in her life?

She ran back out onto the landing and into every room, turning the lights on as she went. Soon the whole house was ablaze, with chandeliers and spotlights alike.

Finally she trudged down the stairs and sank down, her bottom on the last step.

Dad could be anywhere when he was on a drinking spree. She might not see him for days. There were no tears left to cry. She'd used up her supply on the way home from Jake's. The taxi driver must have thought she was a nutcase! Dad was her only point of stability now, and a pretty shaky one at that.

Anger flooded through her. She'd had such hopes for her

father when he'd come home. If he self-destructed this time, she knew there would be no coming back. In her gut, she knew it had been his last chance.

Eventually, her abandoned coat annoyed her enough for her to go and pick it up and sling it over a chair. She threw off her boots and padded down the corridor to the kitchen in her stockinged feet.

As she reached the bottom of the narrow staircase that led to the basement kitchen, she stopped. Something was out of place. A glow of orange light spilled from under a door at the bottom of the stairs. A doorway so little used in recent years she'd almost forgotten it was there.

Gingerly, she pushed the door with her fingertips and it swung open. Their basement was huge. The kitchen occupied the back part that led to the garden, but more than half the area was taken up with her dad's recording studio. She pushed open a second sound-proofed door and stopped in her tracks.

Her father was sitting on a stool in the middle of the room, guitar perched on his knee. Every now and then he stopped playing and scribbled something in a notebook balanced on the edge of the baby grand.

He was writing again?

He hadn't written a song in years.

Now the tears came, hot and fast. She should have had more faith, should have believed a little harder.

Dad didn't even see her. He was facing away from her and a pair of headphones covered his ears. She dragged her hands across her face to wipe away the tears. She could see from his three-quarter profile that he was smiling.

A tiny laugh gurgled up her throat and came out as a hiccup. Then she crept back the way she had come, her shoeless feet making no sound on the rich carpet.

CHAPTER NINE

THERE was no way to sit on the metal bench to make it comfortable, especially after forty minutes. Jake traced one of the holes punched in the seat with the tip of his finger. The dark blue paint was flaking off and he picked at a bit.

The girl behind the desk humphed. He pulled his finger away and gave her an apologetic smile. There wasn't any hint of a thaw. Normally, in the face of such indifference, he'd use the name on the lady's name badge and schmooze a little. Only she wasn't wearing a badge, and he didn't think *Oi, you!* would go down very well.

She looked like an *Olga*. The chunky ribbed jumper of her uniform didn't do her broad physique any favours. Those shoulders wouldn't look out of place on an Olympic shot-putter.

She caught him looking at her and gave him a hard look. 'DC Carlisle will be with you shortly, sir.'

He nodded, and watched as she pulled the pencil out from behind her ear and continued scribbling in an important-looking log. His eyes swept round the small lobby, trying to find anything new of interest. The walls had been painted a soothing blue, to complement the navy of the steel bench. Even so, the foyer of Chelsea police station was the most depressing place he'd ever been.

The righteous anger of the night before had deserted him. All that was left was a creeping sense of guilt. God knew his father deserved this. He shouldn't care.

Mel had burst into tears when he'd told her his plans. She'd even confessed to seeing their father in secret. A cold feeling grew in his stomach every time he thought about how she'd learnt the hard way about Dear Old Dad. He should have done more to protect her, and he would have done if he'd have been less preoccupied. Hopefully DC Carlisle and his team would be able to recover Grandma's engagement ring when they caught up with the mongrel.

He stretched his legs and looked at the door to his right, willing someone to come and collect him. Today was a day for putting the past behind him, for ruling a line under things and getting on with his life. No more *if onlys*. He would forget her and move on to pastures new.

He sighed, pulled a pound coin out of his pocket and dumped it in the charity box on the shelf next to him. Fining himself for wayward thoughts had seemed such an inspired idea half an hour ago. Now his pocket was considerably lighter than it should have been. If he didn't kick this habit soon he was going to have to move on to notes.

However, he couldn't evict the thought of how Serena had looked last night as she'd turned to leave—quiet resignation and hopelessness. He should take the same attitude, but all he could do as he sat and waited for the detective was burn with indignation. She'd given up on him, taken all he had to offer and thrown it back at him. Being a bad risk smarted more than he cared to admit.

He was saved from further poverty by a squat man who appeared through the door.

'Mr Jacobs?'

He stood up and offered his hand. 'Detective Constable Carlisle.'

'I believe you have some information we might find useful?'

He picked up his briefcase and stood ramrod-straight. 'Yes. Yes, I do.'

'Well, if you'd like to come this way, sir?'

Jake hid a smile as DC Carlisle punched the code into the door lock. That tie was hideous. Serena would have had a fit!

Blast!

He peeled a fiver out of his wallet and stuffed it in the slot of the plastic box. Olga gave him a funny look, but he was saved from an explanation when DC Carlisle ushered him through the door to an interview room.

The door to the studio creaked as she opened it with an elbow. The tray she carried tipped at an awkward angle and tea sloshed out of the cup and into the saucer.

'Dad?'

'Over here.'

Through the long horizontal window she could see him standing at the mixing desk, messing around with sliders and buttons.

'I brought you some breakfast. You haven't been up all night, have you?'

He nodded towards the battered old sofa in the main part of the studio. A blanket was falling off one side and the dents in the cushions suggested a makeshift bed.

Hope welled in her heart as she saw him standing there,

only just inhabiting the same world as her, his brain whirring with chords and lyrics.

'What have you been working on?'

He shrugged. 'Just an idea.'

'Play me a bit?'

Music flooded the room. It was soulful and atmospheric, every bit as good as his compositions of twenty years ago—better, even. There was an added depth to it.

'You know, you ought to come and help out at the music project. You've got so much experience. It seems a shame not to share it.'

Her dad made an *as if* face. Did he know how much like a teenager he looked when he did that?

'They won't want an old has-been like me around.'

'Nonsense. And I'm not just talking about music. I'm talking about life experience.'

Dad laughed so hard she thought he was going to fall off the stool he was perched on. 'I'm hardly a poster boy for good clean living.'

'But that's the point! You've made the mistakes, you know first hand what drugs and alcohol can do—and you've kicked it.'

'One day at a time, petal. Don't get ahead of yourself.'

She handed him his cup of tea. 'Just think about it, Dad. Please?'

'Okay. For you.'

'The big performance to mark the end of the project is at the end of term. It'd only be for a few weeks, Dad.'

He took a sip of his tea and smiled at her.

A sudden realisation of how lucky she was hit her like an express train. Life might have been chaotic with Dad, but she had *always* been loved. Just thinking about the contrast between her own father and Jake's made her shiver. No wonder he was so wary of commitment.

'I love you, Dad.'

An uncharacteristic sheen appeared in her father's eyes. 'I know. How could I not? You've looked out for me all this time, when I should have been looking out for you.'

'It doesn't matter.'

'It should.'

She slid her arms around his neck and squeezed him hard.

'I'll do it,' he whispered in her ear.

Just for that she rewarded him with a big kiss on the cheek. Grinning, she balanced herself against the edge of the mixing desk.

'But remember, it's only three weeks until the big performance. After that, we've got to decide what to do with the rest of our lives. We've wasted too much time.'

'Hmm.' She watched him dig a fork into the plate of scrambled eggs. 'Time to decide what I want to be when I grow up.'

'It's in here somewhere.'

Jake waited while Serena threw a purse, three pens and a pot of lip balm out of her handbag. Finally, when there was more junk on the kitchen table than in the bag, she produced a rumpled bus ticket. The innards of a woman's handbag were no longer a mystery, but still a source of fascination.

The way her fingers worked on the ticket, smoothing the wrinkles out, mesmerised him. Not so long ago those fingers had been… No.

'I really appreciate this, Serena. I know it's a little awkward…'

She looked up and smiled at him, but it was all lips and teeth. 'No problem. Really.'

He shouldn't feel the need to defend himself.

'It's going to save the police a lot of time and resources if I can set up a meeting with my father rather than them having to look for him. I'm going to phone and say I want to see him.'

She handed the ticket to him. He made very sure their fingers didn't brush.

'Do you think he'll turn up? You hardly parted on good terms last time. Won't he think it's a little fishy?'

Yup. That was the gaping hole in the plan, but what other option did he have?

'It'll be fine. We're very lucky you kept his mobile number. DC Carlisle will be chuffed. I think he's looking to get brownie points with his sergeant.'

'He's the policeman looking into the case?'

'Mmm-hmm.'

'You said they were already looking for your dad. What do they want him for?'

'Deception. Apparently Sussex police have had a warrant out for his arrest since before he went to Spain two years ago. Some scam involving lonely widows and internet dating sites, I believe.'

'I won't have to go to court, will I?'

'You don't have to press charges unless you want to. They have more than enough to detain him at Her Majesty's pleasure for the rest of the decade even without the blackmailing charges.'

'I don't know what I'm going to do. It wouldn't be very good publicity for Dad.'

Wasn't it about time she cut the apron strings?

'You need to do what *you* want.'

She started stuffing things back into the bottomless pit of her handbag—a good excuse to avoid eye contact, probably. Perhaps her dad was just a good excuse too. If she pressed charges they would keep running into each other, and every look, every bit of her body language, screamed that would never do.

He stood up too fast and bumped his knee on the table. They both ignored it.

She walked a wide path around him and led him back to the front door. He waved the bus ticket with the biro scrawl on the back. 'Thanks for this.' She didn't answer.

He knew he should have said a proper goodbye, but he needed to get away from her before he did anything stupid. If he could just reach the path before he turned around and waved, he'd be far enough away not to want to run back up the steps and pull her into his arms.

'Jake?'

Two steps to go. Don't stop. He skipped down the last steps and waited till his feet were firmly planted on the path before he turned. He'd miscalculated. The urge was as strong as ever.

'Would it help if...if *I* called your father?'

He shook his head.

'He might believe I've weakened more easily than you.'

She had a point.

'I don't want you to get involved.'

'I already am involved.' Her fingers jumped to the yellow bruise on her cheek.

'No.'

She walked down the stairs towards him. 'It would help me too, you know. If he doesn't take the bait we'll always be wondering when he'll pop up again. At least this way we've got a better chance of having some closure.'

Closure. Heaven knew he needed some of that. On more than one front.

He pulled his mobile out of his pocket. 'Let me see what DC Carlisle says.' With any luck the detective would pull the plug on her idea and he and Serena would both be spared any further agony.

Fifteen minutes later the man in question stepped out of a car and walked up to where Jake was leaning against the balustrade. He always looked crumpled, as if he'd just pulled his clothes from a tightly packed suitcase. Jake led him inside to talk to Serena.

'Hello, DC…' her eyes skittered down to his Hawaiian tie and she fought to control her lips '…Carlisle. Nice to meet you.'

If she didn't stop pacing soon she was going to wear a track in the carpet. Serena pressed her nose against the glass and tried to see if there was any hint of a grey overcoat on the horizon.

Two hours. He couldn't be much longer, could he?

She resumed her circuit of the dining room. They'd chosen to sit in here because it overlooked the front steps.

Jake was sprawled across one of the antique chairs. She wasn't sure if she dreaded or looked forward to going past him as she circled the table. Her pulse drummed that little bit faster, whatever the cause.

'Sit down. You're doing my head in.'

She kicked the back of his chair as she went past. 'Well, excuse me. Never mind this is all to help you out! Pardon me for being a bit nervous.'

'I didn't say you shouldn't be nervous.'

She yanked out a chair and plopped herself down on it with a thud. 'Better?'

'Much.'

The silence grew thick.

Jake tapped out the beat to an unknown song on the polished wood of the table. She reached over and slapped his fingers flat. He glared. Her hand curled back and she reddened.

Studying her empty cup seemed as good a diversion as any. 'I need another coffee.'

'You wouldn't be so jumpy if you hadn't pumped yourself full of caffeine.'

He was right. Of course he was right. But she couldn't just sit here waiting. Especially not alone—with him. It was driving her nuts. She gave him a high-handed look and stalked from the room. Making sure her feet clomped down the stairs to the kitchen didn't give nearly enough release. She needed to throw something, break something.

'Black with two sugars.'

The mug almost flew out of her hand.

'Don't do that!'

'What?'

'Sneak up on me.'

'I didn't sneak anywhere. You were making enough noise for the both of us.'

She banged another mug onto the counter.

'Go and ask Dad if he wants one, will you? He's through there.' She waved a hand towards the studio door and turned back towards the kettle. The thud of the door made her flinch.

Her own coffee was finished and Jake's was going cold when she relented and went looking for him. First she shoved his cup in the microwave to warm it up. Who cared if it killed all the flavour?

She found him in the studio with her dad. The pair of them were hunched over acoustic guitars, strumming away.

She plonked Jake's cup down on a shelf. His head jerked up.

'Thanks.'

'I wouldn't drink it if I were you. It probably tastes awful by now.'

Her dad's eyes darted between her and Jake. 'It was my fault, love. I asked him to stay.'

She sighed. 'Well, I suppose it's one way to pass the time. Don't let me interrupt you.' They bent their heads back over their guitars and carried on. They could have protested a little harder before they ignored her again.

If you can't beat them…

She dropped into the couch and swung her legs up. Her eyes drifted closed. All the tension had suddenly gone from her limbs. Her voice came out softly, almost dreamily. 'Jake, why don't you play Dad that thing you played me?'

Rustling from the other side of the room. Silence.

'Go on, don't be shy.'

'I'm not sure I—'

The doorbell. All three of them froze.

She rocketed to her feet, eyes wide. 'What do we do now?' Her chest was thumping. She held out a hand. Her fingers were trembling all on their own, no matter how hard she told them to stop.

'They'll need someone to make a positive ID.' Jake's mobile rang. He picked it up and punched a button. 'Yup… Okay… Will do.'

With that, he sprinted out of the room. She could tell by the rhythm of his feet on the stairs that he'd taken them two at a time. She looked at her dad. He put his guitar down and they stared at each other, ears straining.

Suddenly, she was running. She emerged into the hallway just in time to see Jake shutting the front door. He turned, a look of bemusement on his face.

'Jake? Who was it? Was it him?' Her voice was uncomfortably shrill inside her own skull.

He nodded slowly. 'They got him.'

She ran to the door and wrenched it open. Jacobs was being helped into a police car by two uniformed officers and DC Carlisle. He gave her a thumbs-up sign. She raised a hand and lifted her own thumb in slow motion. The door swung closed.

'So that's it, then? It's over.'

He didn't seem to be looking at her, at anything. 'It's over.'

'I thought it was going to be much more dramatic than that.'

'You've been watching too many cop shows.'

She slumped against the door. Hilarity seemed the only way to cope. 'I was expecting at least one "Shut it!".'

He didn't seem to have heard. So much for lightening the situation.

'Say thanks to your dad for me.' He pulled his coat off the hooks near the door. 'Bye.'

She watched him go, a sense of helplessness paralysing her limbs. 'Are you going to the performance next—?'

He was down the path, even steps carrying him away from her.

She went upstairs, collapsed on her bed, and wallowed in the sense of anticlimax.

He'd drifted out of her life. Just like that.

What she'd felt for him had deserved a momentous farewell, a mourning of what might have been. Not a half-hearted

'Bye' and a backwards wave. How could he just switch it all off like that? It made her want to scream.

She stopped outside Lewisham Theatre and cast an eye over the exterior. It had once been a lovely piece of art deco architecture—it still was under the pigeon droppings and pollution stains. She took a deep breath, smoothed her hair down and told herself she was being stupid. After all, she didn't even know if he was going to show up.

Max would be devastated if he didn't. This was what they'd all been working towards, the big gala performance to mark the end of the Youth Music Project and, hopefully, the start of enough funding to do more in the future.

She could see Cassie waving at her through the diagonal panes on the door. A hefty push and she joined the crowd milling in the foyer. Cassie gave her a peck on the cheek.

'You're looking good tonight, Cass. Finally shaken that stomach bug?'

Cassie shrugged and looked at Steve. 'Steve, tell Ren about the all the celebrities you've invited tonight.'

'Anyone I know?'

'Not apart from your dad and Daddy K.'

'Kevin.'

'Kevin, then. I don't think you've met anyone else. They're mainly homegrown celebs, doing it to raise their profile. I've got the mayor, two footballers and a model. Enough to get the front page of the local paper, I hope.'

Cassie jumped up and down and waved her arms. 'Oh, look, there's Mel!'

She needn't bother with all the flapping. Her pink hair was like a beacon. Mel spotted them in seconds and waved back.

Steve looked at his watch. 'Only five minutes until curtain-up. Let's go. I've put all the helpers and local bigwigs in a block.' He doled out tickets indiscriminately.

Cass grabbed Serena's elbow and held her back as the group set off for the circle. She waited for the others to climb a few more stairs before she hissed in her ear.

'He's here, you know.'

Suddenly her stomach became a gaping cavern and her arms turned to gooseflesh.

'Where?'

'Up there,' said Cassie, with a jerk of her head. 'He arrived ten minutes ago. I thought I should warn you.'

She squeezed Cassie's hand. 'Thanks. I don't know what I'd do without you.'

'Me neither. Now, shake a leg before we both start blubbing!'

Good point. If she was going to be within spitting distance of Jake, she might as well have her armour intact, and panda eyes definitely wouldn't pass muster.

They caught the others up and stood in a clump just inside the door to the auditorium. Steve and Cass went in search of their seats.

'Oh, look what the cat dragged in,' said Mel as Serena checked her ticket stub for the row number.

'Who?' Serena's eyes panned the circle and skidded to a halt three rows back from the balcony. 'Who is *that*, and why is she draped all over your brother?'

'That's Chantelle. She thinks she's a supermodel. Outside of her imagination she just does a lot of catalogue work. Doesn't mean she doesn't swan around like she owns the place. Can't stand the cow.'

'Mel! I've never heard you talk like that!'

'You've never met Chantelle before.'

'And how is she so intimately acquainted with Jake?'

Mel let out a breathy hiss, as if she couldn't believe what she was just about to say. 'When Jake was younger and stupider—much stupider—he almost married her.'

She was Jake's ex-fiancée?

Serena braced herself against the doorway and took a good look at the competition. Blonde, long legs, big boobs—your basic nightmare.

Mel whispered in her ear, grateful for a bitching buddy, it seemed. 'Talk about high-maintenance! No matter what Jake says, as far as I'm concerned, she treated him like dirt, especially just before it ended. Jake, the daft boy, just kept coming back for more like a faithful little lap dog.'

Serena faced Mel and frowned. They were talking about the same Jake, right? The Jake who was always in charge, who never let a woman close enough to walk all over him? If she wanted any more proof she wasn't the woman for him, there it was.

When had he ever followed *her* around like a puppy? The only bright-eyed and over-eager one in their relationship had been her. If Jake had loved her, really loved her, he would have moved mountains, swum the deepest oceans—all those stupid things in the love songs on the radio—to be with her.

A long, slow sigh left her body. Why Chantelle hadn't basked in his adoration confounded her. What she wouldn't give to have him worship her like that, put her needs before his own.

'Why was she like that, Mel? I don't get it.'

Mel looked at the object of their discussion and her eyes narrowed. 'She's a sneaky one, that Chantelle. I always suspected she wanted out of the relationship, but didn't want to be the one to end it. She'd talked her dad into spending a small fortune on the wedding, and he was livid when she pulled the plug.

'I think she was trying to push Jake into dumping her first, so he took all the flak. Then she could act the poor, jilted martyr.' She shook her head. 'Can't believe I didn't work out she'd turn up tonight. The whiff of free publicity alone is enough to make her crawl out of her hole.'

'Excuse me.' Someone barged past. Serena jumped out of the way and stared at her ticket stub. Row B, seat twenty-four. And Jake and the floozy were in…row C. Great. She edged along her row. What were the chances that seat twenty-four was in the far corner?

Eighteen…nineteen…

Oh, no, not… Twenty-four…slap bang in front of… She followed an endless pair of tanned legs up to the face they belonged to. Hah! Hair extensions! Fate was giving her a very small break. The thought gave her enough momentum to stretch her lips over her teeth and smile. She looked pointedly at the occupant of the seat next to the legs.

'Good evening, Jake.'

He looked as if he wanted the red velvet seat to fold up and swallow him. Serve him right.

'Evening.'

'Aren't you going to introduce me to your friend?'

Jake tugged at his shirt collar and mumbled something indecipherable.

Floozy held out a hand and regarded her with a suspicious eye. 'Chantelle. And you are…?' The defensive thrust of her chin spoilt the fairest-of-them-all effect.

'Serendipity Dove. Nice to meet you.' Her cheeks felt taut, keeping the smile in place.

Chantelle's eyes opened wide and the pout she'd been wearing transformed into a smile. 'Oh, you're…'

Serena nodded. Chantelle craned her neck and scanned the auditorium. 'Is your dad here, then?' There was something about her husky voice that rubbed Serena up the wrong way—like being caressed by a cheese grater.

'I'm sure he'll surface sooner or later. Keep your eyes peeled.'

Chantelle displayed her perfectly even, white teeth. 'We must have a chat at the interval. I expect we've got a lot in common, both being in the public eye and all.'

Mel, who had arrived next to Serena, snorted loudly.

'Oh, it's you, Melissa! I hardly recognised you now you're all grown up.' Chantelle lowered her voice to a stage whisper. 'You know, no one would ever guess you had a problem with spots when you were younger.'

Mel had that same evil glint in her eye that a Doberman got before it chewed something's leg off. Thankfully, the house lights dimmed and postponed any further insult-hurling. Serena sat down and tried to focus on what was happening on stage.

The gospel choir were the first act, and she really did try to concentrate on them. They'd improved so much. Feet were tapping and hands clapping in every direction. But not behind her. Oh, no. Chantelle leaned across to whisper into Jake's ear every few seconds. It was bad enough feeling heat creep up her neck just because his knees were only inches away, without being reminded that the floozy was the one who was actually touching him.

When the interval came, she couldn't shoot out of her seat fast enough.

Chantelle called after her. 'Good idea—get to the ladies' first. Hang on, babe. I'll come with you.'

Serena didn't bother waiting for the woman to disentangle herself from Jake. She ran to the circle bar as fast as she could and ordered a rather large gin and tonic. When the tumbler arrived she took a large sip and closed her eyes.

It wasn't long before she became aware of a couple of bodies in close proximity. *Please, no!* Relief flooded her when she opened her eyes to find Steve and Cassie standing there. She gave Cass a bear hug.

'Ren...I think you're cutting off my air supply.'

'Sorry. I'm just very glad to see a friendly face.'

Cassie's eyebrows raised.

'Long story. I'll fill you in later, but first let me get you a drink. The usual?' She turned back to the bar without waiting for an answer and waved at the barmaid. Cassie tugged her sleeve.

'Actually, I'll just have a lemonade.'

Serena spun right round and lost all hope of attracting the barmaid's attention for the next few minutes. The bar was filling up rapidly.

'Since when do you drink...?'

Cass shot a look at Steve, who was trying hard to do sheepish, but kept slipping into just plain jubilant.

'Oh, my goodness, you're not—?'

Cassie nodded.

'You *are!* That's wonderful news!'

She hugged Cassie again, making sure she didn't squeeze as hard this time. Thankfully, Steve had decided to jump in and get the drinks. He didn't see her happy mask slide as she looked over Cass's shoulder. How barren her own life seemed in comparison to her friend's.

She should be ashamed, thinking of herself at a time like this! Cassie had been her rock—the sister she'd never had. She deserved every ounce of happiness she got, and a hundredfold more.

She pulled back and took a slug of her G&T.

Cassie looked concerned. 'Are you okay? I wasn't going to tell you yet.'

'You didn't have to keep it a secret because of me.'

Cassie rubbed her arm. 'I just didn't want to rub your nose in it. I know things haven't been that great for you recently.'

There was a flash of blonde hair over Cassie's shoulder. Serena groaned. 'Don't look now! They're about to get a whole lot worse.'

She tried to hunker down and hide behind Cassie, but it was no good. Chantelle obviously had a homing device.

'There you are! We've just about got time for that chat.' She turned to Jake, who was looking the same shade of grey as his suit. 'Jay, could you get me a white wine? Ta, babes.' He was dismissed with a red-taloned hand. 'Don't mind him. He's been like that all evening. I'm not taking any notice, though. Jay and I go way back—but I'm sure you've heard all about that.'

'Not really.' She was surprised at how clear the words sounded through her gritted teeth.

'Oh. Well, we almost got hitched once upon a time, but I called it off. I don't think he ever got over it. I've heard he hasn't had a long-term relationship since.'

Chantelle gave her an assessing look. A look that told Serena she knew all about her recent relationship with Jake, and found it glaringly obvious why Jake hadn't wanted to march *her* up the aisle.

'How fascinating.'

Mel had been spot-on. Chantelle wasn't as dumb as she looked. She was staking her claim, making sure everyone knew she had first dibs on Jake, and always had. Chantelle tucked her arm into Serena's as if she were a long-lost friend and pulled her into a quiet corner, but she wasn't fooled. It was all part of the act. An act Chantelle was very good at.

Every word the model uttered was another nail in the coffin, hammering her rival into place.

'It was just bad timing, really. Just before the wedding I landed a big modelling contract.'

Holding up a tin of dog food, no doubt.

'Jay was so serious back then. Always working and doing exams. He never wanted to go to the parties I was invited to. He just wanted to settle down—' she mimed a yawn '—and do boring things like get a mortgage and have babies. I wasn't about to swell up like a balloon just as my career was taking off!'

She smoothed her skin-tight top down over her hips and gave a little laugh.

'I must have spoiled him for anyone else. He didn't seem to have any problem proposing to *me*. I expect I was the love of his life.' She looked wistfully over to the crush near the bar. Jake was in there somewhere. 'People said we were too young, and I suppose they were right. But now…well, let's just say I'm older and wiser.'

A grey-suited arm thrust a glass of wine under Chantelle's nose.

'Jay, you melon! This is dry wine. I only like medium sweet—you know that.'

Jake wore a grim look as he squeezed his way back to the bar, and Serena grinned into her glass as she took another sip. Either Jake didn't care enough to remember his ex's favourite tipple, or he was making a point. Either way, he wasn't Chantelle's lap dog any more.

Right then, the cavalry arrived. Cassie and Steve found them, and Steve made the mistake of asking Chantelle if he recognised her from somewhere. Pretty soon she'd launched into a monologue on all the designers she'd worked with, and how many minor-league pop stars she'd left broken-hearted.

Serena searched the sea of heads near the bar and found Jake's within seconds. Maybe the exact shade of his hair had stuck in her memory. It was like spotting the right jigsaw piece and knowing it was the one that was going to fit. She watched him work his way towards their group, diverting her eyes at the last moment, so he wouldn't know she'd been watching him.

Chantelle accepted the glass he offered her and took a gulp or two. 'Oh, good—that's much better!'

Jake elbowed his way round to stand at Serena's other side and whispered in her ear. 'This isn't what it—'

She knocked back the gin and tonic and slammed the glass down on a table. 'Well, I must get back.'

Chantelle's mouth turned down. 'Must you? Well, we'll have to go for a drink afterwards. Maybe after I've met your dad?'

'He's rather busy tonight.'

'Oh, we just want to say hi—don't we, Jay?'

Jay grunted.

Serena fled before she had to face any more. No way was that woman getting within twenty feet of her dad. Jake would be dropped like a hot brick and she'd be calling her *step-mummy* before you could say collagen injection!

Over my dead body. Or hers.

She sat in her seat, arms folded, shoulders hunched, for the second half of the programme. If Chantelle kicked the back of her chair one more time…

She hardly heard a note of the performance. When she actually managed to wrench her attention from the two seats behind her, the thought of watching from the sidelines while Steve and Cassie built their family shredded her like a knife.

She rubbed her forehead. Her friends had a future full of love and sunshine while her own was as bright as a bucket of Thames mud.

Perhaps she should stop planning her tomorrows like a military campaign. Do what Cassie had done. Perhaps she shouldn't hunt love down, but let it find her instead. But she was scared to let go and go with the flow. What if she just ended up washed out to sea—alone?

Grabbing on to any sign of security had seemed a much better plan, but she realised now it wasn't working. The things she grasped for always slipped through her fingers anyway.

Her dad, Max, and a couple of keyboard players filed onto the stage. She'd heard them rehearse all week, and it was going to bring the house down. The song was a fusion of rock guitar and hip hop, with Max's smooth vocal over the top. If that boy didn't have a recording contract in the next six months she'd eat her crocheted hat. Funny how all thoughts led back to Jake.

Chantelle's stilettos made jarring contact with the back of her seat again. She was living her worst nightmare. If the immediate torture of seeing the man she loved being pursued by another woman wasn't bad enough, her long-term plans for her personal life were looking even more bleak. She had no love-life, no husband, no babies—no future.

Of course she could change the *no love-life* part if she moved in with Jake, but that meant giving up her dreams. In the end she'd be back at square one, and maybe too old to find someone else who wanted to have children with her.

She sat very still. What if she got pregnant—with Jake's baby? Even if the relationship didn't last, she'd still have the baby. She looked from side to side, just to make sure no one could tell what she was thinking.

Now, this shows just how desperate I'm getting! Wake up, Serena!

She couldn't do that to him. Jake would want to do the right thing. She'd have him trapped and he would hate her for it eventually. She wanted his heart and soul, not just a family car in the garage and his and hers toothbrushes in the bathroom. The clamour of the auditorium vanished. Her chest rose and fell. Her heart thudded.

She wanted Jake, heart and soul.

The question was: what was she prepared to sacrifice to get him?

CHAPTER TEN

THE SWING DOOR closed and hit her on the bottom. She moved to one side and leant back against the smooth plaster wall. The cool air of the stairwell was delicious. Out here, away from the others, it was easier to see things for what they really were.

Chantelle wasn't any competition really. She was hardly a blip on the radar. Even if she wanted to cast herself in the role of *femme fatale*, it was obvious Jake wasn't interested

Serena knew Jake was *her* man. For now.

But Chantelle was a warning. One day a woman who was a more serious threat might be hanging on his arm, and Serena's chance would be gone. It was time to stuff her fears into the bottom of her handbag and seize the moment.

A few more deep breaths and she was ready to head down the stairs to the dressing rooms. Once in the warren-like basement, she set about tracking down her father. Benny's familiar bulk was placed outside dressing room three.

'Hey, Benny. Did you see any of the show?'

'A bit.'

'Like it?'

A nod. High praise indeed.

She knocked on the door and peeked inside. Dad was sitting on a table at one end of the room, surrounded by yabbering teenagers. They were all shouting over the top of each other, telling anyone who would listen how they'd almost tripped over, or how they'd fluffed a note. All of them had hundred-watt smiles.

She yelled to make herself heard. 'You were all brilliant!'

Raucous cheers of appreciation. She slipped into a seat next to her dad and kissed him on the cheek. 'It sounded great. The best you've played in years.'

'There's a lot to be said for being able to focus on the strings,' he said with a grin.

'Dad, I won't be going out with you and the rest of the gang after the show. There's something I've got to sort out.'

'About time too!'

She frowned.

'I might be over the hill, but I'm not blind! It's about time you and Mr Three-piece-suit sorted yourselves out.'

'Thanks, Dad.'

'Anyway, Max and I have a lot to discuss. I'm going to help him put a demo together.' Max sat on the other side of her father, doing a really bad job of being chilled about the whole idea.

'You're a star!' she mouthed to him, and he blushed. Max actually blushed!

She heard a pair of heels clacking in the corridor and her smile faded. Chantelle's radar must have gone into overdrive, being this close to a *bona fide* rock star. Serena hopped to her feet and marched to the open door.

'Benny, don't let that woman in here, or there'll be hell to pay.'

She stepped out into the corridor and pulled the door to, while Benny folded his arms and stood across the entrance. Chantelle was clomping to and fro, looking in dressing room doors. Jake stood at a distance, hands stuffed in his pockets and a forbidding look on his face.

Then he looked in her direction and they both stopped.

Bodies swarmed around them and Chantelle was forgotten. But she knew Chantelle wasn't meant for him, anyway. That was why he'd got cold feet before their wedding. It had had nothing to do with his ability to commit, that was for sure, but she suspected Jake hadn't woken up to that fact yet.

No guarantees, that was what he'd said. With love there were no sure things, only risks, and while Jake was fixated on the idea that there were no guarantees for success, there were no guarantees for failure either.

She lowered her lashes momentarily, and when she looked at him again she took all the barriers down. All her love and longing for him were there for him to see.

He swallowed, and his Adam's apple bobbed. He wanted her just as much as she wanted him. There was a sense of inevitability about all this. They had no choice, really. How stupid of them to have wasted all this time.

She wove through the moving bodies towards him and he suddenly sprang to life, forging through the crowd too. Finally they stood face to face. It was all she could do to stop herself from leaping into his arms. They were only inches apart, but she held back from touching him. Both of them knew that contact would light the touch paper, and this was neither time nor the place.

Her voice came out all low and breathy. 'We need to talk.'

'I'll give you a lift home.'

His eyes swept over her, drinking her in. Much more was being said than just words. Body to body, man to woman.

'What about Chantelle?' she asked.

'What about her? She came here on her own. She can leave the same way. I didn't bring her. She just…latched on.'

'I know.'

They both turned and watched Chantelle trying to sweet-talk Benny. All her eyelash-flapping was getting her nowhere. Serena and Jake smiled at each other and he reached for her hand. Her fingers slid into his and her fate was sealed, just as surely as if she'd said *I do*.

They didn't break contact until they reached Jake's car. The ride home was made in a silence thick with promise. It reminded her of the first night they'd met, when the boundaries of the universe had shrunk to fit the cabin of her dad's car.

Her heart throbbed like the engine and her nerve-endings were sensitised. Just watching him drive, watching his firm hands and strong wrists, was sending waves of pleasure crashing through her just as if he'd been touching her.

By the time the car screeched to a halt she was shaking with need.

As they climbed the steps to the front door, he caught her hand and pulled her to him. Since she was a step higher than him, they were at eye level with each other. His hands traced the contours of her cheeks, and the look in his eyes made her tremble all the more. It was more than desire, something richer and deeper, which, given enough time and room to grow, *might* turn into love.

She drank in that look.

Then her lashes lowered to her cheeks and she started to close the gap between them, slowly, savouring the ache of anticipation. Jake broke before she did, crushing her to him and claiming her lips with heady need. She clasped her hands round his neck and pulled him closer still, letting him know the heat was raging inside her too.

They stumbled up the next few steps, Jake guiding her as best he could since she was going backwards. Her back crashed into the front door, but all thoughts of keys and lights were banished from her head by the velvet of his lips upon her throat, burning kisses that set her toes alight.

She dragged her hands from the back of his head and fumbled in her pocket. The keys felt like ice. They jangled in her shaking fingers as she tugged them free. Jake refused to let her go when she turned to slide her key into the lock. His hands flew under her coat, caressing her through the clingy wrap-over dress she was wearing. One hand delved under the top layer. She gasped hard and almost dropped her keyring.

Then they were falling through the front door, keys clattering somewhere on the tiles. Coats fell to the floor. Jake's weight shifted as he slammed the door closed with a foot.

He pulled away and looked at her, and her heart almost stopped. Such tenderness, such vulnerability. How did this amazing, intelligent man not understand he was nothing like his father? He was too scared to see the truth. Scared of the loss and rejection that might ensue if his fears were real. That fear had kept him a prisoner too long.

She kissed his nose, his eyelids, his brows.

I was scared too.

But she had thrown away her fears and preconceptions and jumped over the precipice. And instead of a terrifying plummet to the death, she was flying—free to love and give herself without reservation. It was glorious.

She would lead him, step by step, and if they stumbled, they stumbled, but at least they would have tried. She laced her fingers into his and led him towards the stairs. The house was as familiar to her in the dark as it was with the lights on. Jake, however, was blind. But it didn't matter. She would guide him through the darkness.

When the bedroom door clicked shut behind them, the pace slowed, as if they both knew the momentous nature of the occasion. No rushing through without enjoying the scenery. Each moment, each touch, was to be savoured, not wasted.

He stepped towards her and kissed her. His lips were so soft, so gentle, that tears sprang into her eyes. She knew she would never regret taking this path, whatever the future held. Just to experience this bliss once in a lifetime would be enough.

The tips of his fingers skimmed the contours of her body, and the string holding her dress together tensed, then fell loose. She fumbled with his tie, trembling fingers working through the knot, but she wouldn't rush. It slid free and landed by their feet.

She lowered her arms and shimmied out of her dress. It clung to her slightly as it slid down her legs and pooled at her ankles. Jake reached for her, his patience evaporating, and his long fingers slid down her back, sending ripples of delight up her spine.

Knowing she was in her underwear while he was still fully clothed only served to heighten her desire, making her feel feminine and sexy. The cotton of his shirt grazed the skin of her torso as they clung together, finally overbalancing and landing with a thump on the goose-down duvet.

Her hands were everywhere. She couldn't claim enough of him.

He was the one. She didn't care which boxes he ticked and which he didn't. He was the only one. There was no point taking her hunt any further. Any other man would only be second best. He could have her heart on his terms—no strings attached, no regrets.

She pulled his face close to hers and gave him the sweetest kiss she could deliver. 'I love you, Jake.'

He pulled her even closer, his arms so tight it felt as if he wanted to climb inside her skin. She could feel him trembling, his breathing uneven. His voice was warm in her ear. 'Oh, God, Serena, I…'

Say it! Say you love me too!

'I…can't do this.'

The air rushed cold and barren round her body as he pushed himself away. Suddenly she felt naked rather than sexy, underwear or no underwear. This was no longer abandon; it was humiliation. She pulled her arms and legs into herself and curled into a ball.

He was panting. 'I'm sorry, so sorry. I should never have let this happen.'

Her tongue was glued to the roof of her mouth. His pity stung. She closed her eyes and turned her head away.

'I'm sorry.'

She winced.

And then he was gone, his feet thudding down the stairs, the crash of the front door, the squeal of tyres. She sat up and strained for the sound of his car until it melded with the sirens and the rumble of the city. Then she slid off the edge of the bed and collapsed onto the floor.

Her foot touched something silky. His tie. She wound it round her fingers and pulled it to her chest.

No regrets? What a fool!

She was so stupid not to have seen the signs.

Jake *could* do commitment! She'd seen evidence of it in his relationships with Mel and Max, and even Chantelle. The truth was he couldn't—no, *wouldn't*—commit to *her*, not even for a night. She had offered herself to him and he just hadn't been able to bring himself to accept her gift. He didn't want her on any terms at all.

She pulled the tie to her face. It smelled of him. The fabric was soft on her cheek, where his lips had been only moments before. She wasn't sure whether she wanted to rip it to shreds or wind it round her own neck.

She buried her face in the duvet and quivered at the thought of her humiliation.

Her eyelids were stuck together with congealed tears. She stretched them far enough for them to pop apart, lash by lash, then slithered out of bed. Her foot made contact with a soggy tissue, thrown there some time around four a.m. In fact, the whole bedroom floor was a minefield of them.

She pulled on her robe and fluffy slippers, and bent to retrieve her bra and knickers from the night before with thumb and forefinger.

She would never wear them again. Who needed a constant reminder of the most painful moment of her life? They would brush against her skin, touch the places he should have touched but had declined.

I can't do this.

She dodged the tissues and left the bedroom. A cup of tea would have to solve all her problems. She certainly didn't have any other ideas.

Back at square one.

Well, back at square minus one hundred, actually. Last time she'd been planning her happy ever after at least her heart had been in one piece, without boot-marks all over it. The weight of all she'd lost lay heavy on her chest. It hurt to breathe, to think.

Just the slightest thought of him made her stomach roll.

Being lovesick had always sounded so romantic before she'd realised it involved feeling physically ill—as if she'd gone ten rounds with a bout of flu and come off the worst.

She reached the kitchen and wandered over to the sink to stare out of the window. The tint of the sky meant dawn was imminent. A few cups and plates sat in the sink. Hardly enough to bother with the dishwasher. All mind-numbing activities were heartily welcomed for the foreseeable future, so she reached for the washing-up liquid. A puff of air and three tiny bubbles were her reward.

So she stood and stared out of the window again. The bright daylight colours of the garden were hushed into hues of grey and blue and lavender. Everything seemed so peaceful, so empty. She longed to feel like that. Peaceful. Empty. Not bombarded by her senses. Colours were too bright, noises too loud, feelings too...much. She felt an overwhelming urge to let the cold grey light of the garden dampen them until they were bearable.

The instant she opened the back door the cold air hit her like a slap. It was wonderful. Anything to give her a split-second relief from her broken heart. She needed more of the same. She didn't want to think about him, to feel anything for him. She had to numb herself.

She understood her father's addictions a little better this morning. It was the only way he'd been able to cope after her mother died. Now she understood how seductive the thought of oblivion could be.

If only she could escape the gnawing pain, could forget the way his face had looked when he left.

I'm so sorry.

She found herself at the old wooden bench under the oak tree and sat down. Its weathered surface was still rough through the thin protection of her pyjamas and wrap, but she didn't care. She sat facing the blank garden wall and waited for the pre-dawn chill to freeze her heart as it had her fingertips.

The sun had turned the sky a pale apricot when her father found her shivering.

'Come back inside,' he said, reaching for her hand. 'You'll freeze to death out here.'

She let him pull her up and guide her back to the house, too drained to argue. 'It all went horribly wrong, Dad.'

'I guessed as much when I saw you sitting out there. Come on, I'll make you a bacon sandwich. I know how you love them.'

'But, Dad, you're a vegetarian. You hate—'

'It doesn't matter. It's high time I looked after *you* for a change.'

He led her into the kitchen and pulled out a chair near the sturdy table. 'You're a survivor, you know. You'll get through this.' He kissed the top of her head and then started rummaging in the cupboards for a frying pan.

Serena slumped forward and laid her cheek on the cool wood of the table. She stayed there, just watching her breath mist the surface and evaporate over and over again.

Getting through this seemed as likely to her as bungee-jumping off the top of Big Ben.

Jake checked his watch. Two-fifteen. The view from the plane window showed unrelenting grey ocean. He relaxed slightly. He was more than halfway across the Atlantic. Not a totally safe distance, but better.

He leaned his elbows on the drop-down tray and rested his face in his hands.

'Are you all right, sir?'

He twisted his head to look at the stewardess. 'Fine.'

'Air sickness?'

'Something like that. It'll pass.'

'Just press the call button if you need anything.'

'Thanks. I will.'

He pressed his thumbs into his eye sockets. He couldn't cope with the thought of how much he'd hurt her. She'd hate him, but he had to remind himself it was better this way. If she had any idea *why* he'd really done what he had, she'd keep on hoping. If she knew he loved her she'd waste her time waiting for him, instead of finding someone to give her all she needed—all she deserved.

How embarrassing. He hadn't cried since he was thirteen and Millwall had lost to West Ham. He sucked in a breath and held it, willing the stinging at the backs of his eyes to stop. He only just made it.

A few more hours and he'd be in New York. If only he'd stayed away longer last time he wouldn't have put both of them through this. At least with an ocean between them he could hardly foul up her chances of happiness again.

The in-flight movie started—an action flick. He needed something to take his mind off Serena. But, five minutes in, things were exploding left, right and centre and all he could think about was her.

Leaving her had been the hardest thing he'd ever had to do, but he couldn't stay and see her shrivel as all her dreams died. She would be a great mother. He could imagine her covered in finger paint, giving horsey rides to a little girl with chocolate-brown eyes who could wrap her daddy round her little finger.

Rats! His cheek was wet. He might as well just shove his face in the sick bag and pretend.

* * *

Serena reached for the phone. Finally her fingers gripped it and pulled it to her ear. 'Uh-huh?'

'It's nine-thirty. Time to get out of bed!'

Cass!

'I'm not in bed.'

Silence.

'I'm sitting at my computer, fully dressed: hair combed, teeth brushed—the works.'

'Well…good. I'm glad to see you've stopped wallowing. I haven't heard from you in a fortnight.'

'I haven't been wallowing; I've been busy working on something. And, believe it or not, I'm a big girl, Cass. I can actually get out of bed on my own now and then.'

'Well, if that's the way you feel…'

'Cass, please! I know you're just looking out for me, like you've always done, but I need to stand on my own two feet. You've got to stop fussing over me!'

'I'm only trying to look after you.' Cassie sounded really hurt.

'I know! And I love you for it. But pretty soon you're going to have someone else to look after—someone even more helpless than me.'

'Only just.' Cassie tried to make a disapproving noise, but Serena could tell she was stifling a smile.

'I've spent too long hiding behind Dad, pretending I was looking after him, when really I was just playing it safe. It's time to live my life, take some risks.'

'Good for you! What sort of risks?'

'I want you to arrange another blind date for me.'

The series of muffled thumps and clunks that followed gave her a pretty good clue that Cassie had just dropped the phone. When she next spoke, she sounded breathless. 'You're kidding!'

'I'm perfectly serious.'

It took Cassie a good few seconds to stumble the next few words out. 'But…Jake…'

'…is gone, Cass. It's been a month now. I need to move on.'

'Well, if you're sure…'

'I am. Set it up for Lorenzo's.'

'Gino and Maria as back-up? Like before?'

'Too right. They'll tear strips off anyone who even looks at me funny.'

'Thanks a lot! Don't you trust my judgement?'

'Let's just say I'm covering all the bases. Look how it worked out last time.'

'Good point. Lorenzo's it is.'

'Talking of Lorenzo's, can you and Steve make it for lunch tomorrow? Dad and I have an idea we'd like to talk through with you.'

'Sounds intriguing.'

'All will be revealed tomorrow. One o'clock?'

'Sounds good. Look after yourself, sweetie.'

'You too. Bye.'

Serena put down the phone and wrote the lunch date on the calendar. Tomorrow was four weeks to the day since she'd last seen Jake. She hadn't actually marked off the days, but every time she looked at the calendar she imagined those little spiky red crosses there all the same.

She opened her internet browser and clicked on a link in her 'favourites' list. A girl could always do with a little retail therapy at a time like this. There, at the top of the list, was the link to the Jacobs Associates website. The pointer hovered over it. She clicked—and sent it to the recycle bin. A wave of sadness hit her.

It wasn't that she was over Jake. She just needed to move on with her life. Some important lessons had been learned from the whole sorry affair. The most important being that it didn't matter if the packaging wasn't conventional: love and security came in all different disguises.

She'd been so sure her upbringing had lacked stability—and sometimes it had—but she'd always been loved. She just hadn't recognised it for what it was. No more judging by appearances. And men were most definitely included in that edict.

Look at Jake. She'd picked him because he had the right look to fill her fantasy role of Mr Right—a little cardboard cut-out she could tack on to the rose-covered cottage along with the kids and two dogs.

And underneath the layers of crusty accountant she'd found a surprisingly imaginative and wonderful man, even better than her wish list—for all the good it had done her!

Asking Cassie to set her up again wasn't a sign she'd got over him. Her heart still squeezed every time she thought of him. She avoided anywhere they'd ever been together, and she couldn't find a single sensible thing to say to Mel. Just looking into his sister's blue eyes set off a whole string of memories like tiny time bombs.

No, resuming her husband-hunt was more an act of faith. Maybe one day she would find someone to love and support her. It wouldn't be like it had been with Jake. He was the love of her life—such a corny phrase, but she knew now what people meant by it. Maybe she would find someone nice to share her life with, but a little piece of her would always be reserved for Jake.

Next time she would be more prepared.

No! her heart screamed. It didn't want a *next time*.

'So, what do you think?'

Steve clapped his hands together. 'I think it's a great idea!'

Serena and her father exchanged smiles.

'What are you going to call it?' asked Cassie.

'We haven't come up with anything yet.'

Steve sat back in his chair and scratched his chin. 'What about The Phoenix Foundation? Would the other band members mind you using the name?'

Her dad shrugged. 'I'll have to ask, but I can't see it being a problem.'

'It just seems to fit, doesn't it?' Steve continued. 'The whole idea of setting up music projects in inner city areas, breathing new hope into people and places that have been written off.'

Serena squeezed her dad's hand. 'I think it's perfect. In time, once we're up and running, we'd like to offer scholarships for gifted pupils to take their music education further—or even get the music industry to give work experience placements and funded apprenticeship programmes.'

Steve smiled. 'With your contacts, Mike, nothing is impossible.'

'I'm glad you like the idea,' her dad said. 'Because we want to ask you and Cassie to be on the board of trustees. Will you do it?'

'Just try and stop me!'

Her father turned to Cassie. 'How about you?'

Cassie smiled an elfish little smile. 'When's the launch party? You've got to have a launch party! Attract a bit of publicity, get the ball rolling...'

'How about three weeks from now?' Serena said.

Cassie stared at her. 'Three weeks? That's cutting it a bit fine!'

'Not for my daughter! She's been up till all hours most nights, working on this idea. She's a human dynamo!'

'Dad can pull a few strings to get us a venue, and I'll get

to work on the rest—after all, I haven't got anything else to occupy my time.'

While the others started chattering and suggesting ideas for the party, Serena sat back in her chair and folded her hands in her lap. The foundation was going to be a salvation for her—and her father too. Something positive to fill the void left by their differing personal addictions.

She waved over to the bar. 'Gino! Give us another round of Shirley Temples—and this time stick an umbrella in them. We're celebrating!'

CHAPTER ELEVEN

MERV BLUMSTEIN spoke in his nasal Brooklyn accent. 'Did you have a look at that investment opportunity I told you about? What do you think?'

'It looks like a good bet,' Jake replied.

'Are you sure?'

'As sure as I can be.' He flicked through a file. 'Nothing's a dead cert in investment terms, of course. There are no iron-clad guarantees…'

Merv coughed. 'Mr Jacobs?'

Jake snatched his focus back from the ceiling. 'Sorry. I just…remembered something similar I said to someone else.' He shook himself out of it and smiled warmly at the quizzical Mr Blumstein. 'Irrelevant, really. As I was saying, there's no way to guarantee success, but failure isn't certain either. We have to take a risk, yes, but it's a calculated risk.'

Merv nodded, but his face was pinched. For a self-made millionaire he was the most cautious man Jake had ever met. People often made that kind of money by taking chances, but not Merv. He'd probably saved every penny since he was a toddler, refusing to let anything out of his sweaty grasp.

It was daft, really. If only he'd learn to jump in and take a risk, he could be twice as rich as he was now and probably half as stressed! Life was no fun if you always played it safe…

He slapped the folder closed and handed it to his client. 'It's your money, Mr Blumstein, and you can do what you want with it. But I recommend you give this some consideration. Take the report away with you and let me know how you want to proceed when you're ready.'

Merv shook his hand and left, clutching the folder as if it contained the secrets of the ancients. Jake managed to resist wiping his hand on his trouser leg until the door was safely closed. He moved out from behind the desk and wandered to the window. It was a great *thinking* window; the view was never boring. The afternoon sun bounced off the skyscrapers, and traffic and people swarmed like multi-coloured bugs seventy floors below.

Was he really guilty of playing it safe?

He'd always thought he was so sensible in his attitude to love—keeping his distance, never getting involved. He'd told himself it was to protect the innocent, so he didn't break too many hearts. A cold feeling crept up his arms. What a load of…

He was protecting *himself*! The whole keep-'em-at-arm's-length thing had been about self-protection—until Serena, of course. He really had done what was best for her. To see her broken and dejected like his mother would have been more than he could bear. And to know that he was the one responsible for taking that generous heart and squeezing all the life out of it until it was a withered shell… He couldn't do that to her.

No guarantees…

He turned his back on the New York skyline and faced

into the office. It was dingy and claustrophobic by comparison. He thought about his father. Mel had phoned only that morning to let him know when the trial date was. The image of his father as the policeman had put his hand on top of his head and guided him into the police car still hovered in his memory.

There had been no remorse, no compassion on his face, only blind rage. It was as if he believed it was undeserved, that he was not to blame. Jake just didn't get it. He'd looked at it from every angle to get inside his father's head, and still he couldn't fit the pieces of the puzzle together. He would never understand how…

A wave of nausea hit him, so powerful he almost reached for the wastebin.

He was nothing like him! Nothing like his father at all!

In appearance, maybe, but that was where it ended. Inside, they were as different as alien species. His stomach turned again. What if…what if he'd made the most terrible mistake?

He couldn't think about that now. Time was needed to digest the most recent revelation before he plumbed the even greater depths of his own foolishness.

He stabbed the button on the intercom. 'Susan?'

'Yes, Mr Jacobs?'

'Hold all my calls for the next thirty minutes. I'm…something has come up. I'm going out.'

Within five minutes his feet were in contact with the sidewalk and the multi-coloured bugs were a mass of taxis, cars and jostling people. The bustle of the Big Apple was good for crowding out any unwelcome thoughts; that was why he'd come back here.

His favourite coffee house was only just round the corner.

He could buy a double espresso and read a British paper. Café Noir liked to appear cosmopolitan, and stocked a selection of international newspapers for their clientele to peruse.

Just as he was about to turn into the doorway, he stopped in his tracks. All the breath left his body.

How...?

She was hailing a cab. Sleek dark hair fell around her shoulders and her long skirt was ruffled in the light breeze. A silver bracelet danced on the wrist of her raised arm.

Then she turned, and he realised it wasn't her after all. Only a memory superimposed on a similar shell.

How many times was he going to do this? It was getting to be a weekly, if not daily, occurrence. Pretty soon he'd have to barricade himself inside his rented apartment to safeguard his sanity.

He went inside Café Noir, ordered his coffee, and grabbed a paper from the rack by the till. It was a little downmarket from what he usually read, but it was the best he could lay his hands on. A large man with a moustache was hogging the only copy of *The Times*.

Once seated, he read every word on the first three pages— from the date to the regional weather forecasts—but the words swam around his head in a mini-tornado. Not one sentence made sense. He flipped a few more pages, desperate for something to divert his thoughts.

Lord, he was seeing her in here too!

A picture of a model he'd just flicked past had made his stomach lurch. It was a bad idea to fuel his imagination when it was behaving like this, but he flipped the pages back anyway, and smoothed them down.

RISING FROM THE ASHES.

He didn't notice much of the other text apart from the headline. Something about a charity do. His eyes were fixed on the photo in the bottom right corner. *Rock star Damon Blade with Serendipity Dove,* the caption read.

Jake knew enough about the music scene to want to rip the head off the guy with his hand hooked around her waist. His gut clenched at the thought of it. Blade's mouth was only inches from her long, graceful neck as he whispered something in her ear. The tabloids called him a 'love rat', and by the look of him he was trying to take a nibble on Serena.

Look at him! He couldn't even take his eyes off her long enough to smile for the camera. But then, Jake could hardly blame him. She looked stunning, her eyes large and haunting, staring straight into the camera lens. Straight into his soul.

His heart stuttered.

It was as if she were looking right at him—which was ridiculous, of course. Blast that stupid brain of his! Always conjuring up things that weren't there. That was what had got him into this mess in the first place.

No matter. He still couldn't tear his eyes away from the picture. Even after almost two months he was hungry to see her. If a grainy print was all he could get hold of, it would have to do. He wondered if the waitress would shout at him if he tore it out and stuffed it in his pocket.

He looked back at the photo. She wasn't even smiling, really. Her eyes were sad, and her mouth and chin had a defiant set—issuing him a challenge, almost.

If you want me, come and get me—before it's too late.

He advised his clients to take risks, but he'd been guilty of ignoring his own good advice. He loved her, and hadn't she told him she loved him too? They were well suited—her warmth and impulsiveness a perfect complement to his over-analytical reserve. That sounded like a calculated risk, didn't it? Could it have worked?

No guarantees, he'd said. He'd been wrong. He was guaranteed one thing: he would regret it for the rest of his life if he didn't go and convince her to give him another chance.

The kitchen door crashed open and Serena looked up from her magazine. Cassie stood braced in the doorway. Body language like that normally meant trouble.

'We're on!' Cassie announced.

'I beg your pardon?'

'You heard. We're on—or at least you are. Saturday night at Lorenzo's, eight o'clock. You've got a date.'

Oh, flip!

She'd forgotten about her moment of insanity when she'd suggested Cassie start up the whole husband-hunt thing again. Trying to run before she could walk, she supposed.

Cassie sat opposite and leaned forward on her elbows. 'What's the matter? *You* asked me, remember?'

'I know. It's just—'

'Don't tell me you actually agreed to go out with Damon the Dastardly? I know he's phoned you three times a day since the party, but still!'

She shot Cass a *what-kind-of-idiot-do-you-think-I-am?* look. 'No, I'm not seeing Damon.' The very thought made her flesh crawl.

'So what's stopping you, then?'

Serena toyed with her mug of coffee.

'Exactly!' said Cassie, a triumphant gleam in her eye. 'Nothing.'

'I'm just not ready.'

'Nonsense. Time to get back on the horse, plenty more fish in the sea, every dog has its day—that sort of thing.'

Her cheeks creased into a smile. Cassie was priceless when she did her schoolmarm bit. 'Horses, fish, dogs? He's not a zookeeper, by any chance, is he?'

'No. Stop stalling.'

'So spill the beans. Who is candidate number four hundred and twenty-two?'

'Mr Right, of course.'

Sure.

She flapped her magazine closed. 'I really don't want to, Cass.'

'This was your idea, sweetie. You can't back out now! It's going to make me look stupid. Just go and have dinner with the man. If you don't like him, don't see him again. And I promise I won't set you up on any more dates for a few weeks.'

'Months.' Years.

'Okay, for a few months.' Cassie's smirk was the biggest one Serena had ever seen her wear, and that was saying something!

'So, who *is* Mr Right, then?'

'All you need to know is that he's tall, good-looking, and perfect for you.'

How many times had she heard that before?

'We'll see.'

The reflection in the glass of the restaurant door didn't look great. Her hair was wavy on one side and straight the other. Her fingers curled around the door handle. It seemed a lifetime away since she'd been standing here ready to meet a different stranger.

This meant nothing, really. She wouldn't even see the guy again. She was doing it to prove something to herself—a symbolic act to show that there was hope for the future. Far, far into the future.

'Are you gonna stand there all night, love?'

She jumped, and her fingers sprang away from the door handle as if it were red-hot. 'Sorry,' she mumbled, hardly looking at the man who barged past her into Lorenzo's.

Oh, get a grip!

She nipped inside before the door swung shut, and marched herself up to the bar.

'Hi, Gino.'

'Hey, *bambino*!' His eyes twinkled. 'Looking for love again?'

Serena snorted. 'How's Maria?'

'Good. She's in the back at the moment. I'd go and get her for a chat, but we don't want to keep your fella waiting, do we?'

'He's not my *fella*.'

Gino just smiled.

The man who'd barged past her on his way in collected a couple of carrier bags from Marco, the chef—who winked at her—and swept back past her on his way out. At least he wasn't her date. A bucketload of fun that would have been!

Gino herded her towards the main part of the restaurant. She turned the corner and stopped.

'It's empty!'

Gino chuckled behind her. She spun round to look at him.

'It's Saturday night. You should be packed!'

He shrugged. 'Your fella wanted a little privacy.'

Oh, great! A date with a first-class bunny boiler. Her eyes darted around the room and she did a quick calculation of how many seconds it would take her to reach the exit if things went pear-shaped.

'Where is he, then?' When she'd said the room was empty, she hadn't been joking.

Gino led her to a table—her favourite table, the one she'd sat at waiting for Jake.

'Could I sit somewhere else, please?'

Gino shook his head.

'The place is deserted! Surely it wouldn't matter?'

'The gentleman was very specific.' He pulled out a chair and she dropped into it, scowling. She was still in the same pose when Gino returned with two glasses of champagne.

This was a bad sign. She hadn't even met the guy and he was already getting on her nerves. Far too smooth by half!

'Where's this Mr Wonderful, then?'

Gino just winked at her and turned to smile at Maria, who was now behind the bar, hands clasped, eyes shimmering.

She pushed the champagne glass away. 'Could you bring me a mineral water, please, Gino?' She wasn't touching a drop of anything alcoholic until she knew it was safe to let her guard down. Gino disappeared, and she stared at the tablecloth. Her date was obviously building up to a grand entrance, and that did not bode well. It told her he thought he was the icing on the cake. The last thing she needed in her life at the moment was a man addicted to drama.

She traced the pattern in the tablecloth with her finger. Gino was a long time getting her water. She craned her neck to see what he was doing, but she only had a partial view of the bar, and he and Maria were nowhere to be seen.

She guessed he wasn't too far away, because the uncharacteristic silence had been broken by music, billowing chords that stroked the tension out of her shoulders. She smiled to herself as she imagined her date jumping out of a giant cake when the music reached its crescendo. There was something about this evening that was decidedly surreal.

Oh, well. She took a sip of champagne anyway—more for something to do than anything else. Mmm. Just another small sip.

She stilled and put down her glass. That vocal…it was so like…Max! That was Max's voice! What on earth…?

She tipped her head to one side and listened carefully. What was that he was singing? Something about being too scared to let a girl into his heart. It was beautiful. A sad tale of lost love and missed chances. She tried desperately not to mist over. Stupid, really, it just reminded her so much of what had gone wrong between her and Jake, as if he was singing their story.

When the instrumental break arrived she gave herself a stern talking-to. It would not be good if she was all red and puffy when Mr Right arrived. She swiped away some moisture with her finger and sniffed. Then, one by one, all the hairs on the back of her neck stood on end.

She didn't only recognise the voice; she recognised the tune. It was Jake's song! The one he'd played her in his flat the night he'd cooked her dinner. She just hadn't realised because with the other instruments and vocals it sounded fuller, more complete.

And now Max was singing about how he wanted to love her for ever, to have and to hold, to cherish her and never let her go.

Tears rolled down her cheeks, but she was too lost in the song to remember to wipe them away. Then the final chords wove themselves together and faded. She reached for her glass, but her fingers trembled too much to risk picking it up.

'I finished it.'

Her head jolted up and there he was—Jake. She grabbed onto the table, sure the world had just rolled on its axis.

'I discovered all I needed was a little inspiration.' He was walking towards her, trying to smile, but a little nerve twitched in his cheek. '*You* are my inspiration, Serendipity Dove. I needed *you* to make it complete.' He arrived at the table and sat opposite her, all the time keeping eye contact. She needed to remember to breathe every few seconds, she really did.

He took her hand. 'I need you to make *me* complete too.'

That was it. The tears fell like torrential rain. Those clear blue eyes were full of everything she had ever wanted to see in them. She tugged at the elaborately folded napkin in front of her, intending to bury her face in it.

Something flew out as she pulled it open, and tumbled onto her lap. Her fingers reached for it. She looked at him and he swallowed.

Her fingertips brushed against velvet. She grasped it and pulled a little jewellery box from under the table into the light. The air around them fizzed with static electricity. She was still staring at the box when she realised Jake had moved. He was close beside her, but not touching. She met his gaze at eye level.

He was down on one knee.

A shiver ran right through her and the little box slid from her fingers. Jake was ready. He caught it in one deft swipe and held it out to face her. Her eyes grew wide as he eased the lid open.

Inside was a stunning antique ring. A square-cut emerald flanked by diamonds set in white gold. She couldn't have imagined anything more perfect.

His face went slightly grey. 'Serendipity Dove—I won't call you Serena; it's not your name, and it's the real you I love—will you marry me?'

He lifted the ring from its velvet cushion and held it near the tip of her finger, waiting.

Finally her tongue remembered what it was for! 'But you don't want me!'

'I want you more than anything in this world.'

She shook her head. 'You left.'

His eyes clouded over and a shadow passed over his face. 'I'm so sorry.' His thumb reached up and brushed the tears from her cheek. 'I thought I was being noble, but actually I was just being very, very stupid. I thought I was saving you from me. I knew you were desperate for the whole package, husband and babies, and I couldn't steal that dream from you, so I left.'

'But now you're back?'

'Yes. To stay, for ever—if you'll have me.'

If she'd thought her heart was beating fast before, now it doubled its efforts and sprinted off into the sunset.

'I thought you didn't *do* that kind of thing.'

'Only for you.'

She shook her head. This was all too much. She wanted to believe him, she really did, but he'd bolted on her twice before.

'Look at me.'

His deep blue eyes were earnest. She could see right inside, and there wasn't a shred of doubt or fear in them. 'I love you like I've never loved anyone else. I want to spend the next fifty years with you—or sixty, or seventy. I want to fight about who has the remote control and whose turn it is to change the next stinky nappy. I want you to remind me where I've left my false teeth when we're old and crusty. Please marry me. Say yes.'

She blinked, hardly daring to believe it was true. She'd better answer before this lovely dream evaporated.

'Yes. Yes, I'll marry you—*Charlie*.'

She half expected him to wince, understanding now why he hated his name, but he was the one who'd started being picky on the subject. He laughed, a deep guttural sound, and slipped the ring on. It sat comfortably there, as if her finger had always been waiting for it.

And then they were standing, and she was in his arms, his lips pressed against hers, and she thought she was going to pass out from sheer delight.

Slowly, she became aware of other noises in the room: whispers, shuffling, and then, growing in volume, a round of applause. She pulled away and stared at the dozen or so people gathered near the bar.

'Cass! Dad! Mel? All of you! What are you doing here?'

Jake whispered in her ear. 'I hired the restaurant for our engagement party.'

She punched him on the arm. 'You were a little sure of yourself, weren't you?'

'Actually, no. I knew I'd hurt you badly, and I had no idea what you'd say. I was prepared to look like a fool in front of all of them if you made a different decision. I was so fixated on the idea I was going to repeat my father's history I didn't give *us* a chance. I didn't try to prove myself wrong. I'm sorry.'

Champagne corks popped in the background, but she didn't move her eyes from his face. 'I was stubborn too! It wasn't all your fault. I had this picture-perfect idea of my future, and I wouldn't accept anything that didn't fit the template. It was stupid. At first all I saw was your suit and your job, but then I fell in love with you and it didn't matter what you wore or what you did. I just wanted you—any way I could have you.'

'And now you've got me. I hope you realise there's a no returns policy?'

'Oh, shut up and kiss me.'

She pulled him close by the lapels and savoured the taste and the feel of him. She was home.

Someone in the room let out a wolf whistle—probably Cass. They pulled apart, grinning.

'I suppose we'd better go and say hello to all our guests. After all, they made this possible.'

She looked at him, eyebrows raised.

'Cass was a mine of helpful information—and, of course, got you to turn up. Your dad and Max have worked round the clock for the last few days, helping me put down the song. I finished it on the plane journey back to London. It's amazing how much clarity you get when you're racing through the air, hoping to high heaven that you haven't messed up the best thing that ever happened to you.'

'The song is wonderful. You're wonderful. I love you so much.'

Then the crowd descended on them, and there was much hugging and kissing and slapping on backs. Mel was in tears, and Cass was grinning away as if she was responsible for the whole thing—which she was, of course, but it would never do to admit that. Her head was far too large already.

Finally, they found each other again. Their fingers laced together and he smiled down at her. She sighed. She wanted so much to be alone with him, away from all the chatter and clamour.

He read her look and his pupils grew.

'Later,' he whispered, and placed a kiss in the hollow beneath her ear. 'We've got the rest of our lives.'

* * * *

Fiona Harper brings you more emotional romance in
Three Weddings and a Baby.
Coming soon from Mills & Boon® RIVA™!

The Blind Date Surprise

by Barbara Hannay

Barbara Hannay was born in Sydney, educated in Brisbane, and has spent most of her adult life living in tropical North Queensland, where she and her husband have raised four children. While she has enjoyed many happy times camping and canoeing in the bush, she also delights in an urban lifestyle—chamber music, contemporary dance, movies and dining out. An English teacher, she has always loved writing and now, by having her stories published, she is living her most cherished fantasy.

Special thanks to Andrea and Gordon Smith,
my eyes and ears in Brisbane

PROLOGUE

From the Ask Auntie page of the *Mirrabrook Star*. (Circulation 2,500, including Wallaby Flats):

Ask Auntie,
The loneliness of the outback is driving me crazy. I'm two hundred kilometres from the nearest cinema or nightclub and it's so hard to meet guys. The few dates I've had have been spectacularly forgettable, but now I've met a wonderfully warm, funny and clever man over the Internet and I'm in love. I want to dash off to the city to meet him, but all my life I've been accused of being too hasty and impulsive, so I'm seeking guidance. What do you advise?
Marooned in Mirrabrook.

Dear Marooned in Mirrabrook,
If you're as lonely as you sound and your cyber-romance is going well, why shouldn't you meet this man? I suspect you're afraid of disappointment—that you fear you've fallen in love with the idea of the man, but you're worried about the reality. Some tension is understandable, but if you're looking

for a long-term relationship you need real interaction with a real man. You need to meet him.

Of course, a woman from the bush would be wise to approach an e-date in the city with some caution. Perhaps you could arrange for a double date with friends? If not, you should make sure you meet at a public venue and you should have a friend in the city who knows the time and location of your date and who can be reached at the touch of a button on your mobile phone.

However, once these details are organised, go for it. Don't believe the old cliché that good things come to those who wait. Good things come to people who want them so badly they can't sit still…

Good luck!

Ask Auntie.

CHAPTER ONE

CRIKEY, *pink* jeans!

Annie McKinnon hated to guess what her brothers would say if they could see her. Come to think of it, what would anyone from her outback home town, Mirrabrook, say? She'd lived in blue denim jeans since she was three years old—ever since her brother, Kane, first lifted her on to the back of a stock horse.

Never pink. And *never* teamed with stilettos.

And yet here she was in the heart of the city, sashaying into the foyer of one of Brisbane's swankiest hotels in killer heels, the sweetest little white silk camisole top, and low-rise jeans so baby-pink and slim she felt like a pop-star wannabe.

So this was where following your friends' advice got you.

'You'd better listen to Victoria,' Melissa had said. 'She's our in-house fashionista and everyone at work takes her word as gospel.'

Victoria had been definite. 'Annie, when it's an e-date, you have to be super careful. You need to hit exactly the right note.'

And because Annie had known Melissa since boarding

school, and because Victoria was Mel's flatmate, and because both the girls were city born and bred, Annie had deferred to their finely honed understanding of 'How Things Work in the City'.

The trio had hit the shops with Victoria leading the fray, and Annie had quickly discovered how exceedingly lucky she was to have clued-up friends to advise her about clothes. On her own, she would have made so *totally* all the wrong choices.

She'd wanted to head straight for the stunning racks of sparkly after-five wear, but Victoria had dismissed them with a disdainful toss of the corkscrew curls she'd created that morning.

'No way, Annie. You don't want to look as if you're trying too hard to impress Damien. If you look too dressed up or trendy you might scare him off.'

Oh.

After one last wistful glance towards the shimmering, ultra-feminine dresses, Annie allowed herself to be steered towards racks of jeans.

'Never underestimate jeans,' Victoria explained with impressive patience. 'You can dress them up or down and they always look fab.'

'But—um—I live in jeans. And Damien knows I'm a country girl. Don't you think these might make me look a little too *Annie Get Your Gun*?'

Victoria blinked, then eyed Annie with just a tad more respect. 'Point taken.'

But, seconds later, she was struck by her light bulb idea. 'I've got it! *Pink* jeans would be perfect. Team them with a little camisole top.' Grabbing a coat-hanger from a rack, she flourished something white and silky. '*How heaven is this?*'

Annie squashed the thought that a pink and white outfit would make her look like an ice cream. She tried the clothes on and decided that they were comfortable *and* rather gorgeous, actually.

But she put up a stronger fight over the high heels.

'What if Damien's really short?'

This time Mel chipped in. 'He didn't look short in the photo he sent you.'

'Photos can be deceptive.' Annie had spent many sleepless nights worrying about that possibility.

'Annie, if Damien's short, you're going to be taller than him no matter what kind of shoes you wear.'

She tried another tack. 'I can't afford two hundred and fifty dollars for a couple of strips of sequinned leather.'

Victoria grinned. 'Don't worry, that's why God invented credit cards.'

And so here she was in the foyer of the Pinnacle Hotel, dressed by Victoria and getting last-minute advice from both the girls before she took the lift to La Piastra on the twenty-seventh floor. To meet Damien.

Damien. *Eeeeeee!* Just thinking about him made her stomach play leap-frog with her heart. She knew it was foolish to have high hopes for this guy, but she couldn't help it. She'd travelled over a thousand kilometres from her outback cattle station in Southern Cross, North Queensland, just to meet him and she really, *really* wanted their date to work out.

It was going to be fine. It *was*.

Everything she and Damien had chatted about over the Internet during the past six weeks indicated that they meshed. They both loved dogs, world music, books and thinking about deeper things—like destiny and fate, whether life was a wager, and the possibility that animals were happier than humans. Talking to him had been comfortable and inspiring, fun and—and well, to be honest—sexy.

To cap it off, she and Damien both adored everything Italian, *especially* linguini.

That was why they'd settled on La Piastra.

And when Damien had emailed her a photo of himself, she'd completely flipped. Head over heels. He looked so-o-o yummy—with sleepy blue eyes, sun-streaked surfer-boy hair, pash-me-now lips and a cute, crooked smile. She hoped to high heaven that he'd been as impressed with *her* photo as he'd claimed to be, because she could feel in her bones that he was her perfect match.

And now she was about to meet him.

She was six minutes late, which, according to Mel and Victoria, was perfect timing. Her heart thumped as the trio waited for the lift, and she drew several deep breaths while the girls pumped her with last-minute advice.

'Remember, don't be too serious. Try to relax and have fun.'

'But don't drink too much.'

'You have to watch your date's body language. If he's mirroring your gestures, you're on the right track.'

'The danger sign is when he crosses his arms while you're talking.'

'Or if he starts to come on too heavy. He might just want sex.'

Annie shook her head to shush them. The girls meant well, but she wasn't as clueless about men as they feared. Besides, there was a rather conservative, bespectacled fellow a few feet behind Victoria, who must have overheard them. He was looking rather stunned by their conversation and he—*crikey*—he almost walked smack into a marble pillar.

Annie was about to send him a sympathetic smile when the bell above the lift pinged.

The doors were about to open.

'Remember there's always the escape plan,' Mel urged. 'You've got your mobile phone handy, haven't you?'

'Yes.'

'Right. You look gorgeous, Annie.'

'Stunning!'

'Thanks.'

'So break a leg!'

'Have a ball!'

'Go get Damien, kiddo!'

Amidst a flurry of air kisses Annie stepped into the lift, sent the girls a quick wave, and pressed the button for Level twenty-seven. The doors swished closed, Mel and Victoria's encouraging grins disappeared, and with a soft sigh the lift whisked her away from them... skywards.

And her stomach dropped. Oh, crumbs.

She made a last-minute check in the mirror at the back of the lift. No bra showing, no visible panty-line. Lipstick still holding. Hair okay.

Ping! Level twenty-seven.

Gulp.

This was it.

The lift doors swept apart and Annie looked out at an expanse of mega-trendy pale timber and stainless steel. So this was La Piastra. She felt a fleeting rush of nostalgia for Beryl's friendly café in Mirrabrook with its gingham tablecloths, ruffled curtains and bright plastic flowers on every table.

How silly. She'd come to Brisbane to get away from all that. Somewhere in here Damien was waiting. *Oh, please let him like me.* Her legs shook. She was as nervous as she'd been on her first day at boarding school.

A tall, dark, very Italian-looking man in black was watching her from his post directly in front of the lift and as she approached him he bowed stiffly.

'Good evening, madam.'

'Good evening.'

'Welcome to La Piastra.' He looked down a very Roman nose at her.

'Thanks.' She smiled, but her smile faltered as the man waited for her to say something more. What was she supposed to say? She peered into the restaurant, searching for a streaked sandy head among the diners. 'I'm—er—supposed to be meeting someone here.'

'You have a reservation?'

'No.'

He frowned and pursed his lips.

She hurried to explain. 'I mean *I* don't actually have a reservation, but I've come to meet someone—who made a reservation.'

Cringe! Was she a country hick making a complete fool of herself, or what?

He turned to a thick book on a timber and stainless steel lectern. 'What name?'

'You mean his name?'

Her question was met by a sigh that suggested the man in black was quite certain he was dealing with an airhead. 'What name was given when the reservation was made?'

'Grainger,' she said with sudden dignity. 'Mr Damien Grainger.'

Again he peered down his imperious Roman nose and slowly examined the list of names in his book. And Annie felt a moment's panic. Could she have made a mistake? Was this the wrong restaurant...the wrong day, wrong time?

No, it couldn't be. She'd checked and rechecked Damien's email a thousand times.

She peered again into the restaurant. She'd been hoping that Damien would keep an eye out for her. She'd pictured him leaping to his feet when he saw her, hurrying through the restaurant to meet her, his face alight with a welcoming smile.

Perhaps his table was positioned behind a post?

'Ah, yes,' said the rich Italian voice at her side. 'Table thirty-two.'

Phew.

'But I'm afraid Mr Grainger hasn't arrived yet.'

Oh.

Silly of her, but she'd been certain that Damien would be on time, even early.

'Would you care to wait for him at the bar or at your table?'

She glanced at the bar. If she waited there, perched on a stool by herself, she would feel like a prize lemon. 'At the table, please.'

'Then come this way.'

Several heads turned as she followed him to a table set for two near a window. Back in Mirrabrook, people would have been smiling and calling out greetings. Here they merely stared without emotion. Was there something wrong with the way she looked? Were her jeans too pink?

A seat was drawn out for her.

Annie sat and looked at the bare, pale timber table top, set with two round black linen place mats and starched white napkins, solid shining cutlery, gleaming wineglasses and a single square black candle exactly in the middle of a square white saucer.

It was all very urban. Very minimalist.

If Damien had been here, she would have found it exciting.

'Would you care for a drink while you're waiting?'

She tried to remember the name of the trendy drink Mel had ordered for her at a bar the night before. Something with cranberry juice.

When she hesitated, the man in black asked, 'Perhaps you would like to see our wine list?'

'No, thank you. Um, would it be all right if I just have water for now?'

'Certainly. Would you prefer still or sparkling?'

Good grief. At Beryl's café in Mirrabrook, water was simple, uncomplicated H_2O.

'Still water, please.'

He left her then and Annie heaved a sigh of relief. But the relief was only momentary, because now she was very conscious of being alone. A swift glance around her showed that she was the only person in the restaurant sitting by herself.

Shoulders back, Annie. You can't let a little thing like that throw you.

A handsome young waiter approached her, bearing a tray with a frosted bottle of iced water. 'How are you this evening?' he asked, smiling.

She smiled back and the simple act of sharing a smile made her feel a little better. 'Very well, thank you.'

'I'm Roberto and I'll be looking after your table.'

Her smile held. 'I'm Annie and I'll be looking forward to your service.'

His mouth stretched into a broad grin as he poured water into her glass. 'Would you like to see our menu?'

'No, I'll wait for my—' She indicated the empty seat opposite her.

'Girlfriend?'

'Actually, no—it's a guy.'

He managed to look charmingly disappointed before moving away to take orders from a nearby table.

Annie took a sip of water and wished she could press the cool glass against her hot cheeks. She told herself that it didn't matter that Damien was late. He was probably battling his way though a traffic jam, cursing fate. Any minute now he'd come bursting out of the lift, full of apologies.

She counted to a hundred and then took another sip. After reaching three hundred and taking more sips, she watched a couple on the other side of the room reach across their table to hold hands then gaze romantically into each other's eyes.

Somewhere in the background a guitar was playing *Beautiful Dreamer.*

Sigh. How many hours had she spent dreaming about this date in the city? About what Damien would think of her, what she'd think of him.

She'd worried about saying the wrong things, or discovering that he had some terrible off-putting habit. She'd considered endless ways to suss out whether he was married. That was her biggest fear. But she'd never once imagined that she would be sitting here alone. Without him.

The worst thing was that on her own in the city, surrounded by people, she felt even lonelier than she did in the outback, when she was surrounded by nothing but gumtrees and wild mountains.

She turned to look out of the window at the lights in the tall buildings around her, at the flickering neon signs in the distance, at the street lights way below and the headlights and tail-lights of the traffic—red and white rivers flowing in opposite directions...

Where was Damien?

Perhaps she should have given him her mobile phone number, but she'd been playing it cautious until she met him. Now she was tempted to ring Mel and Victoria just for a little friendly reassurance, but she resisted the urge.

She didn't want to look at her watch. Oh, well, perhaps a quick glimpse. Oh, God. Damien was twenty-five minutes late.

Maybe this was a guy thing. Damien was establishing the upper hand, making her wait. And wait...

Around her, people's meals were arriving. The food was

served on enormous white plates. Someone was having linguini drizzled with a pale green sauce and it looked divine.

Roberto came back and asked her if there was anything else he could bring her. Some bruschetta, perhaps? She shook her head, but she realised that other diners were casting curious glances her way. Again.

Oh, Damien. I know you probably can't help it, but this is so disappointing.

How much longer would she have to wait?

When the waiter left, Annie fingered her cute new clutch handbag and reconsidered using her phone to have a quick chat with the girls. But as she flicked the clasp she saw the man who guarded the front of the restaurant walking towards her. What now? Was he going to ask her to order some food or leave?

'Miss McKinnon?' he said as he approached.

'Yes?' Her stomach lurched. How did he know her name?

'We've received a phone call—a message from Mr Grainger.'

'Yes?' she said again and her heart jolted painfully.

'He's had to cancel this evening's engagement.'

Cancel?

Whoosh! Slam! Annie felt as if she'd been tipped through the window and was falling to the pavement twenty-seven floors below.

Damien couldn't cancel. Not like this. 'No,' she squeaked. 'That's not possible. There must be a mistake.'

The man in black's jaw clenched.

Wrong thing to say.

She tried again. 'Did—did Mr Grainger say why he has cancelled?'

She must have looked totally stricken because his face softened a fraction. 'I'm afraid the person who rang didn't offer an explanation. He asked me to apologise, Miss McKinnon. Apparently he's been trying to ring for some time, but our line has been busy. He hopes you will understand.'

Understand? Of course she didn't understand. She couldn't possibly understand. Annie felt so suddenly awful she wondered if she was going to be sick right there in front of everyone. 'Didn't he tell you *anything*? Are you sure he didn't—explain—?'

The man sighed and shook his head as if he found this situation tiresome.

'What should I do?' she asked. 'Do—do I owe you any money?'

'No. And you are still very welcome to dine here. The caller is happy to pay for your meal.'

The caller? Nothing made sense. 'Damien Grainger called, didn't he?'

'No, it was Mr Grainger's uncle.'

His *uncle*? This was really crazy. Where was Damien? Why hadn't he rung? Was he sick? Oh, goodness, yes. That had to be the problem. Damien was suddenly, horribly, un-avoidably, violently ill. From his sickbed he'd begged this uncle to phone her.

'Shall I send for a menu?' the man asked her.

Annie shook her head. Her throat was so choked she couldn't speak and there was no way she could possibly think about eating. Not in the midst of tragedy. This was the single worst moment in her life.

Grabbing her bag, she managed to stand and then she took a deep breath and began to walk…past the other tables…con-scious of the unbearable curiosity of the diners. Holding her head high and her shoulders back, she stared straight ahead, not wanting to catch anyone's eye.

It wasn't until she was safely out of the restaurant and behind the closed doors of the lift that she collapsed against the wall and covered her mouth with her hand and tried to hold back the horrible sobs that swelled in her throat and burned her. Was it possible to bear this disappointment, this horrible humiliation?

As the lift cruised downwards, she fumbled in her purse for her phone.

'Mel,' she sobbed as soon as there was an answer.

'Annie, where are you?'

'I'm in the lift at the Pinnacle.'

'Why? Are you running away?'

'Yes.'

'Oh, my God, what happened?'

'*Nothing!* Where are you?'

'Just up the road,' Mel shouted above a blast of loud background music. 'At The Cactus Flower. It's in the next block from where you are—on the left.'

'Stay there, please. I'm coming.'

'Honey, we won't move.'

Theo Grainger waited in the foyer of the Pinnacle Hotel and watched the blinking lights in the panel beside the lift indicating its journey downward from the twenty-seventh floor. All too soon, those shiny lift doors would slide open and Annie McKinnon would burst out.

A kind of dread tightened his throat muscles as he anticipated the tears streaming down her face. The kid would be a mess. A heartbroken, disillusioned mess.

He cursed himself for handling the whole situation so badly. His cowardly, fickle nephew had caused enough trouble, but Theo had bungled his part in the evening too.

He wasn't sure how he'd managed to make such a hash of things. He'd come to the hotel this evening with the best of intentions. He'd planned to meet the young Internet hopeful and to apologise to her on his nephew's behalf and to explain that the date had been cancelled. To apologise in person—before she headed up to La Piastra.

Theo could pile on the charm when necessary and he'd been confident he could appease Damien's date and send her on her way with her dignity intact, even if her tender young heart was broken. It wasn't the first time he'd had to move into damage control after one of his nephew's pranks.

But somehow Theo hadn't been prepared for Annie McKinnon.

He hadn't anticipated the blinding excitement shining in her face. She'd arrived at the Pinnacle looking so incredibly young and innocent, so unspeakably hopeful. So thrilled!

And he *certainly* hadn't anticipated her cheer squad of friends.

The girlfriends had been his final stumbling block. One mere male couldn't be expected to confront *three* overexcited, chattering females with the bad news that the *big deal* date was off.

In future, he would make sure that Damien was forced to face up to the consequences of his thoughtless pranks, even if he had to drag the wretch to the scene of his crime by the scruff of his neck.

But tonight the result of Theo's bungling was that he'd felt a compunction to hang around for the aftermath—to make sure Annie McKinnon wasn't too terribly heartbroken.

The light beside the lift indicated that it had reached the ground floor and he stood to one side of the foyer with his hands plunged deep in his trouser pockets. There was a clean handkerchief in his right pocket and it would come in handy if he needed to mop her tears before he called a taxi to send her safely homewards.

The doors opened and he held his breath and steeled himself for the sight of Annie's flushed, tear-ravaged face.

But no.

Annie swept out of the lift with her golden head high, looking pale but dignified, almost haughty. No sign of tears. Her pretty blue eyes were dry and glass-clear and her mouth was composed, almost smiling.

Almost. If Theo hadn't been watching her very closely, he might have missed the tremor of her chin and the exceedingly careful way she walked, as if she needed all her strength to hold herself together.

Her unexpected courage shook him. He felt a sudden lump in his throat and an absurd urge to applaud her.

And he remained stock-still as she sailed across the foyer. Even as the huge glass doors at the hotel's entrance parted, he didn't move. It made absolutely no sense but this devastated young woman seemed more composed than he felt.

She disappeared into the night before he came to his senses. By the time he dashed outside she was already hurrying along the footpath, ducking her way past pedestrians with athletic grace.

He called, 'Annie!'

But she didn't hear him and when people turned and stared at him he felt several versions of foolish. What on earth had he thought he was going to do if she'd heard him? Offer her coffee and consolation?

Clearly she needed neither.

He came to a halt in the middle of the footpath. Ahead of him, he saw a flash of pink jeans and white top as Annie turned to her left. Then she hurried up a short flight of steps and vanished inside a bar.

Theo Grainger couldn't remember the last time he'd felt so inadequate.

'The guy's a jerk!'

'An A-grade jerk.'

Mel and Victoria were vehement in their anger.

And never had Annie been happier to see friends.

As the three girls drowned their sorrows in strawberry daiquiris, she found it comforting to listen to their united rant.

'Annie, your Damien has reached an entirely new, utterly despicable level of jerkdom.'

'How dare he behave so jerkily to such a lovely, trusting country mouse?'

But the horrible part was that in between moments of righteous anger Annie still wanted to love Damien. She couldn't let go of her fantasy man in the blink of an eye. She needed to believe he was helpless and guiltless.

Perhaps he really couldn't have helped missing the date. There was still a chance that he was sick, in pain and feeling as bitterly disappointed as she was.

'He might be sick,' she said wistfully.

Victoria sniffed. 'Yeah, that's about as likely as he's fallen under a bus.'

'Or he's found an urgent need to flee the country,' added Mel, rolling her eyes. 'Face it, Annie. If Damien was halfway decent and he had a genuine excuse, he would have gone out of his way to make sure you understood what had kept him.'

Annie sighed. 'I suppose you're right… I guess I just don't want to believe it.'

It was so hard to let go of her happy dreams. She wanted to crawl away and cry for a month.

'The thing is,' said Mel, stirring her icy daiquiri with a slim black straw. 'He's not just a base-level jerk, he's a cowardly jerk. He had to pretend to be someone else.'

'What do you mean?'

'I bet you any cocktail on this menu that the so-called uncle who relayed the message doesn't exist.'

The thought that it might have actually been Damien on the phone, pretending to be someone else, made Annie feel ten times worse.

Victoria patted her shoulder. 'I reckon you should forget about blind dates and concentrate on raising the cocktail drinking statistics for the Greater Brisbane Area.'

Annie nodded miserably. It wasn't her style, but losing herself in an alcoholic fuzz had definite appeal. The problem was that it would only take the edge off her pain momentarily. There would still be tomorrow. And the rest of the week in Brisbane. A whole week in the city. Without Damien.

'I'd rather go back to your place and borrow your computer to send The Jerk a blistering email,' she said.

'Yeah,' agreed Mel. 'Great idea. Besides, Victoria and I still have to go to work tomorrow morning. Let's go home and send Damien a message he won't forget. Let's make sure he absolutely understands just how totally bottom-of-the-pits he's been.'

'If he's a true jerk, it'll be like water off a duck's back,' suggested Victoria gloomily.

But Mel's mind was made up. 'It doesn't matter. Annie will feel a lot better once we've told him off.'

CHAPTER TWO

TOSSING and turning on the lumpy old couch in Mel's lounge, Annie stared into the darkness. This was the worst night of her life. She was never going to sleep.

After helping her compose the email designed to set Damien back on his heels, Mel and Victoria had gone off to their bedrooms and were sound asleep now. Annie was left to get through the long night alone. And, to her dismay, the satisfaction she'd felt when she'd hit the button to shoot their message into cyber space was evaporating.

Rolling on to her side, she punched her pillow and gave vent to a loud groan. It echoed through the house, but no one stirred. That was the one good thing about loneliness; she didn't have to be brave any more. She could finally wallow in her misery.

Now, in a cocoon of silence and darkness, she could tell herself that never in the history of dating had there been a bigger fiasco, and if there had been she didn't want to know about it. Her experience at La Piastra was as bad as it got.

She could admit to herself that she was truly devastated.

Devastated, hurt to the marrow, disappointed to the max! And angry. Yeah, bitter too.

Her *glorious romance* was over before it had begun.

How could Damien have done this to her?

How could he have spent so many weeks courting her in writing, just to leave her stranded at the Big Moment?

And *why*? What had gone wrong? Had she been too forward when she'd suggested they should meet? Should she have waited till he'd broached the subject? The thing was, he'd shown no sign of caution or of having cold feet. Once she'd mentioned the idea of a date he had seemed very keen.

His absence didn't make sense and she couldn't let go of the slim hope that something completely unavoidable had detained him. Problem was, if that was the case, he wouldn't appreciate the savage email the girls had encouraged her to send.

Oh, hell!

It seemed like agonising hours later that she banged the pillow with another thump and flung herself on to her back, still too tense to sleep. Mel's house was in the inner city, not far from a main road, and as she listened to the alien sounds of never-ending traffic, tears seeped beneath her stinging eyelids and she felt a rush of homesickness.

At home the day started when the sun peeped over the Seaview Range and she was nudged awake by her Border collie, Lavender. She would give anything to hear the reassuring thump of Lavender's tail on her bedroom floor. And at Southern Cross she'd be greeted by the friendly laughter of kookaburras and the warbling of magpies, or perhaps the distant soft lowing of cattle.

But thinking about home and her twin brothers, Reid and Kane, brought an added twinge of guilt. The guys had been away mustering cattle when she'd left for her adventure in the city. She'd left them a note, but because she'd been afraid they'd jump right in and put a stop to her plans, she hadn't told them any details.

In her own mind she'd justified her dash to the city. Apart from the compulsion to meet her e-date, she'd felt a strong need for a holiday. But she knew that people usually planned their holidays. They didn't dash away, leaving a note telling family members to look after themselves.

Perhaps she shouldn't have been so secretive. Surely she should have been able to tell at least one of her brothers about the man she'd met over the Internet. But they were so protective of her. Which was why she'd resorted to writing a letter to the *Mirrabrook Star*.

If only her mother wasn't so far away in Scotland...

But thinking about her family only made her feel lonelier than ever. As she waited for morning and for Damien's reply to her email, she almost reached the point where she wished that her brothers *had* stopped her from coming to the city.

'You got a reply.'

At breakfast, Mel came into the kitchen waving a sheet of A4 paper at Annie. 'Here, I printed it out.'

Pain jabbed hard in Annie's chest. There was no escaping the truth now. Very soon she would know Damien's reason for avoiding her.

'It's from the uncle,' Mel said as Annie snatched up the page.

'The *uncle*?' Annie clasped the paper to her chest, too disappointed to read it. 'It's not from Damien?'

''Fraid not.'

Victoria turned from the microwave where she was heating coffee. 'So there really is an uncle?'

'Looks like it,' said Mel, reaching for milk to pour on her cereal.

Annie groaned. 'You mean an *uncle* read that email we sent last night?'

'Seems so.'

'But we were so—' Annie gulped. 'So—'

'Tipsy,' supplied Mel, looking sheepish.

'And rude,' added Annie. 'I had no idea his uncle would read it. Heck, we should have toned it down.'

'Hey, don't sweat,' said Victoria. 'We were relatively sober and we were merely being honest. We told it like it was.'

'Yeah…but to some old uncle!' Annie cringed at the thought of a sweet, elderly uncle reading their message. It had sounded so forceful and feminist last night. But when she thought about it now…

Oh, crumbs…

Fearing the worst, she looked down at the page…

From: **T. G. Grainger**

To: anniem@mymail.com

Date: **Monday, November 14th 6:05 a.m.**

Subject: Re: You'd better have a brilliant excuse, you jerk!

Dear Annie M,

I hope you don't mind my replying to your message, but my nephew is out of town this week and he's asked me to respond to any important emails. I consider your communication to be of the utmost importance. I regret having to intrude into such a personal exchange but I believe you deserve the courtesy of a quick response.

Please accept my sincerest apology for the unpleasant experience you suffered last night as a consequence of my nephew's inexcusable thoughtlessness.

Damien was called away at short notice and I contacted La Piastra restaurant on his behalf. However, I understand your deep distress and I am saddened by my nephew's bad manners. You're absolutely right; you deserved an explanation from him and I will make sure that he contacts you immediately on his return.

In the meantime, I trust that you are still able to enjoy the remainder of your stay in Brisbane.

Yours sincerely,
Dr Theo Grainger.

Annie dropped the page on to the tabletop. 'Oh, my God. Damien was called away at short notice.'

'Oh, yeah,' scoffed Mel. 'And we all came down in the last shower.'

'You don't believe him?'

This question was greeted by a significant silence while Annie watched Mel and Victoria exchange knowing glances that snuffed out her final glimmer of hope. After a bit, Victoria leaned across the table, grabbed the page and scanned the printed message.

'The uncle's a bit of a wordsmith, isn't he?'

Annie nodded sadly. 'I guess "inexcusable thoughtlessness" is a refined way of saying that his nephew's a bottom-of-the-pit jerk.'

Mel grinned. 'I rather liked the way we described his rotten nephew in *our* email.'

'Yeah,' said Victoria. 'There's nothing wrong with short, shoot-from-the-hip language.'

Annie managed a small smile.

'Anyway.' Victoria tapped a French tipped fingernail against the email printout. 'This uncle's a doctor, so you'd expect fancy words.'

'He's not a medical doctor,' said Mel.

Annie and Victoria stared at her. 'How do you know?' they both asked simultaneously.

'Because a Dr Theo Grainger was my philosophy lecturer

at university and it's not a common name. I'm sure this must be the same guy.'

Annie's mouth fell open. 'You studied philosophy?'

'In my first year. I didn't keep it up because I wanted to major in urban planning, but Dr Grainger was a pretty cool lecturer. He had quite a following.'

To Annie the very word philosophy sounded lofty and unbelievably clever, and she found it hard to imagine an ordinary girlfriend like Mel studying the subject.

Suddenly Victoria looked at the clock. 'Hey, look at the time. We'd better get moving or we'll be late for work, Mel.'

The two girls jumped to their feet.

'Don't worry about the kitchen. I'll tidy up,' Annie called after them, but they'd already disappeared into their rooms. It occurred to her that if she stayed in their house much longer the girls would soon treat her the way her brothers did.

At home, Kane and Reid ran around doing important outside work like mustering the cattle, fencing, servicing the bores and machinery, and they left her behind to cook and clean and keep the books, as if she were some outback version of Cinderella.

It was a big part of the reason she'd wanted to get away and it wasn't very comforting to think that in no time at all she was becoming a City Girl Cinders.

A broken-hearted, disillusioned City Girl Cinders.

One thing was sure; she didn't want to spend this week keeping Mel and Victoria's flat clean and tidy. But what were her options? She could reply to Dr Grainger's email and press the issue about Damien by demanding to know when he'd be back. But she was fast losing confidence in the Internet as a form of honest communication.

She lifted the printout from the table and read the uncle's email again. Philosophers were fantastically brilliant and thoughtful and wise, weren't they? Pity some of it hadn't rubbed off on his nephew.

Actually, it was a wonder this philosopher uncle hadn't lectured *her* on her own lack of wisdom. No doubt he took a rather dim view of any girl who dashed recklessly into the city from the far reaches of the outback and expected a blind date to fulfil her silly romantic fantasies.

She was halfway across the kitchen with cereal packets in hand when she paused. Come to think of it, Uncle Theo hadn't expressed any negative opinions about her. He'd been surprisingly sympathetic.

Perhaps there was something deeper behind this—something the uncle understood. A direct approach to Dr Grainger might sort this whole mess out. Rather than mucking around with email, it would be better to deal with him face-to-face. That was the McKinnon way. It was what her brothers would do.

Look the enemy in the eye so you knew what you were dealing with.

But how the heck did you confront a philosopher?

Dropping the dishcloth, she dashed into the bathroom, where Mel was applying mascara.

'Which university does this Dr Grainger teach at?'

Mel frowned at her reflection in the mirror. 'UQ at St Lucia. Why?'

'I—I've always been curious about philosophy and I was thinking that, as I have time on my hands, it might be interesting to sneak into the back of one of his lectures. Is that allowed?'

'Well…yes.' Mel gave her eyelashes a final flick with the mascara wand and turned to face Annie. 'But don't you think you should just let this Damien thing die a natural death?

You know what they say about other fish in the sea. There are some okay guys at my work—'

'This isn't just about Damien,' Annie said quickly. 'It's about me. I want to sort it out. I don't want to be left up in the air until Damien eventually decides to turn up.'

Mel gave a puzzled shrug.

From near the front door Victoria called, 'You ready, Mel?'

'Yeah, coming.' To Annie, she said, 'You do what you like, Annie, but I think you might be out of luck. The university year will be winding down now. Lectures will have finished and the students will be on swot vacation getting ready for exams.'

'Oh.'

As Mel hurried for the door she called over her shoulder, 'If I were you, I'd stick to shopping.'

'No, thank you,' Annie said quietly.

When a knock sounded on his office door Theo Grainger was deep in a mire of student assignments and he grunted a greeting without looking up from the papers on his desk.

'Dr Grainger?'

He'd assumed that Lillian, the philosophy department's receptionist, was dropping off the day's mail. But this voice wasn't Lillian's; it was younger, no doubt a student panicking about forthcoming exams.

He didn't bother to raise his head. 'Do you have an appointment?' he asked just a little too gruffly.

'No.'

His aggrieved sigh drifted downwards to the pile of papers on his desk. 'You must know by now that all students have to make an appointment to see me. Put your name against a time slot on the notice board.'

'All right.'

He returned to the assignment he was grading—a rather badly constructed analysis of utilitarianism.

'One problem,' the voice at the door said. 'Could you please tell me where the notice board is?'

Theo's head snapped up and he glared at the caller. 'How long have you been a student here?'

'No time at all.' Her mouth twisted into an apologetic smile and she pushed a wing of blonde hair back behind her ear. 'You see, I'm not a student.'

The surprise of recognition startled him like a bolt from the blue.

Annie McKinnon.

Just in time, he stopped himself from saying her name aloud. The last thing he wanted was for her to realise that he'd seen her before—that he'd been watching her—virtually spying on her yesterday evening.

He rose slowly to his feet. 'I'm sorry,' he said. 'What did you say your name was?'

'I didn't actually get my name out. I must be nervous.' She gave a self-conscious roll of her eyes. 'I'm almost ashamed to admit it, but I'm Annie McKinnon.' She winced. 'You answered an email I sent to your nephew, Damien.'

'Ah, yes.' Theo knew it was unkind, but he couldn't resist tipping his head forward to appraise Annie with a searching look over the top of his spectacles.

Not surprisingly, she squirmed.

'So,' he said. 'I have the pleasure of meeting the forthright Miss McKinnon.'

'I'm sorry, Dr Grainger. If my friends and I had known *you* were going to read that email we wouldn't have been so—so forthright.'

'I can well believe that.' Theo was still holding the pen

he'd been using to mark the students' assignments. Now, he replaced its lid and set it carefully back on his desk. When he looked at Annie again he felt as if she'd been staring at him intensely. He offered her a cautious smile. 'So why did you want to see me?'

She returned his slow smile measure for cautious measure. 'I wanted to apologise to you.'

'I'm not sure that *you* need to apologise.'

'Well, I also wanted to find out the truth.'

'The truth?'

'About Damien.'

Her gaze locked with his and she stopped smiling. Her eyes were clear blue—the kind of blue that made Theo think of summer sky reflected in spring water, and it occurred to him that their astonishing candour must be an Annie McKinnon trademark.

Standing straight as a soldier, she said, 'I need to know if Damien was really called away on urgent business, or if he simply didn't want to meet me.'

Theo cleared his throat. After observing this young woman last night, he should have known that she wouldn't simply turn tail and give up. 'Perhaps we should discuss this somewhere else,' he said and he glanced at his watch. Best to get her safely away from the curious eyes and ears of his colleagues and departmental secretaries. 'Let me buy you coffee.'

'Thank you,' she said warmly. 'That would be wonderful.'

Seeing the sudden animated brightness in her face, Theo wasn't so sure. He lifted a navy-blue blazer from the back of his chair and shrugged his shoulders into it, then he gestured for her to accompany him down the hallway. It was a warm November day and the formality of the blazer was unnecessary, but it gave Theo a sense of protection and, for some peculiar reason, a glowing, excited Annie McKinnon at his side called for protection.

Their journey took them through the Philosophy department's reception area and Lillian looked up from her desk.

Annie smiled and waved to her. 'I found him,' she called gleefully.

Lillian returned Annie's wave, and then her amused eyes met Theo's. They glimmered with undeniable curiosity and one eyebrow rose, but Theo hurried forward, eager to get his nephew's jilted girlfriend out of the building.

Wow.

As she walked with Theo Grainger through the Great Court of the University of Queensland, Annie was seriously impressed.

Talk about hallowed halls. With its stretch of green lawn encircled by graceful columns and arches, the courtyard was as dignified and atmospheric as any place she'd ever seen. And all the surrounding buildings were made out of beautiful sandstone, too. As she looked around at their impressive façades she felt a sense of awe.

She could almost smell knowledge in the air. How could anyone *not* become earnest and clever in this inspiring environment?

'Do these people have any idea how lucky they are to be here?' she said, casting an envious eye over the students strolling casually past.

Theo smiled. 'Not enough of them, I'm afraid.' He turned to her. 'So you didn't have the chance to go to university?'

'I was planning to go straight after boarding school, but then my father died and things kind of fell apart at home. I live on a cattle station up in North Queensland—so I stayed home for a year, and after that it was just assumed that I would stay on indefinitely.'

'But that wasn't your plan?'

'I didn't mind at first, but in the past few years I've been champing at the bit.'

'It's never too late to start at university.'

'That's what I've been thinking. Twenty-four's still quite young really, isn't it?'

'Very young,' he said in an ambiguous tone that puzzled her.

They reached a café in a leafy garden setting and Theo collected two white coffees and carried them to a secluded table, away from chattering students.

They both opened slim paper sachets of sugar, used half, then twisted the unused halves and set them on their saucers. Annie laughed. 'We could have shared a sugar if we'd known we only wanted half each.'

Theo looked surprised, then smiled and shook his head as if he didn't quite know what to make of her.

Well, that made two of them. She was certainly feeling shocked and unsure about Damien's Uncle Theo. He wasn't *anything* like she'd expected.

She'd had an image in her mind of an absent-minded professor type—a badly groomed academic, aged fifty plus, carelessly dressed in a wrinkled shirt and rumpled trousers. She'd expected untidy hair, a beard perhaps, and most definitely a scowl.

But although this man had scowled at her when she first knocked on his door, he'd quickly become polite. And heck, he couldn't be older than her brothers, who were in their mid-thirties.

As for his appearance—his grooming was impeccable. Neat, dark hair, crisp blue shirt and stone-coloured trousers.

Tall, trim physique. His dark-rimmed glasses gave his hazel eyes a scholarly air, but in no way did they detract from his appearance.

But he was a philosopher, for heaven's sake.

Somehow she hadn't expected someone so painfully thoughtful and clever to look quite so—so worldly. He was actually very *attractive*. But in a way that was refreshingly different from the tough ringers and jackaroos she was used to in the outback.

Then again, perhaps Theo's appearance shouldn't really surprise her since he was related by blood to Damien.

Thinking of Damien, she felt suddenly subdued, and she picked up her coffee and took a sip while she considered the best way to ask this man about his nephew.

'It's very kind of you to take time out to see me,' she said as she placed the cup back in its saucer. 'You must think I'm very foolish really, trying to arrange a date over the Internet.'

'If you're foolish, then so are thousands of other people.' He sent her a reassuring smile. 'Dating on the Internet is becoming more popular every day.'

'Well, thanks. That makes me feel a bit better.'

'But I'm sorry you've come such a long way. And it's a pity you feel let down by Damien.'

'I have a right to feel let down, don't I?'

'Everyone has a right to their feelings.'

Annie frowned at him. 'I have a horrible feeling right now that you're going to start philosophising and I'll get lost. Can you just tell me straight? Is Damien avoiding me?'

He sighed and dropped his gaze to stare hard at his coffee. 'I'm not sure.'

'You must have a fair idea.'

At that he looked up and the glimmer of a smile sparked in

his eyes. 'Have you ever thought of becoming a prosecuting attorney, Miss McKinnon?'

'Why?'

'You have a disturbingly direct manner. I defy anyone to lie to you.'

'Good,' she said quickly. Their gazes met across the table and for a moment she almost lost her train of thought. Drawing a quick breath, she said, 'Does that mean you're going to drop the Miss McKinnon and call me Annie and tell me the truth? Damien's a jerk, isn't he?'

'If you've already made up your mind, I don't need to answer that.' Theo paused, then added softly, 'Annie.'

When he pronounced her name in his lovely deep, educated voice the strangest shiver ran through her. She felt as if she'd been tapped on the shoulder, as if an unheard voice had whispered something important in her ear.

The feeling was so distinct that for a moment she had to close her eyes. When she opened them again, Theo Grainger was watching her and she saw a puzzling tension in his expression.

'Please,' she said softly, feeling strangely shaken. 'Don't play mind games with me. Just tell me, so I can put this whole mess behind me.'

He sighed and pushed his half-empty coffee cup to one side so that he could rest his clasped hands on the table in front of him. 'I honestly don't know Damien's exact reasons for getting out of the city this week, but I'm afraid he was anxious to avoid your date. I'm sorry. My nephew doesn't have a very good track record. He's prone to pranks and he's managed to upset quite a few people one way or another.'

'I see.' She drank some more of her coffee.

'I hope you're not too heartbroken.'

Strange, but she wasn't nearly as upset as she thought she'd be. The news that she was the victim of some kind of prank no longer surprised her. It was more like receiving confirmation of something she'd suspected in theory, but hadn't tested in practice. *Yes, Annie, fire will burn you.*

Damien's uncle was expecting a response from her. She looked at him. 'I can assure you, Dr Grainger, it will take something much worse than being stood up on a blind date before I allow my heart to be broken.'

For a moment he looked startled. 'That's a relief,' he said.

But he didn't look particularly relieved and they both turned quickly to stare over to the distant Brisbane River. Annie watched the slow drift of the water as she finished her coffee.

'Actually, there is *something* I'm very upset about,' she said.

'What's that?'

'I won't get to meet Basil.'

'Basil?'

She turned back to him. 'Damien's dog. His Dalmatian.'

'Is that what he told you? That he has a Dalmatian called Basil?'

'Yes.' She leaned towards him, eager to make her point. 'It was part of the reason we clicked. I'm mad about dogs. Damien and I used to joke about how fabulous it would be if my Border collie, Lavender, fell in love with his Basil. I know it sounds childish, but it was fun. We used to say that if Basil and Lavender mated we would have a pot-pourri of puppies.'

Theo smiled briefly, then frowned and shook his head.

Annie slumped in her chair. 'Don't tell me that's a lie, too. I couldn't bear it if Basil doesn't exist.'

'Oh, don't worry, Basil most certainly exists,' he said quietly. 'But he's *my* dog.'

CHAPTER THREE

'How long would it take me to walk from here to the Goodwill Bridge?' Annie asked Mel, who was in the middle of brushing her teeth before bed.

To her relief, Mel and Victoria had opted for an early night this evening.

Mel turned from the sink. 'Oh, I'd say about half an hour. Why?'

'I want to set my alarm.'

Lowering her toothbrush, Mel frowned at her. 'You're going to walk to the Goodwill Bridge tomorrow morning?'

'Yes.'

'Why on earth would you want to do that?'

'I want to go for an early morning walk and that bridge will take me over the river to the South Bank, won't it?'

'Yes, Annie, but I thought you came to Brisbane for fun, not exercise.'

Annie shrugged. 'A little exercise won't hurt me.' She turned to leave the bathroom. 'Goodnight.'

'Hang on,' Mel called, making a hurried effort to rinse her mouth.

With some reluctance, Annie paused in the hallway. She'd been hoping to avoid an inquisition about this.

Mel came through the doorway, still wiping her mouth with the back of her hand. 'Okay, confession time! You didn't come to the city for a health kick, so who are you going to meet on the bridge?'

Annie sighed extravagantly. 'A dog. A Dalmatian dog called Basil.'

'Oh, yeah?' Mel let her eyes roll towards the ceiling. 'And will Basil be waiting for you all by himself? He doesn't, by any chance, come attached to some yummy guy you've met today, does he?'

'Theo will be there,' Annie mumbled.

'Who?'

'Theo.'

'Theo?' Mel's voice rose an octave. 'Theo as in Dr Theo Grainger?'

'Yes.' In defence Annie added, 'I told you I spoke to him this morning. And he's invited me to meet his dog.'

Mel collapsed against the wall in helpless laughter.

'What's the big joke? You know I'm nuts about dogs.'

'Oh, yeah, sure, Annie. You're fascinated by Theo Grainger's dog. But *hello*—half the UQ philosophy undergraduates are nuts about Dr Theo.'

Annie couldn't hide her surprise.

'The female half, that is,' Mel amended. 'Not that it gets them anywhere. Apparently, he has a policy of never dating students.'

'Good for him.'

'But that's why I'm so gobsmacked. How did you wangle this date with him?'

'For crying out loud, Mel. Walking a dog is *not* a date.'

'Yeah?' Smiling, Mel shook her head. 'That's like saying a foot massage has nothing to do with sex.'

To her dismay, Annie found it difficult to meet her friend's gaze.

There was an awkward silence while she stared at the floor and then Mel said more gently, 'Well, don't worry. We'll just have to keep our fingers crossed that jerkishness doesn't run in Damien's family.'

Impulsive decisions often had unpleasant repercussions, Theo reminded himself the next morning as he waited at the northern end of the Goodwill Bridge and watched the blue and white City Cats ferrying passengers up and down the Brisbane River.

He suspected that the impulse to invite Annie McKinnon to join him on a walk with his dog had been foolish. But she'd been badly misled by his nephew and he consoled himself that his sense of obligation to her was a worthy motivation.

After spending almost a decade as a university lecturer, he was well aware of the pitfalls of offering even the most casual friendship to an attractive young woman. But in Annie's case it should be quite a simple matter to guard against repercussions.

He'd kept the invitation very low-key. He'd even been un-gallant enough to let her find her own way to the bridge, but now he wondered if she might get lost.

He switched his attention from the river to the traffic speeding to join the network of concrete ribbons that formed the freeway system and in his peripheral vision he caught sight of a hand waving.

Annie.

She was waiting at the pedestrian crossing on the other side of the road. The lights changed and within less than a minute she came hurrying up to him.

'I hope I'm not too late,' she said, panting slightly, as if she'd been running.

'Not at all.'

She dropped to her knees, and focused her attention entirely on the dog. 'Oh, Basil, you're beautiful. I could recognise your gorgeous black and white spots when I was still a block away.'

She ruffled Basil's ears and made a great fuss of him and Theo tried not to notice the way her hair shone in the sun, or how slim and lithe she looked in her black shorts and sleeveless pale blue top. He turned quickly to study the clusters of apartment block towers built close to the river.

'So which way are we going?' she asked, jumping to her feet.

'Over the bridge. Ready?'

'Sure.'

The Goodwill Bridge was restricted to pedestrians and cyclists and as they set off across its gentle arc the city buzzed around them. At this early hour the air was still and cool, the sky clear, and the parks and gardens green. Brisbane looked clean and at its best.

'Hey, Theo, is that Italian writing on your T-shirt?'

Annie had the most disturbing way of asking unexpected questions. 'Yes,' he admitted, looking down at the slogan on his chest. 'It's an ad for coffee.'

'Can you read Italian? Do you know what it says?'

'It's something like… For people who really care about the coffee they drink.'

She looked excessively impressed. 'Have you ever been to Italy?'

'Yes, many times.'

'Wow, I'd give anything to see Rome or Venice or Florence. I've read all I can about them and I drool over the pictures.'

'Italy's beautiful. I think it's my favourite European country.'

'Really?'

To his surprise she looked puzzled.

'You have a problem with that?'

'No, it's just that it's Damien's favourite country too.'

'But he's never been to Italy.'

She came to a sudden halt and Theo tugged on Basil's lead. 'Hang on, boy.'

'This is weird,' she said. 'Do you think Damien has been pretending to be someone like you?'

'I can't think why. What makes you think so? Because of the dog and Italy?'

'Not only that.' She turned to look out at the river where an old wooden ferry was chugging from one side to the other. 'He used to tell me things about philosophy, too.'

Theo laughed. 'Philosophy? Damien doesn't know the first thing about philosophy.'

'Well, he sounded knowledgeable to me.' She turned back and offered him a sheepish smile. 'But then I wouldn't have a clue. I'm more of an old movie fan. As far as I know, Scarlett O'Hara's "Tomorrow is another day" could be philosophy.'

'And you wouldn't be too far off the mark.'

She shook her head. 'I'm beginning to feel so stupid about this. I can't believe all the things I lov—liked about Damien were all make-believe.'

Not make-believe, Theo thought. They were me.

Annie's china-blue eyes were round with worry and when their gazes met she chewed her lip and colour stained her neck and cheeks. Had the same idea occurred to her?

When Damien came back he would strangle him.

She let out a long sigh, then shrugged. 'I've got to stop talking about Damien. I'm over him. Let's keep walking. I didn't mean to hold you up.'

They walked on and Annie's gaze darted everywhere, her hungry eyes taking in the towering buildings, the busy traffic on the freeway and the boats on the river. She looked as if she'd never seen anything quite so exciting.

He'd noticed the same sense of delighted engagement with her surroundings at the university yesterday, and now he tried unsuccessfully to suppress the thought that the clever, academic women he'd dated in recent years were a bunch of jaded cynics.

They reached the other side of the bridge and he looked below to the dry dock where volunteers were restoring an ancient tugboat. He'd been taking a keen interest in their progress.

'Oh, look at that.' Annie was pointing ahead to a forest of very modern unit buildings surrounded by landscaped gardens and restaurants.

'What are you looking at?'

'That dear little clock tower peeping over the fig trees.'

'Oh, yes. It's part of the old South Brisbane Town Hall. It's very Victorian, isn't it?'

'Yes, it's all red-bricked and old-fashioned and out of place, but it's gorgeous,' she said. 'I'm sure it disapproves of all these modern aluminium and glass buildings.'

'Just like the old Queen would have.'

'Exactly!' Annie laughed and her hair glinted pale gold in the sunlight and, without warning, she flung her arms skywards and executed a three hundred and sixty degree spin. 'Oh, I lo-o-o-ve this city!'

And bang went Theo's resolve to remain aloof.

'Would you like to stop for breakfast?' he asked.

Breakfast? Annie bit back a cry of surprise. Come to think of it, Theo was looking surprised too. Perhaps he'd realised that adding breakfast to a walk along the river turned the occasion into something that was almost a date. Maybe he was having second thoughts.

She wondered if she should let him off the hook.

But she didn't want to. Something happened to her whenever she was with him. Something deep. Elusive. Nagging.

And it had nothing to do with his dog, and only a little to do with how great he looked in athletic shorts.

'What about our casual clothes?'

'Don't worry. Most of the eateries along here cater to walkers and joggers.'

'What about Basil, then? He won't be allowed in a restaurant, will he?'

'A friend of mine owns one of the cafés on the riverfront and on special occasions he's happy to keep him out the back for me, away from the kitchen and the diners.'

'Does this count as a special occasion?'

He smiled slowly. 'If I say so.'

His smile made her chest grow tight. She bent down and scratched Basil's spotty head. 'Do you mind being tied up, beautiful boy?'

Basil's tail wagged madly and Theo said, 'Giovanni spoils him so much he never minds.'

'Looks like we're having breakfast, then.'

Annie wondered if her heart had burst into song as they walked through a colonnade of purple bougainvillea. Time to calm down. *This is not a date. This is not a date.*

They turned on to the wide walkway close to the river, where cafés and restaurants were already doing a busy breakfast trade.

A rotund, balding Italian turned from adjusting a red and white striped umbrella over a table. When he saw them his face split into an enormous grin and he called in a booming voice, '*Ciao*, Theo.'

'Giovanni! *Ciao*.'

The men exchanged backslaps as they chatted in Italian. Annie watched, enchanted. Giovanni grinned at her too.

'*Buon giorno, signora.*'

Oh, wow. I'm melting. No one had ever called her *signora* and it sounded sensational in Giovanni's Italian baritone. Warming. Like brandy slipping through her veins.

'*Buon giorno*, Giovanni,' she said back to him. Her pronunciation didn't sound quite right, but nevertheless he looked delighted.

Theo looked pleased with her too.

Almost immediately, Giovanni took hold of Basil's lead. '*è un cane bello*,' he said, giving the dog a pat with his massive hand. Then he waved to them both as he disappeared with Basil around the back of the café.

'That's Basil settled,' said Theo. 'Now, let's find a table.'

Annie could hardly contain her excitement as they sat at a table for two overlooking the water. Breakfast by the Brisbane River with a view of skyscrapers and the busy freeway—she felt so urban and classy.

Okay, this wasn't a date, but La Piastra was Dullsville by comparison.

'What are you going to have?' she asked Theo as they studied their menus.

'I think I'll settle for something light. Probably a sourdough bagel and coffee.'

She wondered what her brothers would think of a man who ate a bagel for breakfast. At home, Reid and Kane expected steak and eggs and a mountain of toast. But they headed off to a day of hard physical work, of course. Most likely Theo would be sitting at a desk.

'I can't decide between a croissant or fruit toast,' she said.

'The fruit toast is very good. Especially if you like dried figs.'

'Oh, yum. No contest then. Fruit toast it is.'

'And coffee?'

'Yes, please.' At Southern Cross she always had tea, but here in the city her taste buds were primed for coffee. Just the smell of it was sophisticated.

Once their orders were placed, Theo leaned back in his chair and looked up at the sky. He seemed relaxed. In a good mood.

Prepared to talk?

Annie took a deep breath. 'Do you mind if I ask you a nosy question?'

Behind his glasses his eyes narrowed slightly, but he didn't look annoyed. His mouth tilted into a slow smile. 'That's difficult to answer without knowing the question.'

'Okay, I'll ask it and you don't have to answer if you don't want to.'

Theo nodded. 'Fair enough.'

'It's just that I feel so ignorant. I've been wondering what philosophers actually do.'

'Ah... I should have seen that coming.'

'Sorry,' she said quickly. 'Do a lot of people ask you that?'

'Just about everyone.'

'Ouch. It's just that I can't imagine you just sit and think clever thoughts all day long. You must—' She broke off, suddenly out of her depth.

'You think we must find *something* useful to do?' he suggested.

'I didn't mean to be insulting. I suppose I'm asking this because your life is so different from *mine*. Where I live, people have to be practical. They have no choice. If a bore breaks down they can't sit around waiting for someone to travel hundreds of kilometres to fix it.'

'And philosophers don't build things or grow things or fix things.'

'I don't know. Do you?'

Theo crossed his arms over his chest. And Annie felt a stab of alarm. Hadn't the girls warned her that this was a very negative sign in body language?

'Obviously philosophers don't bake bagels or build sky-scrapers or fix bores,' he said.

The waiter arrived with their breakfast and she was re-lieved to be diverted by delicious thick slices of toast, heavy with fruit. She was happy to drop the subject of Theo's job, especially if he was touchy about it.

He held up a sachet of sugar and smiled at her.

'Want to share?' he asked.

Oh, crumbs, he had such a nice smile. 'Sure.' She grinned back at him and hoped that their awkward moment was behind them.

But as he spread cream cheese on his bagel Theo said, 'Philosophers build things.'

She nodded and popped a piece of toast into her mouth, trying to look casually interested, but not wanting him to feel pressured into further explanation.

'They work out structures for thinking,' he went on. 'And, once you've got those structures in place, you can think through all sorts of problems more easily. But it's not just a matter of mental gymnastics. Philosophers make connections to real life. These days philosophy is being used more and more as therapy.'

'Like in counselling?'

'Yes. Some people find a thoughtful dose of Aristotle or Plato can be more useful than medication.'

'Wow, that sounds really interesting. I could probably do with a dose of philosophy. People are always telling me I'm too impulsive and don't think things through before I act.' She traced the handle of her coffee cup with her finger. 'There's so much I don't know.'

'Nobody can know what they haven't yet experienced.'

'I guess not.' Her eyes met his. 'But I'd like to be wise, especially about things that really matter.'

Theo didn't answer immediately. He cut a piece of bagel, but before he ate it he looked at her and said gently, 'You might be wiser than you think, Annie. Plato decided that his own wisdom lay in realizing how little he knew about the things that matter most.'

A breeze danced across the river and picked up strands of Annie's hair and tossed them on to her face. As she fingered them back into place Theo stared at her arm, frowning.

Bending her elbow to examine it, she saw the purple smudge of bruises. 'I got these from sleeping on Mel's couch,' she explained. 'It's so narrow and lumpy I keep rolling off and I banged my elbow on the coffee table. I suppose I'll have more bruises by the end of the week.'

'Sounds uncomfortable.'

'Yeah. If I'd known how bad it was I would have brought my camp swag and slept on the floor. Mind you, I didn't give Mel much warning that I was coming and she's been very accommodating.'

He looked thoughtful as he drank his coffee.

Annie checked her watch. 'How much time do you have? Don't you need to go to work?'

'Yes, I do, but now lectures have finished I can be a little more flexible with my schedule.' He set down his coffee cup. 'Just the same, I'd better get going.'

'Basil will be restless.'

'Either that or he will have gone to sleep, with a tummy full of the best off-cuts of Giovanni's fillet steak.'

Breakfast over, Theo attended to the bill, and they collected Basil and set off again along the South Bank walkway.

'What do you plan to do with the rest of your week in the city?'

Darn. Annie wished he hadn't asked that.

'You're *what*?' Mel dropped the knife she'd been using to slice mushrooms. Her hands flew to her hips as she almost shouted her question at Annie.

Victoria, who was perched on a kitchen stool and chopping carrots, looked equally stunned.

Annie hastened to appease them. 'It's not that I don't appreciate how generous you've both been, letting me use your couch, and you've been wonderful helping me with the clothes shopping and the date with Damien and everything. I'm very grateful.'

'But I can't believe you're moving in with Dr Grainger,' said Mel.

Victoria shook her head. 'Why would you want to move in with some stuffy old philosopher who's related to the jerk?'

'It's because Theo *is* Damien's uncle that he's offered me Damien's room for the rest of my time here,' Annie explained. 'He feels a sense of obligation.'

Mel hooted. 'Obligation? Is that what he calls it? I reckon he's feeling something much more physical that ends with "tion".'

'Perhaps you're being a tad naïve,' suggested Victoria.

Annie groaned. How could she explain Theo's invitation without making reference to the girls' narrow couch and the bruises?

'I promise you, this is a very platonic arrangement,' she said.

'Listen to her.' Mel winked at Victoria. 'She's had breakfast with a philosopher and already she's throwing around words like platonic.'

'Give me a break, please!'

Annie hadn't meant to shout, but it worked. Mel and Victoria's mouths snapped shut. In unison, they crossed their arms over their chests.

She took a deep breath. 'I thought this was a good idea for several reasons. Number one, you get your couch back.' When Mel opened her mouth, she signalled her to shush. 'Number two, Damien's caused me grief and I may as well enjoy the comfort of his room while he's not using it.' She hurried on. 'Number three, Theo's house is within walking distance of the art gallery and the library, the theatres, and the South Bank. It's a really handy location for me to entertain myself during the day.'

'What about the nights?' came Victoria's predictable response.

Annie swallowed. 'Theo's not going to pounce on me, if that's what you're worried about. He's a gentleman.'

'But he's also rather gorgeous,' said Mel. 'Have you considered the fact that you might fall for him and get hurt all over again?'

'Like nephew, like uncle,' chanted Victoria in a singsong voice.

Suddenly there was silence. Annie avoided their eyes. She knew Mel had a point. There was a very good chance that she was already rather smitten by Theo Grainger and it was unlikely that he was interested in her romantically, so no doubt there was an element of risk.

But then again…her instincts were screaming for her to accept Theo's invitation. To start with, she knew now that the man she'd foolishly fallen in love with over the Internet was more Theo than he was ever Damien. Why Damien had taken his uncle's persona was a mystery. But it was only part of a much bigger mystery now.

When she and Theo were together something happened. She wasn't sure what it was exactly. It was so tenuous and fragile and unexpected that she couldn't give it an obvious name. But she felt its pull and she found it irresistibly thrilling.

'I'm prepared to take that risk,' she said.

Mel's eyes widened in horror. 'Oh, no. You've fallen for him already, haven't you?'

'No! I don't know him well enough for that.'

'Hang on,' broke in Victoria. 'Why would she fall for this uncle? How can he be gorgeous? Isn't he ancient?'

Mel shook her head. 'At a guess, I'd say mid-thirties.'

Victoria's jaw dropped. She stared at Annie and then her face softened into a knowing smile. 'Go, Annie,' she said quietly, her voice rippling with undertone.

'Well, that's that then,' said Mel. 'It looks like Victoria's on your side, Annie. Two against one. So I bow out of this debate.' She heaved a dramatic sigh. 'But you'd better ring your brothers and explain your plans. Reid left a message on our answering machine today and he sounded pretty worried. I'm certainly not prepared to tell him what you're up to.'

'Yes, of course. I'll ring him now.'

'I'm surprised he didn't catch you on your mobile.'

'Um…he might have. I switched it off and I haven't checked for messages.'

Mel's eyebrows rose. 'Been a touch distracted, have we?' Annie didn't reply. Her decision to turn her phone off had been deliberate. Reid and Kane were probably mad at her for running away to the city and she hadn't felt ready to field their calls.

'Well, Annie,' Mel said. 'If your bags are packed, we can drive you over to the south side as soon as we've had dinner.'

Crossing the kitchen quickly, Annie gave her a hug. 'Thanks for everything, Mel. I don't know what I'd do without friends like you and Victoria. But you don't have to give me a lift. I don't mind getting a taxi.'

'No way,' cut in Victoria. 'Apart from the fact that Mel won't rest easy until she's seen you safely delivered, you can't deny us the chance to see where this mystery uncle lives. We might even get a peek at the great man himself.' She caught the expression in Annie's eyes and added, 'Don't worry, I promise not to embarrass you.'

Tummy churning strangely, Annie went into the lounge room to ring her brothers before collecting her belongings. Not sure where on the huge property they might be, she dialled the number of their satellite phone. Reid answered.

'Annie, thank God it's you. I've rung half of Brisbane trying to track you down.'

She felt instantly contrite. 'I'm sorry. I've been meaning to ring you. How are you?'

'Much better now that I'm hearing your voice and know you're alive.' After a beat, he added, 'I had my fingers crossed that no news meant good news. You must be having a good time.'

'Yes, I am—a wonderful time, but I must admit I've been feeling guilty about taking off the way I did without warning you or Kane.'

'Well—to be totally honest I can't really blame you, Annie. Kane and I both tend to take you for granted and we chauvinist types deserve a bit of a shake up now and again. And *you* deserve some fun in the city if that's what you're hankering for.'

Dear old Reid. In her heart of hearts, Annie had known he would understand.

'So how long will you be staying at Melissa's?' he asked.

'A-ah—' Annie gulped. She spoke slowly while her mind

raced. 'I'm not actually staying at Melissa's place any more. I'm moving to another—friend's place for a few days. There's more room there and it's closer to the galleries and the theatre and everything, so it's terrific. But you'll still be able to reach me on this mobile number. How's everything at home?'

'Lavender's missing you like crazy. She's taken to moping again.'

'Oh, the poor darling.' Instantly she saw a picture of her Border collie, lying in a dispirited sprawl on the back veranda at Southern Cross with her head slumped across her paws. 'Please give her an extra hug from me.'

'I'm afraid I can't. I'm not at home. I've had to come over to Lacey Downs because Mary Rogers went into premature labour.'

'Oh, no. Is everything all right?'

'She's fine now. Had a baby girl.'

'Lovely. She was hoping for a girl.'

'I'll be out here for a week or so.'

Annie grimaced guiltily. 'Sounds like I picked a bad time to take off. Maybe I should come home?' She crossed her fingers, hoping that Reid would say no. She couldn't bear to go home now.

'No, it's okay. Kane's found an English girl to help out at Southern Cross.'

She tried not to sound too relieved. 'That was handy.'

'Yeah.' Reid paused. 'I hope he knows what he's doing.'

The doubt in his voice caused her a twinge of concern, but she decided not to question Reid too closely about Kane and the English girl. It might prompt him to change his mind and say that she was needed at home or, worse still, he might put some more questions to her about her new accommodation.

'I'll have a better idea of my plans in a few days time,' she assured him. 'I'll ring next week and let you know.'

'Okay. Have fun, little sis.'

'Thanks, big brother. I will. Love you, Reid.'

'Love you too, chicken. Take care now.'

It was only after she'd disconnected that she thought again about Kane and the English girl, alone together now at Southern Cross. Why had Reid sounded concerned? It wasn't like him to make a fuss over nothing.

But all thoughts of Kane were banished when Victoria suddenly dashed into the room. 'He's here,' she hissed. 'He's at the front door now.'

Annie's heart rocked. 'Who?' she asked, knowing that there could really only be one answer.

'The uncle. Cripes, Annie, you didn't tell me your philosopher was a hunk. I have never seen glasses make a man look so sexy. *And* he drives a silver convertible with a Dalmatian in the back!'

'Does he?' Annie squeaked. 'I told him not to bother picking me up. I—'

'Didn't want us to be jealous when we saw him?' asked Victoria. 'Oh, baby, I can't blame you.'

CHAPTER FOUR

As Theo drove Annie back across the river to his place, he steeled himself to remain immune to her infectious enthusiasm.

His plan was solid. He would be the perfect gentleman, friendly but reserved. Yes, he would play the role of an attentive host while maintaining an avuncular distance from her. It should be easy enough given the gap in their ages and their backgrounds.

The only wild card in his tidy scheme was Annie herself. She had an unnerving knack for throwing him off guard.

As soon as they arrived at his town house he carried her bag straight up to the second floor where the bedrooms were, and set it on a rug just inside the doorway of Damien's room.

She stepped into the room and looked around at the double bed covered with a plain navy bedspread, and the glass topped table beside it. 'Damien's very neat and tidy.'

'His room looks a little bare because I asked Mrs Feather, who cleans for me, to tidy away the clutter of Damien's personal things.'

'She did a great job.'

Indeed. Perhaps Mrs Feather had followed his instructions just a little too conscientiously. The room did look unnaturally austere. The only ornaments were the lamp on the bedside table and a novelty alarm clock shaped like a television set.

The computer on the pine desk in the corner was switched off and covered with a plastic protector. The timber shutters were drawn across the windows and the walls were completely bare, although Theo could see faint marks where posters of pop groups had hung.

'You have your own *en suite* bathroom. It's through there,' he said, pointing to a doorway. 'So you'll be quite private.'

'That's wonderful. Thank you.'

She lifted her arms to run her fingers through her wind-tousled hair and the movement made her top separate from her jeans to reveal a section of her midriff. Theo saw a couple of inches of smooth, soft skin, and the curve of an exceptionally feminine hip bone and slender waist.

'I'll be down in the kitchen,' he said, backing towards the doorway. 'Do you like mussels?'

She turned, her blue eyes shining with amusement. 'Muscles?'

'The shellfish.'

'Oh, I don't know. I don't think I've ever eaten them, but I'll try anything once.'

'Do you usually like seafood?'

'Yes, I love it.'

'Then mussels should be fine.'

She frowned. 'You're not cooking them, are you?'

'Yes.' He shrugged to make light of it. 'Don't you trust me?'

'But I should be doing the cooking. Heck, Theo, you go to work all day and you've given me this lovely accommodation.

The least I can do is cook. Mind you, most of the recipes I'm used to have beef in them.'

He smiled. 'Another night, perhaps.'

When Theo left, Annie took her toiletry bag through to the neat little bathroom and washed her face and brushed the tangles from her hair, caused by the windy but thrilling drive in Theo's convertible. She thought about adding a touch of lipstick, but decided against it. At home she hardly ever wore make-up and she felt uncomfortable using it unless she was all dolled up for a special occasion.

Besides, she didn't want Theo to think she was trying too hard to impress him. She would unpack later, she decided. She felt a little uncomfortable in Damien's too neat room and she was keen to check out the rest of the house.

On the way to the stairs she passed Theo's bedroom. The last of the twilight was pooling through open floor-to-ceiling timber shutters on to a rich cream bedspread and an artistic tumble of black and cream cushions. His king-size bed was framed by carved timber posts. All sorts of books were piled on one of the matching side tables.

She looked at the sumptuous bed and pictured it at night, looking even more sumptuous in the glow cast by the impressive bedside lamps with heavy gold bases and black shades… But then she pictured Theo in the bed…and she wanted to put herself in the picture, too.

As if…

She hurried downstairs.

Theo's kitchen was at the back of the ground floor section of his narrow town house and as she made her way through the living area she couldn't help admiring his taste in interior decor.

The furnishings were similar to his bedroom—masculine colours like charcoal grey, black and cream that blended

wonderfully with the honeyed tones of the polished timber
floors and the floor-to-ceiling timber bookshelves. One wall
was painted dark red, and set against it were abstract black
and white paintings in thick gold frames.

Music drifted from the kitchen—a rhythmic drumbeat, a
thrumming guitar and the alluring, smoky voice of one of
her favourite Gypsy singers—another passion she'd thought
she'd shared with Damien.

And there was a sensational aroma wafting through the
house. She sniffed the air, trying to identify the ingredients
and decided that it was lemon and crushed garlic and a herb,
perhaps parsley, being heated in olive oil. Then she walked into
Theo's kitchen and it was like walking into another world.

To start with, Theo was at the stove.

For a girl who'd grown up in the McKinnon household,
where a man only stepped up to a kitchen stove in a dire
emergency, it was a remarkable sight, especially as Theo
looked convincingly masculine and yet so totally at home
with a striped tea towel draped over one broad shoulder while
he stirred something in a heavy enamel pot.

But the music and the smells enchanted her, too...

And then the room itself...gleaming white walls and smart
black granite bench tops...a white platter piled with lemons,
and elegant wrought iron stools pulled up to a tall bench...
sliding doors leading to a leafy courtyard strung with tiny
lights. And a table set for two.

'This is almost ready,' Theo said over his shoulder. 'I have
a nice white wine chilled. Would you like some?'

He turned and smiled at her.

And Annie feared she might actually swoon.

The mussels were as delicious as they smelled. Theo served
them in their shells, accompanied by linguini, which he'd
tossed in a simple sauce made from tomatoes and basil leaves.

The meal had an uncomplicated, direct combination of flavours that Annie loved and she couldn't resist licking her lips.

'Does this dish have a name?' she asked.

'*Spaghetti della Paulo.*'

'And what does that mean?'

'That it's Paulo's recipe. He's a restaurateur who lives in Rome. I met him on one of my trips to Italy.'

'I should have guessed that,' she said, smiling. 'Wow! I suppose you'd never need to go to La Piastra.'

'On the contrary, it's one of my favourite restaurants.'

Of course.

There it was again. The unnerving connection between Damien and Theo that she tried not to think about.

She glanced down at Basil, lying at their feet as they dined in the courtyard, then she sipped some wine.

'Tell me a little about your home at Southern Cross,' said Theo. 'I'm sure my understanding of life on a cattle station is very romanticised. I hardly know anything about what happens on a day to day basis.'

Annie shrugged. 'It depends on the time of the year. In the mustering season it's fun to get out in the bush for weeks at a time, sleeping in swags under the stars. But at other times it's pretty routine. There's always general maintenance work—fixing fences, checking water, putting out feed supplements.'

He asked more questions, surprising her with his eagerness to hear details about these tasks and other aspects of handling stock. Then he looked thoughtful for a moment. 'It's ages since I've slept under the stars.'

'You should come to Star Valley, then. It's big sky country. You can see all the stars you like.'

'It sounds wonderful.' He topped up their wineglasses. 'In a way it was star-gazing that led me into philosophy.'

'Really?'

'Yes. It was the summer after I left school and I was on a holiday with some mates, and we camped out on the beach at Byron Bay. It was the first time I'd really taken a good long look at the stars. You know, really looked at the sheer vastness and immensity of the universe.'

'It's a pretty awesome sight, isn't it?'

'It certainly is. It got me wondering how we humans fit into the scheme of things.'

'Does philosophy give answers to questions like that?'

'Not definitive answers necessarily, but it gives theories and possibilities. And it gives you guidance to work through all the existing answers till you work out your own.'

'And you've worked out yours?'

His eyes regarded her warmly. 'I'm getting there.'

Annie sighed. There was so much she wanted to ask Theo. Deep questions about the existence of God, about life and its possible meaning, but she didn't really know where to begin. 'So you went straight from school into philosophy?'

'No. My father wanted me to study something more practical, so I started out studying economics. I got into philosophy by accident.'

'How?'

He pulled a sheepish grin. 'You wouldn't be very impressed.'

'Try me.'

Hooking one arm over the back of his chair, he leaned back and sent her another self-conscious smile. 'I'm talking about centuries ago, remember, when I was eighteen and desperate to win on to girls, but terribly shy.'

Theo had been shy with girls? That was a surprise, but she refrained from saying so.

'I can't quite believe I'm telling you this, but at the time my older sister assured me that girls love brainy guys, so I hit

on the idea of sitting in the backs of bars with a big fat book
and a pipe and trying to look impressively clever.'

'A pipe, Theo?'

'It was unlit. I saw it as a symbol that linked me to all the
great twentieth century thinkers.'

'And were the chicks impressed?'

'Actually, it was amazing how well it worked.'

I'll bet. Annie felt a surge of ridiculous jealousy for all the
girls who'd scored a date with him. She took another deeper
sip of her wine. 'Forgive me for being slow, but I don't quite
get the connection between attracting girls and philosophy.
Or do I have totally the wrong idea about philosophy?'

Theo laughed. 'One of the books I took along with me
was about Seneca, a philosopher who lived in Roman times.
I got so damned interested in him and his ideas that I forgot
to keep an eye out for the girls. Apparently several tried to get
my attention and gave up. From that night on I was hooked
on philosophy.'

'And you gave up girls?' Annie feigned innocence.

'Well…no. Not exactly.'

Across their table their eyes met. Annie saw in Theo's gaze
an unmistakable flash that sent shivers feathering her skin.

Taking a deep breath, she said, 'So what did this Roman
guy have to say that impressed you so much?'

'Oh, many things.' He looked away again as he thought for
a moment. 'Actually, you'd probably like him too, because
you come from the outback.'

'There's a link between the outback and an ancient Roman
philosopher?'

'You folk in the outback have adjusted your lives to cope
with your environment. You accept that there are forces stronger than humans, forces that are completely indifferent to
our desires. You've learned to endure bushfires and drought.

Things that can't be changed. Seneca was big on accepting lessons from nature.'

Annie chuckled.

'What's so funny?'

'I wouldn't be too quick to congratulate us on accepting our lot in the bush, Theo. Why do you think I was cracking my neck to get to the city?'

He blinked.

'Heck, in the bush we get sick of making adjustments for *everything*—even something as simple as ordering books over the Internet.'

'That's a problem?'

'On most websites my postal address is invalid. They won't accept Southern Cross, via Mirrabrook. They tell me I need a street number and suburb or town. So I have to invent an address that keeps them happy.'

Theo smiled. 'And that's before you get to the big problems like droughts and floods.'

'Exactly.'

The next minute his expression grew sombre. And Annie knew she'd spoiled the mood. He'd remembered Damien and the email and how desperate she'd been to find a city boyfriend.

He cleared his throat. 'Anyhow… I'm afraid I can't spend more time chatting this evening. I have some pressing work that I must attend to tonight.'

She jumped to her feet. 'Of course. Let me clean up. You get on with what you have to do.'

'I'll need to show you where things go.'

In the kitchen they were terribly efficient. No more cosy chats as utensils and china were rinsed and the dishwasher was stacked.

Theo made coffee. As he offered Annie a cup he said, 'I'll take mine through to the study.'

'Okay.'

'Good night.'

''Night, Theo.' She watched him disappear, then thumbed through a current affairs magazine as she drank coffee in the empty kitchen with the humming dishwasher as her only companion.

Then she went back upstairs to Damien's bedroom, unzipped her bag and transferred her clothes into the wardrobe. Crumbs, it was empty. All Damien's clothes had been removed. How weird.

The room gave absolutely no hint of Damien's personality. Had that been deliberate? Sinking on to the edge of his bed, Annie looked around her and felt a faint stirring of unease. Surely it shouldn't have been necessary to remove everything from this room?

Then a sharper tingle of fear skittered down her spine as a horrible thought struck her. Perhaps Damien didn't exist!

No, that was silly. It would mean that Theo wasn't his uncle. Oh, God. Sudden panic sluiced through her. Could Theo *be* Damien? Was that why they both had the same tastes and ideas?

Could Theo have used Damien as an Internet code name and then hidden behind his real identity when she came to the city? Oh, God. The very thought made her head spin. Surely she was letting her imagination get the better of her. There had to be a more logical explanation.

But if there was it eluded her.

She'd moved in with a man she knew nothing about. For all she knew he could be leading two lives. That couldn't be very healthy.

A kind of fearful desolation descended on her as she prepared for bed. And she knew she was looking down the barrel of another sleepless night.

CHAPTER FIVE

MEL rang early the next afternoon.

'Just checking to see how everything's going,' she said, her voice purring suggestively.

'Fine,' Annie told her. 'I'm making risotto with smoked salmon and asparagus.'

'At this time of day?'

'Well, I'm starting from scratch. Making my own stock and everything.'

'Crumbs, Annie. I thought you'd be out, strolling around an art gallery, soaking up culture.'

'I did that this morning, but I wanted to—'

'Impress Dr Theo with your culinary skills?'

Yes. It was probably foolish of her to hope that she could impress Theo. A man had to be interested in her before he could be impressed, and Theo had been so remote this morning.

After her restless night she'd slept in and Theo hadn't woken her when he'd taken Basil for his walk. And he'd kept his nose in a newspaper while he had his breakfast coffee and toast. It was almost as an afterthought as he was heading out of the door that he'd mentioned he had theatre tickets for this evening and would she like to come.

But, foolish though it might be, she *wanted* to impress him with this meal.

Despite the mystery surrounding the whole Damien-Theo connection, she fancied the heck out of Theo and heaven knew, she was never going to impress him with her dazzling intellect.

'Theo's the most amazing cook, Mel. I can't just feed him sausages and mash.'

'Don't forget to have some fun, Annie. You told me you came down here to get out of the kitchen. I was going to ask if you wanted to do something tonight, but it sounds like you're busy.'

'Thanks for thinking of me. Theo said something about going to see a play.'

'Oh, nice.'

'I hope so. I haven't seen a stage play since our English teacher took us to see *A Midsummer Night's Dream*. Perhaps I can meet you for lunch tomorrow or the next day?'

'Okay. Keep in touch.' Mel sighed. 'I'm still not confident you're doing the right thing, Annie.'

'Relax, Mel. I'm totally on top of this,' Annie lied.

When the theatre lights came up at the end of the play, Theo discovered Annie dabbing at her eyes with a tissue.

'That was a terrible ending,' she said. 'I was expecting it to turn out happily.'

'So you insist on happy endings, do you?'

'Not necessarily, but when a play starts out like a romantic comedy I do. I was sure James and Erica would end up together, then in the last five minutes everything fell apart. That shouldn't be allowed. I was devastated.' She shoved the bunched tissue back into her purse and sniffed. 'Sorry.'

'No need to apologise.'

'I enjoyed every minute of it until the end.'

Annie looked so disappointed that Theo was tempted to throw a reassuring arm around her shoulders. He might have done so if she hadn't also been looking so lovely this evening.

Despite the hint of tears still shimmering in her eyes, she was radiant in her simple, sleeveless dark red dress. Slim and womanly. Breathtakingly so.

But he was determined to keep his distance, and as they joined the people filing out of the theatre he shoved his hands deep in the pockets of his trousers. He kept them there as he and Annie walked side by side back to his place, even though it was a perfect summery November's night.

A trip to the theatre had seemed a good idea, far safer than staying at home with Annie, being bewitched by the changing nuances in her animated face, or being flattered by her rapt attention during conversations; safer than waiting in pleasant anticipation of being ambushed by another of her unexpected questions, or thinking about an ambush or two of his own... that didn't involve quite so much talking...

And, as if that wasn't bad enough... Tonight the scent of frangipani lingered in the air and fallen jacaranda bells formed a carpet beneath their feet. A half moon rode at a tilt above the rooftops. It was the kind of night that cried out for a little romantic hand-holding, but he had to nip those kinds of thoughts in the bud.

Fat chance.

As they walked beneath trees and street lamps, passing in and out of shadows, he couldn't resist stealing glimpses in Annie's direction. She walked with an easy grace, a barely contained vitality. And whenever the light touched her hair it gleamed like a silken reflection of the pale gold moon. He longed to touch it.

Longed to feel the smooth curve of her shoulders, the slenderness of her waist. And more.

He would be wiser to reserve his admiration for the brave tilt of her chin and the pert jut of her nose. But on a night like this wisdom crumbled so easily. *Damn!* He had always prided himself on his self-control and yet now he was thinking about Annie's legs. How was a man expected to remain immune to them? They were so devastatingly long and lovely beneath her red skirt.

To his dismay, he was forced to admit that he was losing the will to remain at a safe distance from Annie McKinnon. But he had to, damn it. There were a thousand reasons why getting close to her was unwise. Besides, she hadn't come to the city to meet *him*. She was far too young and spirited and lively to get involved with a boring university lecturer.

Annie felt strangely nervous by the time they reached Theo's house. There seemed to be a new tension between them, an almost tangible sexual tension. Or was she imagining that?

The mystery of Damien still loomed in the background of her thoughts, but she didn't know how to broach the subject without spoiling the mood of the evening. And tonight she didn't want to spoil anything. Every minute she spent with Theo convinced her that she was becoming helplessly attracted to him.

They entered his house by the front door and he paused in the middle of his lounge. 'Would you like coffee or brandy or both?'

'I think I'd like brandy but no coffee,' she said. 'Coffee tends to keep me awake.'

'Brandy it is, then. Take a seat.'

She sat in an armchair while he removed his coat and fetched glasses and brandy from a drinks cabinet. He handed her a glass and took a seat on the sofa, which was positioned at right angles to her chair.

Settling back, he loosened the knot of his tie and crossed an ankle over a knee. Then he slipped his glasses up on to his forehead while he massaged the bridge of his nose. He seemed relaxed, but Annie couldn't help wondering if, like her, he was making a conscious effort to look more relaxed than he felt.

His glasses back in place, he smiled at her and raised his drink. 'Cheers. Thanks for your company this evening.'

'Thank you for taking me, Theo. I really enjoyed the play, despite my fuss at the end.'

'Here's to happier endings.'

'I'll second that. Happy endings.'

Their gazes met and the sudden heat in Theo's eyes was so electrifying that Annie was glad she was sitting down.

He took a deep sip of his drink. 'Thanks again for dinner, too. Your risotto was truly superb.'

'Glad you liked it.'

For a while they sat without talking, enjoying the fine brandy. But the prolonged quiet was too much for Annie.

'Theo, can I spoil this golden silence by asking another of my nosy questions?'

He smiled. 'Wait till I brace myself.' He drew an exaggerated deep breath. 'Okay. I suppose I'm as ready as I'll ever be. Fire when you're ready.'

'It's nothing too confronting. Well, perhaps it is a bit—it's just that ever since our conversation last night, I've been curious about your girlfriends.'

'Oh, dear.'

'Do you have a girlfriend at the moment?'

He didn't speak immediately. Keeping his gaze lowered, he said, 'I date women from time to time, but there's no one special at the moment.'

'Are you still shy with women?'

His face broke into a helpless grin and a knowing light sparked in his eyes. 'I don't hang around in bars with a book and a pipe, if that's what you're asking.'

The warmth of his amused gaze flowed over her and her cheeks felt hot. 'Fair enough. I'll let you off that particular hook for now.' Suddenly she kicked off her shoes and settled more comfortably into the armchair with her legs curled beneath her.

'That's the hard questions over. Now for the easy one.'

'I can hardly wait.'

'What do philosophers have to say about romance?'

His smile lurked, but he eyed her cautiously and he took a deep sip of brandy before he answered. 'On the whole, philosophers haven't been too impressed by romantic love. I think they feel it's best left to song writers and poets.'

'Why do they avoid it?'

'Well—romance interrupts more serious projects.'

She made a faintly scoffing sound.

'Even the greatest minds can become bewildered by the power of love.'

'Of course! So they should be.' Leaning over the arm of the chair, she challenged him. 'But surely you can't expect me to believe that all the philosophers, supposedly the greatest thinkers in the world, have put the entire subject of romantic love into the too hard basket?'

'Well, no, they haven't. Not entirely.'

'So?'

'You want examples? Okay, there was a German philosopher called Schopenhauer, who decided that love is perplexing and yet very important to us because the composition of the next generation depends on it.'

Annie stared at him in disbelief. 'Good grief, Theo. Was he serious?'

'Quite.'

'But that's the most unromantic, boring explanation anyone could ever think of. Is that the best philosophers can do?'

His smile was wry as he lifted his glass and watched the movement of the brandy as he gave it a little swirl. 'I admit that most fellows aren't really concerned about the continuation of the species when they ask a girl for her telephone number, but that's no reason to knock the idea.'

'Convince me.'

'The theory is that we are attracted to people whose genes will combine well with our own. For example, a man with a very big nose might be attracted to a woman with a rather small one and together they'll produce a child with a more acceptably sized nose.'

Annie tried hard not to stare at Theo's nose. She already knew that it was quite perfect, neither too big nor too small.

'But that's got next to nothing to do with romance,' she said. 'Not with the emotions and longings we feel deep in our hearts.'

He looked away for a moment and the muscles in his throat worked. 'We're speaking theoretically, Annie. And the theory is that this selection process works at a subconscious level. Apparently it explains why humans have an alarming propensity for falling in love with the wrong people.'

'Do they?'

'Yes. We've all seen it, haven't we? A man or a woman falls in love with someone who doesn't seem at all compatible, and yet they feel no sexual attraction whatsoever to someone who would be much more suitable.'

A sudden chill turned Annie's skin to goose-bumps. 'Do you think that happens very often?'

'Of course. James and Erica in that play tonight were a very good example, but it happens all the time.'

She sat back and took another deeper sip of brandy. Staring down into her glass, she murmured, 'Perhaps that's why I'm so incredibly attracted to you.'

'I beg your pardon?'

Her heart pounded. 'I said perhaps that's why I'm so attracted to you.'

She looked up to find Theo staring at her. He looked predictably stunned, but at least he didn't look horrified.

'We're incompatible, aren't we? Take the education factor for starters.' She dropped her gaze back to her glass. 'Which is a pretty big factor.'

There was a stretch of silence. Then Theo said gently, 'I would have thought the gap in our ages was more of a problem.'

'It's not that big a gap. You could only be, what—ten years older than me?'

'Nine,' he amended quickly.

The speed of his answer and the scratchy sound in his voice, as if he'd swallowed a prickle, gave her courage. Leaning forward, she set her glass on the coffee table. 'Well, there you go, Theo. The incompatibilities are toppling by the minute.'

'Yes.' Without taking his eyes from hers, he set his glass down beside her glass. 'Perhaps they are.'

There was a moment of breathless stillness and silence while they both sat, watching each other, aware that they hovered on the brink of something momentous.

Then, to her dismay, Theo closed his eyes and released a soft groan. 'Annie, your honesty is refreshing but we shouldn't be talking like this.'

'Why not?'

'We need to step back from this for a moment and think.'

'Do we?' Annie winced when she heard the disappointment

in her voice. She sighed and repositioned herself, uncurling her legs and sitting straight in the armchair once more. 'What do you suggest we think about?'

'Why you came to the city. What you really want. I assume you were hoping for adventure and romance, but you expected to find it with another younger person. And now I've intruded into the scene.'

She suspected that this was the moment to bring up her worries about Damien. Problem was, whenever she was with Theo, her whacko theories that he was leading a double life just didn't make any kind of sense. He was too grounded, too balanced, for subterfuge. And why would a man as gorgeous as Theo need to hunt for a woman using the Internet?

'To be honest, I'm not too interested in Damien any more,' she said.

'Nevertheless you should be out on the town—hitting the top night spots with your girlfriends. Meeting younger men.'

'I enjoy being with you.'

He sighed. 'I'm not the kind of man you want to get involved with.'

'Why?' Nerves tightened in her stomach. Was this confession time? 'What's wrong with you?'

'I'm an excessively boring academic.'

'Boring?' She gaped at him. 'Is that all?'

He frowned. 'Were you expecting me to offer you a list of character faults?'

'No, no, not a list exactly.'

'You've already dismissed my claim that I'm too old for you, although I think that deserves closer consideration.'

'It's just that I thought you were going to bring some surprise skeleton out of the closet.'

He favoured her with a small smile and shook his head, and she felt a heady rush of relief.

'No skeletons,' he said. 'But perhaps you think that in itself is boring?'

'Theo, in no way are you boring. Honestly, from where I'm looking, you're shaping up to be the single most interesting man I've ever met.'

A dark colour stained his cheekbones. His eyes flashed with sudden heat. For a breathless moment Annie thought he was going to leap out of his chair and haul her on to the sofa with him.

If only...

Clenching a fist on his knee, he looked away, and she saw his jaw tighten with tension.

After a clamouring stretch of silence he said, 'What surprises me is that a lovely girl like you had to come to Brisbane to search for a boyfriend. I would have thought you'd have plenty of offers, even though you're relatively isolated in the outback.'

For a moment she couldn't answer. She was too busy indulging in a private celebration because Theo had said she was lovely. *Wow!* With an effort, she forced her mind to process the rest of his comment.

'I've tried dating guys from the bush,' she said, 'but after a while I lost interest in them. I suppose I fit right in with that German philosopher's theory. It would have been sensible of me to fall for a man in the outback, but no one clicked. I don't know why. Maybe it's because I've had a steady diet of cowboys all my life that I find city men much more interesting.'

Theo's response was to sit very still and scowl at a spot on the floor, which made Annie feel suddenly flooded by doubts. And very foolish. And exposed.

Had she completely misinterpreted their situation? She'd

thought there was a mutual 'something' happening between them, but perhaps she'd got it all wrong. Maybe Theo was trying to suggest kindly, indirectly, that he was regretting his offer of hospitality?

A horrible flash of chilling panic slithered through her. She bent down and picked up her shoes, then stood. No doubt it was an immature, reckless, *un*-philosophical way to respond, but she couldn't help herself. 'I can move back to Mel's in the morning, if that's what you want.'

Then, because she suddenly felt the need to cry, she turned and hurried across the room without waiting for his reply.

'Goodnight,' she called over her shoulder before scooting up the stairs.

Theo watched her go.

Common sense and logic told him it was best for Annie to return to her girlfriends in the morning. He'd invited her to his house on an impulsive, foolish whim, fuelled by more self-interest than he'd cared to admit at the time, but it was not too late to correct his mistake.

In a flash of images, he pictured himself doing the right thing—driving her back to her friends and then returning to this house without her. Saw himself walking with Basil along the South Bank. Morning after morning. Without her. Saw himself dating sensible academic colleagues—taking them to see plays—women who would never dissolve into tears over the ending, however unsatisfactory.

And the thought appalled him so fiercely that he jumped to his feet, charged across the room and took the stairs three at a time.

Annie was in the doorway of Damien's room—about to close the door.

'I don't want you to go, Annie,' he said.

With her hand on the doorknob, she turned back to him, her face pale and her eyes shining with a suspicious brightness. 'No?'

He shook his head and smiled. 'In fact, I'd very much like you to stay.'

She lifted the shoes she'd been holding and cradled them against her chest in a kind of defensive gesture. 'Why have you changed your mind?'

'One very good reason.' He smiled. 'Honestly, from where I'm looking, you're shaping up to be the single most interesting woman I've ever met.'

For a moment she looked confused. Her clear blue eyes reflected disbelief warring with wonder. But then a slow, warm smile suffused her face. 'That's nice to know,' she said.

But instead of running into his arms with the open-hearted impulsiveness he'd come to expect from her, she said a demure goodnight and closed her bedroom door.

And yet again, Dr Theo Grainger was left with a feeling of puzzled inadequacy.

CHAPTER SIX

YES! Yes! Yes!

Annie danced in happy circles, waving her shoes above her head. Theo found her interesting. Not just any old interesting, but terribly interesting—the *most* interesting woman ever. And he'd also said she was lovely.

She waltzed around Damien's room. *Lovely.* Wasn't that the most scrumptious word in the whole dictionary?

Spinning another ecstatic circle, she knew that Theo was lovely too. Exceptionally lovely. In a completely masculine way, of course. She loved everything about him, from the topmost hair on his head to—

A curt knock sounded on her door.

In the middle of executing a wicked pirouette, she wobbled precariously. Then promptly lost her balance. Her shoes flew from her hands as she tumbled to the floor at the precise moment the door opened.

Theo.

From an undignified heap at his feet, and with her dress riding high up her thighs, she looked up at him and blushed.

'I'm so sorry,' he said, bending to offer her a helping hand. 'I didn't mean to startle you.'

There was little she could do except take the hand he offered and allow herself to be helped to her feet.

'Are you hurt?'

'No, not at all.' Blushing again, she smoothed her dress over her hips and thighs, and took a calming deep breath before lifting her eyes to meet his. 'Did you—um—want something, Theo?'

'Yes.' Amusement danced in his hazel eyes. 'I wanted to double-check something you said earlier. I have an urgent need to be quite clear about it.'

She stared at him blankly for a moment. She'd said so many things this evening. 'Which something would that be?'

His smile was the sexy kind that turned her insides to marshmallow.

'Was it my imagination, or did you say something about being attracted to me?'

'Oh.' Heat suffused her. 'Well, yes, I did, because it's true. I *am* attracted to you, Theo.'

Taking her hands in his, he smiled again. 'Good. Because, in case you haven't guessed, the attraction's mutual.'

'It is?'

'Very.'

For a heartbeat they smiled into each other's eyes, and then Theo drew Annie gently towards him, and it was as easy as spring slipping into summer, the way she melted into his arms.

His lips brushed her cheek. 'I'm very, very attracted.'

'Same here. Think of me as a dropped pin and you're a magnet.'

His chuckle caressed her skin. 'There's no way I'm going to think of you as a dropped pin.'

Her eyes drifted closed as his lips explored her jawline. 'I suppose it does sound dangerous.'

He pressed a kiss to the corner of her mouth. 'You *are* dangerous, Annie McKinnon.'

'No, I'm—'

He stopped her protest with a kiss on the lips.

Oh, man!

Oh, bliss, to be kissed by Theo. Bliss to be enclosed within the strong circle of his arms and to feel his lovely lips tracing dreamy patterns on hers. Joy to let her lips drift open as his kiss turned hot and brandy-flavoured. Heaven as his mouth seduced her.

She pressed closer, wriggling her hips against his hard, masculine body. And Theo's gentlemanly reserve became a thing of the past.

His mouth became demanding. His tongue delved deep while his hands moulded her shoulders, then the shape of her breasts through her dress. Soft groans rumbled low in his throat as he began to walk her slowly backwards to Damien's bed.

Damien!

Oh, help!

A wretched alarm bell pierced Annie's consciousness.

The thought of Damien pulled her up sharply, like a rough hand dragging her back from the point of drowning.

Damn, Damien. The spectre of him was beside them, like a ghostly presence in this strangely bare room...

Darn. Why did she have to think of the jerk now? Why did her worries about the Theo-Damien connection have to surface at this crucial point in time—possibly the most decisive moment in her lifetime?

Theo, sensing her sudden tension, grew still. 'Is something the matter?'

She didn't want to speak, didn't want to spoil this delicious, all-important moment, but the word spilled out. 'Damien.'

'Damien?'

She could hear the raggedness of his breathing. His eyes met hers and for long seconds he stared at her, looking puzzled and worried, before he released her and took a step back.

'You're still infatuated with Damien?'

'No, of course not.' She felt so overcome she had to cover her face with her hands.

'What is it, Annie? Have I frightened you?'

'No, no, Theo.' She dropped her hands to her sides again, then looked around her. 'It's just this room—I just don't understand who Damien is, where he's gone, or why he pretended to be you, or why you've stripped his room bare. It's kind of getting to me. It makes me nervous. Half the time I'm afraid that—that—'

'What? What are you afraid of?'

She was almost too afraid to say it. 'That he's you.'

'Me?'

Theo looked so clearly appalled that Annie felt instant relief.

'I've been plagued by this horrible thought that Damien might have been your Internet persona. You know, like a code name.'

'Oh, Annie.' Theo shook his head and raked a hand through his thick dark hair. Staring at the floor, he let out a huff of irritation. 'It's time that wretched nephew of mine faced up to the consequences of his own foolishness.'

Annie gulped. 'I'm so sorry, Theo. I didn't mean to blab it out now. I didn't want to spoil things.'

'No, you're right,' he said. 'It's better to clear the air. I'm going to get on to Damien right away and insist he comes back to apologise to you.'

His eyes shimmered darkly with emotion as he reached out and traced his fingers down the curve of her cheek. His mouth quirked into a lopsided smile. 'It was probably best that you spoke up when you did. Someone needed to apply the brakes.'

Her hand closed over his as it lay against her cheek. Turning her face, she kissed the inner curve of his palm.

His breath escaped on a soft sigh. Bending closer, he pressed a warm kiss to the back of her neck. 'I'll say goodnight, Annie, before I'm tempted to go back on my word. Hopefully, you'll have your answer about Damien tomorrow.'

He left her room quickly and she turned back to look around Damien's bedroom, awash with a tumble of emotions—with relief, with happiness, but also with regret and longing.

But, with the imprint of Theo's lovely kisses lingering warmly on her lips, she knew she would sleep well tonight.

Next morning, after a pre-breakfast run with Theo and Basil, Annie was in the shower when she heard a young man's voice penetrate the hiss of water streaming over her.

'What the hell's going on? Where are my things?'

She paused in the process of rinsing shampoo from her hair. Was there someone in her room?

'Where's my stereo and my CD collection?' the voice shouted again. It was louder. Angrier. 'And where's my DVD player? What have you done to my flaming room?'

Snapping off the taps, she stood, naked and dripping.

Fists hammered on the bathroom door. 'Who's in there?'

'Hold your horses!' she yelled back, scrambling out of the shower cubicle so quickly she stubbed her toe.

In panicky haste she snatched a towel and wrapped it

around her. Her wet feet threatened to slip on the tiled bathroom floor as she hurried to the rattling door. With one hand clutching the towel tightly over her chest, she opened the door six inches.

And blinked.

A gangling, bespectacled boy stood there—an angry looking boy in his late teens, wearing a T-shirt and Hawaiian print board shorts. And sandals.

At the sight of her his jaw dropped so fast he risked dislocation. His eyes practically popped out of his head.

Annie was just as shocked. 'Who— w-what—?'

She was rescued from her stammering question by Theo charging through the bedroom doorway like a cattle truck out of control.

'Get out of this room immediately,' he roared at the boy.

'Hey, steady on, Theo. You can't order me back from the Gold Coast and then tell me to get out of my own bedroom.'

'You've abdicated all rights to this room for the foreseeable future.'

Stunned, Annie stared at them both.

This couldn't be Damien. Not this boy. For heaven's sake, he couldn't be more than seventeen or eighteen. He still had spots on his chin. Where was the surfer streaked hair from the photo he'd sent her? The movie-star-sexy good looks?

The intruder switched his attention from Theo to her and his face turned beetroot. 'Oh, God. It's Annie, isn't it?'

Her last lingering hope sank without a trace. No chance for error now. This was Damien. *This was her Dream Date!*

Sick to the stomach, she sagged against the doorjamb. Then, as Damien continued to stare at her, she remembered with a jolt of embarrassment that a bath towel was not appropriate clothing for this encounter.

Theo, who was similarly damp but at least dressed, must

have realised the same thing. Grabbing Damien by the neck of his T-shirt, he hauled him out of the room.

'But how was I to know?' the boy shouted. 'You sent me a text message ordering me back home and here I am. How did Annie get here? What's going on?'

She could hear Damien's continued protests and Theo's raised voice as he dragged the boy downstairs.

Good grief! Closing the bathroom door, she leaned against it and her stomach churned. Damien—a kid *barely out of school*. She felt such a fool as she thought of all the weeks she'd blissfully exchanged emails with him. For crying out loud, she'd flirted with him. Shamelessly. In her typical, take-no-prisoners fashion, she'd spilled out her heart and soul in those emails. She'd even discussed her feelings for him with the agony aunt in the *Mirrabrook Star.*

How humiliating! All that excitement she'd felt had been over a date with a skinny kid still clawing his way out of puberty.

Her mind cringed. But then, hot on the heels of her embarrassment, came a burst of anger. The nerve of him to deceive her, to play games with her like that! What a grub!

She remembered all the names Mel and Victoria had used to describe him after the disastrous non-date. He deserved every one of them.

Peeling the towel away from her, she wrenched the bathroom door open again, hurried into the bedroom and dragged on jeans and a T-shirt. No way was she going to hide away in the bathroom feeling humiliated when she could give the little twerp a piece of her mind.

Without a care for her messy wet hair, she hurried downstairs.

Theo and Damien were glaring at each other across the kitchen.

'I don't care where you go,' Theo growled. 'You're not

welcome here. Once you've apologised to Annie, you can go back to your mates at the Gold Coast.'

'So I'm being thrown out because Annie McKinnon's moved in?'

An embarrassed grimace flickered over Theo's face, but he covered it with fresh anger. 'It's time you accepted the consequences of your actions, Damien. You've caused Miss McKinnon inconvenience and expense and embarrassment. It's time to grow up. You're legally an adult, but no one would know it from the way you behave.'

Realising that Annie was in the room, Damien turned her way and he reddened again when he saw her. 'I'm sorry, Annie.'

'So you jolly well should be,' she said sternly.

'And how about a proper apology?' added Theo.

Damien scowled at him. 'What do you mean?'

'You can do better than merely mumbling you're sorry. I want you to stand here in front of Miss McKinnon and look her in the eye and tell her exactly what you're apologising for.'

'There's no need to jump down my throat. She knows why I'm sorry.'

Theo's fists clenched as if Damien had tested his patience once too often. 'Tell her, or you'll get a good clip on the ear.'

Annie didn't believe Theo would carry out his threat. Nevertheless, tension quivered in the air as Damien glowered back at his uncle and his own fists curled in response. But the nephew knew he was in the wrong and his defiance wilted.

He dropped his gaze to the floor. 'I apologise—' he began.

'Speak to Annie,' ordered Theo. 'Look at her.'

Another flash of resentment flared, but then Damien took a deep breath, squared his shoulders and turned to Annie. 'I really am sorry, Annie.' His Adam's apple slid up and down in his youthful throat. 'I guess I shouldn't have gone to a dating chat room in the first place, and when you told me how old you were, I shouldn't have strung you along. It all started out as a bit of fun and it went too far. I—I'm sorry about the d—date and everything. I didn't really think you'd show up.'

Her eyes narrowed. 'It's not very pleasant to discover I've been used, Damien. I value myself more highly than a form of amusement for a youngster with raging hormones.'

He flushed more brightly.

'You don't look much like your photo,' she added and he looked so hugely embarrassed that she began to feel sorry for him.

Theo chipped in. 'And I didn't appreciate the way you dashed off leaving some garbled message and expecting me to pick up the pieces. So I've told Annie that she's welcome to use your room for as long as she wants to stay in Brisbane.'

About to protest, Damien thought better of it. 'So where's all my gear?'

'It's been stored at Pop's.'

He seemed relieved to hear that and he nodded slowly. 'Maybe Pop will take pity on me and let me stay at his place.'

'You don't deserve any kind of pity,' said Theo. 'But no doubt your grandfather will relent. It'll be up to you to explain to him why you don't have a roof over your head.'

'No roof?' Annie felt suddenly guilty.

Theo shot her a quick warning frown. 'Don't worry about him. My father will take him in.'

Apparently resigned to his fate now, Damien slung a small blue backpack over his shoulder. Annie couldn't help noticing the family resemblance between the youth and the uncle. It wasn't just that they both had steady hazel eyes, or the fact that they were both tall and had the same shiny dark hair—or that they both wore glasses.

With his confession behind him, Damien's face showed the beginnings of the same intelligence and strength of character she'd found so readily in Theo's. In another six or seven years, when Damien filled out and matured, the resemblance would be even stronger.

Now, he backed towards the door. 'I hope you enjoy my room, Annie.' He spoke with a polite dignity that was another echo of his uncle. But then the effect was spoiled by a cheeky smirk. 'But it can't be much fun for you hanging around here with old Uncle Theo.'

'Get going,' barked Theo.

Damien went.

'Oh, boy.' Annie felt shaken and she sank on to a kitchen stool.

Theo was watching her, his eyes shadowed with concern. 'I'm sorry you had to find out about him so abruptly.'

She frowned. 'Why did you keep him a secret? Couldn't you have told me sooner?'

He began to fill the coffee maker. 'I was trying to spare you.'

'From embarrassment?' She managed a wan smile. 'So you cleared all his things out of his room because you didn't want me to realise how young he was?'

'Yes.'

She nodded, then sighed. 'Actually, that was kind of you. I must admit I feel pretty small when I think how gullible I was to come charging down here for a big city date—with a *teenager*.'

She stared at the dazzle of morning sunlight streaming through the glass doors from the courtyard, thinking of that happy, excited self who'd come rushing to the city, full of high hopes.

'I was so worked up about coming away for that date I actually asked for advice from a columnist in the *Mirrabrook Star*.'

'What's that?'

She rolled her eyes. 'Our little local newspaper.'

Theo smiled. 'Were you given good advice?'

'Yes, it was excellent. It was exactly what I wanted to hear.' Annie's answering smile was cheeky as she rose and walked across the room and stood in the sun's warmth, fluffing her damp hair with her hands to help it to dry.

Behind her, the room began to fill with the delicious aroma of coffee and she began to feel calmer. After all, anger was a choice, and why spoil a beautiful morning when the mystery of the Damien-Theo link had finally been laid to rest.

'How did Damien come to live with you?' she asked. 'Are you his guardian?'

'No, he's my sister's boy, but she's a single mother and when Damien hit his teens he became too much for her to handle. As I'm sure you can imagine from this latest stunt!'

'You took over raising him?'

'Jane felt he was lacking in male guidance and I volunteered to lend a hand. It ended up becoming more or less a permanent arrangement.'

She stared at him as she digested this. 'So you've looked after Damien all though his high school years?'

'That's right.'

'Solo?'

He nodded.

'It can't have been easy for you.'

Theo shrugged. 'I'll admit he's been a challenge. But Jane was working flat out to make a go of her career and she and Damien were having terrible clashes.'

He reached into an overhead cupboard for coffee cups. 'I

must admit there have been occasions when he's almost been too much for me. But, on the whole, he's not a bad kid—just *young*. Half his problem is he's too damn smart.'

'Is he a university student?'

'Not yet. He decided to take a year off between school and university. And I supported that decision. I thought it was a good idea to let him mature a bit before he started studying. He's been working as a waiter in a bar, but it's not enough to keep him occupied. And, as you said, his hormones are rampant. Spare time and eighteen-year-old hormones are not a good combination.'

'Maybe he'll settle down next year when he gets his teeth into some serious study.'

'Yes, I'm quietly confident that he'll turn out okay.'

Annie nodded. 'I don't doubt that Damien's very clever. He certainly has a way with words. I got no hint from his emails that he was a teenager.' She shot Theo a shy smile. 'He obviously holds you in very high regard.'

'What makes you say that?'

'When he was writing to me he modelled himself on you.'

'By claiming to love Italy and philosophy?'

'And Basil. He was very entertaining, very interesting. Sweet and charming, too.'

A wave of heat swept over her as she remembered the way she'd described him in the Ask Auntie letter. 'I thought he was a wonderfully warm, funny and clever man.' She shot him a coy smile. 'A man like you.'

Across the kitchen their eyes met and Annie felt a sweet pang of longing, that tug of attraction that snatched at her breath.

She distracted herself by hurrying to help with breakfast—dropping slices of bread into the toaster and fetching plates from the cupboard. And she was relieved when the toast popped up and she could busy herself buttering it while Theo poured their coffees.

But as they carried their mugs and plates out to the little table in the courtyard, she laughed suddenly.

'What's the joke?' he asked.

'I just saw the funny side of this.'

'Which is?'

'Damien's efforts on the Internet aren't all that different from the antics of a certain young man, who shall remain nameless, who used to try to attract girls by sitting in the backs of bars with a scholarly book and a pipe.'

Theo's valiant attempt to look angry failed. 'You'll keep, Annie McKinnon,' he said as a reluctant smile twitched his lips. 'You'll keep.'

'Theo's invited me to some sort of staff social function at the university,' Annie told Mel when she phoned her mid-morning.

'Far out, Annie! Do you really have to go?'

'I guess so,' she said, feeling a little taken aback by Mel's reaction. 'I told Theo I'd go, but I must say I'm a bit nervous. I've been trying to swot up on philosophy this morning and I've been thumbing through some of his books, but not much is sticking. Do you have any tips?'

'Heck, no. I've forgotten most of the philosophy I ever learned.'

'The ideas are so hard to hang on to. I get to the point where I think I've got my head around a concept, but the minute I try to move on to the next idea, the first one slides straight out of my head. I feel so dumb.'

Mel chuckled. 'Believe me, you're not dumb, Annie. Why do you think people spend years studying philosophy in incremental stages, rather than trying to cram centuries of accumulated wisdom into a half an hour?'

'I guess.' Annie sighed. 'Do you think philosophers talk about the weather and the quality of the wine like ordinary people?'

'For Pete's sake, they *are* ordinary people. But, whatever you do, don't let them know you've figured that out.' There was a pause and then Mel said, 'Annie, you're going all out to impress this guy, aren't you?'

'He's worth it, Mel.' Annie closed her eyes. She tingled all over whenever she thought about tonight—especially when she thought about coming home from this function—and taking up where she and Theo had left off last night—exploring their mutual attraction.

'If you want my advice,' said Mel, 'take a nice long bubble bath and shampoo your hair and paint your toenails. Forget the cramming. Just wear a short skirt and those professors won't be grilling you to find out what you know about Socrates.'

'Mel, you used to be such a feminist. What happened?'

'I slammed up against real life. Hey, I've got to go, Annie. The boss is looking daggers. Catch you tomorrow.'

'Okay.'

'And try to have fun tonight.'

'I'll do my best.'

The minute Annie and Theo arrived at the faculty cocktail party, she realised that enjoying herself was going to be a bigger challenge than she'd feared. For starters, she'd made a terrible mistake. Her dress was totally wrong.

She should have paid attention this morning when Theo assured her that the dark red dress she'd worn to the play last night would be fine for this evening's function. She certainly shouldn't have gone back to the shop where she'd bought the pink jeans and she most definitely should not have gone anywhere near the racks of glittery party wear that Victoria had warned her against.

But they'd been calling to her.

And she'd fallen head over heels in love with the most divine little dress, covered with tawny pink pearls and softly shimmering sequins.

When she'd tried it on she'd been blown away by the transformation. It was as if she'd been touched by a magic wand and turned into a film star. She loved it. From the fine spaghetti straps to the scalloped knee-length hem, the dress was gorgeous. It clung softly to her shape, but was tastefully demure and its understated colour toned fabulously with her complexion.

But it was fabulously wrong.

She realised that now as she stood, frozen in horror, in the doorway of the university's Staff and Graduates Club. Her spirits sank through the soles of her sequinned sandals.

She turned to Theo. 'Why didn't you warn me?'

'What about?'

'My dress. It's all wrong.'

'It isn't, Annie. It's wonderful.'

'But everyone else is in black.'

'Not everyone.'

Her eyes skirted the room. 'Just about.'

In the far corner, surrounded by a little forest of potted palms, earnest, black-clad musicians were playing a string quartet. Everywhere else, people with drinks in their hands were standing and talking quietly in dignified groups.

The men were wearing dinner suits, but apart from a very arty looking woman draped in an exotic profusion of scarves, the women were wearing elegant, conservative dresses in subdued hues like black, dark smoky-blue or deep claret. Even brown.

Nothing pink—tawny or otherwise. And certainly nothing sparkly. Unless you counted the occasional head of silver hair.

If only she could run away and hide.

These people belonged together. They were an exclusive club. And for Annie they spelled *other*. Not her crowd.

But Theo placed a protective hand at the small of her back and ushered her forward.

And a woman who looked a well-preserved, supremely confident, sixty years of age, hurried towards them. 'Theo, dear, I'm so pleased you could come.' She had one of those deep, mellifluous, cultured voices that made Annie instantly nervous. She smiled at Annie. 'How do you do, my dear? I'm Harriet Fletcher.'

'Hello, Harriet.' At least Annie's hand wasn't trembling visibly as she held it out.

Shaking hands, Harriet said, 'You haven't been to one of these evenings before, have you?'

'No.'

To Annie's surprise, Harriet took her arm as if they'd been friends for years. 'Then let me prise you away from Theo so you can meet everyone. Theo, you can look after Annie's drink.'

'Champagne?' he called to her as she was led away.

'Yes, please.'

Before she knew it, Annie had a glass of champagne in her hand and, under Harriet Fletcher's supervision, had been introduced to a dizzying whirlwind of strangers. But, too soon, more new guests arrived and Harriet hurried away to greet them. Annie looked around for Theo, but couldn't catch sight of him, which meant she was left alone with a group of people whose names she couldn't remember.

Shoulders back, Annie.

She turned to her right and discovered a bearded, balding fellow with a pleasant face. When she smiled and said hello, he patiently reintroduced himself and she responded warmly.

'Are you staff?' he asked.

'No. I'm a guest of Theo Grainger.'

He nodded. 'And what's your field?'

'My field?' For a frantic moment her mind flew into a panic. In desperation, she tried to jest. 'Would a paddock of Brahman steers count?'

This was met by a look of utter bewilderment.

'I'm sorry, that was a very bad joke. I don't have a field of study. Not yet, at any rate. You see, I help my brothers to run a cattle property in North Queensland.'

'How fascinating,' he said, returning her smile.

And, to her surprise, she realised he meant it. He really was interested. He told her that he was an environmental scientist and that he'd conducted studies on the river systems in North Queensland.

By the time Theo found her, she and the scientist were deep in a discussion of the varieties of fish that inhabited the Star River. They chatted for another five minutes or so and then Theo said, 'I'm afraid I must drag Annie away to meet some members of the philosophy staff.'

And Annie's nervousness returned. These people would be Theo's particular friends. What would they think of her? Her stomach clenched as she crossed the room beside him.

'Are they all terribly clever?' she asked.

He smiled. 'Terribly.'

Oh, crumbs. She couldn't remember a thing she'd read in his philosophy books this morning.

Halfway across the room, she gripped his hand. 'I'm scared,' she said.

He stopped and looked down at her. 'You can't be, Annie. You're fearless.'

'What makes you think that?'

'I saw how brave you were when—' He suddenly shut his mouth as if he'd had second thoughts.

'When?'

Instead of answering, he lifted her hand to his lips and he kissed her fingers. Right there in front of everyone. And his tender smile was so beautiful she felt she might burst into tears.

'Just be yourself, Annie,' he said. 'These people will love you. Come on.'

They'd been heading for a group in the corner and now several faces, both friendly and curious, watched their approach. Annie couldn't help noticing that none of the men in the group had beards or looked remotely like scruffy absent-minded professors. Nor, for that matter, did the women.

Introductions were made and the atmosphere was relaxed and friendly as Theo explained that Annie was on a short visit from North Queensland.

'How did you stumble across our Theo?' asked a tall, dark, rather elegant woman, who'd been introduced simply as Claudia.

Annie hadn't been prepared for that question and her mouth turned dry as desert dust, but Theo rescued her.

'Through my young nephew, Damien,' he said. 'The two of them met chatting about philosophy over the Internet.'

'So you're a fellow philosopher?' someone else asked.

Somehow, Annie managed to unglue her tongue from the roof of her mouth. 'Oh, no,' she said. 'I'm interested—fascinated, actually. But my understanding is very superficial.

I think it might take me a thousand years to come to grips with Aristotle alone.'

This was met by sympathetic smiles.

'What's young Damien doing these days?' a man called Rex asked Theo.

'All the wrong things,' Theo growled.

'How old is he now? About eighteen?'

Theo nodded.

'Six months working on a cattle property as a jackaroo would do him good,' Annie suggested, and behind her back she crossed her fingers, hoping that she hadn't been too outspoken.

To her relief, her comment was met with unanimous agreement.

'I read about a young eighteen-year-old who spent three months droving two thousand head of cattle across Queensland on his own,' Rex said.

'That's pretty amazing,' said Theo.

A middle-aged man shook his head. 'My kids could never cope with that kind of challenge. Apart from anything else, they couldn't go anywhere without their Discmans.'

'Or home-delivered pizzas,' added a woman who was probably his wife.

A plate of smoked oysters was passed around.

'That colour suits you wonderfully, Annie,' a woman in the group commented.

'Actually, I've been wondering what you'd call a colour like that,' said Claudia, less kindly.

There was something about Claudia that unsettled Annie. Now, recognising that a deliberate shot had been fired, she couldn't resist firing back. 'The girl in the shop called it naked shimmer.'

Rex chuckled. 'Naked shimmer. I like that. Whatever it's called, it should be compulsory.'

Claudia rolled her eyes and pulled her mouth into a tightly contemptuous pout.

And Annie prayed that the conversation would steer on to something else. Surely these people had deeper, more serious things to talk about? But it seemed that Claudia didn't want to let her off the hook.

'How are you coping with life in the city?' Her smile was faintly patronising.

'I think I'm coping just fine, thank you. I love it here.'

'Don't you miss the wholesomeness of the country—those wide open spaces and all that fresh air?'

'I can't say that I do.' Annie smiled pleasantly. 'I miss my dog, but Theo's Dalmatian, Basil, makes up for her.'

Claudia's right eyebrow hiked high. 'Basil's a darling, isn't he?'

Despite the warm words, there was a new brittle edge in Claudia's voice. She shot a swift glance towards Theo and a disturbing watchfulness dimmed her dark eyes. And Annie realised with a prickle of alarm that this woman had almost certainly been involved with Theo at some time in the past. Had they been lovers?

And swiftly following that thought came another. It was quite, *quite* possible that Theo's gesture of kissing her hand in full view of everyone had been more significant than she'd realised.

CHAPTER SEVEN

THEO doubted he could take much more of sharing Annie with a crowd. His colleagues were finding her as intriguing as he did. But ever since last night when he'd kissed her the sole focus of his thoughts had been kissing her again.

Tonight, in her fascinating skin-toned dress, she was driving him wild with the need to touch her, to hold her and taste her.

At last the buzz of conversation was interrupted by Professor Gilmore clearing his throat into a microphone, and everyone's attention turned to the little dais near the musicians where a microphone had been set up. Taking Annie's hand, he drew her away from the crowd, towards the back of the room.

'This is the formal part of the evening. Speeches and presentations,' he told her. 'So from now on the night gets even more boring.'

'But I haven't been bored. Your friends are very nice.' *Correction, most of them are nice.*

'You've been a big hit,' he murmured. 'But let's get out of here.'

She turned to him, her blue eyes round with surprise. 'Already?'

He hoped his smile didn't look wolfish. 'Yes, we've done our duty. There's no need to hang around. Come on, let's go while no one's looking.'

Still holding her hand, he led the way out through a side door.

'Where are we going?' she asked.

'Home.'

'Oh.' A pink tide rose from her neck to her face.

'Is that okay with you, Annie?'

'Yes,' she said quickly. 'Yes, of course.'

As they walked through the university grounds to the car park, it took every ounce of Theo's restraint to stop himself from hauling her into one of the dark recesses along the way and pressing her against a wall while he kissed her senseless. What the hell had come over him? It was years and years since he'd felt so out of control.

And yet, he'd never needed control more.

Annie might be enthusiastic and uninhibited, but there was an air of trusting innocence about her too. She was young. She was vulnerable.

He had no idea how experienced she was with men. She needed to be wooed. She deserved gentle loving.

Over the past twenty-four hours he'd thought it through a thousand times in his imagination. And he burned with his plans for making love to her—slowly, with exquisite restraint and sensitivity.

At least, that was the plan.

Annie could hardly breathe. Her sense of anticipation was excruciating.

Although nothing had been said, she knew deep in her

bones why Theo was leaving the function early. Their physical awareness of each other had been building ever since last night and now they were both so turned on the atmosphere between them was almost crackling with electricity.

When they reached Theo's car he opened the door for her. She was too self-conscious to look at him. She slipped quickly into the passenger seat and when her bare shoulder brushed against his coat sleeve a flame of heat shot through her.

The heat burned inside her while she listened to his footsteps crunching on gravel as he walked around the back of the car. Her chest grew tight as he opened his door and lowered his long body into the driver's seat beside her. Tonight he'd pulled the car's hood in place so she wouldn't be blown about, and the tang of his aftershave reached her in the confined space.

Without speaking, he turned the key in the ignition, revved the motor and his sports car took off, zooming through the night like a low-flying jet. *Omigosh.* Annie had to remind herself to breathe.

Theo was taking her home...to make love to her.

She was acutely aware of every inch of his body so close beside her. She watched his hands resting lightly on the steering wheel, watched the purposeful movements of his left hand as he shifted the gear stick. He had very nice hands—strong, confident, capable. Perfect.

Crumbs, I'm forgetting to breathe again.

She leaned back against the cool leather of the car seat and closed her eyes. But that was no good because it encouraged her to imagine Theo's hands touching her. Another burst of heat flared inside her.

Eyes open again, she tried to concentrate on the city scape that flashed past them. In a kind of daze she watched flickering neon signs and the traffic lights changing from red to green, the yellow rectangles of windows in office blocks. She looked at the traffic, which seemed to be engaged in a wickedly daring dance of ducking and weaving between lanes. After the bumpy and unlit outback tracks she was used to, everything in the city was so exciting and dangerous.

Closer to the city centre the buildings grew taller. No chance to see the moon or the stars. But it didn't matter. Tonight, everything she wanted was right beside her, driving expertly, hurrying home.

If only she wasn't feeling so nervous. Why couldn't she be cool about this? *Come off it, Annie. No girl could be cool about sex with Dr Theo Grainger.* This was a Big Deal! No doubt about it.

Would Theo be able to tell how long it was since she'd made love? Was he used to experienced, sophisticated lovers? Women like Claudia?

His voice broke the silence. 'I half-expected you to bombard me with questions all the way home.'

'I'm—um—I'm fresh out of questions.'

For once, she couldn't think of *anything* to say. And neither, it seemed, could Theo. He drove on in silence till they reached his house and he parked the car in the garage. They both made a fuss of Basil, who was prancing about their legs with his tail wagging madly as they walked to the back door. In the kitchen, Theo's keys made a clinking sound as he dropped them on to the granite-topped bench. Then there was silence.

And, out of the blue, Annie found herself rushing to speak at last, to say something… *anything.* 'Are you hungry?'

'Hungry?'

'My brothers are always starving when they come home from cocktail parties. As far as they're concerned, canapés aren't real food and they always complain that they can never get enough to eat.'

Theo looked mildly surprised. 'I guess we could have some supper.'

'Would you like something light? Scrambled eggs, perhaps?'

'That sounds—er—fine.'

While Annie busied herself finding eggs and milk and a saucepan, he took off his coat, removed his bow-tie and loosened his collar. She dashed out into the courtyard and snipped some parsley and chives from the potted herbs and returned to find Theo observing her assembled ingredients with a puzzled frown.

'Shall I put on some music?' she asked.

'Yes, whatever you like.'

Without stopping to choose, she grabbed a CD from the stack and slipped it into the player and next minute the slow, sexy sounds of a romantic ballad rippled around them. *What a dumb, dumb selection.*

As she turned back to the bench she felt so tense she thought she might crack in two.

'Annie.' Theo came up behind her. She was holding an egg and his hand closed gently over hers. 'Are you really hungry?'

She almost crushed the fragile eggshell as she turned to face him. 'No. I mean, yes. Well, I just thought—'

What was the matter with her? This wasn't the way tonight was supposed to happen. Everything was turning out wrong, wrong, *wrong.*

He smiled slowly, took the egg from her grasp and set it back in the bowl with the others. 'Why on earth are we making scrambled eggs when neither of us is hungry?'

'I—I—because I suggested it, I guess. I—thought per- haps—'

He placed a finger against her lips. A finger that was strong, confident, capable. Perfect.

Her heart thumped so loudly she was sure he must hear it.

'Let's forget supper,' he said.

She nodded.

Holding her by the shoulders, he let his thumbs trace the line of her collarbones. 'I'm afraid this attraction thing isn't going away. Not for me, at any rate.'

'No, not for me, either.'

His fingers traced back and forth over her shoulders, following the superfine silken straps. 'All evening I've been wanting to tell you how incredible you look. This *naked shimmer* is a major distraction for me.'

Now she could feel her heart thumping in her chest and in a pulse in her throat. 'That's what I was hoping when I bought it.' Crikey, that sounded much, much braver than she felt.

'So—you planned to seduce me?'

'Yes, I—um—toyed with the idea.'

His face broke into one of his lovely smiles. 'I must say I like the way your mind works, Annie McKinnon.'

Then, dropping his hands to her waist, he tested the texture of the shimmering fabric. His hands spanned her ribs and he lowered his head till their lips touched. He teased her with a hardly-there brush of his mouth over hers and Annie hoped he didn't mind that she seemed to be shaking.

Apparently not. Next minute his hands cradled her face and he kissed her properly, and his lips were slow, soft and tantalising. Swoon-worthy.

'So this attraction thing…' he murmured. 'Want to do something about it?'

'Yes… I do.'

Annie was definitely trembling now and there was every

chance her knees might give way, but the next minute Theo lifted her up in his arms.

Goodness, this was the sort of caveman stunt a man like her brothers might have pulled, but she hadn't expected anything so macho from Theo. 'I'm too heavy!'

Ignoring her protests, he carried her across the kitchen, through the lounge, to the stairs.

'Not the stairs, Theo. You can't. You'll strain something.'

Without any sign of strain, he carried her up the stairs and into his room.

His room.

The room with the sumptuous bed, the rich cream bedspread and the tumble of black and cream silk cushions. The glow of timber shutters closed against the night. Lamplight.

And Theo.

Theo, lowering her on to his bed, then joining her and kissing her some more. She let her eyes drift closed as he kissed her slowly, lazily, as if he had all the time in the world for nothing but kisses. She surrendered with total complicity to the leisurely caress of his sensuous lips, to the playful flirtation of his gentle little bites, and the arousing dance of his tongue meeting and mating with hers.

The last of her nervousness melted away as she luxuriated in the warmth of his unhurried, easy seduction.

'You have the most gorgeous mouth,' he murmured.

'Your kisses are sensational,' she whispered back.

He kissed some more while his hands traced slow, circling patterns on her shoulders and up and down her arms. Beneath his easy touch her body turned languid and warm. Why had she ever been nervous? This was Theo and he was perfect. He knew exactly what was right for her.

Then he stole her breath as his hand slipped lower to caress her thighs. A flowering of longing spilled deep inside her and suddenly she was impatient to feel his touch all over.

She gasped. 'I've got to get out of this dress.'

A surprised little laugh escaped him as she rolled into a sitting position.

'Can you undo my zip?'

Theo obliged, and she wriggled in a frantic attempt to shed her clothing.

'Whoa, Annie, don't tear your dress. It's too lovely to wreck the first time you wear it.'

She raised her hands over her head. 'Can you help?'

Theo could. And she watched in a fever of anticipation as he carried her dress across the room and draped it carefully over the chair in the corner, but when he removed his own clothes he let them fall to the floor without paying them any attention.

His attention was for Annie.

And she couldn't drag her eyes from him. He was everything she'd ever wanted in a man. Her heart pounded, her skin burned, her body yearned for his.

His eyes paid homage to her as he moved back on to the bed, and everything in her world became perfect when his lips found hers once more. His hands began to glide down her arms, over the bumps of her hips, into the dip of her waist and then to the swell of her breasts.

And she explored him the way he was touching her, tracing the wonderfully muscular contours of his shoulders, the smooth sweep of his back, the hair on his chest. Then lower.

With each kiss, each tender touch, their hunger mounted and their sense of intimacy deepened. Sweet, poignant longing coiled and built inside her, making her body arch with pleasure. She felt heavy-limbed and anchored by desire and yet blissfully free, happy that the soft, needy little sounds that escaped her would let Theo know how much she loved his touch, was grateful for each daring caress.

And her eagerness released a new kind of wildness in them both. The tempo of their lovemaking changed as Theo's gentle, lazy seduction gave way to focused passion.

Annie whispered his name and he whispered hers back to her, turning her name into a breathless caress as he murmured it over and over, until at last the words were lost inside one long, hungry kiss before they were both swept beyond recall—hot-blooded lovers drowning in a flood of desperate need.

Theo lay in the stillness of midnight, in the slanted moonlight that stole through the shutters, with Annie's head resting against his chest and her soft breath warm on his skin, and he waited for regret to attack him.

He had every reason to feel remorse. He had just made love to a woman who was almost certainly too young and trusting for an uncommitted, casual relationship. Annie McKinnon was the kind of girl who needed to believe that the act of sex was an act of commitment. An act of faith.

Now, as she slept, he threaded his fingers through the soft golden strands of her hair and examined his motives again and again, searching for blame.

But the search was in vain. Although Theo tormented himself with self-recrimination, he had absolutely no sense of regret. Sane, logical reason and theories about incompatibility simply refused to stack up against the overwhelming force of his feelings.

With Annie tonight, he'd felt a helpless tenderness and a depth of emotion that made absolute nonsense of theory and reason. Perhaps he'd lost his head, but he'd found his heart.

And while common sense pointed to the fact that tonight had been an error of judgement, something far deeper told Theo Grainger that it was quite possible he'd made a deliberate choice and that the passion he'd shared with Annie McKinnon was neither casual nor uncommitted.

Which led him to one surprising conclusion.

It was quite, quite possible that he was falling in love with her. And nothing about it felt like a mistake.

CHAPTER EIGHT

BREAKFAST next morning was lazy, luxurious…and late.

Basil missed out on his early walk while Annie and Theo stayed in bed. It was almost mid-morning before they wandered downstairs.

Theo didn't seem to be in a rush to get to work and he was more than happy to hang around while Annie made a special breakfast of pancakes with strawberries and cream.

Sitting in the courtyard under a smiling sky, they took time over coffee, stealing kisses that tasted of strawberries, and basking as only new lovers can in the warmth of their exquisite happiness.

They talked about happiness. Their happiness. About whether Basil, who was stretched blissfully over their feet, could sense their happiness. And was it possible for dogs to ever be as happy as Annie and Theo were right now, on this bright, beautiful, beaming morning?

Neither of them dared to suggest that the state of happiness could be slippery—that happiness could slide from beneath your feet when you least expected it.

'What's the Italian word for happiness?' Annie asked instead.

'*Felicità.*'

'Oh, I like that. Italian always sounds so amazingly sexy.'

They might have spent ages talking and gently flirting, just as they'd spent ages making love last night and again that morning, but eventually Theo looked at his watch and sighed. 'I had better get to work.'

'I'll take Basil for his walk,' she volunteered.

'It won't hurt him to miss a day.'

'No, but I'd like to take him. I need to walk off these pancakes so I have room for lunch with Mel.'

Theo made a teasing comment about ladies who lunch and they kissed some more, before he left.

Mel took one look at Annie and gasped. 'Omigosh, it's happened, hasn't it?'

'What?'

It took several seconds of panic before Annie reassured herself that it wasn't possible for the whole world to guess what she'd been doing last night just by looking at her. Just the same, the knowing gleam in Mel's eyes brought a rush of embarrassment. And she blushed.

'You're up to your eyebrows in love,' Mel said.

'It shows?'

'Of course it shows, Annie. Your glow is bright enough to light up the Power House.'

There wasn't much point in trying to pretend otherwise, so she nodded.

'And?' Mel prompted.

'And what?'

'And what about Theo? Is he wrapped, too?'

'It…it seems…yes, I think he is, Mel.'

'Wow, Annie, scoring with Dr Theo is such a coup.'

Annie drew a deep breath. A coup? Scoring? Was that what she'd done? Surely not. Making love with Theo had felt ever so much more special than notching up points in some kind of competition.

She made an unnecessary show of studying the menu. 'Are you having a salad, Mel?'

''Fraid so. I don't dare have anything else. One of the guys at work has invited me to a gala ball next month and I'm trying to lose weight so I can squeeze into something red and strapless.'

'A guy at work?' Annie seized on the chance to divert attention from herself. 'Come on, tell me more.'

To her relief, Mel was happy to explain about Bill Brown, a cute, lanky, thirty-something guy in Planning. And then Mel went on to tell Annie about Victoria's latest foray into the heady world of speed-dating and their girl talk steered into safer, Theo-free waters.

It wasn't till near the end of their lunch that Mel said, 'So what happens next, Annie? Are you still going home to North Queensland next week, or are you planning to move in permanently with Theo?'

'If everything works out, I won't be going back to Southern Cross,' Annie said and then she felt a slam of shock as she realised how easy it was to make such an astonishing statement.

The days that followed were pure magic. First there was the weekend. Two whole days with Theo's undivided attention; two days to explore Brisbane together.

'Your enthusiasm is like a tonic,' he told her. 'I love seeing my home town through your eyes.'

After his return to work on Monday, Annie took Basil for extra walks, or pottered about the house and courtyard garden.

She continued her exploration of the galleries, and in the evenings she talked with Theo about what she'd discovered.

It was pretty phenomenal the way she'd morphed so easily into a lust-pot. But Theo's transformation was just as dramatic. It was hard to believe this amazing, red-hot lover was the same polite, rather formal 'uncle' she'd met such a short time ago.

It was almost like waking up in one of those perfume commercials where a girl used a certain scent and suddenly there was a guy who needed to chase her with a bunch of flowers or murmur nonsense in her ear at the oddest moments, just because he loved the smell of her.

And then there was the soul mate thing. It kind of got shoved aside in the heat of passion, but it crept in at other times. Annie couldn't get enough of talking with Theo. They talked about *everything* and she was as crazy about his mind as she was about his body. And his smile.

And the most fabulous thing was that Theo was absolutely committed to discovering the real Annie. She'd never met anyone so interested in *her* thoughts. He was intrigued by her past, her reactions to the present and her dreams for the future. She felt totally flattered.

'Tell me more about your home at Southern Cross,' he said one evening as she lay beside him in a stream of silver starlight.

'What would you like to know?'

'Do you have a favourite haunt?'

'Lots.'

'Any special place that you escape to when you want to be on your own?'

'Yes, there's a spot down by the creek.'

Drawing her close, he pressed a warm kiss into the curve of her neck. 'Tell me about it. I'd like to picture it. Shut your eyes and go there in your mind. Describe it to me.'

With her eyes closed, she snuggled more comfortably against him. 'Okay. I'm sitting on the creek bank.'

'A high bank?'

'Yes, a reasonably high, grassy bank with clumps of reeds growing down near the water's edge. The water is dark green and still. You wouldn't think it was moving at all, but there's a leaf floating past very slowly. And there are little water spiders dimpling the surface.' She turned to him. 'They make little circular ripples all over the top of the water.'

He nodded. 'And is the water very clear?'

'Yes, you can see through it to mossy logs on the bottom.'

'Sounds lovely. What else?'

'Well…there are lily pads all along the edge of the creek with tiny white flowers. And there's a melaleuca tree on the opposite bank with branches leaning right out, low over the water at an impossible angle, and you half-expect the tree to topple into the creek. And…there's a tangle of lantana bushes and a small wattle with yellow flowers that really stand out against all the green. And right on the top of the bank there are massive eucalypt trees towering up to the sky.'

'Is it quiet there?'

'Yes, absolutely.'

'Can you hear anything?'

'Mmm…every so often there's a breeze that runs up the creek and you hear the sound of it whispering through the treetops.'

'Birds?'

'A peaceful dove. Honey-eaters. Chip chips.'

He lifted a curl from her forehead and kissed her brow. 'Annie, are you quite sure you're not missing the bush?'

His face was in shadow, but she thought she heard a throaty tension in his voice. She rubbed her cheek against the smooth cradle of his shoulder. 'I'm sure, Theo. I love the bush and

I guess it will always be my home, and I'll be happy to go back to visit, but I've never felt I belonged there the way my brothers do. Lately, I've felt as if the outback was stifling me. I *needed* to escape. Damien was just an excuse. I was already desperate for a city life.'

He seemed content with that.

After a bit, Annie rolled on to her tummy and poked his shoulder. 'Your turn,' she said.

He mumbled sleepily.

'Come on, tell me one of your favourite places. Tell me about somewhere in Italy.'

'Which city?'

'I don't mind. It's all exciting to me.'

'Give me a kiss first.'

Annie was happy to oblige.

'Okay, I'll describe the view from the apartment I rented when I was studying in Rome. It's in an ancient quarter called Trastevere, the place where musicians, writers and artists from all over the world like to stay—a bit like Greenwich Village in New York.'

'It sounds wonderful. Are you looking out of a window?'

'Yes.' With his arms around her, he spoke softly in his lovely deep voice. 'I've opened the shutters and it's early. The light is still soft—and in the distance I can see the rounded outline of a hill with cypresses and umbrella pines silhouetted against the sky.'

She felt an unexpected thrill as if she were there with him. She could see it all. 'What about the buildings?'

'Oh, there are plenty of them. I can see sloping, tiled rooftops, television aerials, spires and domes. There are ancient temples and Roman ruins crowding shoulder to shoulder with modern architecture. And if I look straight below me, I see a little cobbled piazza.'

'Oh, wow! What else? Can you see any people?'

'An old man sitting on the steps in front of a small fountain. A fellow putting up umbrellas on the tables outside a café. And another man opening up his news-stand.'

'Where are the women? Still in bed?'

Theo laughed. 'There's a woman watering her geraniums and herbs on a little balcony.'

'Can you smell anything?'

'Freshly baked bread and pizza.'

'Oh, yum. It sounds truly amazing, Theo.'

'It is.'

'I'd love to see it one day.'

'I'll take you there.'

Another wild thrill sent her sitting bolt upright. 'You really mean that?'

'Yes,' he said, sounding almost as surprised as she was. 'I really do.'

On the days she took Basil for bonus walks Annie liked to explore the streets closer to Theo's place, where humble, old-fashioned workers' cottages were still scattered among the modern townhouses and apartment blocks.

Friendly, elderly folk lived in the cottages, she noticed. Several were sitting on their front porches or working in their front gardens when she passed, and they smiled and nodded to her the way people in Mirrabrook did.

She felt almost at home.

That was how she met George.

She saw the elderly man leaning on his front gate as she walked down his street and she smiled and called, 'Good morning.'

He returned her greeting with a wave and suddenly Basil

charged towards him, straining on the leash, his tail wagging madly.

'Hello, Basil, old mate,' the man said, leaning down to give the top of the Dalmatian's head an affectionate scruff.

'Do you two know each other?' Annie asked.

'We sure do.' He beamed broadly. 'I'm Basil's grandfather.'

Annie laughed, but her laugh turned into an exclamation of surprise as she watched the delirious way Basil responded to the old man. *Basil's grandfather?* It was obvious these two knew each other very well. Did that mean…?

Recognising her confusion, he grinned again. 'I'm George Grainger, Theo's father.'

'Oh, my.' She stared at him in amazement. It had never occurred to her that Theo's father might live so close by. 'So you're Pop?'

'That's right.'

'Well—how nice.'

'And you must be Annie.'

'You've heard about me?'

'Of course I have, love. From Damien and from Theo.' He shook her proffered hand. 'How do you do?'

'I'm very pleased to meet you, Mr Grainger.'

Now that she looked more carefully, she could see the likeness to both Theo and Damien. George Grainger was shorter, probably because he was a little stooped, and his hair was white, his face lined and his knuckles knobbly with arthritis, but behind his glasses his eyes were the same alert hazel as his son's and grandson's.

And he was looking at her with an intense interest that bordered on delight.

'How is Damien?' she asked, wondering exactly what

George had been told about her connection to his son and his grandson.

'Right as rain,' he said. 'He's at work this morning.' Then he surprised her by unlatching his gate and swinging it open. 'Why don't you come on in, Annie?'

Basil pulled frantically on the leash in an effort to dive through the gateway. 'Looks like Basil loves coming here,' she said, giving in.

'We're old mates. I'm his favourite ear-scratcher and I look after him whenever Theo goes away.'

Annie wondered what Theo would think if he could see her following his father down a shady path that took them around the side of his simple weatherboard cottage to a sunny back garden filled with plots of vegetables.

'Wow! These are doing well,' she said, looking around at staked tomato plants, rows of corn, silverbeet, carrots and lettuce. 'You must have a wonderful green thumb.'

He nodded, smiling. 'Gardening keeps me active.' Then he added, 'This was Theo's home when he was a boy, you know.'

'No, I didn't,' she said. 'So he's lived in this part of Brisbane all his life?'

'Yep. Apart from the couple of semesters he's spent studying overseas. He bought the town house around the corner when his mother took ill, so he could stay in close contact. We lost her four years ago.'

'I'm sorry.'

'He's a good son.'

Annie tried to picture Theo here, growing up with his sister and parents in this tiny cottage, and she felt a touch embarrassed. What must a man from George Grainger's generation think of a young woman who'd moved in with his son—who'd *slept* with his son—after such a short acquaintance?

'You're probably wondering why Damien moved out,' she said.

'Theo explained,' George assured her. 'He popped in last week to check whether Damien arrived here and he filled me in. His version was a little different from Damien's, of course.'

She would have loved to ask what George Grainger had been told, but refrained.

'Would you like a cool drink?' George looked at her eagerly, almost pleading with her to say yes. 'Come along inside. Basil will be happy to lie here in the sun.'

'Thank you,' she said, recognising the loneliness behind his request. She'd experienced her share of loneliness at Southern Cross. 'But I mustn't stay long.'

In the kitchen he invited her to sit at a small wooden table painted a fresh mint green and he took a jug from the refrigerator and poured her a glass of old-fashioned lemon and barley water.

She looked around her and thought about Theo being here in this kitchen every day of his boyhood, eating breakfast at this table. She could imagine him coming in from playing outside and forgetting to wipe his feet, raiding the old pottery cookie jar, reading with a torch after lights out in a little bedroom down the hallway.

She remembered to take a sip of her drink. 'This is delicious, Mr Grainger.'

'Call me George,' he said and he smiled and began to ask her about her home in the outback.

Ten minutes later, she realised she'd told him a potted history of almost everything about herself—about her brothers, their cattle property, her years at boarding school, her father's death and her mother's return to Scotland. She'd even confessed about her loneliness—and meeting Damien over the Internet.

'You must miss your mother,' he said.

'Yes.' She drew a deep breath and tried to ignore the little niggle of hurt she felt whenever she remembered how easily her mother had resettled on the other side of the world.

George's keen eyes watched her for a moment or two, but when she didn't volunteer anything else about her mother he told her stories about Theo—about what a terrific Rugby Union player he'd been, representing Queensland during his undergraduate days. And what a brilliant student he'd been. George confessed that he and his wife had never understood how they'd produced such a clever son—and then he added details of how wonderfully well Theo had looked after Damien.

Annie would have happily stayed on with George. Between them they could have formed a Theo Grainger Admiration Society, but she had promised to meet Mel again for lunch, and so eventually she made her excuses.

George accompanied her as she collected Basil. 'Come and visit me again,' he said.

'I'd love to,' she promised.

At the front gate he said simply, 'You're the one, Annie.'

'Th-the one?'

His eyes shone shyly. 'The one I've been waiting for Theo to find.'

She felt a bright blush burning her cheeks. 'You've shocked me, George. I don't know what to say.'

'I'm sorry,' he said. 'I know that was very forward of me. I'm a silly old man. But don't worry, I won't make trouble by saying anything to Theo.' He bent down and patted Basil's head. 'I don't reckon I'll have to. Do you, mate? Not if Theo's as smart as he makes out.'

* * *

Driving home to Annie with a bright bouquet of flowers on the seat beside him, a bottle of expensive wine stowed in the glove box and tubs of aromatic Thai take-away packed in a box on the floor, Theo was comfortably confident that all was right with his world.

He'd rung Annie mid-afternoon, but she'd still been out, so he'd left a message on the answering machine telling her not to worry about preparing dinner. He'd briefly toyed with the idea of taking her out to a restaurant—to La Piastra per-haps—but he was still feeling too selfish to share her with a room full of people.

That was what infatuation did to a guy. Theo wanted, no, needed, to be alone with Annie. At home. Just the two of them. All night.

He pictured how it would be when he walked into the kitchen this evening. Pictured the way Annie's face would light up when she saw the flowers. She was so delightfully appreciative of the smallest gestures and she never held back in expressing her pleasure. Her eyes, her face, her whole body responded.

Her uncomplicated spontaneity was contagious. Theo had caught himself whistling at work a couple of times this week. Whistling, for heaven's sake. And his extravagant outbursts of cheerfulness had not gone unnoticed by the staff.

However, he couldn't be bothered about the wry glances of colleagues and their cryptic comments about his *Ode to Joy*. He was almost home.

And, as he thought of home, he recognised another dramatic shift in his thinking. Already he'd begun to suppose that Annie belonged in his home. The idea of her leaving to return to the wilds of North Queensland appalled him. He must make sure she understood how much he wanted her to stay.

He wanted to introduce her to his father, too. The two

of them were sure to hit it off. He'd even begun to consider contingency plans for Damien's future. It was too much to expect old George to care for his grandson indefinitely and Damien's mother was still tied up with her job in Sydney.

But Damien would be attending UQ next year... Perhaps he would enjoy a year in a student residential college? Living on campus with other students would be good for him. St John's College would suit him down to the ground...and Theo had good connections there.

Pleased with that possibility, he smiled as his car rounded the corner into his street. But his smile and his musings were zapped instantly by the sight of a dark green sedan parked in front of his house.

Claudia.

What on earth was she doing here?

Theo wasn't given to overreaction, or to fanciful notions of telepathy, or premonitions for that matter, but at the sight of Claudia's car a voice in his head whispered a distinct and chilling warning.

He scowled as he parked his car in the garage. How long had Claudia been here? And how was Annie handling her visit?

His scowl sharpened as he anticipated Claudia's cynical reaction to his arrival with his arms full of telling purchases, and he almost left the flowers behind on the car seat but sudden loyalty to Annie changed his mind.

Claudia could make of them whatever she wished.

The two women were sitting in the courtyard drinking wine and as soon as Claudia spotted him she waved and called hello.

He crossed the lawn and saw that the wine was one of her favourites. Almost certainly she'd brought it with her.

'Oh, what a charming picture,' Claudia said as he drew

nearer. 'Those flowers suit you beautifully, Theo. You should carry bouquets more often.'

'Hello, Claudia.' He tried to inject a degree of polite welcome into his voice but it fell rather flat.

Turning to Annie, he offered his warmest smile. 'Hi, there,' he said softly. 'How was lunch?'

'*Lunch* was lovely,' Annie said with a subtle emphasis on the first word and a quick glance that implied that things had gone rapidly downhill since then. 'What gorgeous lilies, Theo.'

'I'll take everything through to the kitchen and then I'll grab a glass and join you,' he said.

To his surprise, Claudia jumped to her feet. 'I'll come inside too, Theo. There's something I need to discuss with you.'

A steel band seemed to clamp around his chest.

'A business matter,' Claudia said, averting her eyes momentarily before sighing significantly. 'I'm afraid I have some rather bad news.'

A grim kind of dread settled inside him. He had no idea what was going on, but nothing about Claudia's visit felt right.

Determined to remain calm, he allowed himself a small frown. 'Couldn't you have shared this bad news with me at work?'

'I was held up in meetings all afternoon.' Claudia lifted her gaze slowly. 'And then I couldn't find you. You must have been out hunting for these delightful purchases.' Her mouth flickered into a smile that was too thin, almost cruel. 'But because we're old friends I didn't want to leave you in the dark, so I came straight here. I'd hate you to find out from anyone else.'

'What don't you want me to find out, Claudia? For God's sake, what's happened?'

She cast a speaking glance in Annie's direction, and Theo saw that Annie's cheeks were flushed and her eyes worried.

'I need to discuss this with you in private,' Claudia said.

'You had better come into my study then.' He struggled to hold back a mounting sense of alarm. 'Please excuse us, Annie.'

Annie felt sick as she placed Theo's bottle of white wine in the fridge and put the tubs of food in the microwave and then arranged his flowers in a tall rectangular glass vase and carried them through to the lounge. The flowers were gorgeous, long-stemmed lilies—deep red, golden and cream—and they teamed beautifully with the colours and mood of this room.

But she couldn't enjoy them. Not when she could hear the sombre murmur of voices from behind the closed door of Theo's study.

Setting the vase on the coffee table, she made a few adjustments to the arrangement, but as she straightened she found herself stalled in the middle of the room, hypnotised by the threat of those muffled voices. She wound her arms across her stomach, as if to protect herself.

Perhaps it was pathetically paranoid of her, but she knew just knew that this bad news of Claudia's was somehow linked to her.

The half hour she'd spent alone with Claudia before Theo had arrived home had been hideous. Claudia had feigned an interest in Annie's life in North Queensland, but her boredom had been thinly veiled and when Annie tried to talk about Brisbane or the university Claudia's manner had been patronising in the extreme.

Without actually saying so, the other woman had conveyed with crystalline clarity that she couldn't imagine how dear, clever Theo had become infatuated with such a brainless little bimbo from the back of beyond. It had taken all Annie's self-control to refrain from acquainting Claudia with the truly astonishing fact that the Star Valley was not populated by a mob of inbred, illiterate, banjo-playing yokels.

The voices in the study stopped abruptly and Annie hurried back to the kitchen, terrified that it might look as if she'd been eavesdropping.

Basil was sprawled on the back step and she crossed the room and dropped on to the step beside him. Seeking comfort, she gave him a huge hug. 'If only you could tell me what you know about Claudia,' she whispered to the dog. 'Has she been here often? Is she in love with Theo? What do you think is going on in there?'

Basil pushed his wet nose against her neck and gave her a loving lick. He made a gentle, whimpering sound as if he were trying to comfort her. 'You dear old boy,' she said, rubbing her cheek against his magnificent black and white spotted neck. 'You understand, don't you?'

'You really do get on well with Basil, don't you?'

Annie jumped at the sound of Claudia's voice. She hadn't heard footsteps. Whipping around, she was startled to see the other woman standing in the kitchen behind her. She shot a quick glance past her, hoping to see Theo, but there was no sign of him.

She jumped to her feet. 'Have you and Theo finished your discussion?'

'Yes.' Claudia fished in her handbag and extracted her car keys. 'I imagine you'll want to go inside and offer the poor man some comfort.'

Horrified, Annie whispered, 'W—what's happened?'

'I've had to let him go.'

'Let him go?' Annie felt ill. 'What on earth do you mean?'

'Theo's contract as a lecturer was up for renewal at the end of this year, but our department has had severe funding cuts and we were left with a very difficult decision.'

Annie gasped. 'You can't mean that he's lost his job?'

'Believe me, Annie, it's a grave disappointment for all of us. But I can imagine how distressed you particularly must feel. I saw how hard you tried to fit in at the soirée last week. I'm terribly sorry but all that's going to be lost to you now.'

Appalled, Annie stared at her, unable to think of anything to say.

Claudia's long, nimble fingers sorted through her key ring and she made a selection. Tapping the key against her elegant chin, she eyed Annie thoughtfully. 'I'm sorry if you feel badly about this.'

'Well, of course I feel badly. I feel terrible for Theo.'

Claudia looked pained, then she shook her head and rolled her eyes before releasing an impatient, huffing sigh.

'What is it?' challenged Annie, too fraught to decide whether this woman was displaying an Oscar-winning performance or genuine emotion. 'Is there something I'm supposed to understand? Something else I should feel bad about?'

Claudia turned as if she were leaving, then looked back at Annie and said almost gently, 'You don't see the problem, do you, Annie?'

Annie felt a terrible urge to slap her. 'I might if you gave me a clue.'

Again Claudia sighed. 'Sometimes we don't want to accept that we might be a burden or a hindrance to people we're very fond of.'

'A—a burden?' Annie's legs threatened to buckle beneath her. 'Are you telling me this is m-my fault? Theo's losing his job because of me?'

The brief but unmistakable flash of triumph in Claudia's eyes indicated that this was the exact message she'd intended.

'How can I be a hindrance to Theo's career? I only met him a week ago.'

But now Claudia chose not to answer. She'd planted the necessary seeds. Without another word, she turned and walked purposefully out of the house without looking back.

A wave of nausea swept through Annie. This didn't make sense. How could she have caused so much havoc in Theo's life in such a short space of time?

She thought of last week at the cocktail party, and remembered her dress and the silly comment about naked shimmer. She remembered the way Theo had kissed her hand in full view of everyone, and the way he'd stolen away early with her...

No doubt a few tongues had wagged, but surely in this day and age something like that didn't amount to a scandal? Not the kind of scandal that got a man sacked. *Unless...*

From the street outside came the sound of Claudia's car starting up. Last week Annie had suspected that Claudia and Theo had a past relationship. Now she was almost certain of it.

And she was just as certain that Claudia wasn't over Theo.

CHAPTER NINE

HEARTSICK, Annie hurried through the house to Theo's study. He was sitting in a black leather chair with his elbows propped on the desk, his head slumped in his hands.

She stopped in the doorway. Although she wanted to run to him, to throw her arms around him and to comfort him, Claudia's words had undermined her confidence.

Had she really cost Theo his job? Her throat burned with a painful, rocky clump of mounting fear. Fisting a hand against her mouth to stop herself from making a noise, she drew a deep breath, trying to calm down. The last thing Theo needed was hysterics from her. For the moment, until she heard his side of the story, she would have to be strong and put Claudia's accusations behind her.

It was growing dark outside and the only light in the study came from the lamp on Theo's desk. In spite of her agitation, she couldn't help admiring his bowed head—the dark sheen of his hair in the lamp's light and the neat, essentially masculine way his hair ended in a straight line across the back of his neck.

What am I going to do? I'm so in love with this man. I couldn't bear to walk away from him now.

After a minute or two he lowered his hands and looked up, surprised to see her there. 'Hi,' he said. 'I didn't hear you.'

She stepped into the room. 'Theo, I'm so sorry.'

'Claudia told you?'

'Yes, it's terrible.'

He sighed. 'I must admit I'm feeling a bit shell-shocked.' Then he smiled faintly and said, 'Come here.'

Moving closer, Annie hitched a hip on to the edge of his desk and leaned forward to touch her fingers lightly against his cheekbone. The little laughter creases around his eyes looked as if they'd been etched deeper by pain. He was hurt more than he was letting on and she couldn't bear it.

'I don't understand, Theo. How can the university do this to you?'

'Very easily, it would seem.'

'But how can they dump news like this out of the blue, without warning?'

He shrugged. 'Normally a lecturer would have some idea that a contract might not be renewed, but it's still legitimate for it to happen as quickly as this.'

'It might be legitimate, but it's too cruel.' When he didn't respond she couldn't help adding, 'Why was Claudia the one to tell you?'

'She's the head of the department.'

'Really?' She couldn't hold back a choked cry of dismay. 'Claudia's your boss?'

'Yes.' He saw the look on her face and added, 'She's a highly intelligent, very qualified academic, Annie.'

She sniffed. 'Maybe she is, but there was nothing high-minded or ethical about the way she sacked you.'

'I'm sure she would argue that she conducted herself in a very civilised manner.'

Annie shook her head and almost snarled.

'Don't look so worried, Annie. I'll be okay. Losing a job isn't the end of the world.'

She might have guessed that Theo would be stoical about such an unexpected disappointment. 'I'm more angry than worried,' she said and she had to compress her lips to stop herself from saying more. Would Theo think her suspicions about Claudia were catty?

But it was impossible for impetuous Annie McKinnon to hold back for long. Moments later the question that burned inside her burst out. 'Is Claudia in love with you, Theo?'

He let out a little huff of surprise and looked away quickly. 'Of course not.'

'Do you and she have a history?' She pressed her hand against the burning knot of panic in her stomach.

His eyes were worried as he turned back to her. His hand sought hers. 'Yes, but it was over long ago. Almost two years ago now.'

'I wouldn't be too sure that it's over.'

'Believe me, Annie. Claudia and I are *ancient* history.'

'You may think so, Theo, but I suspect Claudia is still hung up on you. I think it's very possible that what happened today was the green-eyed monster in action.'

He frowned and shook his head. 'Claudia's above that.'

Oh, boy. He had no idea.

He knew nothing of the half hour she'd spent squirming in Claudia's unpleasant company. Annie was sure the woman could stoop to murky depths if it suited her. 'I'm sorry, Theo, but I can't agree with you. Claudia might have top credentials, but I don't believe she's a philosopher's boot lace.'

A corner of his mouth twitched upwards. 'What makes you say that?'

'If she was trying to think rationally and logically and for the greater good, why would she choose to get rid of one of her most valuable lecturers?'

'You don't know anything about my value at work.'

'Yes, I do. People were falling over themselves last week to tell me what a popular and effective lecturer you are.' She dropped a quick kiss on his cheek, then slipped from the desk and walked quickly away from him.

I mustn't cry. I mustn't cry. Hunching her shoulders, she wrapped her arms over her stomach and she kept her back to him as she stared through a long, narrow window to the dusky outline of a lipstick palm growing in the courtyard.

'This sacking has nothing to do with the quality of your teaching.' A sob threatened and she gulped it down. 'It's about me, Theo. *I'm* your problem.'

'For God's sake, Annie, *no!*'

The shocked pain in his voice almost tore her in two. *Claudia hadn't said anything to him.*

It made sense. Claudia was too smart to openly point to Annie as the reason for Theo's dismissal. And he, poor lamb, didn't have the benefit of feminine intuition, so he probably hadn't noticed that haunted watchfulness in Claudia's eyes whenever she looked at him. And he hadn't heard the lethal parting shot his boss had fired at Annie.

'I'm afraid it's true.' With her back to him, Annie drew a deep breath and once again willed herself not to cry. 'If I left you, you'd have your job back in no time.'

Close behind her now, Theo clasped her by the elbows. 'That's not how it works.'

At his touch she almost sobbed aloud. She closed her eyes to hold back the tears, but the telltale moisture slid from beneath her lashes and down her cheeks.

Theo hauled her backwards hard against him. 'Don't even

think of leaving me.' Binding her with his arms, he pressed hot kisses to the back of her neck.

She was helpless, overcome by heartbreak. She didn't want to go…didn't want to…didn't want to. And Theo was holding her so tightly, he was kissing her hair, her wet cheek, her neck.

'This is not your fault,' he whispered.

But she knew it was. It *was* her fault. She was the reason Theo had lost his job. Nevertheless, when he whispered, 'Come here,' she turned in his arms, powerless to resist him as he covered her damp face with kisses.

'I want you in my life, Annie.'

Oh, Theo. Lovely, lovely Theo.

Cradling her face, he kissed her mouth. And she was lost, lost on the riding tide of her emotions, on a cresting wave of despair and longing.

Later she would think about what she must do to get Theo's job back, but not now. Not now when he was kissing her with a tenderness that blocked all sensible thought. Not now when his hands and his mouth left her no choice but to submit to sensation…when they were both trembling with the accelerating force of their feelings.

Not now when he was undoing the buttons of her blouse… when she was undoing the snap fastener at the waist of her jeans…when he was peeling her blouse away from her shoulders, when his lips were tracing the lacy patterns on her bra… while she tugged his shirt free from his trousers…

Only this…now…

The future and the past vanished and they let the urgency of the present take them by storm, expressing their emotions in the most honest and intimate way, the only way possible now.

All that mattered was this moment…and their sensitivity to each other's touch. Nothing else counted but their heightening need…the act of giving and receiving…and their rapturous, passionate drive for completion.

And afterwards…after they'd dressed again and after they'd giggled as they gathered and sorted the papers that had fallen from Theo's desk and scattered all over the study…after they'd heated the Thai take-away and poured fresh glasses of wine and eaten their dinner, picnic style on the floor of the lounge, and admired the lilies on the coffee table…

After all this, Theo still refused to accept that his dismissal had anything to do with Annie. And, because she couldn't bear to start a fight with him, she let the matter drop. For now.

'What will you do?' she asked as they carried the take-away cartons back to the kitchen.

'The only thing I can do. Look around for a new job.'

'But will there be another job like yours going in Brisbane?'

'It's highly unlikely. Actually, I'm almost certain there won't be anything on offer here for next semester.'

'But if you have to go away, what will happen to Damien? And George? He'll be terribly disappointed.'

'George?' Theo's eyebrows became question marks.

'Your father. You know that nice elderly gentleman who lives in the little white cottage around the corner?'

'But—' He smiled and frowned simultaneously, clearly puzzled. 'How do you know about him?'

Annie smiled back. 'I met him today when I took Basil for his walk.'

'Did you, now? So you've been spying behind my back?'

'It was more like the inaugural meeting of the Theo Grainger Fan Club.'

Theo grinned. 'What a charming idea.'

It was the first time he'd grinned all evening. 'I could scrounge up a few more members,' she said, hoping to cheer

him some more. *Everyone who knows you loves you, Theo.*
'My friend Victoria was smitten at first sight.' Remembering
the Italian café owner she'd met on the first morning, she
added, 'I'm sure Giovanni would join us if he was invited.'

'Perhaps they will write me a good reference,' Theo said,
with a grimace that was more rueful than cheerful.

*You won't need a reference, Theo. Not when I've done what
I have to do.*

But at the thought of the task that awaited her in the morning, Annie shuddered.

'What's the matter?' he asked.

She forced a weak smile. 'I just wish this hadn't happened.'

'It'll turn out all right. I'm going to look on this as a challenge, a new bend in the road. Who knows what I'll find
waiting around the corner?'

'Now you're being philosophical.'

'Of course. Why not?'

'Because this should never have happened. It's unfair.' She
caught the quizzical expression in Theo's eyes and shook
her head. 'I know, I know, we can't expect life to always be
fair.'

Just the same... She looked around her at Theo's lovely
home. It would be a wrench for him to leave it. She thought
of Damien, who still needed his uncle's guidance, of George,
Theo's ageing father, who was so pleased to have his son
living close by. Theo was losing more than his job. He was
losing his home, his family, his lifestyle. All because of
her.

Which was why, ultimately, it was up to her and her alone
to set matters right.

Stepping close, he slipped his arms around her. 'I'm surprised you're letting this get to you, Annie.'

She shrugged. 'It's been a big week. A bit of a roller coaster, actually.'

'It has indeed.' He began to massage her shoulders. 'You need to relax.' Nuzzling her neck, he murmured, 'Why don't you put yourself in my tender care? I suggest an early night. Problems always look much better in the morning.'

Not this time, Theo.

Oh, God. The very thought of the action she must take in the morning made her tremble with terror. How could she do it?

She mustn't think of it now, or she would break down in front of him. She had to focus on what was left to her. This night.

'Your tender care is exactly what I need,' she told him and she turned and slipped into his welcoming embrace.

CHAPTER TEN

ANNIE had known it was going to be hard, but not this hard.

Three times she'd tried to dial Claudia's number and three times she'd chickened out. How could she ever bring herself to do what she knew she must?

Dripping with dread, she stood in the middle of the kitchen and forced herself to stare at the phone. *It will only get worse if I keep putting it off. I've got to do it this time.*

There was no other way. She'd lain awake for most of the night thinking and agonising and she knew this was the only solution.

It broke her heart to realise that she'd caused Theo so much trouble by falling in love with him. At first she told herself it was okay because she hadn't known, hadn't dreamed that she could be creating problems for him.

But she'd read in one of his books about Chinese philosophy that even when you're not wholly responsible for a situation, you have an obligation to find the best way through it. Which meant she had to accept the awful reality that her presence here was a problem for Theo. She was a threat to his career, and to his happiness as well. And it was up to her to do something about it.

It wasn't fair. It wasn't fair at all that a jealous, vindictive woman like Claudia could cause so much unhappiness, but Annie knew she had to be the one to make amends.

Last night she'd lain beside Theo while he slept and she'd held his hand against her heart and covered him with soft, secret kisses and worshipped him in silence. And then this morning he'd woken refreshed and ready to go to the university to begin grading examination papers and she'd had to find the courage to say goodbye to him, knowing—heaven help her—that it was for the last time.

It had nearly killed her to stand at the back door and watch him walk out of the house with no idea that he'd never see her again. When he turned back and waved to her she'd almost weakened and run to him.

But somehow she'd managed to let him go.

All that was left to do now was this…

Just remember you're doing it for Theo. Think of him, not yourself.

A scared little cry broke from her lips as she dashed across the kitchen and snatched up the phone. *Think of Theo.* She'd already found the direct number for Claudia's office in a notebook beside Theo's phone and her hand shook as she punched the digits.

Oh, please let the connection go through. I couldn't bear it if I have to spend ages waiting, or if I'm asked to call back later.

'Claudia Stanhope speaking.'

Gulp. *Oh, help.* 'Claudia, good morning. This is Annie— Annie McKinnon.'

'Good morning, Annie.' Claudia's response was cool, but she didn't quite manage to hide her surprise. 'How can I help you?'

'I think you'll be able to work that out for yourself.'

'I beg your pardon?'

'I'm ringing to let you know that I'm leaving Brisbane and I'm leaving Theo. I'm getting out of his life—going home to Southern Cross.' The words spilled out in a rush, an emotional landslide.

For too long there was silence on the other end of the phone. Then... 'Poor Theo.' And a little later, 'Why are you telling me this, Annie?'

Annie suppressed an urge to scream. 'You know very well why.'

'I do?'

'I'm not going to put myself through the humiliation of spelling it out, Claudia. You've umpteen degrees, so I'm going to trust you to be clever enough to fill in the blanks. Just remember—' Her courage almost failed and she was shaking so badly the trembling vibrated in her voice. 'I'm going to be out of Theo's life. Gone. For *good!*' The last word exploded on a sob.

Oh, Theo.

Slamming the receiver down, she slumped on to a stool.

She'd done it.

She'd done the unbearable. Now all she had to do was get out of here and she would have atoned for the damage she'd caused. Within a day or so, Theo would have his job back and he wouldn't have to leave this house, or his life here in Brisbane.

Oh, God. She'd given him up.

As the full force of her heartbreak crashed over her, she caved forward on to the kitchen bench, unable to control her horrible, noisy, desolate sobbing.

How could she bear this? Theo was the most wonderful man she'd ever met—was ever likely to meet. She loved everything about him—his beautiful smile, his quiet dignity, his mind, his body, his kisses, his touch—his *passion*.

Oh, dear heaven. She had to get a grip. If she thought about the way Theo made love to her, she would be crying for the next hundred years.

A scratching sound on the glass door caught her attention and she turned to see Basil on his hind legs, trying to get inside the kitchen, no doubt worried because he could see how upset she was. Hurrying over to him, she slid the door open, then dropped to her haunches to hug him.

'Oh, you darling boy, I'm going to miss you too.' Still sobbing, she let him lick her tears. 'Look after Theo for me, won't you, mate?'

She hugged Basil hard, rubbing her cheek into his soft coat. When at last she released him, something tugged at her hair and she realised that the old piece of ribbon that she'd used to tie back her hair had caught in his collar. She stared at the narrow strip of yellow silk and then, on impulse, threaded it through the metal ring on Basil's collar and twisted it several times before knotting it.

'This is a friendship band for you, Basil,' she said.

It was a hopelessly teenage-angst sort of gesture, but it made her feel a little better to leave something behind. And it looked kind of cute—that little band of gold against Basil's dramatic black and white coat.

Then, before the tears could start again, Annie jumped to her feet. It was time to call a taxi.

'Is Annie here?'

The question burst from Theo the instant Mel opened her front door and he could hardly believe he'd asked it so calmly. Inside he was *roaring*.

Mel gaped at him. 'Dr Grainger, what a surprise.'

'I'm looking for Annie. Is she here?'

'Here?' Mel repeated, frowning, and the blank look on her face sent Theo's hopes plummeting. 'I thought she was at your place,' she said.

He muttered a curse beneath his breath.

'What's happened?' Mel stepped forward on to the porch and let the door close behind her.

He tried not to feel put off by her lack of welcome. 'Annie's gone and I have to find her.'

'You mean she's packed her bags and left you?'

Left you. The finality of those words echoed and clanged in the cold, hollow emptiness inside him. 'Yes,' he admitted, although it killed him to do so. 'She left a note, but it doesn't make sense.'

Mel's fine eyebrows lowered over worried eyes as she held out her hand. 'May I see the note?'

Theo hesitated. He hadn't intended to hand over something so personal.

'Do you want my help?' asked Mel.

With reluctance he accepted that he had little choice. Mel was an important connection and, the truth of it was, he was desperate. Taking the creased paper from his shirt pocket, he handed over the message he knew by heart.

Dear Theo,

I have to go, and you mustn't try to stop me. Soon you'll understand why and then everything will be fine for you.

All my love,

Annie

After scanning it quickly Mel looked up and fixed him with an even grimmer glare as she folded her arms across her chest. Her manner was so fierce that he felt like a very naughty schoolboy being carpeted by the headmistress.

'What have you done to upset her?' she demanded.

'Nothing that I know of.' He sighed. 'I don't think this is about something I've done.'

'Then what's happened?' Mel's eyes shimmered with fury.

'I think it must be a—a situation that's arisen.'

'A situation?' she snapped like a bossy little guard dog.

'It's kind of complicated.'

'Oh, God. Not another woman?'

'Yes.' One glance at her horrified face and Theo rushed to redress his mistake. 'I mean no. I'm not seeing another woman or anything like that, but Annie thinks—' He groaned and shoved anguished fingers through his short dark hair. 'It's way too complicated to explain, but Annie's decided that she's to blame for something that happened—' He sighed again.

'So I take it she hasn't tried to contact you?'

'I'm afraid not. Do you know what time she left?'

'I think it was some time this morning. If she's not here, she might have headed back to Southern Cross.'

'Probably.' She scowled at him again. 'I knew this was going to turn out badly.'

Theo wanted to protest but decided it was wiser not to begin an argument with Annie's friend. 'If you hear from her will you please let me know straight away?'

Her gaze narrowed. Cocking her head to one side, she leant one hip against the porch railing. 'That depends on what Annie has to say, Dr Grainger. She may not wish to have anything more to do with you.'

'Please,' he begged, not caring how desperate he sounded. 'I've got to find her and speak to her.'

Mel didn't answer immediately and if Theo hadn't been so distressed he might have admired her caution.

'You're obviously a very good friend of Annie's,' he said. 'I can see that you're as worried about her as I am but, I promise you, I have her best interests at heart.'

'You do know she's hopelessly in love with you, don't you?' Mel said carefully.

His heart rocked. 'That's why I have to find her.'

There was another agonising stretch of silence, but at last Mel's expression softened. 'Okay,' she said. 'If Annie rings, I'll try to persuade her to contact you.'

'The minute you hear from her?'

She smiled gently. 'Yes, Theo.'

Bouncing on the front seat of the mail truck as it rattled along a dirt track that cut through the heart of the Star Valley, Annie peered through the dusty windscreen, straining to catch her first sight of home. Now that she'd almost completed the long journey from Brisbane via Townsville and Mirrabrook, she wanted this last leg to be over. The closer she got the safer she felt.

She tried to squash memories of the overexcited, bubbly young woman who had raced away from Southern Cross for her date with Damien. She'd known then that she was taking a risk, that things might not work out in the city, but she could never have anticipated that she would be coming home with such a broken and battered pain-filled heart.

Ahead of her a flash of green and white told her that Southern Cross homestead was coming into view and as the truck bumped along the gumtree-lined track, she glimpsed more and more details—the silver flash of the ripple iron roof, the smooth green sweep of lawn in front of the house, the bullnosed overhang on the deep, shady verandas—and then—a black and white streak shooting around the side of the house.

Lavender, her Border collie.

Leaning out of the open side window, Annie waved to her. 'Poor Lavender's missed me,' she told Ted, the mail truck's driver. But Ted wasn't a talker so a nod and a grin were the most she could expect from him.

It was so weird the way Lavender always knew when she was coming home. Weird, but wonderful. Wonderful to know that, whatever else happened in this crazy world, faithful Lavender's loyalty would never falter. Her dog's love would always be waiting for her.

Oh, help. She forced herself to mentally edit out the other black and white dog she'd farewelled yesterday.

'Are you going to stop for a cup of tea?' she asked Ted.

He grinned and nodded. 'I could do with a cuppa. Throat's a bit parched.' It was the longest speech he'd made all morning.

As soon as he'd guided the truck to a halt near the homestead's front steps, Annie threw the door open and succumbed to Lavender's enthusiastic greeting. 'Hey, baby, you've got to calm down,' she said with a laugh. 'Yeah, I love you, too, sweetheart. Okay, why not lick me to death?'

When at last Lavender calmed down and Annie stood up, she looked around expectantly. Where was everyone? She knew that Reid was still filling in for the manager at Lacey Downs, but there was no sign of Vic, the gardener, or her brother Kane, or the English housekeeper who'd been filling in while she'd been away.

Somehow she didn't think she could bear to come home to an empty house.

'Hey, Kane, where are you?' she called.

It was quite possible that he was out working on one of the back blocks, but what about the English girl he'd hired? Annie had hoped that she would still be here, even if she only stayed on for another day or so.

It would be rather nice to have some female company. A welcome distraction from all the thoughts that were tearing her apart.

She walked around to the back of the truck and lifted her bag down and then at last she heard Kane's voice. 'Coming, Annie.'

Thank goodness. With something of a shock, she realised how much she wanted to see Kane. There had been many times, particularly in her teenage years, when her big brothers' teasing had been the bane of her existence, but that had changed after their father had died, and right now she couldn't think of anyone she'd rather see.

Then suddenly there was Kane, loping down the front steps—a tall, sandy-haired figure in typical outback working clothes—cotton shirt, blue jeans and dusty riding boots. Annie threw herself into his big, strong embrace and clung to him. And Kane, bless him, hugged her tightly and pressed her head against his massive shoulder and held her as if he understood exactly how she felt.

When he released her, he held her at arm's length and studied her. 'I wasn't expecting you so soon. How are you, sis?' he asked gently.

'I'm—' She drew a deep breath. 'I'm okay.'

He frowned. 'You sure?'

'Yep.'

'You look a little—strained.'

She shrugged and looked away. It was going to be hard to keep a stiff upper lip, but it would be worse to start talking about her heartache. Her pain was still too fresh and raw and she just knew that she'd break down and upset Kane. Next thing *he'd* be on a flight to Brisbane threatening to rip poor Theo to shreds.

But she couldn't just stand here staring at her toes. She

looked up at Kane and was suddenly shocked by the scary bleakness in his blue eyes and the uncharacteristic tension in the set of his jaw and his shoulders.

'You don't look so great yourself,' she said. 'Is everything okay?'

Kane seemed distracted and turned abruptly away from her to the mailman. 'Hey, Ted,' he said. 'Sorry I didn't say good day. Will you be able to take another passenger with you on your way back into town?'

'I reckon I could,' Ted said, nodding.

'Who's that?' Annie asked. 'Not the English girl?'

Kane shot her a sharp glance. 'You know about Charity?'

'Reid told me you had someone here to do the house-work.'

He nodded slowly.

'Is she leaving already?'

'Yeah.' He kicked at a clump of grass with the toe of his riding boot.

'That's a pity. I was hoping she could stay on for a bit.'

'She's rather keen to get away.'

Kane's voice was casual enough, but he stared so sadly into the distance that Annie was suddenly certain her brother was hiding something—something that could only have happened while she'd been gone.

Given her own misery as well as Kane's, it was becoming horribly clear that she should never have left Southern Cross for the city.

When Reid McKinnon came back from his stint at Lacey Downs it took him no time at all to work out that something was very much amiss with both his siblings.

'What's been going on while I was away?' he demanded at dinner on the first evening. 'Have you two been sick or something? Annie looks as if she hasn't slept for a month. And Kane, you look like you've been sentenced to life imprisonment.'

Annie and Kane exchanged self-conscious shrugs. They'd both been sympathetic to each other's misery, but they'd avoided delving too deeply into their problems. Even so, Annie was almost certain that Kane's gloominess was directly related to the departure of the English girl, Charity Denham.

Charity was incredibly pretty, with lovely auburn hair, clear green eyes and gorgeous skin, and when she'd said goodbye to Kane it had been impossible to miss the chemistry between them. Why had Kane let her go?

Crikey! What a pair she and Kane were—both lovelorn losers.

When neither of them replied, Reid gave up and resumed eating, but Annie knew he wouldn't let the matter drop, even though he diplomatically changed the subject and gave them a report on the condition of the stock at Lacey Downs instead. She knew that Reid was doing his Big Brother act—watching them carefully and waiting for the right moment to question them separately.

As it turned out, he confronted Annie mid-morning the following day.

'Wow! They look snazzy,' he said, coming into the washroom when she was in the middle of ironing her pink jeans.

'Thanks,' she said cautiously.

He lounged a denim-clad hip against the door frame and she waited for him to follow up with a wisecrack about her new citified taste in fashion.

'I guess you bought them in Brisbane.'

'Yep, under the expert guidance of Mel and Victoria.'

Shifting his weight to lean a bulky shoulder against the doorjamb, Reid watched her in silence for a moment or two. 'So how was the break in Brisbane?'

'Great.'

'Was it long enough?'

Surprised, she stared at him. 'I—I guess so.'

'You came home in a bit of a hurry, didn't you?'

She shrugged.

'And you look like hell, Annie.'

Oh, help. His grey eyes were regarding her with such obvious concern and he had said this so gently that she almost broke down.

I feel absolutely awful, Reid. There are so many broken pieces inside me, I'm not sure I'll ever heal. And it's getting worse every day.

'Hey, Annie, watch out, you'll burn a hole in those new jeans.'

Quickly setting the iron upright, she turned it off at the wall, then hooked the jeans over a coathanger on a cupboard door, and turned to face him once more. She loved both her brothers, but Reid had always been the one she'd turned to when she had really been in trouble. He wasn't a saint. There were times when he'd teased her mercilessly, but he wasn't as hot-headed as Kane; he was more sensitive and a terrific listener. Now, however, he was bent on firing questions.

'Kane tells me you've been refusing to take phone calls from some guy in Brisbane.'

She felt her face flame. 'I can't talk to him.'

'Why? Who is he?'

How on earth could she explain? Her poor tormented brain seemed to be tied in knots and everything about her trip to Brisbane felt too painful and complicated. If she tried to explain about Theo, everything would unravel too fast and she'd probably make a hash of it. She might not be able to make Reid understand that Theo was wonderful and kind and not at all to blame for her misery.

'You look terrible, Annie. What's the matter? What's this bloke in the smoke done to you?'

'Nothing,' she said quickly.

'You can at least tell me his name.'

'It doesn't matter, Reid. He's—he's just a guy—who—who wants to keep in touch but—' She hesitated.

'But you want to give him the cold shoulder?'

'Yes,' she said in a small voice.

'He's not a stalker, is he?'

'No.'

'Is he making a nuisance of himself, Annie?'

Horrified, she insisted, 'No, nothing like that.'

'Then why do you look so flattened?'

'I think I overdid things in the city. Too much partying. Don't worry about me, Reid. I'll be okay.'

At first Reid let out an irritated grunt and looked as if he wasn't going to accept her weak explanation, but then he seemed to have second thoughts.

With an excessive lack of haste, he relaxed in the doorway again, crossed his arms over his chest and hooked one riding boot in front of the other. 'Maybe a proper holiday would do you good.'

Surprised, she managed, 'Perhaps.'

'How about a total change of scene?'

It occurred to her then that her brother had probably been leading this conversation in a pre-programmed direction from the start. 'Did you have somewhere in mind?'

He shoved his hands deep in the pockets of his jeans. 'I had a long chat with Kane last night.'

'Did he admit that he's in love with Charity Denham?

Reid smiled slowly. 'I dragged it out of him.'

'Good.' Annie blinked. 'I can't blame him. Charity's very lovely.'

'She's that all right. Kane's eating his heart out over her,' Reid said. 'So I've told him he should get cracking over to England to sort things out.'

She felt a rush of excitement for Kane. 'Good for you, Reid. That's excellent advice and he'll listen to you. If you say it's okay, he'll probably go.'

'And I think you should go with him.'

She gaped at him, then rolled her eyes. 'As if Kane would want me tagging along while he sorts out his love life.'

'But you could fly with him to the UK and visit Mum in Scotland.'

Goodness! Averting her gaze, so Reid couldn't see her reaction, she noticed a fallen clothes peg on the floor and she quickly bent to pick it up, then dusted a fine layer of red outback dirt from it with her fingers.

'Wouldn't you like to go?' Reid asked.

'Y—yes, of course.' At any other time she would love to go. She'd be there in a shot. She'd missed her mother terribly and longed to see her again.

But—she knew it didn't make a jot of sense—but she didn't think she could bear to travel so far from Theo. Even though she could never be a part of his life, the thought of putting so much distance between them was too painful. Scotland was on the other side of the world. 'That would leave you here on your own,' she said.

'Don't worry about me. I can get another ringer from Starburst station if I need to, and I've got a new cook coming over from Richmond in a day or two.'

'What about the book work? I've been away and I need to catch up.'

'I'm sure I'll manage. Those spreadsheets you've set up on the computer are great, but if there's a problem with the books, Sarah Rossiter will lend a hand.'

Annie waggled the peg at him. 'You mustn't take Sarah for granted, Reid. Heading a one-teacher school must keep her busy enough without running to your beck and call.'

To her surprise, Reid's face darkened. Icy sparks flashed in his grey eyes and a muscle twitched in his jaw. 'Don't ever accuse me of taking Sarah for granted.'

Jeepers, where had *that* come from? Since when had Reid become so touchy about Sarah? 'I'm sorry.'

'Listen,' he said, quickly recovering his usual composure. 'The mustering's finished and it'll be the wet season soon, so we shouldn't be too busy. Kane needs to go now, and you could do with a diversion. I'll be fine. It's perfect timing.'

Reid had it all worked out.

'Can we afford two overseas plane flights? I'm afraid I went ballistic with my credit card in Brisbane.'

He fired a quick gaze at the jeans she'd just ironed and smiled. 'We can manage.'

Dropping the peg back in the appropriate basket, Annie crossed to the washroom window and stared out at the big expanse of sunny blue sky and the stretch of dry, buff-coloured paddock that ran down to the trees lining the creek.

Common sense told her that it didn't matter where in the world she was in relation to Theo. She couldn't communicate with him or see him, so if she was going to be separated from him in the isolated outback she might as well be on the other side of the globe.

Her terrible task was to try to forget about him. She had to avoid Theo at all costs. If she stayed in Queensland she might weaken.

Perhaps being on the other side of the world was her wisest option.

She took a deep breath and then another before she turned back to Reid. 'Thanks for the offer. I'll definitely give it some thought.'

'Don't take too long to make your mind up. Kane's raring to go.'

Theo dropped his pen and pushed away from his desk. It was so difficult to work, so hard to focus. The end of year examination papers had started flooding in and he had a mountain of marking to wade through, but all he could think of was Annie.

Where was she?

Whenever he tried to ring Southern Cross or her mobile he got an answering machine, but none of his messages were returned. His emails to Annie's address had been blocked as well, so he couldn't reach her that way. And yesterday even her friend Melissa had gone silent on him.

If he could, he would jump on a plane and fly to Townsville, then hire a car and drive himself out to the McKinnons' cattle property in the Star Valley. And if Annie wasn't there he wouldn't leave until he'd found someone who would tell him where she was. But he had all these exam papers waiting to be assessed. Unavoidable deadlines loomed.

He'd never felt so hellish, so frustrated, so anguished.

Until now, he'd taken life's setbacks on the chin. He was a philosopher and he'd trained himself to react to disappointments with a certain sang-froid. But Annie's disappearance had dealt a blow that no amount of reason or logic could heal.

He'd told her once that philosophers avoided discussions about romantic love because the emotions involved disrupted more serious occupations.

Damn right. He was a mess. The famous Theo Grainger equanimity had been shot to pieces.

The downhill run had started from the moment he'd seen Annie McKinnon in the lobby at the Pinnacle Hotel. That night he'd been so distracted by her animated, lively loveliness that he'd almost walked into a marble pillar.

And that had been before he'd got to know her.

Since then he'd been totally distracted and walking into metaphorical pillars every step of the way.

Vivacious, fun-loving, gutsy, inquisitive, sensuous—Annie McKinnon was a weapon of mass distraction. She'd worked her way under his skin and straight into his heart. And now she was gone. And Theo was so undone he couldn't think straight.

If only he'd taken more notice of the way she'd blamed herself for his dismissal. At the time her fears about Claudia had seemed so ludicrous that he couldn't possibly take them seriously. But Annie had been convinced, and now—

At the squeak of a door opening behind him, Theo turned to discover Rex Bradley, a fellow lecturer, poking his head into his office.

'Oh, you are here,' Rex said. 'I knocked but there was no answer.'

'I'm sorry, Rex. I didn't hear you.' He raised a hand and made a quick, beckoning gesture. 'Come on in.'

To his surprise his colleague almost skipped into the room.

'You look chipper.'

'I am. I've just come from Claudia's office and I bring glad tidings.'

'You've been promoted?' Theo hoped he would be able to dredge up the necessary enthusiasm.

'Good heavens, man, credit me with some tact. I haven't

come to crow over you with news about myself. No, it's great news for you, Theo. For all of us, actually. Her Highness has just announced there will be enough funding for your course to continue after all.'

'She's what?' Theo felt the blood drain from his face.

'Claudia's changed her mind. She's going to renew your contract.'

'That—that's incredible. Why?'

'Who knows? Our Claudia works in mysterious ways. I can only suppose she's had an attack of sanity and remembered what a fabulous lecturer you are and that she'd made a stupid mistake with the budget. But I don't give a hoot for her reasons. The whys and wherefores aren't half so important as the fact that we're not going to lose you.'

'No one else has been sacked instead of me, have they?'

'No, Theo. Trust you to worry about others at a time like this.' Rex paused. 'Curiously enough, Claudia seems to have found a loophole in the funding cut problem.'

Theo stared at Rex and felt an icy flood sluice through him from head to toe. *Annie had been right.* He hadn't believed it possible, but Claudia's sudden about-face was so implausible there could be no other explanation.

'Why hasn't Claudia come to tell me this herself?' he asked.

Rex cleared his throat. 'She made some excuse about a meeting in Sydney and having to rush away to catch a plane. I suspect she might be feeling a bit sheepish about her sudden turnaround. But I promise you, Theo, it's genuine. She asked me to give you the news.'

He held out a memo and Theo shoved it on to his desk without even glancing at it. He was too appalled by the realisation that Annie had sacrificed herself for him. She'd seen through Claudia's game.

It was all so sickeningly obvious now. Just yesterday Claudia had called by his office to see how he was bearing up, and she'd posed several carefully casual questions about Annie. And, poor, ignorant fool that he was, he'd confessed honestly that Annie had disappeared. And when Claudia had pressed him, he'd admitted that he hadn't really known why.

Now it was patently clear that the damned manipulating woman *had* been jealous of Annie. She'd been playing games with his life, with his personal happiness. And, just as Annie had predicted, within a few days of her disappearance his job had been reinstated.

'You don't look too happy, Theo.'

Rex had to be joking. How on earth could he possibly be happy?

CHAPTER ELEVEN

THE week before Christmas was not the best time for a girl from tropical North Queensland to be visiting Scotland. As Annie walked beside the Lake of Menteith, she tried to imagine this scene in summer when it was bathed in sunshine, bordered by lush, green forests and busy with busloads of tourists and fishermen in boats. Now the shores of this romantic lake in the heart of the Trossachs were white and stark. And *so-o-o-o* cold.

Then again, lonely, cold, windswept shores suited Annie's mood. Out here she could feel as bleak as she liked and no one could bother her with well-meaning questions.

Fat snowflakes fell, settling on her head and shoulders as she stared out to the little island in the middle of the lake.

And thought of Theo.

It happened all the time now. It didn't matter what she looked at, where she visited or whom she talked to…she thought about Theo and longed for him. He commanded centre stage in her thoughts first thing in the morning, at noon, and into the long, lonely nights.

Coming to Scotland hadn't helped at all.

It was wonderful to see her mother, of course. Lovely to meet her mother's friends and to get to know the quaint town of Aberfoyle where her mother and her Aunt Flora lived. But Annie hadn't been able to bring herself to talk to her mother about Theo.

What was the point? How would it help to *talk* about him, when what she craved was to see him, to feel his arms around her, to have him with her, in her life. She needed him here beside her.

She longed to share these new sights with Theo. If only she could slip her arm through his and walk with him over this ground. She longed to talk with him...

They would talk about everything...

She could almost hear their voices above the crunching sounds of her boots treading on icy snowflakes...

They would discuss the fascinating history of Rob Roy and the monks at Inchmahome, an ancient priory that had been built centuries ago on the little island in the middle of this lake. She could take him to see her favourite sights so far—the charm of a cluster of pines beside the wee kirk in Aberfoyle, the breathtaking grandeur of Stirling Castle, or the gorgeous stone bridge over the falls at Killin.

But without Theo, Scotland's attractions seemed insignificant and colourless—as stodgy as porridge and as bleak as the leaden skies looming low over the lake.

It was shameful how weak she was. If he rang again, she was sure she would have to speak to him. She should be disciplining her mind, training herself to forget about him, instead of obsessing about him night and day. But how could she ever forget Theo? She knew he was the one, the man she'd been searching for all her life. Her soul cried out for him.

Except... I've given him up and I must forget him.

Oh, help... Time to drive on to check out Loch Katrine.

As she crossed the icy ground to her parked car, her mobile phone beeped and her heart took off like a duck at the sound of a shotgun. How stupid of her. It wouldn't be Theo.

Digging a thickly gloved hand deep in the pocket of her coat, she extracted the phone, but her woollen gloves were so thick she almost pressed the wrong button as she tried to receive the call.

It was Kane's number.

She let out her breath with a whoosh and willed herself to relax.

'Hi, Kane,' she said, raising her voice above the wind. 'How are you?'

'I'm terrific,' he said and she knew immediately that it was true. She could hear his happiness ringing in his voice. 'Charity and I are getting married.'

'Oh, Kane! Oh, wow! That's fantastic!' She let out an excited little squeal. 'When?'

'In a few weeks' time. Here in Derbyshire. You and Mum and Aunt Flora will all have to come, of course.'

'Of course we'll come. We'll be there with bells on. Oh, Kane, I'm so happy for you. Congratulations. You sound so excited.'

'I'm over the moon, Annie. I can't believe Charity wants me. You've no idea how good this feels.'

'I—I guess not.'

'I'll get back to you soon with details, dates, venues et cetera.'

'Yes, okay.'

'Oh, I forgot to ask. How's Scotland?'

'Lovely. I'm driving around the lochs today. How's Derbyshire?'

'It's amazing—has a cute factor right off the scale. Hollydean, where Charity lives, is the sort of place we only get to see on Christmas cards.'

'Everything over here is so pretty, isn't it? Have you rung Reid?'

'Yes, I wanted to tell him first. If it wasn't for the pair of you urging me over here, I'd probably still be at home moping around Southern Cross like a wounded dog.'

'Our pleasure, mate.'

They said their farewells and Annie dropped the mobile back into her pocket. Kane was ecstatic. And she was so happy for him. She was, she really was.

Just the same, as she continued to the car she almost collapsed beneath the weight of a sudden cloud of despair. She tried not to let Kane's happiness highlight her own misery, but she couldn't help it. She felt so instantly black and hopeless; it was as if she'd stumbled into a bottomless hole with no hope of rescue.

She needed Theo more than ever. Now. This moment. Suddenly she knew she had to make contact. She couldn't face another day, another hour, without speaking to him.

Her heart raced frantically as she pictured herself dredging up the emotional courage to telephone him. It would be nighttime in Australia, but not so late that he would be asleep. Yes, she would do it. She could justify her call on the grounds that she needed to make sure he'd been reinstated at the university and that her sacrifice had been worthwhile.

Leaning against the side of the car, she pulled off one glove so that she could punch in the international code followed by Theo's number.

Oh, God, what could she say? *I just need to hear your voice?*

Her chest felt so tight she could hardly breathe. At this rate, when Theo answered she would be too breathless to say anything. But she would feel better once she knew that he was all right.

Closing her eyes, she dragged in a deeper breath as she listened to the phone ringing.

Then it stopped and her heart almost shot clear out of her throat.

'Hi, Theo Grainger speaking.'

She experienced a jolt of pure elation. It was so, so good to hear his lovely voice. 'Hi, Theo.'

'I'm afraid I can't take your call. I'm on an extended vacation. Please leave a message after the beep…'

'Oh, no, *no!*'

Extended vacation? Oh, God, no.

That meant the worst had happened—the very worst. He didn't have his job back; her sacrifice had been wasted.

And now he'd gone away—disappeared beyond her reach.

She couldn't hold back a horrible, harrowing moan. And she was too blinded by tears to find the disconnect button and too devastated to care that her heartbreak was being recorded.

She'd made a mess of everything. Everything! And coming to the other side of the world, which she'd thought was the best, the wisest, thing to do, had been a stupid, terrible mistake.

Standing on the bottom step at Southern Cross homestead Theo felt at a distinct disadvantage, especially as Annie's brother was glaring down at him from the top step, and more especially because the brother's welcome smile had vanished the moment Theo had mentioned Annie's name.

'You came all the way from Brisbane just to speak to my little sister?'

'That's right.' Theo mounted the steps slowly and felt marginally better when he reached the top and discovered that he was much the same height as the scowling brother. Holding out his hand, he said, 'How do you do? I'm Theo Grainger.'

The brother nodded and, although he shook hands, a wary caution lingered in his cool grey eyes. 'Reid McKinnon,' he said, then his lips snapped tightly shut.

'I was hoping to find Annie. Is she at home?'

'I'm not sure that's any of your business.'

So this encounter would be as tough as Theo had feared. He squared his shoulders. 'Your sister may feel differently.'

'I doubt it. You're the fellow who's been ringing her, aren't you? She's refused to answer your calls.'

'Yes, I'm afraid that's right.'

'Can't you take a hint, mate?'

'Believe me, I do understand your concern.'

Reid's eyes betrayed a brief flicker of surprise before he resorted to scowling again. 'You're dead right I'm concerned about Annie. And if you had anything to do with the state she's in, you should be bloody ashamed of yourself, Grainger.'

'State? What do you mean?' Theo's voice seemed to crack and, in spite of his intention to remain calm and polite, he found himself shouting. 'What state? What are you talking about?'

Reid didn't answer.

Pain filled Theo's throat and he felt as if he'd swallowed a block of marble. 'Where is Annie? What's happened to her?'

At last Reid looked as if he was about to say something, but then he hesitated again.

Theo groaned and slammed one fisted hand into the palm of the other. 'You must understand how I feel about your sister. Do you really think I would travel over a thousand kilometres just to see her if she wasn't immensely important to me?'

Suddenly, from behind him came an explosion of barking and he whirled around to see Basil straining to get out through the passenger window of his hire truck. A Border collie, her tail wagging madly, was barking just as loudly as she leaped to greet him.

Theo spun back to Reid. 'Is that Lavender?'

'Annie told you about Lavender?'

'Of course she did. It isn't possible to know Annie without knowing all about Lavender, is it?'

'I don't suppose it is,' Reid said, looking slightly stunned. 'Hey, Lavender,' he bawled. 'Cut that out.'

The collie ignored him and the tail wagging and frenzied barking continued.

'What's got into her?' Reid muttered. 'Anyone would think those dogs were long lost friends.'

He hurried down the steps and Theo followed him. By now, Lavender was leaping so high she was almost doing back flips and Basil was trying to squeeze through the too narrow gap of open window.

'Stop that right now,' Theo ordered his dog. 'You'll wreck the hire truck.' When Basil ignored him, he strode around to the driver's door and swung it open. Next minute Basil whipped past him.

'Well, I'll be…' said Reid as the dogs found each other. Almost immediately the barking diminished. Lavender began to sniff excitedly at the piece of yellow ribbon on Basil's collar and Theo realised what had caused the fuss.

'That's Annie's hair ribbon,' he explained.

Reid's face flushed and for a moment he looked confused. But then, as he watched the dogs continue to check each other out, his mouth twitched into a puzzled half-smile.

He dropped his gaze to the toes of his riding boots, gave this some thought for a moment or two, then looked up to Theo and assessed him coolly, but his smile was warm as he said, 'Perhaps you'd better come inside. Then you can explain exactly why you're here.'

Jessie McKinnon pushed a plate towards her daughter. 'Have another scone, Annie.'

'I couldn't possibly.'

Sighing, Jessie set her cup and saucer aside and leaned forward. 'You're not well, are you, dear?'

'Of course I am, Mum. I'm fine.'

To Annie's dismay, silver tears glinted in Jessie's eyes. 'I haven't been much of a mother in the past few years,' she said unexpectedly. 'I feel as if I've let my children down.'

'No, Mum.' Despite the loneliness she'd felt over the past six years, Annie knew this wasn't a moment for brutal honesty. Besides, during her time in Aberfoyle, she'd begun to suspect that there were stronger reasons for her mother's absence than she or her brothers had ever guessed.

'We've been fine at home,' Annie said. 'The boys have been fantastic. Anyhow, we bullied you into coming back to Scotland after Dad died and you've simply been a very obedient parent.'

Jessie looked down at her hands in her lap. 'Just the same, my dear, if I'd been a better mother to you, you might have been able to talk to me and tell me what's troubling you.'

Annie's teacup rattled as she set it back on the saucer.

'I've been watching you for weeks now and you're getting paler and thinner. Flora's noticed it, too. You can't pretend that you're not terribly upset about something, Annie.'

'No,' Annie said softly.

'Is it a man, darling?'

Closing her eyes against the sudden rush of hot tears, Annie nodded.

'You love him?'

Again Annie nodded.

'But he doesn't love you?'

Her eyes flashed open. 'Oh, no, Mum. It's not like that.' Seconds stretched into eternity as their gazes linked and held. Dusky shadows were creeping into the kitchen and in the fading light Jessie McKinnon's lovely blue eyes seemed to shimmer with a dark, secret wisdom as if to say, *You can trust me, Annie. I've had my share of pain and I understand...*

Perhaps it was the compassion in her mother's eyes, or perhaps it was simply the right time, but suddenly Annie knew that she couldn't hold back any longer. She had to tell her mother about Theo before she collapsed from the strain.

It was almost dark by the time she finished her story.

Jessie listened quietly with very few interruptions. Then she rose and hurried to Annie, giving her a long, hard hug and Annie clung to her, treasuring the comforting warmth of motherly arms so long denied to her.

'You poor darling,' Jessie said. 'My poor, brave girl.'

She didn't offer further comment at first, and Annie felt suddenly nervous as Jessie moved quietly about the snug kitchen, turning on the lights, checking the casserole in the oven and drawing the pretty floral curtains to block out the encroaching night.

'How about a pre-dinner sherry while we talk about this?' she said.

'Thanks.' Annie's nerves tightened a notch. There was something about the tone of her mother's voice that suggested she would need this drink.

As soon as Jessie was seated again and they each had a

glass of sherry in front of them, Annie said, 'You do think I did the right thing, don't you, Mum? Don't you agree that I had no choice but to leave Theo?'

She held her breath as she waited for her mother's quick reassurance.

But the answer didn't come immediately. Jessie stared at her sherry glass, twisting its stem to make it turn slowly.

'Mum?'

Lifting her gaze from the glass to her daughter, Jessie reached out and clasped Annie's hand. 'You've been very brave, Annie. And I'm proud of you.' She paused and seemed to be carefully thinking through what she would say next. 'In every situation there is a better and a worse way to behave, and you saw what you thought was the only right thing to do and found the courage to do what you felt you must.'

'But?' whispered Annie. 'There's a but, isn't there? I can hear it in your voice.' Her insides flinched. Was she strong enough for this? She'd thought she would feel better if she told her mother about Theo. 'What is it, Mum? Tell me quickly.'

Jessie sighed softly. 'I—I can't help thinking that you made one serious mistake.'

'What's that?'

'You didn't consult Theo.'

'But I couldn't!'

'I know that was how you felt, dear, but try just for a moment to think about the situation from his point of view.'

'Of course I've been thinking about it from his point of view. All I ever did was think about what I had cost him. It was because of me that he lost his job. And he was probably losing his house, his life in Brisbane. Everything.'

'So you made a rash decision by yourself and then you left without allowing him any chance to discuss it.'

'But he would have tried to persuade me to stay.'

'Didn't you want to stay?'

Annie moaned. 'Yes, of course I did.' She dropped her head into her hands, then jerked upright again. 'I can't believe you're so down on me.'

'Annie, I'm not down on you. But I know how impetuous you are, darling. Sometimes—' She sighed and left that sentence unfinished. 'What bothers me is that you weren't totally honest with Theo. You didn't tell him everything that Claudia said to you.'

'Because I was sure he wouldn't believe me. I wouldn't have believed it, if I hadn't heard it with my own ears. Claudia's quite beautiful and she's the Top Gun of the philosophy department. Why would a woman in that position be jealous of a clueless little ditzy chick from the bush?'

'I think you're underselling your assets, Annie.' Jessie sighed. 'Okay, even if we leave that aside, you didn't give Theo a chance to come up with his own solution to the problem.'

'That—that's true.'

'Surely it was up to him to decide what was best for his career.'

Oh, God. Annie stared at her mother. She felt winded. Winded *and* wounded. She didn't want to hear this. Struggling to her feet, she began to pace the room. Was her mother right? Had she been totally, totally foolish? A martyr without a just cause?

She'd thought she'd offered Theo a gift of freedom, but had she denied him the chance to make a choice? Theo was mature and patient—a philosopher, trained to think through crises till he reached a reasonable outcome. She, on the other hand, had always been impetuous and rash, swept away by emotions, eager to make the grand gesture.

'What have I done?' she whispered. 'Oh, God, Mum, I've lost him and it's all my own fault.'

CHAPTER TWELVE

IN THE heart of midwinter in the middle of Derbyshire Theo
stood in the foyer of the Hollydean Arms and listened to the
sounds of dance music and laughter coming from the other
side of a set of double doors. Kane McKinnon's wedding
reception was in full swing.

And Annie was in there among the wedding guests.

He looked at his watch and wondered when the celebrations would finish. Desperate as he was to see Annie, he had
no intention of gatecrashing another man's wedding. He'd
convinced himself that it was okay to be here, hovering about
outside a function he hadn't been invited to, but he felt uneasy,
like an infatuated fan hoping to catch a glimpse of the star
he idolised.

Nevertheless, he was prepared to wait here in the foyer and
reflect on a sad truth he'd experienced firsthand during the
past weeks—a harrowing lesson of the human heart—that
the source of a man's greatest joy could become the source
of his greatest torment and pain.

He swallowed to rid himself of the knot of tension in his

throat. This meeting with Annie would be the most vitally important in his life. He would wait all night if necessary.

Without warning, one of the doors of the reception area opened and a tall, broad-shouldered fellow came into the foyer, tugging at his bow-tie.

He saw Theo and grinned. 'I can't wait to get out of this clobber.'

The clues fell into place in an instant—the man's Australian accent, his blue eyes so like Annie's, his formal suit and bridegroom's buttonhole.

Theo hurried forward, offering an outstretched hand. 'You must be Kane McKinnon.'

'Yeah, that's right.'

'Congratulations.'

'Thanks.' As the bridegroom shook hands, his silver-blue gaze narrowed and gave Theo the once-over. 'Have we met?'

'No. I'm Theo Grainger. Your brother, Reid, directed me here.'

'Grainger…ah, yes.' Kane's face broke into a grin. 'Now I know who you are.'

'Reid mentioned me?'

'When he rang yesterday to wish me luck for the wedding, he told me all about you, Theo.' Kane thumped his shoulder. 'I must say you made a pretty good impression on my brother.'

'I think we hit it off—quite well.'

'Two of you got on like a bushfire, from what I hear.' Kane cocked his head to one side and his eyes turned shrewd. 'Sounds like you've made a big impact on my sister, too.'

Bingo. The raw knot in Theo's throat tightened. Again he tried to swallow. 'That—that's why I'm here. I need to speak to Annie.'

Kane chuckled and he gave Theo's shoulder another friendly thump. 'Looks like the airlines are doing a roaring trade with lovelorn Aussie blokes. I know exactly what you're going through, mate. You feel like hell, don't you? Listen, I'm supposed to be getting changed. Charity and I are heading off soon, but I'll just duck inside and find Annie for you.'

'There's no need to disturb her. She's probably enjoying herself. I—I can wait a little longer.'

Kane favoured him with a who-are-you-trying-to-kid smile. 'Don't talk rubbish, man. Of course you can't wait.'

How much longer could she last? All around Annie, wedding guests were smiling, chatting, laughing and drinking and her face was aching with the effort of holding her smile in place.

It hadn't been so bad at the church. The groom's sister was more or less expected to sniffle and weep during the beautiful and moving wedding ceremony, but it would be rather bad form if she sobbed her way through the reception as well.

Not that she wasn't happy for Kane and Charity. They were both so obviously in love it was impossible not to be thrilled for them. And the reception had been very enjoyable so far— even when she'd been dragged around the dance floor by the local headmaster, the bank manager and by Charity's young brother, Tim.

Problem was, a wedding celebration and a badly broken heart were not a comfortable combination. And it was so hard to avoid thinking about what might have been—if she hadn't been such an impulsive fool. Instead she was left with the consequences of her recklessness—this ghastly cold, unbearable emptiness inside her.

'Annie.'

There was a tap on her shoulder and she turned to find Kane grinning down at her.

'Hey,' she said. 'Aren't you supposed to be getting changed?'

'Yeah. I just ducked back because I've got a message for you.'

'Oh? What is it?'

'There's someone outside who wants to speak to you.'

'Really? Where?'

'Waiting in the foyer.'

She frowned. 'But no one here knows me. Are you sure I'm the one wanted?'

His grin grew wider. 'Absolutely.' Reaching down, he grabbed her elbow. 'Come on. Get a wriggle on.'

'All right.' Puzzled, she stood and smoothed the softly flaring skirt of her fine woollen dress. Across the table she caught her mother's eye. 'I'm just popping outside for a moment.'

Jessie smiled, gave her a brief wave, and continued chatting to the bride's uncle, who was sitting beside her.

'Go through those doors over there,' Kane said, pointing and giving her a gentle shove.

'Who am I looking for?'

'You'll see.' Then he muttered that he had to go, and he took off quickly, heading for a different exit.

How weird.

Making her way through the throng of happy wedding guests, Annie tried to think who could possibly want her. Her mother and Aunt Flora were both here in this room. Charity was upstairs, getting changed out of her bridal gown, and she didn't need Annie because she had a swag of girlfriends to help her. Annie didn't really know anyone else in Hollydean.

There was always Charity's brother, Tim, of course. He'd

worked at Southern Cross as a jackaroo. It could be him. Perhaps he was planning to tamper with the honeymooners' car—tin cans on the bumper bar—Just Married written in shaving cream—confetti in their suitcases. But surely the bridegroom wouldn't have fetched her for that task?

Pushing the nearest of the double-doors open, she stepped out into the hotel's reception area.

And her heart almost stopped.

The foyer was practically empty, but over by the stand of tourist brochures there was a man who looked so much like...

It *was*...

Theo.

It really was him.

She couldn't move. Her heart seemed to lie still in her chest and her body was frozen to the spot by a sudden deluge of emotion. But her eyes were drinking him in.

Theo.

Theo, looking absolutely gorgeous—tall and cuddly in a thick cream cable-knit sweater and brown corduroy trousers. Theo, looking drop-dead sexy in his dark-rimmed glasses. Theo, looking unbelievably worried, his face drawn and his eyes almost haunted. Oh, the poor darling.

It felt like an age but must have been seconds before her sense of paralysis faded. Her heartbeats returned and kicked up to a frantic pace. She was trembling all over, but she took a shaky step towards him and then another.

'Hello, Annie,' he said in a strangely rough, tight voice.

'Hi, Theo.'

She stared at him, hardly daring to believe that this was really happening. She couldn't be dreaming, could she?

'I—I was passing through.'

Passing through? What did that mean? Was he here for five

minutes? Five days? She felt terribly confused. There seemed to be a thousand questions she needed to ask, but she couldn't deal with them. Not now. Not when a miracle had occurred and Theo was *here*.

'I'm so pleased to see you,' she said.

'Are you?' He still looked impossibly worried.

'Oh, yes, Theo. I've almost died from missing you.'

And Theo, darling man that he was, held out his arms to her. And suddenly she was rushing, hurtling forward, falling into his embrace.

'Oh, Theo, I can't believe it's you.'

He was real. She clung to him and he hugged her tight against his bulky sweater. Oh, how good it was to touch him, to know for sure that she wasn't dreaming.

He felt huge and wonderful. His body was deliciously strong and hard beneath the layer of soft wool and, as his arms held her close, she could hear his heart beating as fast and hard as her own. Oh, he felt so, so good.

She touched his cheek.

He touched her hair.

Ignoring the group of curious hotel guests walking past, they leaned apart to gaze into each other's eyes with wondrous, disbelieving delight and then they embraced again, holding each other tightly, fiercely, both too overcome, too thankful, too happy for words.

But at last Annie felt compelled to confess. 'I tried to ring you in Brisbane, but I only got your answering machine and I didn't know how else to find you. I've done everything wrong. I'm so sorry.' She looked up into his dear, familiar face. 'I've been terrified that I might never see you again.'

His smile wobbled and his throat worked as if he were dealing with emotions as strong as her own. It was too much for Annie. Her vision turned watery and her eyes filled with tears and she had to press her face into his chest and will herself not to spoil this miracle by sobbing all over him. But she did cry and he seemed to understand and for quite some time he stood there, not saying anything, simply holding her and gently stroking her hair.

At last she was calmer and she lifted her face, swiping at it with one freed hand while she clung to him with the other. She tried to smile. 'You've no idea how good it is to see you.'

He managed a beautiful smile. 'I think you may have mentioned it. I've missed you, too, you know.'

'Theo, I'm so sorry. I'm sorry I left the way I did. I thought I was doing the right thing.'

'I know. I know.'

'I made a mess of everything.'

'*Claudia* made a mess of everything.'

'But I shouldn't have run away and I was so silly. I wouldn't answer your calls and I blocked your emails.'

He toyed gently with a straying curl near her ear. 'You've been a thorough nuisance, Annie.'

'Will you ever forgive me?'

'What do you think?'

She could read the answer in his eyes and she almost expected that he would kiss her.

But instead he touched the V neckline of her heather blue wool dress. 'This is very elegant.'

She shrugged and smiled. 'I thought naked shimmer might be a bit much for the good folk of Hollydean.'

'They don't know what they're missing.'

His smile was of the very private, bone-melting kind, and she wanted so badly to kiss him, but then she remembered exactly where they were.

'How on earth did you know about Kane's wedding? How did you know where to find me?'

He smiled slowly. 'I'm lucky to have your brothers on side. Reid sent me here.'

'Dear old Reid. He's done good turns for both Kane and me now. But you didn't come all this way just to—to see me, did you?'

'Why shouldn't I?'

'You've got so many problems to sort out. Your phone message said you were on extended leave. That's a polite way of saying you've been sacked, isn't it? I was so devastated when I realised that I didn't even save your job.'

'But you did, Annie.'

She blinked at him. 'What do you mean?'

'It happened exactly the way you predicted. As soon as Claudia knew that you were gone, my contract was miraculously up for renewal again.'

'Really?' Already she could feel a layer of guilt peeling away. 'That's wonderful.'

'But I told Claudia she could stick her job some place that's highly uncomfortable.'

Annie gasped. 'Crumbs, Theo, I wish I'd been there. I can't imagine you telling anyone to do that. You're always such a perfect gentleman.'

'You know very well that I'm not.' His eyes flashed with a sudden unmistakable hunger that sent a thrill shimmying straight to her centre. With reverent fingers he traced the curve of her cheek. 'Annie, you don't get it, do you? You're more important to me than any job. There's no way I would consider working for Claudia after what she did to us.'

She wanted to laugh and cry at once. Was it possible to feel this happy without bursting? 'Theo, you mustn't say such lovely things to me in a public place. I'm likely to show my gratitude in an unseemly manner.'

'That's my responsibility,' he said and, without a care for the people in the foyer, he pulled her in to him and kissed her and he took a scrumptiously long time about it.

'You've no idea how much I missed you,' he murmured against her lips.

'Show me again,' she murmured back, winding her arms around his neck.

And he kissed her some more and Annie could feel all the hurt and broken pieces inside her becoming whole again.

'Oh, good, you two found each other.'

They were reluctant to separate, but turned to find Kane coming down the stairs, changed into travelling clothes. His grin was wide. 'Looks like it's a happy reunion.'

Theo and Annie shared rapturous smiles.

Kane crossed over to them and dropped a kiss on her cheek and slapped Theo's shoulder. 'The name Theo Grainger rings a bell,' he said.

'Theo's a philosopher,' Annie told him proudly.

'A philosopher? Oh, must be a different guy then. The one I was thinking of played Rugby Union for Queensland.'

Theo looked surprised. 'I played a couple of seasons for the state team. Years ago.'

Kane nodded. 'Thought it must be you. You were a brilliant winger.' He winked at Annie. 'You did well to catch this guy. He can run like the wind.' He glanced towards the hotel entrance. 'It's a pity I can't hang around and be sociable, but my wife will be down soon and she's expecting a honeymoon.'

'You bet I am.'

Charity, with her lovely auburn hair bouncing about her shoulders and dressed in an elegantly long black coat and boots with a multicoloured scarf at her throat, came hurrying down the stairs. Following her came her bridesmaid, carrying the bridal bouquet.

Annie made hasty introductions.

'Nice to meet you, Theo.' Charity tucked her arm through her husband's and smiled at them. 'I suppose I should join Kane in saying it's a pity we're leaving so quickly, but you wouldn't believe me, would you?'

'No way.'

'We've kept it a secret, but we're off to Paris,' Charity whispered, her eyes shining with excitement and happiness.

'How fantastic.' Annie kissed them both. 'Have an absolute ball.'

Word soon spread that Charity and Kane were downstairs and ready to leave and soon the wedding guests were crowding through the doors into the foyer, all keen to farewell them. Among them was Jessie McKinnon and when she saw that her daughter was holding hands with a tall, dark and handsome man, her eyes widened with delighted interest.

'Theo?' she mouthed to Annie across the foyer.

Annie nodded and they exchanged excited grins and Annie tingled with happy pride.

Then the guests were all crowding around Kane and Charity as they headed for their car, which was parked in the street outside.

'The bride's about to toss the bouquet,' Theo said. 'Do you want to stay to catch it?'

'I didn't think philosophers would hold with such superstitions.'

He smiled. 'You're right. Besides, you don't need to catch a bouquet. As your brother said, you've already caught me.'

Her heart clattered. Good heavens, was she terribly focused on weddings at the moment, or did that almost sound like a proposal? Electrified, Annie glanced quickly around her at the crowd of people. Everyone's attention was focused on the bridal couple in the doorway.

Theo's attention however, was concentrated directly on her. And now she couldn't drag her eyes from him—even when an excited babble broke out behind them, which she presumed was Charity's girlfriends trying to catch the bouquet.

Theo took her hand. 'Do you think anyone would mind if we slipped away somewhere?'

'No, it's what my mother has been suggesting with her not very subtle handwaving gestures.'

'She has?'

'Absolutely.'

Hungry for privacy, they almost ran out of view through the doorway into the now empty dining room. Surrounded by the flowers, candlelight and streamers that had decorated the wedding reception, Theo swept Annie close.

'I love you, Annie.'

'Oh, Theo, I love *you*.'

Hearts hammering in unison, they kissed impatiently, hungrily, deeply, their bodies pressing closer, desperate for intimate contact.

When at last he released her, Theo took Annie's hands in his. 'You're coming with me to Rome.'

'To *where*?' she whispered, breathless with shock.

He smiled and dropped a quick kiss on her nose. 'To Rome—in Italy—that country you claim to love—the one where everyone speaks Italian.'

'But—but—'

'I'm on my way there now. I've scored a Research Fellowship and I'll be working at the University of Rome for the next six months.'

'Oh, Theo, how fantastic for you.'

'Fantastic for us, Annie. I'm not going to let you out of my sight again. Besides, I promised I'd take you to Rome and now it's going to happen.'

She stared at him, too stunned to speak.

Watching her, Theo frowned and he looked so endearingly anxious she couldn't resist a playful smile. 'But I've—um—made a New Year's resolution to be less impulsive.'

He released a soft little sound, half-sigh, half-chuckle. 'Trust you to become sensible just when I need you to be reckless.' With a hand beneath her chin, he tipped it up so that her mouth was angled just so and he kissed her again, more slowly this time. Against her lips, he murmured, 'You can learn the language and then we can seduce each other in sexy Italian.'

'Goodness,' she said in a breathless voice, 'you sure know how to make things difficult for a girl who's decided to become less impulsive.'

'Don't worry, Annie, I've done enough deep and serious thinking for both of us. I've even squared this plan away with your brother, Reid. *And* with your dog.'

'My dog?'

'I've left Basil at Southern Cross. He and Lavender are the best of mates and she's stopped moping, so you won't have to feel bad about abandoning her for six months.'

Annie's mouth gaped open.

Theo smiled and kissed her open lips and then he nuzzled her cheek close to her ear. 'Everything's organised, Annie, so you'd better prepare yourself for the fact that you're coming to Rome with me. If you try to say no, I'm just going to pick you up and carry you off.'

Annie grinned. 'No need, Theo. I'd swim to Italy to be with you.'

They arrived in Rome in the early hours of the next day, after a night that had passed like a dream. First they'd shared their news with Jessie McKinnon and received her enthusiastic blessing, and then they'd packed Annie's things and driven in Theo's hire car from Hollydean to London, slept in snatches on the flight from Heathrow to Fiumicino Airport, and taken in the first sights of Rome as their taxi sped them to their apartment.

Finally they set their bags down.

'You must be exhausted,' said Theo.

'I'm too happy and excited to be tired. I can be tired later.' Annie spun in a circle to take it all in. 'This is just lovely.'

The apartment had a tiny kitchen and a large living room, cool tiled floors, stucco walls and wooden beams. The furniture was simple—old-fashioned couches and a timber table with two chairs by a shuttered window. A bowl on the table held a welcome gift of luscious, ripe pears. And in the next room there was an enormous iron bed covered with a white woven spread.

Taking Annie's hand, Theo led her to the window and pushed open faded blue door-length shutters. 'What do you think of the view?'

In the pearl-grey light of dawn, she stepped out on to a tiny balcony with lace ironwork and pots planted with pink geraniums and wild mint. In the distance she could see the rounded curve of a hill, and the silhouette of trees against the lightening Roman sky. She let her gaze travel over the sea of dark rooftops and the occasional dome or spire.

Closer, illuminated by a streetlight, she saw a row of apartment buildings, centuries old and painted bitter lemon, tomato and rosy grey. Then she looked below and saw a little cobbled square where tables and chairs were set outside a café, and a fountain trickled water from the mouths of two stone dolphins.

'This is it,' she said in breathless awe, leaning back against

Theo as he wrapped his arms around her. 'This is Trastevere, isn't it? And it's exactly the same view that you told me about.'

'Do you like it?'

'Oh, Theo, I *adore* it.' She turned in his arms and kissed him, let her lips trail from his gorgeous mouth to the scrumptious underside of his jaw, to his delectable earlobe.

Theo closed his eyes. 'Annie... Annie, have you any idea what you do to me?'

'Mmm.' With her fingers, she traced the line of his jaw then slipped them inside the open neck of his shirt and played with the lovely straight line of his collarbone, savouring the knowledge that soon, very soon now, she would be able to touch all of him.

His hands bracketed her hips, keeping them hard against his as he kissed her brow, her cheek, her chin, her ear. 'You do know how much I love you, don't you?'

He had already told her this in Hollydean, at Heathrow, and on the plane...but it was perfectly wonderful to hear it again now that they were so very alone. Together at last in their own fascinating, exciting, private home from home. She nuzzled his neck. 'I love you more, Theo.'

'Uh-uh. I don't think you understand how very important you are to me.'

'Well, I need *you* to understand that I'd go with you anywhere. It's wonderful to be here in Rome, but I would have been deliriously happy with you in a grass hut in the jungle.'

'Will you marry me, Annie?'

Goodness, how much excitement could a girl handle? Was it possible to melt from happiness?

Just the same, Annie found herself hesitating... She looked away. There was just one little problem...

'Sweetheart, you're welcome to be as impulsive as you like.'

She lifted her gaze back to his. 'Theo, I'd marry you anywhere, any time, just as I'd live with you anywhere. The only thing is—'

'What?' His voice cracked beneath the terrible weight of that single syllable.

'I told my father before he died that when I got married it would be at Southern Cross. It was a silly promise to make, I realise that now—but it's been a—a girlish dream of mine.'

There was a fleeting flash of disappointment in his eyes, impossible to hide, but he recovered in a moment and the tender smile he gave her was his most beautiful yet. 'I wouldn't want to tread on your dreams, Annie.'

'You really are the most darling, darling man.'

'But we can be engaged,' he insisted. 'In fact, we'll go out and buy an engagement ring today. I want to announce to the world that Annie McKinnon is my woman.'

She had thought she was as happy as it was possible to be, but now as the sun climbed above the distant hill, coating the rooftops of Rome with an apricot glaze, and as she and Theo turned back into their new little home, Annie experienced the deepest happiness of all.

She knew now that whatever the future brought she would share it with this man. A lifetime of loving awaited her.

And this was just the beginning.

* * * *

More long-distance dates lead to long-term romance in
Molly Cooper's Dream Date.
Coming soon from Barbara Hannay in
Mills & Boon® Riva™.

are proud to present our...

Book of the Month

Walk on the Wild Side
by Natalie Anderson

from Mills & Boon® RIVA™

Jack Greene has Kelsi throwing caution to the wind
—it's hard to stay grounded with a man who turns
your world upside down! Until they crash with
a bump—of the baby kind…

Available 4th February

*Something to say about our Book of the Month?
Tell us what you think!*

millsandboon.co.uk/community
facebook.com/romancehq
twitter.com/millsandboonuk

Is the *It* girl losing it?

At the helm of must-read *Snap* magazine,
veteran style guru Sara B. has had the joy of
eviscerating the city's fashion victims in her
legendary DOs and DON'Ts photo spread.

But now on the unhip edge of forty, Sara's
being spat out like an old Polaroid picture:
blurry, undeveloped and obsolete.

After launching into a comic series of blow-ups,
Sara realises she's made her living by cutting people
down...and somehow she must make amends.

Available 21st January 2011

www.mirabooks.co.uk